H.A.L

BOOK THREE

ORIGINS

NATALIE WRIGHT

A BOADICEA PRESS BOOK

NATALIE WRIGHT
- NatalieWrightAuthor.com -

Publisher's Cataloging-In-Publication Data

Wright, Natalie, 1966-
  H.A.L.F.: ORIGINS / Natalie Wright
ISBN 978-15453-7109-1 (CreateSpace tr. pbk.)
Subjects: LCSH: Extraterrestrial beings--Juvenile fiction. | Human-alien encounters--Juvenile fiction. | Teenagers--Juvenile fiction. | Official secrets--Juvenile fiction. | Transgenic organisms--Juvenile fiction. | CYAC: Extraterrestrial beings--Fiction. | Human-alien encounters--Fiction. | Teenagers--Fiction. | Secrets--Fiction. | LCGFT: Science fiction. | Fantasy fiction.
Classification: LCC PZ7.W75 Had 2015 (print) | LCC PZ7.W75 (ebook) | DDC [Fic]--dc23

First Edition

ISBN: 1545371091
ISBN-13: 978-1545371091

FOR THE READERS WHO HAVE
LOVED H.A.L.F.

CONTENTS

ACKNOWLEDGMENTS

August 2017

The idea that became the H.A.L.F. series first arrived in 2010. Seven years, over 300,000 written words, more drafts than I can count, and enough coffee to fill a pool later, the H.A.L.F. writing journey has come to an end. And what a strange trip it has been!

The H.A.L.F. series launched at Salt Lake Fan X in January 2015. The Salt Lake folks gave it an enthusiastic reception, and I will be eternally grateful for the amazing support of Salt Lake folks for authors and artists. My mascot, "Baby Tex," and I have traveled over ten thousand miles since then, meeting readers and fans at comic cons and book festivals throughout the western US. We've had a blast! A huge thank-you to all who have supported my work. When you buy books, whether at an online retailer or in person, you're a patron of the arts! I appreciate all patrons.

Every finished book is a team effort, and I have an amazing team. Much gratitude to Alyssa, content editor extraordinaire at Red Adept Editing and Publishing; thank you to Jason G. Anderson for flawless eBook formatting; to Dane at eBook Launch for another fabulous cover; and to Kelly at Red Adept for final line editing. A special thank-you to Dylan White for inspired narration of the audiobook edition. I am so blessed to have found a voice that matches the work so perfectly. Cheers to a great team!

And thank you, as always, to Pete and Sarah. Together, you form the shore to my sea. The ocean pitched and rolled this year, but you kept the light on for me.

PRONUNCIATION & DEFINITION GUIDE

	Pronunciation	Definition
Council of U	Council of ū	The ruling body of the M'Uktah people.
Doj	ZHō	The One God of the M'Uktah people.
Doj'Madi	ZHō madi	Female half of the One God
Doj'Owa	ZHō ouä	The head of the Temple of Doj.
Dra'Knar	Dreknar	U'Vol's intergalactic starship.
drosh	drō SH	A black, hard, carbon-like metal.
Eponia Tu'Vol	epōnēya too väl	U'Vol's third wife.
Ghapta	gäptä	A lush, watery planet with plentiful game. Harvested by the M'Uktah.
kiknari	kick nari	A lotus-like flower on Ghapta
K'Sarhi	k sari	The M'Uktah name for Earth.
kracht	crock	Beg forgiveness; apologize.
Kreelan	krēlan	A planet harvested by the M'Uktah and sight of an uprising against the M'Uktah.
krindor	krin door	Mechanized exoskeleton.
M'Uktah	mooktä	A race of hunters from the planet Uktah.
Mocht Bogha	mäk bōZHä	A warp in space within the Uktah planetary system.
Navimbi	nävimbi	One of the planets that the M'Uktah have harvested.
phlegering	flegi(e)rng	A large, feathered, winged beast from Ghapta.
Rik'Nar	rick nar	A landing ship similar to *Wa'Nar*
Sarhi	sari	The M'Uktah name for humans; earthlings.
scryr	skrier	A psychic and seer.
thukna	thuknä	A hairless, horned beast that lives on the planet Ghapta.
Tu'Nai	too nye	First Officer of the Vree hunter ground crew
Tu'Rhen	too ren	Chief Pilot and Captain of the *Wa'Nar*

Tu'Vagh	too vah	First Officer of the *Dra'Knar*
U'Baht	ōō bäht	U'Vol's friend and mentor. The representative of the Vree class to the Council of U.
U'Vol Vree	ōō väl vrē	Captain of the *Dra'Knar*.
Uktah	ooktä	The M'Uktah planet in a star system in the Milky Way but 1000 light years from Earth.
ulv	ōōlv	The wolf-like ancestors of the M'Uktah.
Valo'Kar	Val ō car	A single-person pod used for short-distance travel through warped space.
Vrath	vraTH	The current Lij of the M'Uktah.
Vree	vrē	The space-faring hunting and harvesting class of the M'Uktah.
Vree'Kah	vrēkä	The hunters of the Vree class.
Vree'Sho	vrē shō	Farmers/ranchers of the Vree class.
Wa'Nar	wā nar	U'Vol's landing ship.

ERIKA

Raindrops pelted the windshield of the rust-bucket truck Erika had borrowed from Ian's dad. Nearly an hour had passed since she'd seen the lights of the last police car recede in her rearview mirror, but her fingers still shook as she turned on the windshield wipers. They were little help. The spittle of rain turned the dusty windshield into a muddy mess, and the sun-rotted rubber of the wipers streaked the glass.

The jacked-up truck tackled the harsh terrain of the desert like a pro. The police cars were no match for barrel cacti and creosote bushes as large as small cars. The local Ajo police that had tried to stop them likely didn't know that they were chasing a human-alien hybrid that had escaped, again, from a secret underground lab controlled by the clandestine organization known as the Makers. The Makers had surely spun the lies necessary to convince local law enforcement that Tex was a dangerous fugitive. Ironic. The lie had become the truth. Erika and Tex were, in fact, fugitives on the run and again fighting for their lives. It was like déjà vu all over again.

Erika's bottom was bruised from bouncing on the seat. Her wrists ached from gripping the wheel. After nearly an hour of rough riding, they hit a two-lane road going east. Erika was heading to New Mexico, where her Aunt Dana, her father's sister, lived. Without complications, they would get to Aunt Dana's in about eight hours. *If she'll have us.*

Tex had been quiet but awake as Erika navigated the bumpy ground. Once they reached the smooth pavement, he tucked his knees to his chest, hugged his arms around his legs, and became a silent, egg-shaped blob on the seat next to her. Erika had seen him withdraw into himself before, but he was even more quiet and still than usual.

Erika wished he'd stayed awake longer. She wanted to pry answers out of him. She had questions about his time with the

Conexus, when he had been linked directly to their hive-mind collective. Ever since Dr. Randall had unhooked Tex from the Conexus, he was acting distant and short-tempered. Erika wondered what had really happened to him during his time with the Conexus. *And what did he mean when he spoke of struggles for humans to come and the knowledge he got from the Conexus?* She hoped he would answer these questions and more when they got to Aunt Dana's.

The dribble of rain became a hailstorm. Peanut-sized ice balls pinged the metal roof of the truck. Within minutes, the hail turned into a deluge. Erika turned the wipers to full blast, but that only smeared the windshield faster. The Tex blob remained eerily quiet and unperturbed.

Erika's swollen right eye, a gift from one of the Makers' guards during their escape from the school, made it difficult to see. Both eyes were heavy with fatigue. She blinked rapidly and shook her head, trying to clear the drowsiness. She switched on the radio, and raucous Tejano music blasted. She wasn't a fan of the accordion-heavy genre. The ancient truck speakers distorted the sound, making it nothing but noise to her ears, but at least the booming music helped keep her awake.

Erika had never been much of a life planner. Her current situation of living day-to-day did not bother her as much as it might have irritated some people. She was focused on her current task, getting Tex safely to a location where he could heal. She'd help him find a place to stay hidden from the Makers and Sturgis. She wasn't sure what came after that. *Just stay awake. And alive.*

Tex didn't stir or acknowledge the radio. *Is he dead?* She poked at him with a finger. "Tex? You okay?"

With his head still to his knees, his voice was muffled but cool and even. "I am alive, if that is what you mean."

"You've been so quiet. With the escape back there at the school, the dogs, and now the rain... I was just hoping that you're all right."

Tex raised his head slightly and turned toward her, his large eyes peeking over his arm. "I have been through worse."

The understatement of the century. She'd been through worse, too: the days of fever she endured after the Conexus gave her the virus, the long hours of watching Ian wracked with pain when she could do nothing but watch him inch toward death, weeks of hunger and thirst. She had been forced to take the lives of others or lose her own, and she had watched her mom breathe her last breath. They'd all been through hell and back.

Tex's indifference was still better than silence between them. The tinny horns and the beat of the music stopped abruptly.

The radio announcer broke in, speaking in Spanish. "There has been a massive terrorist attack in Europe. The entire continent is without power. Communication systems are down. Though reports are sketchy, US authorities state that the attacks appear to be focused on London and Paris."

Erika's chest tightened. For a moment, she forgot to breathe. "He said that communication systems are down in Europe and there's been a massive terrorist attack. The terrorists hit London and Paris."

Tex unwound his arms from around his legs. "I understood what he said." He sounded condescending, as though everyone could understand Spanish as well as English.

"Oh. I just assumed that—"

"You assume a great many things."

Erika didn't know what he meant, but she was more worried about what the heck was going on in Europe than her traveling companion's surly attitude. The radio announcer spoke of the apparent sophistication and coordination of the attacks. He stated that the terrorists had clearly used an advanced technology that took out the power grid across Europe. *Terrorists with advanced technology? Could the Makers be behind this?*

Continuing in Spanish, the announcer said, "The US has raised the terrorist alert level to high and has closed all borders, effective immediately. There are reports of disruption to GPS and cellular service in the United States, indicating possible destruction or interference with multiple satellites."

"Just what we don't need. First the virus to deal with, now terrorists run amok."

"It is not a terrorist attack," Tex said with total conviction.

"You just heard the guy say it's a terrorist attack. He said the report came from NORAD."

"Then this NORAD fellow is wrong... or lying."

During her time at Casa Sturgis, Erika had lost most of her faith in the authorities. Getting locked up in an underground city run by crazy government scientists and black-budget military would do that to you. Even if the Makers were behind A.H.D.N.A., that didn't negate the fact that, somewhere along the line, some important people were very corrupt. Maybe even a lot of people.

Even after all she'd seen, though, she still believed most of the people working for the government weren't crooked, self-serving traitors who would sell out the lives of millions just for their own little piece of the post-virus pie. People like Dr. Montoya worked for the government. Dr. Montoya had risked her life to help them to keep the antivirus out of the hands of the Makers so it could be synthesized to help the masses rather than the elite few chosen by William Croft and company.

"Why would the military lie about terrorists?" she asked. "And if it's not terrorists, then who would cause a massive power failure?"

"Something far worse than extremists with a vendetta. Pull over. I will drive now."

"Have you ever driven before?"

Tex shook his head. "Pull over," he repeated.

"And what do you mean 'worse'?"

"Erika, I tire of questions every time I ask something of you. There is a helicopter on its way. You did not think that the Makers would send only a few local law-enforcement vehicles after me, did you? Shall we argue further? Or shall I attempt to lose those that tail us?"

Erika had been the driver of her own destiny since her dad died. She wasn't used to taking orders. Instinct told her to hold tight to the wheel and tell him to pound salt.

She turned off the radio. The hard rain pounded the roof and battered the windshield. She heard the unmistakable sound of a helicopter over the din of the rain. "They're too close. There's no time to switch places."

After a few seconds of silence, Tex said, "We need to vacate the vehicle."

"We don't exactly stand a chance to outrun a helicopter on foot." An image of Tex running with his preternatural speed came to mind. "I don't, anyway."

They were in the wee hours of the morning. The minor road they were on was practically abandoned. Storm clouds obscured the dim light of the half-moon. Darkness enveloped them like an oily black stain—obvious, persistent and impossible to remove. If the men in the copter took them prisoner, no one would be there to witness it.

"I think we should stay in the truck," Erika said. "We've got to be getting close to I-10 now. It's a busy highway, even at this hour. They won't do anything to us on that road. Too many witnesses."

Tex shot her a sidelong look. Even with his unreadable eyes, Erika felt the disdain and disagreement seeping out of him.

"You must pull over," he said. "Now."

Erika nearly did as Tex commanded, but Tex wasn't himself since they'd come back from the world of the Conexus. He admitted that the Conexus had experimented on him and that he feared his mind wasn't whole. She couldn't be sure he was thinking clearly. *Shouldn't we drive away from the people chasing us?*

A bright spotlight shone down from above and circled in front of the truck. Erika mashed her foot on the accelerator, trying in vain to coax more juice out of the beater, but it was already pushed to the floorboards. The needle of the speedometer trembled at nearly a hundred miles an hour, but it would not budge further. *Not fast enough to outrun a helicopter. Not by a long shot.*

The cone of light circled back and hit its mark, filling the truck cabin with bright white light. Tex's arm shot up to shield his sensitive eyes. The spotlight found them, and they were ensnared in photons, stuck just as surely as if a giant net had been thrown on them. Despite the cool autumn night air, slick sweat covered Erika's back. They'd come so far. They'd gotten away from Commander Sturgis and escaped the Conexus and the Regina. She'd gotten Tex out of the militarized school hospital. She'd had to kill a man to do it, a fact she was trying not to dwell on.

Erika held fast to the steering wheel. Her shoulders ached from gripping the wheel for so many hours. Her palms were so wet with sweat she feared her hands would slide off and she'd lose control. The knowledge that they wanted Tex alive staved off complete panic. He had, after all, been created as a personal bodyguard for William Croft. *I haven't come this far to give up. Let them try to take us. I'm not going to make it easy for them.*

She removed her right hand from the wheel and reached for the pistol she'd laid on the seat between them. She'd taken it from the dead soldier back at the school. Keeping the truck on the road with only one hand took effort. Its steering wasn't exactly capable of finesse, but she kept them going straight while she tucked the gun into the back waistband of her pants.

Gunfire exploded as loud as thunder splitting the night sky. A bullet hit the bed of the truck, making an unmistakable sound of metal being torn to pieces.

"We cannot outrun them," Tex said. He might as well have been reading from a grocery list.

"Really? You think? Got any help for me, or are you just going to sit over there like a lump and state the obvious?"

Tex didn't seem bothered by her sarcasm. Maybe he didn't even notice it. "They are attempting to terminate us."

Erika sighed loudly and rolled her eyes even though Tex couldn't see it. "Yes, well, bullets hitting your vehicle generally are a sign that someone's trying to kill you." She sucked in a deep breath. "What I don't understand is why. I thought they wanted you alive."

A shot hit the back window, sending a shower of glass across their backs and covering the seat between them. Erika instinctively ducked. Her leg strained, but she pushed even harder on the gas pedal as though that would somehow persuade more power from the old machine.

They were in the open and vulnerable, staying on the road, but if she swerved down the embankment, they'd be back in the desert, fighting cactus and scrub. They'd be like sitting ducks then. She kept the truck on the two-lane.

"It appears that Croft has decided that I have become more of a liability than a potential asset. If you want to live, Erika Holt, we must abandon this vehicle."

Another bullet hit the roof of the truck, tore through the metal, and buried itself in the upholstery of the seat only a few inches from Erika.

"You may be right, but we can't jump out of a car at a hundred miles an hour. The impact will kill us."

"I am well aware of the laws of motion and the physics of an impact with the pavement."

A spray of bullets coming from the front shattered the windshield.

"We have no more time," Tex said. He placed a thin hand on Erika's hand, her knuckles white from her death grip on the steering wheel. "You must trust me. Let go of the wheel, Erika. We must escape on your motorcycle."

Erika had insisted they throw her Yamaha into the back of the truck before they left Ajo. The motorcycle had been like a companion for her, and she hadn't wanted to leave it behind.

Erika wanted to live. She wanted to trust Tex. She also wanted to get on that bike and ride. Riding had been her escape from reality many times in the past. It was a fitting means of escape from the Makers. She had difficulty convincing her fingers to let go of the wheel and the false security that the metal roof over her head provided.

Tex slipped out through the truck's back window. His small, emaciated body fit easily. He held out his hand to her. "I do not want to leave you behind, but I will. There is no more time."

She unwound her fingers from the wheel. She put her hand in his, and he pulled her through the opening just as a barrage of bullets tore into the driver's seat.

Her stomach scraped across the sharp edge of the rusty metal window opening, and shards of safety glass prickled her skin even through her clothes. By the time she landed on the glass-strewn truck bed, Tex had the cycle up on the truck's bed and was straddling it.

With her foot no longer pressing the gas pedal, the truck had slowed considerably as it careened. The old truck's steering had pulled hard to the right all night while Erika drove, and staying true to form, the truck pulled right and set them on a course over an embankment.

"Hurry," he said as he started the cycle. "I have created a shield around myself. It will protect you too, but I am too weak to hold it for long."

She thought she should drive since it was her bike, but a bullet zinged past her head, and she gave up the argument. She hiked a leg up and over the seat to settle in behind Tex as he readied to jump the motorcycle out of the moving truck.

The truck bounced over the rough terrain and picked up speed slightly as it went down the hill that led to a ditch. Erika wound her arms around Tex's tiny waist as he throttled and spun the bike around. The truck jostled them as it tottered down the hill.

The bouncing they'd experienced that night had already knocked the rusty truck gate down, and it banged wildly against the back of the truck. Tex gave the cycle gas. The motorcycle skidded and nearly fell over on them, but Tex managed to keep it upright. The cycle landed hard on the embankment just as the truck careened to a halt, crashing into the ditch. Erika squeezed her thighs tightly against the machine and gripped Tex, but she kept herself on the cycle mainly by force of will.

The truck crashed into the gully behind them. Tex drove into the desert in a sideways trajectory away from the crashed truck. He didn't turn the cycle's headlamps on. Tex could see in the night as well as Erika could during the day.

Before they'd gone twenty yards, the truck exploded into a fireball. The heat of it warmed Erika's back.

"Guess you made the right call. They shot the gas tank. Definitely wanted us dead," Erika said.

Tex kept his head fixed forward, his eyes on the road. He deftly steered them around clumps of creosote and cactus as he twisted this way and that through the desert.

The helicopter circled overhead, its lights searching. Tex changed directions often and bobbed this way and that while always moving away from the crashed truck.

Erika's thighs burned from squeezing tightly to keep from being flung off of the machine as Tex made abrupt and sharp turn after turn. "Do you know where you're going?"

"Away from the helicopter," he said.

Good plan. She wanted to trust in him, but since she and Dr. Randall had taken him from the Conexus, Tex had been indifferent—hostile even—to both of them. She wasn't sure any trust was left between them.

But he got you out of that truck alive. She tightened her grip around the bony ribs of the person whose fate seemed irrevocably intertwined with her own. "Head northeast," she said.

"Why?"

"Trust *me*," she said.

They had put distance between themselves and the helicopter, but they weren't in the clear yet. Erika continued to grip tightly with her thighs as Tex drove in a northeasterly direction, the *pfft pfft pfft* of the helicopter blades receding, the blaze of the truck soon a memory.

2
WILLIAM CROFT

William Croft threw his cellular phone across the room. It smashed the glass of the case that held his numerous awards and recognitions for philanthropic work and achievements from his over forty years in business. His hands shook, and his heart beat wildly.

William quaked, not with fear but with anger. His daughter Lizzy had botched things badly in New York. She'd lost number ten, the hybrid code-named Alecto. Even worse, she had killed Robert Sturgis.

Of the two bungles, the death of Robert was by far the worse. Croft had not authorized her to kill one of the blood. the Makers were already a small group. They could not afford to lose someone of the caliber of Robert unless it was absolutely essential.

William's assistant knocked on the door. "Sir Croft? Do you require assistance?"

He was ready to tell the inept girl to leave him be, but he decided he needed her help after all. "Get in here! Quickly." He yelled the command, a touch of spittle on his lips. William pulled the monogrammed handkerchief from his inside jacket pocket and wiped his lip on the silk threads that read WJC.

Ms. Beauregard cracked the door open. She peeked her cherub-round face, complete with tight blond curls, through the opening. When Croft waved her in, she scurried forward as quickly as her high-heeled feet and too-tight pencil skirt would carry her. Ms. Beauregard's fingers trembled as she swiped her phone on and opened the app to record his commands. After numerous assistants over the years had proven unable to transcribe adequate notes to do as he asked, he required them to record his directives so there could be no doubt as to his requests. She put the phone on his mahogany desk so she could take notes as well.

"I must be on a plane to New York as soon as possible. Phone Kip, and have him ready the jet." William was not certain of what irked him more: having to clean up Lizzy's messes or having to make the trip across the pond to do it. He much preferred London to New York and did not relish time amongst the Yanks.

Ms. Beauregard's fingers still trembled as she wrote notes on her stenographer's pad. "Will anyone else be joining you, sir?"

He thought for a moment. "No. Let Kip know *minimal staff.* There's no time for a chef and sommelier. I want to be wheels up within the hour."

Ms. Beauregard checked her watch. "But sir—"

Croft shot her a look that could peel paint off of a car. "Within the hour, Ms. Beauregard."

She nodded furiously. "Yes, sir. And you'll be landing at JFK as usual?"

"Of course." He proceeded to spew forth additional directives at such a feverish pace Ms. Beauregard's fingers were likely cramped when he gave her leave to exit the room.

William Croft's father had begun hatching the Makers' master plan in the late 1940s after the Roswell crash. William had carried out his father's plans. For over sixty years, he and the Inner Circle had worked tirelessly and meticulously, building the Makers and the underground facilities that would house them when the time came. Billions of dollars were spent to create the human-alien hybrids that would be their insurance policy against the coming alien threat. Negotiations and a successful treaty were arranged with the Conexus so that the Makers would be the sole recipients of the antivirus. But number 9 and Robert's inept sister, Lillian Sturgis, had nearly obliterated the elaborate and meticulous insurance policy.

William's upper lip involuntarily curled up in disgust as he considered his daughter Lizzy's failure to reprogram Alecto. Presently, she was off-grid somewhere with Anna Sturgis.

"What am I to do with her?" he asked himself aloud. If Lizzy were not of the blood, he would simply have had her terminated. In fact, in his anger, he might have dispatched her himself. *If she was not of the blood.*

She was, though, as was Lillian, and he could not leave Thomas and Anna out of the ring of culpability. *All of the blood.* How could he take a pound of flesh when all that had betrayed him were part of the Makers?

He was in his seat on his plane and wheels up within sixty-two minutes. He took note that Ms. Beauregard had failed his command to get him into the air within sixty minutes. That would give him cause to fire her when he got back to London. *If I come back to London.*

The virus had already spread through much of Arizona. Cases had been reported in California and Texas, as well as a second ground zero in China. Dr. Montoya of the CDC had the antivirus, though. William was not so much concerned that millions of ordinary people might become inoculated as he was irritated that he had not gotten the antiviral injection himself and that his company would not profit from the cure. He had a mole planted in Montoya's organization, though. By the time he landed in New York, the mole might well have the antivirus to put into William's hands.

He watched the sky turn orange as the sun set on the day that had cost him so much. His mind worked feverishly on machinations to set his empire straight.

Jack kept his foot to the pedal and his eyes on the road. Fueled by adrenaline and coffee, his cells were more caffeine than water.

Alecto had pulled herself into an egg-shaped blob in the back of the van. She slept so soundly she could be mistaken for dead. Thomas also slept in the back, only slightly more alive than the human-alien hybrid he shared the space with. Alecto had healed his bullet wound, but the trauma had robbed Thomas's energy.

Anna was more awake than asleep but no more company to Jack than the rest of them. Lizzy's attack had left Anna with a slash of pinkish-red skin running diagonally across her left eye. The knife wound would heal in time. Jack was more concerned about how Anna would emotionally heal from watching Lizzy gun down her father. Anna was staring off toward the horizon in a nearly catatonic stupor. Jack figured she needed comfort and encouraging words after the ordeal of being kidnapped, watching her brother get shot, and witnessing the execution of her father. But Jack was fresh out of comfort and encouragement at the moment.

They had accomplished phase one of their mission and freed Alecto from the Crofts, but the price of their success had been high. Thomas had been shot. Anna had been brutally knifed. Jack's hands were stained with the blood of the Makers men that he'd had to kill in order to free Alecto and survive the ordeal. Worst of all, Lizzy Croft had shot Anna and Thomas's father, Robert, in the back.

They were through only phase one of what Jack had signed on for. They still had to somehow break Anna's aunt, Lilly Sturgis, out of federal military prison in Miramar, California. And so Jack was driving west to Miramar. The sooner he completed the job, the sooner he would be free of the whole thing.

Exhaustion finally won out when they hit St. Louis. "I have to stop for the night," Jack said.

Anna gave no argument. She numbly paid cash for two adjoining rooms at an inexpensive motor inn. She quickly pushed Alecto into one of the rooms, said a quiet good night, and closed the door.

Jack stood outside her door and stared at it.

"You were expecting a good-night kiss?" Thomas asked. His voice dripped sarcasm.

Jack ran his hand through his wavy, newly dyed brown locks. He hadn't bathed for two days, and his hair felt stringy and greasy in his fingers. "No." He shuffled to the door of the room next to Anna's and unlocked it. "Just hoping she's okay is all." He would have gladly returned a good-night kiss if Anna had offered it, but he didn't want Thomas to know that. The memory of kissing Erika flitted through his mind. He felt instantly guilty for envisioning a kiss from Anna.

He turned the light on, and before he had a chance to say anything else, Thomas breezed past him, flopped onto the bed nearest the door, and clicked on the television. Thomas flipped through channels until he found CNN. Jack would have preferred silence. Even a shower could wait. He only wanted to bury his face in a pillow and sleep until someone forced him awake.

Jack stripped out of the blue work shirt with the name "Steve" embroidered on the left chest pocket. The shirt reeked of BO and was spattered with the blood of Makers guards he had shot in the Croft penthouse. *I'll never put that back on.* He shrugged out of his pants as well and stood in a pair of boxers and an undershirt.

"I'm beat. Can you turn that off so I can sleep?"

Thomas shushed him, glared, and turned the sound up. "Listen."

Wolf Blitzer's face was mouthing words that Jack's tired brain strained to fully comprehend. Blitzer said something about a coalition of Mideast forces that had attacked France and Great Britain. Jack's exhausted brain tried to wrap itself around the phrase "turn into World War III."

Jack was confused. "What the—"

Thomas shushed him again.

The camera panned from Blitzer to a middle-aged guy who was supposedly an expert on electromagnetic pulses, which he referred to as EMPs. The man's voice talked over a computer animation illustrating how a large enough EMP could take out the electrical grid of a country or even a whole continent. The video ended with the lights blinking out over Europe and faded into a live satellite image of Europe. It was as black as the animated simulation of it in the video.

"This is not good," Thomas said.

As usual, the guy was a walking understatement. Jack's mind recalled images of dead men torn into pieces by the laser weapons fired by the alien ship and strewn across the red bricks of Apthartos. Europe had gone black. Jack's conspiracy senses tingled.

"There's no way this news is legit," he said.

Thomas rolled his eyes, his voice clipped. "Jack Wilson, high-school senior from BFE Arizona, authority on news?"

"No. But I've spent enough time now with black ops and the Croft/Sturgis clan to spot bullshit news when I see it."

Thomas raised an eyebrow, but the angry crinkle in his forehead eased. "What specifically do you find unbelievable?"

"First, the Middle East countries have been fighting amongst themselves for thousands of years. Like they're going to suddenly unify into one cohesive force? I don't buy it."

"Perhaps they were more unified than we knew?"

Jack shook his head. "Second, why attack Europe? Lots of people in the Middle East hate Americans, so why not attack us?"

"Simple. Europe is closer."

Jack sighed loudly. His head pounded from lack of sleep. "Just think about it for a minute. Whoever did this had tech that not only wiped the entire European power grid but also disrupted satellites. You think any country in the Middle East has that kind of capability?"

Thomas stared at the television screen, but his eyes weren't focused. He looked as though he was doing complex math in his head. He turned down the talking heads on the TV and asked, "Do you have more evidence to support your theory?"

Jack shrugged. "Not sure I've got any evidence. It's more a hunch. Don't you think it's an awfully big coincidence that the Greys recently shot Apthartos to hell and now the Middle East has allegedly not only put thousands of years of grievances behind them but miraculously developed the technology to pull this attack off? No, I'm saying it's an alien attack and the government's keeping it from the public. They're using the Middle East terrorist story as a cover because it's an easy lie that people are more than willing to believe." The memory of men cut in half and disemboweled, strewn across the red brick of Apthartos, made Jack shudder. He could almost smell the blood and urine and gunpowder from rounds the humans had fired to no avail. Those same aliens had taken Erika and Ian away. Bile rose in his throat as his worry for them was renewed.

Thomas considered what Jack had said for a few minutes then asked, "Why would the government cover up an alien attack?"

Jack rolled his eyes. "Come on, Thomas. Why have they hidden the truth about aliens since the 1940s? Build an entire underground city and create human-alien hybrids and keep all that secret? You really think, after all the lies and deceit, that they're going to just admit that aliens took out the power grid of Europe and, oh yeah, they're probably on their way over here to do the same?"

Thomas steepled his fingers under his chin and rested his elbows on his knees. "You actually make a lot of sense. We need to be wary and stay alert. The war is starting, and Croft is likely more motivated than ever to get Alecto back into his slimy hands."

"We should tell Anna." Jack was already a few steps toward the door when Thomas stopped him.

"No." He put his body between Jack and the door.

"But—"

Thomas held up a hand. "She's exhausted. We all are, and we're going to need our rest. Let her sleep tonight, Jack. Tomorrow, we'll let her know that the alien war has begun."

Prickly branches of dry desert scrub scraped Tex's legs as he tried to evade the copter chasing them. The time he had spent in deep meditation, both at the makeshift hospital and in the truck, had served him well. His senses were nearly as acute as they had ever been. He could also maintain a shield of repellant energy, for a time anyway. Bullets from the copter had zinged and ricocheted as he jumped the motorcycle out of the truck, but they hadn't been hit.

He had not been sure of his ability to protect them, though he had kept his doubts to himself. Other powers remained untested, but at least he knew he still had the ability to create a protective shield, despite the rain and the missing pieces of himself that the Conexus had taken from him.

Erika's body warmed his back. Her arms, wrapped around his waist, were distracting him more than he cared to admit. Her touch aroused in him confusing emotions and memories. *I know her, do I not?* The memories of his time with the Conexus and even the false memories implanted into his mind by the Regina were more vivid than the hazy memories of his time before the Conexus.

Erika's warmth was real, though. She was with him right then, her body heat seeping into him, her scent clinging to his nostrils. His head swam with dizziness. His mental resources, already compromised, were being spread thin by the need to maintain the shield while at the same time navigating his way through the desert. He tried to stop thinking about the maddening sensation of Erika's body against his own, the scent of her driving him to a nearly crazed state.

He tore through the desert scrub and whizzed past cactus and mesquite trees. The fabric of his pants was likely shredded at the ankles, torn to bits by the sharp thorns and prickly branches of the desert plants that grew more thickly than he had imagined.

Tex came upon a two-lane paved road. He crossed it and continued into the desert on the other side. Knowing Erika had been driving them northeast toward New Mexico, he continued in the same direction.

"Wait. Why didn't you take that road?" Erika asked. "It'd be faster and save what little flesh I have left on my legs."

"We need to stay off of the road. We are too exposed on this open-air vehicle."

Erika had to yell to be heard over the high-pitched whine of the bike. "What we need is another car."

She was correct, and they had only one way to procure a new vehicle.

"At the next road, we will abandon the motorcycle and obtain new transportation."

Tex assumed Erika would argue with him, but she remained quiet. Her arms were locked tightly around his waist as if he was a life raft that she clung to on a stormy sea.

He had put at least two kilometers between themselves and the crashed truck. Tex thought he had lost them, but his sensitive ears picked up the sound of helicopter blades. *Croft's men must have determined that there are no bodies in the burning truck.* He threw a glance over his shoulder. The searchlights roamed the desert floor but appeared to be searching to the west of where they were. *As long as they do not have canines, we stand a chance.*

After being chased by dogs at the school during their escape, Tex had taken a dislike to the beasts. When dealing with humans, Tex's ability to sense the environment more keenly than them was an advantage. Before a human could form the intention to pull a weapon on him, Tex had already smelled their surge of adrenaline.

Dogs were as tapped into their surroundings as Tex was, though. He had no sensory advantage over canines. *But they cannot manipulate matter as I can.* The thought gave him a small measure of comfort.

Tex brought his sensory attention back fully to the world around him. He detected exhaust fumes in a far greater quantity than he had smelled at the two-lane road he had recently passed over.

"I believe we are close to the highway that you mentioned previously," he said as the barest hint of light peeked over the eastern horizon. The night had been their ally. "We must get a car before the sun rises."

"Agreed. But it's not like we'll just walk up to a parking lot and find a car with keys in the ignition, waiting for us to take it."

Tex chose to ignore her barbed tongue. She was unlikely to agree with his idea of how to get what they needed. He did not have the energy to fight with her about every detail of their forward progress.

A new sound caught Tex's attention, making the hairs on the back of his neck stand on end. Dogs yipped and barked.

"Great. Dogs. They must have our scent," Erika said.

The yips grew louder. The dogs were quickly erasing the distance he had put between life and a bullet.

The smell of diesel overwhelmed his sensitive nose. In the daylight, they would be too exposed on a motorcycle, and Tex wanted to ditch the cycle in the scrub, where it would be more difficult to find than on the road. "We must abandon the motorcycle now. The freeway is just ahead."

Tex skidded to a stop, dismounted, and was nearly ten yards away from Erika in just a few seconds.

"Wait for me," she called.

"Hurry." His legs were wobbly, but he quickly scrambled up the embankment and easily jumped the guardrail. That was no more of a challenge for him than it would be for a deer. He stopped and looked back for Erika.

She stumbled and kicked up a puff of dust. He was ready to run back to her, but she got up and scrambled up the embankment to the road.

Behind her, the call of the dogs was louder still, and the copter's searchlights swept the desert floor less than a kilometer away from them. *They will catch up to us before I have the opportunity to procure a vehicle.* Running was not much of an effort, and it raised his heart rate but little, but the sound of the dogs made his heart gallop in his chest, the flutter of it causing a loud rush of blood in his ears.

Tex had never attempted to use his telepathic weapon on a dog. He recalled his first time in the desert. He had killed a snake simply because he could. The memory still brought heat to his cheeks. In his mind, he heard Dr. Randall's reproachful lecture for killing an innocent creature.

"But they will find us." He said the words aloud even though Dr. Randall was not there to hear them.

Erika hoisted her legs over the guardrail and stood looking at him, her chest heaving and her hands on her hips. "You don't have to kill them." She panted hard. "In Apthartos, you made that soldier unconscious rather than dead. Remember?"

Hazy images of Erika in trouble, pleading with Tex to spare her attacker, filled his mind. Since that time, though, she had killed Conexus and human too. Tex did not understand why she seemed to apply one standard to him and another to herself.

Tex reached out with his mind. Three dogs and six men were on the ground, closing in on them.

"While you take care of the posse hunting us, I'll get us a ride." She took a few steps toward the road but stopped beside him. Erika put her hand lightly on his shoulder. "You don't have to kill them. Just knock them out." She let go and stood at the edge of the pavement, her arm out and her thumb up.

He remained fixed on establishing a telepathic link with the dogs. He had been able to use his powers since leaving the school, but he was not at the strength he had been that night in the desert when he first met Erika—and nearly killed half a dozen soldiers. *I am no longer whole. I may never have those abilities again.*

During his years held against his will at A.H.D.N.A., he had longed to be more human. Tex had resented his abilities as they were the reason he was not free. Now, though, the idea of not having them both saddened and frightened him. He had taken his power for granted, and it certainly had come in handy to save his life—and Erika's—on several occasions. *How can I protect her if I cannot even protect myself?*

A semi passed them on the road behind him, and the strong gust of wind coming off the truck nearly knocked him over. Tex was having trouble closing the windpipes of all the dogs at once, at such a significant distance. He funneled his focus instead to the one that he sensed was the closest, and it finally fell away, unconscious but alive.

Erika yelled a curse at a car that slowed down but sped back up and left them still at the side of the road.

Another dog went down. A string of cars threw up a breeze at his back, and his skin prickled. Tex pulled his focus back to the men still advancing despite the fact that the dogs were down. They were less than a quarter of a mile away.

"I must look like a pile of horse crap," Erika said.

As much as Tex was concentrating, the statement was so odd that it pulled his attention back to her. "Why do you say that?"

"Because I can't even get a trucker to stop for me."

"You look good to me."

The words had tumbled out of his mouth. His cheeks were aflame, but his back was to her, so she likely had not seen how clearly flummoxed he was by such a bold admission of his feelings. She said nothing in response.

He was perhaps as surprised as she was by his statement. His mind had been a jumble ever since Dr. Randall unhooked him from his interface with the Conexus. He still recalled holding Xenos in his arms, kissing her. The implanted memory was as fresh and real as any memory in his mind. He recalled loving Xenos as fully as if he had spent his entire life with her. The fact that it was a virtual memory, gifted to him by the Regina, did not matter. In his mind, he had loved her, and Xenos had loved him back.

He meant what he'd said, though. He enjoyed looking at Erika—even when her golden-brown eyes were rimmed with red, puffy, and circled by darkness. Even when her clothes were tattered and dirty, her black hair a ratty, greasy mess, Erika was beautiful to him, and he suspected nothing she could do would ever change that.

Tex shook his head slightly. Nothing rattled his concentration more than musing about her. Five men still remained. As he redoubled his efforts, soon only four were left standing.

"Come on. We've got someone stopping." Erika waved at a car pulling onto the shoulder, its headlights catching them in a bright beam of light.

The car was a late-model sedan. It likely did not have the power Tex would have liked, but it appeared to be in much better shape than the old truck.

The driver was a middle-aged man with gray hair and glasses. The man reminded Tex of Dr. Randall, and a hollow feeling took up residence in the pit of Tex's stomach. *Guilt for what I may have to do to this fellow.*

As they approached the car, Erika said, "You should get in the back. And keep your hat on and your eyes averted. Maybe in the dark, he won't notice."

The men pursuing them were closer. Tex reached out with all his strength and simultaneously sent a piercing knife of pain through the heads of their pursuers. Though Tex couldn't see them, he imagined they were on their knees from the agony.

He had to drop his mental connection to the men to get into the car, but they would need a few seconds to recover. That was the best he could do. Tex did as Erika asked and eased himself onto the cloth seat in the back. He had to shove a stack of magazines and newspapers out of the way to make room.

The man's voice was gravelly. "What 'r you two doin' out here so late? You're not runaways, are you?" Though they were both strapped in, the man did not make any moves to get the car back onto the highway.

The man looked into the rearview mirror as he spoke. Tex turned to look out the window so the man would not get the full view of Tex's eyes.

The driver stared into the rearview mirror. "What the—"

"We need to go northeast," Erika said. "How far can you take us?"

Though the humans likely could not hear them yet, Tex knew choppers were close. Soon, they would be near enough to identify the car.

"They are almost here." Tex's voice was low but urgent. "You must drive. Now."

In the time Tex took to give the command, the helicopters had gotten close enough that even the humans heard them. The driver looked up through the top of his windshield, searching for the source of the sound.

He rounded on Erika. "Get outta my car. I figured you were two young people maybe broken down or something, but I'm not about to help two fugitives. Best you turn yourselves in. Turns out badly for people who run." The man reached toward the ignition to turn off the car.

Before his hand reached the key, the car accelerated wildly and pulled back onto the highway. The sudden thrust forward whipped Erika and the driver, and they slammed back into their seats. Tex had already used a lot of his stored energy to prevent the dogs and men from reaching them. The effort of manipulating the car's gas pedal made his head throb. He ignored the pain and kept his mind focused on making the car go as fast as it was capable of.

The man again said, "What the—" and stomped on the brake, but it did nothing to slow the car. "What's goin' on here?" The man's eyes searched the rearview mirror, frantic to find answers.

One of the first lessons Commander Sturgis had taught him was that fear was a powerful tool to obtain obedience. Sturgis had used it on Tex with great effect. He despised Sturgis's teachings. He had vowed that if he were ever free of her, he would shun her lessons. When in danger, though, he found himself resorting to her playbook.

Tex turned his head so that the man saw him clearly. Tex removed the knit cap that had covered his slightly pointy ears and large head, covered in silky, silver-blond hair falling in soft waves to his shoulders. With the first pink-tinged light of dawn spilling into the car, Tex's features were clearly visible to the man. His eyes were much too large and dark to be normal, to be human.

The man's mouth flew open and moved as though he was trying to get words out but couldn't quite formulate the question he longed to ask. He mumbled a prayer while he made the sign of the cross on his chest with his right hand while he kept his left hand on the wheel. He was apparently unwilling to concede that Tex had control over his car now, not him. Finally, he got his mouth to work. "Who... What are you?

Tex did not answer the question, and Erika remained silent. She stared straight ahead, and though she appeared calm on the outside, Tex heard her heart thrumming wildly in her chest.

"Do as I say, and you will live," Tex said.

5
WILLIAM CROFT

The flight attendant woke Croft when his jet was somewhere over the Atlantic Ocean.

His eyes were bleary. "Have we arrived? You know I require to be awoken no more than one hour prior to arrival." His voice showed his impatience at the flight attendant's incompetence.

The flight attendant, Frank, quickly corrected him. "No, sir, we have not arrived. There is urgent news that we believe you should be briefed on before landing."

Croft wiped sleep from his eyes and shifted himself to sit more upright. Frank had jettisoned his jacket and wore only a black vest and white shirt. Frank wiped his clean-shaven neck and slight chin with a handkerchief that he quickly stowed in a pants pocket.

Croft motioned for Frank to sit in the seat across from and facing him so that he did not have to crane his neck to look up while they spoke. As Frank sat, the odor of gin wafted off of him, his nose and cheeks red from drink. Frank had worked on William Croft's private plane for nearly twenty years. Croft had never seen him drink before.

Frank's eyes were wide and his brows crinkled. He fidgeted his hands in his lap as he advised William of the massive EMP and ensuing power outage throughout Europe. William did not interrupt or show the slightest emotion as Frank detailed the news of horrendous terrorist attacks in both London and Paris with great concern and emotion. The man's eyes watered. He nearly cried more than once during his recitation of the events that had befallen Europe while they flew to America.

"Early reports indicate that as many as three thousand people have been killed." Frank shook his head in disbelief and wiped sweat from his upper lip. "Officials say it could be weeks before power is completely restored in England."

While the events were certainly a shock to most, they were all expected—predictable even—for William Croft. The Conexus had told his father years before that a warrior species would arrive to harvest the Earth's most plentiful source of protein. The Conexus had been vague, however, about the date. The Conexus were from a far-off future, and the knowledge of an attack was from their past. Details had been lost to time. What remained in Conexus archives was more legend than clearly detailed history.

"So it has begun," Croft said. His voice was a low whisper meant more for himself than for Frank.

"Sir?"

Croft waved him off. "It is not important. Carry on."

Frank hesitated, his hands clasped in his lap, and he rubbed his right thumb nervously over his left hand. "Sir, what shall I tell the crew? Are we to be on standby to return to London at your command?"

Frank had no way of grasping the truth. They were likely never going back to England. Croft decided against telling him. If the British and US governments wanted to spread the lie of a terror attack to prevent widespread hysteria, he would not interfere with their disinformation campaign.

"Yes, remain on standby, Frank. I have some business here in New York, but be ready to leave at any time."

"Yes, sir." Frank hurried down the aisle toward the cockpit.

William had, as his father before him, spent his life preparing for the very events that were unfolding. Two lifetimes of preparation lay nearly in ruins, thanks to Lillian Sturgis and his daughter. Sturgis had let that teenage hybrid escape. Somehow, he and his friends had ended up with the antivirus the Conexus had promised to William. Rage filled him, and he pounded the armrest in frustration.

Croft gripped both armrests in his hands and took deep breaths. Losing his temper would do no good. The antivirus would be his again. He had simply to steal it back. It was, after all, promised to him.

Once he properly scolded Lizzy, they would head to Arizona. His lip curled at the thought of it. He detested the heat and dust and lack of green in the place. He would have much preferred his underground city to be built nearly anywhere else on the planet. Once underground, though, it would not matter. A mile beneath the surface was the same, the world over.

He had unfinished business there—one hybrid to rid himself of rather than risk it destroying what he had worked toward, another hybrid to recapture. *This time I will see personally to her reprogramming.*

The hour was well past noon when Jack finally woke. He was shocked Anna had let him sleep so long. They'd lost nearly eighteen hours of driving time.

Thomas wasn't in the room, and Jack was relieved to have a bit of time to himself. He stood under the spittle of lukewarm water coming from the lime-encrusted showerhead and tried not to see the faces of the men he'd killed. Whenever he tried to think about something other than death and hell breaking loose in Europe, his mind drifted to Anna. Those thoughts weren't much better. Inevitably, he'd imagine running his hands through her silky hair and kissing the divot at the base of her neck. Then he'd feel guilty for daydreaming about making out with Anna when he should have been worried about Erika, Ian, and his mom.

His stomach hurt. He couldn't remember when they'd last eaten. After what had gone down at the Croft penthouse, none of them felt much like eating. Jack skipped shaving and shoved the blood-spattered "Steve Harper" work clothes to the bottom of his duffel.

He walked to Anna's room in search of Thomas. Before he even knocked on the door, he heard the TV blaring from inside. *Found Thomas.*

The lock clicked, and the door slowly opened. Jack's heart quickened at the sight of Anna. Her freshly washed hair was hanging in blond curtains. Her face was cleaned of dried blood. Even the scar across her eye seemed paler and less angry, though the iris in that eye was still milky. Her face brightened at the sight of him, and she forced a small smile.

"You sure do clean up well, Jack Wilson." Her voice was a breathy, hushed whisper.

He bowed slightly. "As do you, Anna Sturgis."

She blushed, and he flashed her a mischievous smile as he entered, leaving her standing at the door.

Thomas sat on the edge of the bed, his eyes glued to the television screen. Alecto was again curled into an upright ball with her back against the headboard, her head tucked to her knees.

How long is she going to do that?

"I don't know about you guys, but I'm starved," Jack said. "Anybody want to go to the diner across the street for some grub?"

Anna answered by tucking her room key and a small black wallet into a back jeans pocket. "Let's go," she said while putting on her jacket.

Thomas answered by gesturing for Anna to get out of the way of the TV screen. For her part, Alecto remained a motionless blob, her head a shiny dome over her knees.

Jack was glad of the chance to spend time alone with Anna. He'd grown accustomed to her company on the trip to NYC and their days of stakeout. That seemed like months before even though less than a week had passed, and his life in Ajo seemed like a hazy dream or perhaps a movie he'd seen once.

The diner was nearly empty, but they asked for a booth in the back corner. They drank hot black coffee and avoided talking about Anna's dead father, men Jack had killed, battle wounds they nursed, and the threat of world war looming in Europe.

Steering clear of topics that would allow their open wounds to fester left them with little to talk about. They downed enough greasy-spoon food to feed four people without saying much more than "pass the salt," but the silence between them was not the uncomfortable, awkward silence of a new relationship. Jack felt as though he'd been with Anna for years instead of weeks. *Only we're not really together.*

Anna finally pushed a plate covered in syrup and pancake crumbs away from her. "I can't believe I ate so much of this horrid food." She looked disgusted.

Jack stuffed another large forkful into his mouth, thinking he'd had worse. "What's our plan for the day?"

Anna glanced around as if making sure no one was listening. She leaned across the table slightly and whispered, "I should contact Mr. Sewell."

Jack washed down the pasty pancake with a long draw of coffee. "Probably a good idea. With all that's happened." He hoped Sewell had more information about the Miramar prison than he had given them about Croft's penthouse. Since Sewell still had one foot in the door of the Croft organization, he should be able to fill them in on what the Crofts had been up to since leaving NYC.

Anna wrapped her hands around her coffee mug and stared at the black liquid inside as if the mug was a scrying bowl and she could divine the future by staring at it.

Jack pushed his plate to one side and touched her hand. Despite the warmth of the mug, her delicate hand was still cold.

"Anna?"

She looked up at him. Her eyes glistened.

Jack's voice was low and soft. "Talk to me."

She put her cup down, their contact broken. Anna wiped her eyes with the back of her hand. Then she took a deep breath, and within seconds, she had put on a mask of calm. The false smile she plastered on would have fooled most people into believing that all was right with her world, but Jack knew better. He was a bit disturbed by how quickly she could go from looking as though she was on the edge of losing it to the picture of serenity.

"For Christ's sake, Anna, your dad just got killed. Your brother was shot, you were kidnapped and tortured by your friggin' cousin, and your mom—"

"I know what happened," she hissed. As quickly as she had put on a mask of calm, her face was a storm of anger.

Jack put up his hands in a conciliatory don't-shoot gesture. "I'm just trying to help. You shouldn't keep stuff all bottled up."

Anna took a last swig of coffee and rose, grabbing the check to pay. "Don't presume to tell me what I need." She walked toward the register before Jack could say anything else to piss her off further.

She was acting as though he'd been an asshat to her, but as far as he could see, all he'd tried to do was help. Rich girls from NYC were no less a mystery to him than poor girls from rural Arizona. He seemed to be in perpetual hot water with both despite wanting nothing more than to see them smile.

Anna paid the bill and got several dollars' worth of quarters that she stuffed into her pockets. Jack followed as she pushed through the door. He had to practically run to keep up with her.

She hurried to the pay phone up the street as she pulled the collar closer to her neck. Winter had finally arrived in Missouri.

They were still off grid, which still sucked. Jack would have preferred making the call on a cell phone in the relative comfort of the grungy hotel room rather than freezing his nads off at a pay phone. He blew on his cupped hands and wished for gloves. Anna pulled the door to the pay phone closed, putting a glass wall between them, her back to him. He watched her feed quarters into the antiquated public phone.

He tried to listen in on Anna's conversation. Her back was toward him, so he went to the other side so he could see her face. Her left hand was to her ear so she could hear better. She looked up when she saw him. The look on her face was indecipherable.

Jack couldn't hear much of what she said. She mainly listened, and at one point she shook her head and said no. The crease in her brow was back.

Anna finally hung up. Her gloved hand lingered on the receiver, and she stared at it as she'd stared at the cup of coffee. She swung the glass door open, gave Jack a curt nod, and walked back to the hotel.

Jack was the hired help, but Anna had never treated him as such—until then.

He ran after her and tugged on her arm. "Hey. What'd he say? Or am I too lowly to talk to now?"

Anna stopped and stared at him, her upper lip curled in disgust.

He was ashamed that her look of repugnance was directed at him.

"Really? You think now is a good time to be needy?" She shook her head and continued her walk away from him.

A part of him begged himself to let it go. It was the part of himself that avoided conflict and that played along when girls said things like "Just friends, okay?"

Jack was tired of playing along and keeping his thoughts to himself, though. It wasn't "needy" to want to know what Anna and

Sewell had planned for them. Their plans would affect his life too after all.

Jack caught up to her easily and pulled her again, that time more forcefully. "Stop, Anna."

She stopped and shot him a look that could melt glass.

"It's not needy to want to know the plan for my life. I was conscripted into this, remember?"

Her look remained fiery. "Well, you'll be happy to know that your torture will soon be over."

Jack was afraid to ask the inevitable question. Their original goal had been to free her Aunt Lilly from prison. *If I'm being cut loose, does that mean her Aunt Lilly is dead?*

"What happened?" he asked.

"My Aunt Lilly has been set free."

7
ERIKA

A statue of the Virgin Mary wobbled back and forth on the dash of the Olds Cutlass that Erika and Tex had hijacked. The driver clasped his hands at his chest, his head bowed as he mumbled prayers. Tex drove the car from the back seat.

Erika no longer heard helicopters chasing them, which was little comfort. She'd thought they were free before, only to have something hunting them around the next corner.

"What's your name?" Erika asked.

The man shot her a furtive look. "Gary."

"We're going to switch places, Gary. You scoot across, and I'm going to skittle over top of you. Got it?"

"But we'll... I've got to steer, or—"

"You're not steering now," Erika said.

Gary's eyes were red, his cheeks wet with tears.

"Do as she says." Tex's voice was cold and ominous from the back seat. He could be so boyish and naïve at times that it was difficult to remember what he was capable of. *Please, Gary, just do what he asks.*

Gary scooched across the seat while Erika climbed over him. They were a tangle of limbs. At one point, she was awkwardly stuck with her butt in his face, but finally Erika was behind the wheel.

"I can take over now," she said.

Erika made eye contact with Tex in the rearview mirror. His face was so calm and pale that he looked like a statue.

"You need to rest."

"I need to stay awake. The copters still search."

Erika didn't doubt that. If Croft were anything like Sturgis, he wouldn't easily give up the effort to find Tex. The exploding truck was evidence that Croft no longer cared about taking Tex alive. *If they find us in this car, they'll kill us all.*

Erika pressed down on the accelerator, but it was already to the floor. Tex still had control. "Look, if I hear or see the choppers, I'll wake you. Besides, I know the location of Dana's house. You don't."

Tex didn't say anything, but the car slowed and started to veer off the road. Erika hurriedly grabbed the wheel and pressed the accelerator to the floor. They were on I-10, headed east. In another hour, they'd be to Tucson, and if she continued on main roads, they'd make it to her Aunt Dana's place in New Mexico in about seven hours. Their only advantage was that Croft's men had no idea where Erika and Tex were headed. *We'll find a place to let Gary out after we get north of Tucson.*

Erika adjusted the seat so her feet more readily reached the pedals. The pistol she'd jammed into her waist pressed uncomfortably into her back. She pulled it out of her waistband and placed it on the seat next to her. Gary's eyes grew wide.

"Don't worry. I'm not going to shoot you. This is for protection only."

Gary didn't look relieved.

"I'm just caught up in a bad mess, but I'm not a bad person," Erika said.

"Said the girl who carries a gun, hijacks cars, and kidnaps people," Gary said.

Erika averted her gaze from his eyes. He was right. She didn't feel like a good person, at least not anymore. She'd never tried to be goody-goody before, and no one was likely to have accused her of that before she got involved in the mess with Tex, but she had never considered herself a bad person. *And I've killed a man too, Gary. Don't forget to add that to the list.*

Tex took Erika's suggestion and withdrew into himself. His eyes shut, and he pulled into a tight ball in the back seat. Gary sat silent and still on the seat next to her, his eyes glassy and fixed forward. Erika drove in silence.

They hit Tucson before morning rush hour and breezed past it with little traffic to slow them. Though the speed limit was seventy-five, she kept the speedometer needle pushed past one hundred. She hoped she wouldn't get pulled over for speeding. She didn't want to see what Tex might do to a hapless cop who tried to give Erika a speeding ticket.

After two hours of driving, they were well east of Tucson and less than an hour from the border of Arizona and New Mexico. Even when they'd hit Tucson, she hadn't slowed down. She'd seen no more signs that the Makers pursued them, and she hadn't been pulled over. *No one has luck that good, especially not me.*

Erika remembered how Tex had immobilized police cars that tried to chase them that first night Jack drove his Jetta into the night. She glanced in the rearview mirror. Tex was as still as a stone. He didn't appear to be paying a bit of attention to anything going on in the world around them, but she had no idea where he went when he withdrew. *Maybe he's aware on a level humans don't understand.*

The sun was well up, a bright October day. Erika pulled some cheap, wire-frame sunglasses from the visor. They were so large on her small head that they covered her face from above her brows to midcheekbone.

Erika had put the car on cruise control set at one hundred. The road was smooth, flat, and straight. Without anyone talking, she had nearly dozed off when she came upon signs announcing a border-patrol checkpoint.

She slammed on the brakes and slowed the car. "Border patrol. Gary, you're not an illegal alien, are you?"

Gary glared at her.

Tex's voice, low, soft, and muffled, came from the back seat. "He may not be, but I am. We cannot go through that checkpoint."

Erika tore the large sunglasses from her face and attempted to hand them back to Tex. "Here. Put these on and your hat, and—"

"No," Tex said. "Black uniforms, Erika."

They were still far enough away that Erika couldn't tell the color of the uniforms the men wore, but Tex's senses were keener than hers. If he said the uniforms were black, she believed him. The Makers men had worn all black. Her dad had never worn black in all the years he was with border patrol.

"You must turn around. Now."

They had nowhere to go but across the wide median covered in desert plants and high, scrubby grass. Erika turned sharply to the left, and the car bounced over the rumble strips and hit the median. She was going so quickly and had turned so sharply that the car nearly rolled, but Erika got the steering under control and sped across the median.

She checked the rearview mirror. Black-clad men that had been standing by orange cones funneling cars to a central checkpoint were scrambling toward a patrol vehicle. Erika pressed the accelerator to the floor.

"Looks like they're in pursuit," she said.

Tex did not respond.

Gary grabbed the gun from the seat and pointed it at Erika. "I don't know who you are or why you're runnin', but I'm turning you in. Get back to that checkpoint."

In normal circumstances, Erika would have been terrified of a gun pointing at her. Even though Gary's hands trembled visibly, she had no doubt that fear would just as easily urge him to pull the trigger as prevent it.

Those weren't normal circumstances, though. Tex might have been distant and cool toward her, but she knew he wouldn't allow Gary to kill her. She didn't want Tex to kill Gary either, though.

Erika kept her hands on the wheel and the pedal to the floor. "Just be cool. Put the gun down. We don't want to hurt you. We just need your car and—"

Gary pulled the steering wheel with his left hand while he tried to point the gun at her with his right. The car jerked, but Erika pulled the wheel hard in the opposite direction with her left hand while she beat at Gary's hand with her right. She nearly ran into a Ford pickup as she pulled into westbound traffic.

Gary shouted at her, "Stop, or so help me, I'll shoot yer ass!"

Blood rushed in her ears, and her voice was no longer calm. "Put the gun down, Gary. Now! Before—"

The gun dropped to the floor of the car as Gary choked and spat, gasping for air.

"Tex, stop!" she screamed. "You don't need to kill this guy."

He ignored her, though. He had gotten even more efficient at the business of killing. Terminating Gary took less than two minutes. His body was a lifeless mass slumped against the passenger window in the front seat.

Erika wiped her drippy nose and wet eyes with the back of a shirtsleeve. She had difficulty seeing through bleary eyes, and it was hard to hear with the sound of blood rushing in her ears. She thought she heard sirens. She avoided looking toward the dead man just a few feet away from her.

Her ankle and foot ached from pressing the accelerator to the floor, but she didn't dare let up. If an authentic border patrol or law enforcement officer caught up to them, they'd find the dead body and arrest first, ask questions later.

A green sign came into view, and she took the exit. She hoped it was the one for Safford.

Erika took the ramp at sixty and nearly wiped out as she rounded the curve. Somehow, she kept it on the road, but the speed of the turn made Gary's body fling toward her. His dead head landed on the seat next to her, his wisp of white hair brushing against her thigh.

She wanted to scream—to cry—to stop the car, jump out, and run away from dead Gary and dangerous, unpredictable Tex. She wanted to run until she got home. The thought of home reminded her that she no longer had one.

Stop it, Erika. Stop, stop, stop. She sniffed one more time, took a deep breath, and blinked away the tears from her eyes. Erika ignored the stop sign at the intersection and hoped no semi was barreling toward her as she gunned it onto the road leading northeast.

"Are we being followed?" she asked.

Tex remained curled into a tight ball, his voice muffled as he spoke. "I took care of them. For now."

She tried not to think about what Tex meant exactly by "took care of them." They'd spent enough time together in danger to have a pretty good idea what he meant.

"Do you think they saw enough of us to ID the car?" she asked.

"Unknown."

Erika didn't want to ditch yet another car. Worse still, she didn't want to repeat how they'd gotten the Olds and put another human at risk for the same fate Gary got. "Any chance you can manipulate the matter of this car to change how it looks?"

Tex cocked his head to the side, his eyes far off as if thinking about her question. Finally he said, "Perhaps. I have not tried such a task before, at least not on such a grand scale. But I will attempt it."

He closed his eyes and sat with his legs curled beneath him. He looked like a small, thin, big-headed Buddha.

The change was subtle at first. The color of the car's hood went from a dark, navy blue to dark green. That might have been enough to throw someone off a little, but it was unlikely to foil the Makers men completely.

A thin film of sweat shone on Tex's forehead.

One moment Erika was driving a four-door sedan, and the next, she was behind the wheel of a Jetta.

"Jack's car?" she asked.

It was, even down to a pine-tree air freshener hanging from the mirror. The only difference was that Tex had made the car a light tan rather than white.

"Besides the truck that I ignited, it is the only other car that I know."

Erika drove them northeast toward New Mexico, her eyes glued to her mirrors, waiting for a copter or police car to catch up to them. Running for her life on a lack of sleep had exhausted her. *I can't remember a time when I wasn't running from something.*

She got off the two-lane highway, worried that even a two-lane road was too obvious. Using the narrow, twisty road would take them even longer to make it to the wooded, remote, mountainous area where her Aunt Dana lived, but she thought going slow and shaking them off the trail was better than fast and running into them again.

As they traveled on the back roads, no sign announced, "Welcome to the Land of Enchantment" to let them know they'd entered New Mexico. She knew they had left Arizona only because she'd traveled to Aunt Dana's house many times when she was younger. She remembered the subtle changes in the surroundings—the climb in elevation and the scrub giving way to squatty evergreens and sagebrush.

Erika rolled down her window and took in the scent of juniper and dirt. The cool air had a bright crispness to it that said fall but that was rarely felt as far south as Ajo. She breathed it in, relishing the clean air in her lungs after weeks in the dank, musty, oxygen-lacking underground world of the Conexus.

"Let me know if it gets too cold for you," Erika said.

She wasn't sure if Tex was still awake. He'd gone silent again.

Then he said, "It feels... good." His eyes were wide and bright in the midmorning light, his skin less pale than it had been when they'd first left the school. "New Mexico is different."

"Yes. A subtle change, but definitely not the same as Arizona."

"I think I will like this New Mexico," Tex said.

Erika chose to let him bask in a small moment of wonder and apparent happiness, at least as content as she generally ever saw him. She decided to keep to herself the gnawing fear that Aunt Dana wouldn't welcome her with open arms.

Tex's head spun as he catalogued the new sights and odors of the unfamiliar place called New Mexico. Erika had referred to it as the "Land of Enchantment." Tex didn't know if humans actually believed the land had magical properties, but he understood how the superstition could arise.

The light of the place was different from that in Arizona. It was somehow softer, more gentle yet still bright and sunny. A scientific explanation for the difference in the quality of the light escaped him, but it was unmistakable. *Even a human would notice it.*

Fewer particles of air pollution from manufacturing and vehicle exhaust were there. He breathed deeply of the clean air. His chest ached from the effort as his remaining lung tried to compensate for the missing one, stolen from him by the Conexus. His anger at them over the loss of his lung collided with the implanted memories of belonging to the hive. The cognitive dissonance made his head throb. He breathed the cool air more deeply and calmed himself. The anger served no purpose. He would simply have to adapt to having only half the lung capacity. *I cannot grow a new lung, after all. Can I?*

Tex wanted to examine every piñon tree and antelope, to sear those new images into his brain. He considered asking Erika to stop the car so he could run with a herd of animals galloping in a nearby meadow, but he was not strong enough to keep up. Using his powers to create shields, immobilize chase cars, and alter the structure of the vehicle had taken out of him what little energy he had built up since they'd come back from the world of the Conexus.

During his time with the Conexus collective, he'd had access to all their cumulative knowledge. It was a wisdom and history that stretched back for millennia—back to before the Regina existed, back to a time the Conexus considered legend and myth. *Back to human history.* He knew what was coming, and he would need all the strength he could muster to survive.

The news report about the attacks in Europe had confirmed that. *That is how it began.* They had very little time before things would get very tough. He knew of a way to prevent the human world from ending up like the Conexus, cut off from the sky and living in the dark. Even at his full powers and without missing pieces of himself, though, it would've been a long shot.

Tex forced himself to seek rest. He grudgingly withdrew from the joy of discovery of new sensations in the place called New Mexico. Though he tried to enter the quantum realm and heal, his fractured mind flitted from one thought to another.

Erika had held him against herself in the dark hallway of A.H.D.N.A., the red lights blinking, her body warm and soft. The Regina's long, thin finger traced a line down his face. Her touch sent chills down his spine, and he shivered now as he recalled it. Dr. Randall's eyes were misty with tears when they rescued him from house arrest in Apthartos. He smelled the acrid odor of dead bodies befouled with their own urine and the stench of blood—or perhaps that was own blood he had detected as he lay on the cold table in the world of the Conexus.

Tex touched the back of his head, half expecting to feel the metal clamps that had held the cable connecting him to the hive mind. On and on his turmoil went, his fractured mind unable to focus. He was restless and fidgety.

"Are you okay back there?" Erika asked.

He was not okay, but he did not want to alarm her with the knowledge of just how unokay he was. He slowly blinked his eyes and tried to clear the blurriness. "I am here."

"Oh, good. I've got to stop for gas when we hit the next town, and I'm thinking we should dispose of Gary somehow and—"

Tex rubbed at his temples. "Erika, please slow down your speech." His voice was harsher and more impatient than he had intended.

"You don't have to bite my head off. I'm exhausted, okay? I've been driving for hours while you were sleeping—"

"Meditating."

"Whatever. You got to rest. I didn't. And I'm up here with a dead guy decomposing next to me, so I'd appreciate it if you'd stop acting like Emperor Asshole for a minute and help me find a way to get rid of the body so I don't have to sit with a dead guy."

The longer Erika talked, the pitchier her voice became. At the end of her tirade, her voice was downright shrill, and her eyes glistened with angry tears.

Tex had no logical reason to fear Erika. She could not harm him. Even if she picked up the gun and tried to shoot him, he could stop the bullet in midair and even turn it on her if he wanted.

Yet she had a way of compelling him to attempt to avoid her wrath. Tex didn't understand it. No one else made him feel that way. *No one except Commander Sturgis.* He didn't want her to be angry with him, but the issue was more than that. He had never cared what humans thought of him before, but he cared what Erika thought. *Perhaps too much.*

He was unaccustomed to apologizing, but he gave it a try. "I am... sorry."

"It's..." Erika wiped her face with the back of her sleeve. "It's okay." Her eyes were puffy and surrounded by dark circles. Her dark hair clung to her head from days of accumulated grime. She was only slightly less gaunt and pale than she'd been the day they arrived at the school.

Though she looked like a worn-out shell of the woman he had first met, he could not help feeling every bit as drawn to her now as he had then. He practically heard Commander Sturgis's voice in his head, admonishing him to avoid attraction to others. She had trained him to deny himself friendships or even family. He was meant to be a weapon, a guardian of humans against alien threat.

"You will need all of your focus for your job," Commander Sturgis had said. "Attractions—relationships—will only distract you. Allowing yourself even a single dalliance with a woman will undo you, 9. Don't forget that."

Tex hated Sturgis so much that he assumed she'd lied about everything. But as he stared at the back of Erika's angry head, wishing beyond all wishes that he could find a way to simply make her care for him as much as he found himself caring for her, he wondered if

Commander Sturgis had spoken the truth, about that one topic anyway. *Erika, you will be the death of me.*

Tex turned his attention back to the immediate issue. Erika was right. They could not continue to drive around with a dead man in the car. "Pull onto that side road. The one ahead."

Erika did as he requested without argument and turned onto an unpaved forest-service spur road. After about a mile, the dirt road became not much more than a wide trail. They drove slowly over the rutted road but met no other cars on it.

Dust billowed behind them. A layer of rusty-red dirt was covering the tan car. After another mile or so of rough driving, Erika pulled off the narrow trail and forced the car over a patch of sagebrush. She finally stopped in a spot of barren dirt.

Erika flung her door open and escaped the car without a word. A cloud of dust wafted around her, and she coughed. "Must not have rained here last night."

Tex's muscles were more limber than a human's, but he too was glad to exit the vehicle. He stretched his arms overhead then bent over to stretch his calves. His eyes caught the side of the car, and he could not help the chortle that escaped his throat.

"What's so funny?" Erika stretched too.

"I do not think I have a career ahead of me painting cars." Though he had managed to force the paint molecules into a different color, the effect was uneven. The car looked as though it had been spray-painted with a sprayer filled with several different paints. Splotches of tan were layered over patches of dark blue and even bits of white, green, and orange showing here and there. "I have made a mess of this car."

Erika shrugged. "Doesn't matter. We're likely going to have to ditch it soon anyway. I gotta pee. Stay here. And no peeking."

"Where are you going?"

"Into the woods over there. Just stay here, okay?"

She scurried off through the sagebrush and into a thin stand of piñon. Tex had spent enough time around humans to know that they all had a rather peculiar need for privacy regarding the basic functions of their bodies, facts of biology shared by all.

Erika cursed softly at a bramble bush and a few seconds later had choice words for the thorns on an acacia tree. She finally stopped, and Tex withdrew his attention before he sensed too much. Even from a distance, he could hear her unzip her jeans and smell the results of her makeshift bathroom. He had spent enough time with Erika to know she would likely be upset with him even for hearing her pee, let alone watching her.

He turned his back to her and instead stared at the dead body in the car. The man's face was already bloated and pale.

Erika had cried over the man's death. Tex knew human morals dictated he should regret killing the man, but the truth was he did not regret it. Though he wanted to deny all that Sturgis had taught him—all she had genetically programmed into him—he had been trained not to feel remorse, regret, or guilt about killing. The only feeling he had about Gary was relief that the man no longer posed a threat to reveal Tex to those that hunted him.

Tex popped the trunk in the off chance that Gary had been carrying around a shovel. A musty blanket covered in grass was there, along with a rickety aluminum-frame lawn chair, two road flares covered in a thick layer of dust, a spare tire with almost no tread, and a tire iron. Tex picked up the iron and examined it. The steel rod could be a useful weapon, but it would make a lousy shovel. He put the flares in his pockets, tossed the tire iron into the back seat, and closed the trunk.

Erika appeared from behind a nearby juniper tree. "Ah. So much better." Her stomach rumbled loudly as she approached him.

"You need to eat."

Her eyes landed on Gary's bloated body. "Not anymore." Her brows knitted into a deep furrow, and she scowled at Tex.

He avoided her angry glare. "It would be best if we could bury the body to prevent anyone finding it, but we have no tools, and I am not strong enough to create a hole via telekinesis. We'll have to dump the body and cover it as best we can." Tex grabbed Gary's shoulders and began to pull the heavy body out of the car.

Erika's arms were crossed over herself. "We may have another option. Unfortunately, it will require us to carry Gary for a ways."

Gary's body was half out of the car, his legs still lying on the seat.

"Why?" Tex asked.

"It's an awful thing to do to him, really." Erika wrung her hands. "I mean, if I was dead, I wouldn't want it to end like this for me. But I don't see another choice."

Tex resumed dragging Gary out of the car. "What are you talking about, Erika?"

The man landed with a thud, and a poof of rusty-red dirt billowed around him.

"When I was doing my business, I noticed an old water tank for cattle. I haven't seen any cattle on our drive, so maybe it's abandoned. But with the rains lately, it's probably got water in it. It's about a hundred yards from where I was, so it's a ways to take him. We can dump the body there. Even if it's still being used, in this remote area, it could be weeks before anyone's out here to check the tank."

Even a few weeks in water would cause the body to decompose more rapidly than if buried in the dry, sun-packed dirt. For their purposes, that was a good thing.

"I am not strong enough yet to carry the body on my own. I will need your assistance. Are you able to help with his legs?"

Erika's nose wrinkled, her lip curled, and she swallowed. She stared down at Gary, and her eyes filled with tears. "I can help." Her voice was barely more than a whisper. She checked Gary's pants pockets both front and back and retrieved a black wallet. She opened it, her face still ghostly pale, her lip still curled. She pulled out some bills and counted them. "Forty-two dollars." She shrugged. "This should at least buy us some gas and a bit to eat." She stuffed the money in her front jeans pocket, shoved the wallet back into Gary's pants, then lifted Gary's legs.

Though Tex had spent some time in deep meditation, trying his best to heal and recover his strength, Gary's body was like a sack of lead. Tex's arms ached after only twenty yards. After another fifty yards of dragging Gary, Tex's back felt as though someone had beaten it, but he did not voice his agony. He did not want to show weakness to Erika.

For her part, Erika kept her head down and looked only at Gary's feet, her brow furrowed and upper lip still curled as though she had smelled something rank.

They took nearly twenty minutes to get to the watering tank. It was round, steel, and open at the top, standing about four feet tall. The water level was about six inches below the rim. *Plenty of water to cover a body.*

Tex bent to grab Gary's shoulders again. "Let us get this done so we can be on our way."

Erika did not bend. "We should say a few words."

Tex did not let go. "Now is not the time for a discussion."

"No. I mean we should say something about him. It's rude to just dump him in the drink. No funeral. No burial. And his family's not here." She stared off across the small meadow and toward the horizon. "They must be worried sick for him by now." She wiped her eye.

Tex drew in a breath. "We did not know this man. Sentimentality over the death of a person you did not even know is— well, it is a waste of time." He bent again to grab the body.

"That's the thing I'll never understand about you, Tex. You were supposedly created and trained to protect humans, but you sure don't value human life very much."

"Perhaps humans have not shown me reason to value them."

Erika's eyes narrowed, and her lips were set in a thin line. "Thanks a lot."

Her voice did not sound appreciative. *She is being sarcastic.* He had not intended to anger her, yet everything he said seemed to rankle her. "I did not mean offense toward you." *Never toward you.*

Her eyes softened, but only slightly. Erika turned her attention back to Gary. "Dear Lord, we're sorry for what we did to Gary." She sniffled. "He was probably a good man. Probably loved. And, well, he didn't deserve to end up this way, so I hope he's going someplace better than this." Erika wiped her face. "Rest in peace."

"Why are you crying over a person that you did not know? He may have been a horrible person, Erika."

Erika's lips tightened again. She closed her eyes, sucked in a deep breath, and looked as though she had to restrain herself from hitting Tex. "Sometimes I forget how little experience you have with the world." She sighed. "My mom just died, Tex. Seeing this dead guy makes me think about her. And thinking about her being dead makes me think about losing my dad. It's like tearing a whole new hole in my heart."

"One thought leads to another?"

"Yes. It's like a new loss connects to an old loss and somehow makes it grow."

The concept was foreign to Tex. In his mind, each event was unique and not shared with others. Each memory was in its own separate box in his mind. But as Erika described how seeing Gary reminded her of her mother, Tex recalled Xenos flying apart before his eyes, and the memory renewed the ache in his heart.

Tex looked down at the bloated, ghastly white face of dead Gary. "Goodbye, Gary." His words were stilted, the emotions new to him. He repeated the sentiment Erika had offered, though he was not sure he understood the full meaning of it: "Rest in peace."

Erika nodded and patted him lightly on the arm. "Ready?"

Tex nodded, and they heaved the body upward. Erika grunted from the effort, and Tex let out a loud breath. Erika shoved Gary's posterior to get it over the rim, and Tex pushed the shoulders. The body splashed them with surprisingly cold water.

Tex leapt back as if he jumped away from a fire. He quickly took his wet shirt off and instinctively threw it to the ground. The cool mountain air prickled his wet skin. He was glad for the sunny day, otherwise the cool air would have chilled him unbearably.

A mocking smile replaced Erika's grimace. "You look like you were jumping away from a viper's nest."

"It is not funny."

Erika did not stop smiling. "It is a little. You should have seen yourself."

"I do not need to see myself. I am aware of how I look."

Erika picked up his shirt and shook off the dirt. The soil had melded with the splash of water, creating muddy streaks that she could not shake out no matter how hard she tried. "You need to lighten up a bit, Tex." She handed him the dirty shirt and headed back toward the car.

I doubt she will say that when she learns what is coming. "Maybe humans are too light. Perhaps you should take things more seriously, not less."

She stopped abruptly, and Tex nearly ran into her back. "No, I disagree. I'm thinking that the only thing that's kept me from going stark raving mad, like seriously over-the-top bonkers through this whole thing, is that I had Ian with me. And even during the worst crapstorm that life throws at us, he makes me stop and laugh. For years, he's been saying to me, 'Lighten up, Erika.' And you know what? He's right. Life is a daily run through a minefield of cow shite, and the only thing that keeps it from utterly sucking is a laugh with friends."

She stared into his eyes as if looking for something. Apparently, she did not find what she looked for. Erika threw up her hands, rolled her eyes, groaned, and resumed walking.

"Erika."

She kept walking. "What?"

"Stop. Please. I need to—"

She stopped and blew out an exasperated breath. "What, Tex? My stomach is doubling back on itself in hunger."

"I need to tell you something. You will not like it."

Her dark eyes narrowed on him. "You've been keeping something from me? Well? Out with it." She had one hand on her hip, and with the other, she made a rolling motion.

She will be angry beyond repair if I do not tell her the truth. Most of it, anyway. "When I was interfaced with the Conexus, I learned things about their history. About Earth history."

Her intense gaze continued.

"The attacks in Europe are definitely not terrorists. It is an attack by an alien species. They call themselves M'Uktah, 'people of Uktah.' They come from the far side of the galaxy and have come here using a dimensional gateway."

"You mean like a wormhole?"

"Yes. They are predators, Erika. Deadly predators."

Her face grew paler than he had ever seen it. She gripped her stomach and looked as though she would vomit.

He wanted to provide comfort to her and ease her fear, but he had little experience with such interactions and was afraid to attempt to touch her for fear she'd recoil.

She took a deep breath, swallowed, and said, "You knew this all along. From the moment we found you, lying on that table, and you said nothing?"

Tex had assumed she would be fearful from the new information he'd given her, not angry at him. *I do not comprehend her.*

"Do not be angry with me. When you first found me—when we were at the school—I was not myself. My memories were—still are—confused. But when we heard the announcement on the radio, of the attacks, I knew it was not what they are reporting. I knew it was the alien war that the Makers, and Commander Sturgis, have been preparing for all these years. Do you see?"

Erika closed her eyes and rubbed her brows. Finally, she said, "I understand that you've been ill. I get that. But you can't keep things like that from me, okay? If we're going to work together—to be a team—you've got to be honest with me. Always. Do you understand?"

"It is you who do not understand. I did not want—"

"I didn't want what? To be prepared to be attacked? To possibly be someone's dinner?" Her nose wrinkled in disgust.

She was twisting everything he said until even he wondered why he had done what he had. Within the blink of her eye, he was within inches of her, their eyes locked. Only inches separated them.

His voice was a low whisper. "I wanted to protect you."

Her cheeks flushed, her breathing ragged. He felt her heart fluttering away in her chest. "Oh."

Tex stepped back from her, allowing space to come between them. Erika stood motionless as if frozen in place.

"Erika?"

She sucked in a breath. "Yes, well, we should probably get going." Her stomach rumbled loudly as if to accentuate her point. She stared at him for a few moments more with an expression Tex could not read. Abruptly, she said, "Okay then," and continued back to the car.

Since they'd disposed of Gary, Tex sat in the front seat. Erika drove but said nothing. She looked deep in thought.

They got back to the main, paved road, and in less than fifteen minutes, a sign announced they were entering a town called Luna, New Mexico. It was more a grouping of buildings at a wide spot in the road than a town. Despite the fact that it was midday, there were no cars on the streets, no people going in and out of the handful of businesses.

Erika pulled the car up to the pump at a small gas station also serving as a Mexican restaurant and convenience store. Erika said she'd fill they tank while Tex got food. She pleaded with Tex not to kill anyone.

"Surely it takes more mental energy to kill someone than to simply convince them to give you what you want, doesn't it?" she'd asked.

He wanted to tell her killing someone was in fact easier because the human body was more intelligent than the human mind. He could "converse" with the body in a way that he was unable to "speak" to most human minds because humans lacked the capacity to interact in that way. He did not tell her that, though, for fear he would offend her even further than he already had. Instead, he simply promised not to kill anyone. *This whole business would be a lot easier if I did not need to restrain myself.*

Tex donned the large sunglasses and put the cap back on. He had no sooner stepped onto the wooden porch than Erika let out a string of curse words and kicked the car tire.

"While you're in there, ask them to turn on pump two." She leaned against the car, her arms folded across her chest, waiting to pump the gas.

Bells hanging from the door tinkled as Tex opened it. The wooden floor creaked, and dust motes filled the air. Short aisles of metal shelves usually filled with snack foods and household staples were nearly bare. The doors of the refrigerated cases at the back of the store were open and the cases empty. Tex's nose wrinkled at the odor of spoiled milk and rotten food.

No other customers were in the store and no clerk behind the counter. Tex grabbed a bag of something called Funyuns and a smashed package of snack cakes that had gotten wedged in one corner. Then he grabbed two other bags of chips. *I will not have to restrain myself from killing anyone, after all.* He pushed aside the rising tide of anxiety about why the store had been picked over and left unattended.

On a bottom shelf, he found a bag of red twisted-rope candy of the kind Ian had once shared with Tex. The memory was vivid, as though it had happened the previous day rather than weeks before. He could nearly taste the melted sugary goo in his mouth. He grabbed the last two bags of the candy and headed toward the counter to find a way to turn the gas pump on for Erika.

He rounded the corner and met a rifle barrel pointed at him by a large, middle-aged woman. She wore her wavy gray hair pulled back, but wispy tendrils of it flew about her red, round face.

Tex's voice was low and calm. "Do not be alarmed. We came for food and gas." His words did not seem to alleviate her need to point a gun at him. The tip of the rifle was only a few inches from his nose.

She held the rifle steady. "We got no gas." She eyed him up and down. "No one's got no gas. Where you from that you don't know that?"

"*No one's got no gas.*" The woman's words chilled him. *And so it has begun.*

"We have been... camping. For about a week now. We have not eaten for two days. We barely made it to town." Tex tried to sound desperate and to soften his features so the woman would want to help him.

She stared down the barrel at him, unmoved by his explanation. The woman pulled back on the trigger, and a shell clicked into the chamber.

Erika burst into the place. The door slammed behind her, and the bells crashed against the glass rather than gently tinkling as they had when Tex had come in. She muttered to herself about having to take care of things herself, but she stopped mumbling when she came to the end of the aisle and saw the gun trained on Tex.

He smelled her adrenaline and sensed her fear, though he was fairly certain she was not afraid for him but rather for the woman with the gun.

"There is no gas," Tex said. "She was just filling me in on what happened last week while we were camping."

"Yeah? So why is there no gas?"

The woman kept her gun on Tex but looked furtively at Erika. "My gas shipment was supposed to get here yesterday, but 'cause of that outbreak of some new virus crud over'n Arizona, they got blockades and crap. Don't know when I'll be gettin' my gas, but everybody 'round here's freakin' out 'bout the virus and the terror attacks o'er there'n France. A new damned world war is what it is, and we'll be sucked into it soon, no doubt."

"Go camping for a few days, come off the mountain, and the whole world has gone to shit." Erika shook her head. "Come on, put the gun down. Do we look like we're from the Middle East or terrorists to you?"

Erika stared at the woman evenly, and the gun-toting woman stared back. "Terrorists? No. But you guys don't look—well, he don't look—right." She used the gun to point toward Tex as though Erika would not know whom among the three of them in the store she was talking about.

Erika kept her hands in the air and moved closer to Tex. "My friend isn't like us." Her words were matter-of-fact, and the truth of her statement softened the woman's stare.

"I have a rare genetic disorder." Tex tried to make his voice calm and soothing. Erika had made up a name for his fake disease. Tex wracked his brain, trying to pull that tiny detail from the fog. As the woman stared at him, he blurted out, "Bender's disease. That's what it's called."

"He may not look like you and me, but that doesn't give you the right to shoot him just 'cause he's different." Erika injected her words with a righteous tone that made the woman swallow and pull in her lips in shame.

Tex forced his best congenial smile. "Please, put the gun down so we can talk like civilized people."

The woman stared at Tex as if trying to determine if he was a threat or not. She hesitated a few seconds more then reluctantly lowered her weapon. She looked a bit disappointed to not have cause to use it. "I ain't never seen you around here before, and I know everybody. Where you from?"

To Tex's surprise, Erika told the truth. "We're from Ajo, Arizona."

"I never heard of it." The woman's brow was still crinkled.

"It's in Arizona. Down south near the border. We're up here to visit my Aunt Dana. Camped for a few days before going to her place."

"Aunt Dana? You mean Dana Holt?"

Erika's brows rose. "You know her?"

"Course I know her. I already said I know everybody round here. If she's your aunt, you must be—what did she say her niece's name was, now?"

"Erika."

The woman slapped her thigh. "Erika! That's it. I'll be damned. She said she didn't figure on ever seein' you again." The woman's face had lost its skeptical sneer.

Erika's smile disappeared. "Yeah, well, you know, in times like this, family's got to stick together."

The woman nodded. "Ain't that the truth." She put the shotgun on a shelf behind the counter. "My name's Dottie, by the way. Come on over. Let me get that stuff in a bag."

Tex hesitated. She had seemed so ready to put a bullet in him.

Erika grabbed a few bags from Tex's arms. She put them on the counter, and Tex slowly approached Dottie and put the rest of the bags on the glass counter.

Erika pulled the bills she'd taken from Gary's wallet out of her pants pocket.

Dottie waved her hand at the money. "Put that away." She stuffed the chips and candy into a thin white plastic bag. "Your money's no good here."

Erika put a twenty-dollar bill on the counter. "I insist. I'm no freeloader."

Dottie's plump hand pushed the bill back. "I know you're not. But I'm not greedy, either. I'm not gonna charge you for some smashed-up chips. 'Sides, your Aunt Dana's a good customer and a friend. Hell, she'll prolly be down here helping me with my generator soon, and it'll be more than repayment for some junk food." Dottie winked as she finished bagging the food. "In fact, can you tell her I need her to come down when she gets a chance? She's the only one that can get my old generator to work when it's acting up, and I figure I'll be needin' it soon."

Erika flashed a smile at Dottie. "Thanks so much. And I'll tell Aunt Dana what you said."

As the bells tinkled behind them, Dottie yelled, "Take care of yourselves."

Erika had the dark-orange nacho chip bag open and a handful in her mouth before they got back to the car. "Guess we'll have to ditch the car sooner than expected."

"How much gas is left?"

Erika squinted at the gauge. "So little that the needle is below the E for empty."

"How far is it to your Aunt Dana's? You were telling the truth about going there, right?"

"Yes, it was all true." Erika's gaze was far away for a second. She turned the key in the ignition, and the car actually started.

"We cannot leave the car parked here," Tex said.

"I got an idea of where to put it." She pulled a lever on the steering-wheel column and drove slowly away from Dottie's gas station, which no longer sold gas.

5
JACK

Jack had to nearly jog to keep up with Anna as she stormed back to the motel.

She threw open the motel-room door, grabbed the remote from Thomas's hand, and hastily clicked off the television. "Get your stuff together. We're leaving."

Alecto had been curled into herself, but she raised her head and blinked. She unwound her arms from around her knees and rose. Her movements were slow, as if she moved through air the consistency of gelatin.

Thomas made no move to follow Anna's direction. "Did you talk to Sewell?"

Anna stood in the bathroom and shoved toothpaste and other toiletries into a small bag. "Yes."

Thomas turned his attention to Jack. "Well? What did he say?"

Jack shrugged. "Don't ask me. She's the one that talked to him. I'm just the hired help, so need-to-know basis. Apparently, I don't need to know."

Anna emerged from the bathroom and glared at Jack as she stuffed her toiletry bag into her duffel. "He said our Aunt Lilly is out of prison." She didn't stop her frenetic packing while she gave the news to Thomas as if it were no more momentous than news that rain was falling outside.

Thomas swiveled himself around on the bed and grabbed Anna's wrists. "Stop." His voice was a low hiss.

Anna tried to pull her wrists out of his grasp. "Let go."

Thomas held her firmly. "No. Not until you slow down and tell us what's going on." He looked back at Jack then returned his gaze to Anna. "All of us."

Alecto was at Anna's side before Jack even noticed she had moved. If Thomas had half as much common sense as he had genius, he would have let Anna go. Before Jack had the chance to tell Thomas to let Anna go, Thomas flew backward off of the bed.

Alecto hadn't moved a muscle.

"Stand down, Alecto," Jack said. He tried to pitch his voice downward and put as much authority into it as he could despite the fact that, in her presence, he was pretty much perpetually close to pissing his pants with fear.

She turned her head toward him slowly and raised her hand in the air toward him.

She's apparently not going to take orders from me. Jack put his hands up and out to the sides. "He's her brother. It's between them."

Alecto cocked her head to one side, and her hand dropped. Thomas rose slowly, his eyes on her. He looked rattled but uninjured.

Anna gingerly touched Alecto's shoulder. Her voice was calm. "I'm okay. And Jack's right. Sometimes, Thomas and I argue. But he's my brother. He won't hurt me."

"My brother tried to hurt me. I attempted to terminate him."

Jack recalled his Jetta tumbling off the road and into a ditch and bursting into flames.

"Okay, clearly we need to calm this down. I'm sorry I got everyone so jacked up." Anna dropped the pair of socks from her hand into the duffel and flopped onto the bed on top of the pillows. "Everyone sit and chill for a minute while I tell you what Sewell said."

Thomas sat cross-legged on the second bed, and Alecto sat on the edge of the bed. Her feet barely reached the floor. Her back was as straight as a board. Jack remained standing. He leaned against the TV cabinet, his arms across his chest.

Anna twisted the end of her hair in her fingers then let it go. "Sewell wanted to make sure we knew how relieved he was that we're all still alive."

Thomas clapped his hands slowly and wore a smirk on his face. "Yay for the Sturgis clan. Two survivors."

Anna's brow furrowed again. "Don't be so cynical. Anyway, apparently within hours of our escape, Aunt Lilly was released from military prison."

Alecto stood up. "I must go to her."

"Sit down and listen," Thomas said.

Anna nodded and motioned for her to sit. "I would have thought that too, Alecto. After all, that's why we liberated you from the Croft house, so you could help us break her out of prison. But Sewell said we can't go anywhere near Aunt Lilly, though he didn't have time or inclination to go into details as to why."

"I think it's obvious. He didn't need to spell it out," Jack said.

Anna and Alecto both asked "Why?" simultaneously.

"Because it's what Croft wants."

Thomas uncurled his legs. "Jack's right. It's the only conclusion that makes sense." He gave Jack an irritated look, as though irked that Jack had gotten to the idea before he did.

"So what, he thinks he can use Aunt Lilly as bait to recapture Alecto?" Anna asked.

Jack and Thomas both nodded.

"But why release her? He could keep her in prison and track us. We may be off grid, but we're not exactly an inconspicuous group."

"Tracking takes time," Jack said. "Especially when we're not using electronics or credit cards."

"And with what's going on in Europe, he knows time is running out," Thomas said.

"What did Sewell say we're supposed to do now?" Jack asked. He was a bit afraid of the answer. Breaking Sturgis out of jail wasn't his dream job, but he'd lived with the idea for over a month. He'd gotten used to it the way one gets used to having an irritating wart.

"Thomas, Alecto, and I are supposed to help with a new project that Aunt Lilly has for us. You, Mr. Wilson, are a free man." Anna's face was an unreadable mask.

Jack had thought that Anna had warmed to him. He even thought that maybe she had begun to think about him as much and in the same way that he thought about her, but she didn't seem too torn up over the fact that they'd soon part ways. *I'm just one less piece of baggage for her to haul around.*

The lot he'd recently been handed in life sucked, but being with Anna had made it bearable. In truth, despite the ugliness they'd faced at Croft's penthouse, the month he'd spent with Anna was the best time of his life. He wanted to see his mom again, and he missed Ian and Erika, but the idea of being without Anna made him feel hollow inside.

Anna continued. "We're to go to Phoenix. From there, we'll get you to Ajo. Okay, Jack?"

Jack managed to mumble, "Okay."

Thomas asked, "What's the new project?"

Anna directed her answer to Alecto. "It's something to benefit Alecto."

Alecto tilted her head. "For me?"

Anna nodded. "Apparently, while Aunt Lilly was in prison, she worked on a gene therapy to help you with a problem you have."

"I did not know that I need help." She blinked her huge eyes.

"Sewell said you have an Achilles' heel. A weakness."

"Humidity," Jack said.

"Yes," Anna said. "And this new gene therapy—if it works—will make you less vulnerable to the effects of humidity and water."

As far as Jack had seen, humidity and water were the sole ways to control the hybrid beings. He'd also seen plenty of reason humans should want a Stop button on them. Jack found it hard to believe that Sturgis considered it a good idea to surrender control over Alecto. He didn't want to rile Alecto, though, so he kept his thoughts to himself. Besides, he'd soon be home, and all of the Sturgis, Croft, and hybrid crap would be none of his business anymore.

Thomas asked, "If we're to stay away from Aunt Lilly, then who will be heading up this new project? You have a degree in molecular biology, but you're hardly qualified for something like this. And you don't have a lab."

"This is the really interesting part." Anna turned her attention to Jack. "We'll be working with the founder of the H.A.L.F. program."

"Dr. Randall," Alecto said in a hushed whisper.

The information took a few seconds to fully percolate through the folds of Jack's gray matter. If Dr. Randall was in Arizona again, that meant he was back from the planet the Greys had taken him to. *And if he's back, then maybe...*

"Erika," Jack whispered.

He caught Anna's gaze. For the briefest moment, he thought he saw sadness there, but in an instant, the look was gone, and she put on her well-practiced mask of indifference.

The idea that Erika could be in Ajo should have made him eager to get home. Instead, he wished he had a reason to stay in Phoenix a bit longer. Guilt made his stomach do flip-flops.

Alecto spoke in a barely audible whisper. "9."

"What's that?" Thomas asked.

"She's talking about Tex, the other hybrid. They have the same genetic parents, so in a way they're brother and sister," Jack said.

Alecto nodded her bowling ball of a head. "If Dr. Randall is back... Was 9 with him? Will I see 9 again?" Her voice was more animated than Jack had ever heard it.

"Mr. Sewell didn't mention 9," Anna said.

Alecto's shoulders drooped.

"In fact, Mr. Sewell only mentioned Dr. Randall." Anna's eyes softened a bit, and she looked at Jack. "But that doesn't mean the others aren't there." She clapped Alecto lightly on the shoulder. "There's only one way to find out. Let's get back on the road and get you to warm, sunny Arizona." Anna plastered on her best fake smile.

They needed less than fifteen minutes to get back on the road headed west. As Jack watched the Gateway Arch of St. Louis recede in the rearview mirror, feelings of guilt gave way to a calm happiness. He was going home. Even if he was confused about his feelings for Erika, seeing her and Ian again would be good. Also, his mom would know he was alive.

First a layover in Phoenix. Then this nightmare will be behind me.

Erika headed north out of town but turned onto the first forest-service road she came to. They'd gone less than a mile when the engine sputtered, chugged, and finally died. The car stalled on a narrow, deeply rutted dirt road headed up a steep hill.

She hit the steering wheel in frustration. "So close."

"This spot is quite open. It will be easily spotted," Tex said.

"Yeah, I know that. This wasn't part of the plan. We'll have to push it the rest of the way."

Tex got out and asked, "Rest of the way to where?"

Erika pointed up the hill.

"I do not understand."

Erika put the car in neutral. "Aunt Dana brought me out to this area a lot before... well, when I was younger. I'm guessing there's a perfect spot at the top of the hill." She stood behind the back bumper. "Come on. Push."

She put her hands on the trunk, and Tex followed her lead. She expected to have to rock the car hard to get it out of the rut it had stalled in. Even in a weakened state, though, Tex was stronger than most people. The car easily rolled forward.

The going became tougher once the terrain sloped more steeply. By the time they got the car to the top of the hill, sweat was covering her forehead, and her back muscles burned.

When the ground leveled out, Erika yelled, "Whoa!"

Tex stopped pushing, and the car came to a stop at the edge of a cliff that dropped off at least a hundred feet to the canyon below.

"Let's get our stuff before we shove it over." Erika grabbed the handgun from the front seat and a few bags of food while Tex got the rest. "We need to push it hard so it will have enough momentum to make it farther than just a few feet and get hung up on the trees."

"I can give it an assist."

"If you have the strength for it, that would be great."

Erika pushed with all she had but doubted Tex needed her at all. The car levitated out from the ledge as if flying. It cleared the edge by nearly twenty feet then picked up speed before dropping from the air. The car crashed nose first and toppled back over front as it rolled down the hill. It finally landed in the canyon below, hidden from view by the thick trees and bushes.

"Someone will find it eventually, but this should hold us over for a few days," Erika said.

"Long enough to rest before we move on."

She hadn't planned on moving on, whatever he meant by that. She was exhausted. She was thinking only about getting to Aunt Dana's and sleeping. She didn't know what she'd do after that.

Erika shielded her eyes with her hand and stared at the sky. The sun was already well on its way to the western horizon.

"Come on. We gotta scoot if we're to make it there by nightfall." She headed back down the hill as Tex followed.

Erika hadn't been in the New Mexico forest for several years, but she'd spent a lot of time in the area when she was younger, back before her dad died. She wasn't sure how to find Aunt Dana's traipsing through the forest, and that way would take longer anyway, so she headed back down the main road and toward Luna. From there, she knew the way.

After nearly an hour of walking, they made it to the forest-service road leading to Dana's cabin. They didn't see a single car on the road. *Strange, even for this remote area.* She didn't know if the reason was the lack of gas due to the closed Arizona border or that news of the virus had spread and people were too worried to leave their houses. Whatever the cause, the trek was eerily quiet.

After another thirty minutes trudging uphill on a narrow, deeply rutted dirt road, they got to Aunt Dana's cabin. It was tucked into a forest of piñon and juniper. They came upon the little house at dusk, the western sky ablaze with deep crimson and purple. The cabin's windows were filled with welcoming yellow light, and a truck was parked in the gravel drive. *She's home, at least.*

Erika stopped at the edge of the clearing. "Before we go in, we need to get our story straight."

Tex cocked his head to one side.

"My Aunt Dana is with the forest service. She's law and order, like my dad was. So she's going to be full of questions about why we're here and who—and what—you are. And yeah, it's not going to work with her to say you have a genetic anomaly. She's too sharp for that kind of lie. And..."

"And what, Erika?"

"And, well, I haven't seen or talked to her since my dad's funeral, so she may not be all that thrilled to see me." Her throat was suddenly dry. She had always been close to her Aunt Dana and had practically lived in the New Mexico forest during the summers of her childhood. Being separated from Aunt Dana had made her father's death even more painful.

Normally, Erika couldn't read Tex's face, but he was clearly angry with her. His brows came together, and his jaw set.

His voice came out as a low hiss. "You mean you brought us all this way, and now you tell me that this woman may not welcome you? And if she's 'law and order' as you say, she may well turn me over to the authorities." Tex's hands were fists at his side.

Erika spat back, "Yeah, well, where the hell else were we going to go? I don't recall you having any ideas."

She turned her attention to the cabin. "Just follow my lead. Try not to talk much. And whatever you do, do not harm her. She's the only family I have left on my dad's side. Be cool."

She walked slowly to the porch and tiptoed to the door. Erika rapped lightly on the wooden screen door. The knock caused the hook latch to rattle. In the quiet of the mountain twilight, the knock sounded like an explosion.

Erika heard Dana's footfalls on the wooden floor inside. The porch light came on and bathed them in the nearly fluorescent yellow of a bug light. The inner door opened, and Erika stared through the screen at her Aunt Dana.

Dana's hair had been dark brown the last time Erika saw her, but it was streaked with gray and pulled back in a tail exactly the way Erika wore hers. Dana's eyes were the same clear blue that Erika's father had been. Erika loved the color and had often wished she had it. The lines in Dana's forehead were deeper, the crow's feet at the edges of her eyes more apparent, but otherwise, she still had the athletic build and natural, no-nonsense beauty Erika remembered.

"Well, I'll be..." Dana's face lit up in a smile that quickly faded to a tight mask of anger. "What kind of trouble you get in that's so bad you gotta show up at my doorstep?" Her eyes landed on Tex, and her brows knitted into a tighter knot. She looked Erika up and down, taking in Erika's dirt-covered clothes and unwashed hair. "What's wrong, Erika? Tina kick you out? I woulda figured she'd understand if you got pregnant, seeing as how she did the same thing when she was your age."

Erika needed every ounce of strength left in her not to put her fist through the screen door and land a punch on Dana. If she didn't need the woman's help so badly, she would have told her where to stick it and walked away without looking back.

She did need Dana's help, though—desperately.

Erika's hands were balled up at her sides, but she took a deep breath and said, "I'm not pregnant. And Tina didn't kick me out. She's dead."

Dana's face went from smug to shocked pain in less than a nanosecond. "Oh. Oh, Erika, I'm sorry. I didn't—I hadn't heard. Come on. Get in here out of the chill."

Dana stood aside so they could come in then quickly strode to the kitchen. Her eyes were fixed on Tex. "Who's your friend?"

"His name is Tex."

Dana gave a soft laugh. "Strange name for a young person." She held her hand out to shake his hand.

Tex did not join her laughter. He stared at her hand.

Erika coughed lightly and used her head to gesture for Tex to take Dana's hand. She didn't know how Dana would react to having a fugitive human-alien hybrid in her house, but she didn't know how to hide the truth from her astute aunt when Tex couldn't even abide by simple human customs like a handshake.

He got the hint, took Dana's hand, and they shook briefly.

Dana kept an eye on him as she spoke. "Can I get you something to eat? You look like a scarecrow. How long has it been since you ate a meal?" She didn't wait for them to answer, opening cupboards, rattling dishes, and grabbing things out of the refrigerator.

Erika fell into a wooden chair at the kitchen table, and Tex took the seat next to her. His head swiveled as he took in the small kitchen, seeming to catalog every wood plank and speck of dust.

Dana chopped onions and potatoes while Erika filled her in on what had happened to Erika's mom. Erika cried as she recounted it. Dana placed a warm hand on her shoulder and handed her a box of tissues. That was the kind of quiet comfort Erika had grown up with from the Holt side of her family, and she was craving it more than she had let herself realize. Seeing Aunt Dana was good, and so was talking about the death.

Tex remained quiet and listened as though that was the first time he was hearing of any of the events she recounted. His presence comforted her as well.

Erika told Dana a lot but left out the part about her time in A.H.D.N.A. and the Conexus. She didn't tell Dana about the H.A.L.F. program or the Makers, either.

By the time Erika finished the story of her mom's death and the terrible illness that had taken hold of her hometown, Dana had heaping plates of fried potatoes, pork chops, and green beans on the table. It was the kind of Midwestern meat-and-potatoes food that Erika's dad had preferred but that her mom had never quite mastered how to cook. Erika blew her nose and wiped her eyes.

The smell of home-cooked food nearly made Erika cry with joy. Her plate held a mountain of potatoes and a small forest of green beans. She took two pork chops. Her stomach won over her conscience as she devoured the meat.

For his part, Tex began by taking a bit of each item. After a few bites of the potatoes, though, he heaped several large spoonfuls on and ate greedily, still wearing his hat and sunglasses. He was quiet throughout the meal.

I wonder what he's thinking about all this.

Dana stared at them with a look of mixed wonderment and skepticism. She especially eyed Tex. Erika practically heard Aunt Dana's thought bubbles as she likely churned over in her mind what could cause a person to look so very odd.

Erika's stomach had hurt from hunger but was aching from fullness. She regretfully had to push the half-full plate back from herself before she ate so much she got sick.

"Don't you like it? Oh yeah, I forgot you don't eat meat, do you?"

"Oh, I love it. I'm just full."

They stared at each other, so much unsaid filling the air between them. Dana had begun their reunion with a snarky attitude, but from where Erika sat, Dana seemed to have no cause to be upset. After all, she was the one who hadn't stayed in contact with Erika.

Dana took a sip of her tea and set the cup down. "I know your momma just died. But before you get too cozy here, I gotta know. Why didn't you answer any of my letters? And not so much as a call or thank-you note for the things I sent you. I know your momma never liked me, but what did I ever do to you to be treated that way?"

"Things you sent me? Letters? Aunt Dana, I haven't heard from you since my dad's funeral. You stood there, looked me in the eye, and said you'd be there for me. And you bailed."

Erika's lower lip quivered, but she pulled it in and refused to allow the angry tears to fall.

Dana closed her eyes, and when she opened them, they glistened with tears. "I know you loved your mom." Dana sipped her tea again. "But she and I... Well, we never saw eye to eye. After your dad died, I sent you letters every week. I sent you cards and presents for your birthday and Christmas. I did that for over two years, but I never heard from you. I called too, at first, but your mom got a new phone and never gave me a new number, so I had no way to contact you."

Erika had spent many hours of her life being mad at her mom for a variety of things. When her mom died, she vowed to let all her anger go and focus on what few happy memories she had. Now, though, Dana was heaping on a whole new layer of reasons to be angry with her dead mother. *She intentionally cut me off from my dad's only family.*

Dana reached out a freckled, weatherworn hand and put it on Erika's. Her pale lips drew up in a wan smile. "Don't be mad at her. Water under the bridge. You're here now."

Erika wanted to be angry, to shout and scream and cry and kick things, but she was too exhausted at the moment to do any of those things.

Dana's smile faded as she looked at Tex. He was sitting so silently Erika had nearly forgotten he was there. He had a way of becoming a quiet observer, fading into the background. She was glad of it in that instance. She didn't need or want him trying to interfere in her family business or, worse, doing something to reveal the truth about his powers.

"We've been rude, leaving your young man out of the conversation."

Erika's cheeks colored. "He's not my 'young man.'" *But God help me, maybe I want him to be.*

"Tex. Is that a nickname or something?"

"Sort of," Erika said. She shifted in her seat, wishing she could skip the inevitable conversation about to happen and fall into a bed instead.

"Can't he talk?" Dana's eyes had never strayed from Tex.

His voice was low and steady. "I can."

Dana shook her head slightly and blinked. Hearing Tex had that kind of effect on people. The voice didn't match the body.

"Okay, Erika, I know why you're here, but that doesn't explain why you've got him with you. Tex, do your parents know where you are?"

Erika tried to answer for him, but Tex talked over her.

"I do not have parents." He wiped his forehead with his paper napkin.

Tiny beads of sweat had broken out on his forehead. That was something that wouldn't seem strange if not for the fact that Erika had never seen Tex sweat. Even after pushing the car up the hill, her face had been covered with sweat, but his skin was dry. Erika didn't know what to make of that. He did not show signs of alarm, so she ignored the twitch in her gut.

"You're an orphan too?" Her hand flew to her face. "Oh, no. Did your parents die from the virus?"

Erika and Tex both spoke at the same time, but Erika talked more loudly and interceded with "Yes" before Tex could start down the road of telling Aunt Dana more than she needed to know. He remained calm and did not protest the interruption. His fingers shook as he wiped his neck with the napkin.

Something is up with him. She wanted to talk to him privately but didn't want to be rude after not having seen Dana for so long. Erika yawned. "I know you have a lot of questions, and we have catching up to do, but we're beat from the long trip. Do you think we can bunk down somewhere and talk more tomorrow?"

Aunt Dana nodded. "Of course. Place is so small, you can practically brush your teeth while still in bed, but I'll show Tex here around."

They all rose, but before Dana could make it to the narrow hallway leading to the bedrooms and bath, Tex fell to the ground. He lay on his stomach, his head turned to one side, the metal-framed sunglasses pushed up and askew, revealing his alien eyes.

Erika knelt beside him and put her fingers to his neck. His pulse was weak, and his skin was even colder and grayer than usual.

Dana stood behind Erika and gasped. "What the—"

"He's very ill," Erika said.

"More than sick. He's not—"

"Human." *So much for hiding from her what he is.*

Erika had hoped she could keep that fact from Aunt Dana for Tex's protection. In hindsight, the idea was ridiculous. Tex couldn't wear sunglasses twenty-four hours a day.

Erika picked up Tex's hand and tried to rouse him, but he remained still. His condition wasn't like the trance he voluntarily went into when he withdrew from the world and meditated to heal. She had no idea what to do for him.

"Does he need a doctor?"

Erika nodded but then sighed and shook her head. "We can't take him to a regular doctor." She stood and looked into Aunt Dana's eyes. "If he falls back into the hands of the Makers, they'll kill him. Or worse."

"I've got a lot of questions," Aunt Dana said.

"I'm sure you do, but we've got no time right now for answers." Erika took Aunt Dana's hand in hers. "I need your help. *He* needs your help." She looked down at Tex, lying like a lifeless sack of flour on the floor. Her throat tightened again at the notion that he could die. He had become a part of her life that she didn't want to let go.

Dana's crinkled brow smoothed, and she nodded. "Niyol."

Erika had no idea what Aunt Dana was talking about. The question must have shown on her face.

"He's an old friend. We'll have to drive there. Niyol doesn't have a phone. Help me get him to my truck."

Dana hoisted Tex by the shoulders while Erika lifted his feet. They struggled through the door and got Tex into the back seat of Dana's crew-cab truck.

Erika had been sure she could fall asleep while standing, but she was fully awake and alert again. She scrambled up into the passenger seat.

Tex's collapse was a mystery. She had seen him weakened and pass out from high humidity and exposure to water. She'd also watched him fade from overuse of his powers while weakened by moisture, but the humidity was super low at the cabin. He'd used his abilities all day and, though tired, had not complained of any ill effects. *How can I help him when I have no idea what is wrong?*

They drove in silence on the twisty, rutted dirt roads of rural New Mexico. They headed west and were soon in Arizona again. The sign announcing they were back in Arizona made Erika's stomach twist. She had wanted to get out of the state, not back into it.

"Where are we going?" Her voice had an edge to it that revealed her nervousness.

"I told you. To see if my friend Niyol can help your friend."

"But Tex and I just came from Arizona." *More like escaped it.*

Dana turned onto a deserted two-lane paved road without using her blinker or even looking for oncoming traffic. "Yeah, well, you're back."

The sun had completely set and the air had turned cold by the time they pulled onto a primitive dirt forest-service road winding its way up a mesa. Dana finally came to a stop next to a pickup truck parked near a small house. The truck could have been the twin of the one Erika had taken from Ian's house.

"Let me go in first and talk to him. Stay in the truck. Niyol wouldn't like you out snooping around his property."

Erika hadn't planned on leaving Tex. She nodded and blew a warm breath into her cupped hands. "Don't be too long, or we'll both be frozen when you get back." Though no immediate danger seemed apparent, the things Erika had been through made her jumpy about new situations. She wished she had had the presence of mind to bring the pistol with her.

Dana knocked on the door of the small, stucco-covered house and rubbed her arms to stay warm. Someone peeked through the curtains in the front window, then the door opened, just a sliver at first then wider.

Yellow light spilled out of the open doorway, casting the person at the threshold into a silhouette. Whoever it was, he was small in stature, standing at least a few inches shorter than Aunt Dana. He threw his arms around her, and Dana hugged back then went inside. The door closed behind them, sealing them off from Erika.

Tex had been entirely silent on the drive to that lonely house at the top of a mesa. Erika leaned over the seat and whispered, "Tex?"

He did not answer, not that she had expected him to. She took his wrist in her hand and felt for a pulse. It was still there but even slower and weaker than before. His skin was covered in a thin film of sweat, but she saw no evidence of injury.

"Dammit, don't die on me. Come on, Aunt Dana. He's running out of time."

Erika sat back in her seat, her eyes boring a hole in the door through which Dana had disappeared. She hadn't planned on leaving the truck, but as the minutes passed, her urge to barge into the house grew.

She was about to disobey Aunt Dana's request to stay put when the door to the house opened, and three figures emerged. The small man and a woman flanked Aunt Dana.

Aunt Dana opened the door on Erika's side of the truck. "Erika, this is Niyol Taya and his wife, Kai. He's a healer."

Erika jumped out of the truck and took Niyol's outstretched hand in hers. His hand was warm, the skin leathery. His face was weathered with age. Even in the dark, his eyes shone brightly, and his lips offered a small smile.

"It's very nice to meet you. I'm Erika, and this is Tex." She motioned to the truck with her head. "He's very ill. Do you think you can help him?"

The smile disappeared from Niyol's lips. He looked down then cast a glance backward to his short, round wife. Her deep brown eyes looked sad, and her lips were pulled down in a frown.

"I do not know if I can help," Niyol said. He quickly added, "But it will be my honor to try. Let's hurry and get him inside. I have many questions for you before I will know what medicine your friend needs."

11
JACK

Jack was more than motivated to get to Phoenix. As the cities gave way to open range and the range gave way to distant mountains and mesas, Jack felt more and more at home.

Jack considered giving Alecto a chance to sit in the front seat so she could see the towering spires of rock that made up Monument Valley, but they couldn't risk someone sighting her. Even at eighty miles an hour, she was hard not to notice.

The directions Sewell had given Anna were detailed and accurate. Jack had no problem finding the building housing the regional office of the Centers for Disease Control in Phoenix. They arrived at midafternoon on a Friday. Traffic into the city was light, by Phoenix standards.

He pulled into the visitor parking lot. "I'm guessing Alecto should stay here. For now."

Anna agreed. "Thomas, will you stay with her? Jack and I will go in and see what's up."

Thomas had his head buried in the *New York Times* crossword puzzle. He didn't look up but grunted, "Whatever."

Though November and chilly in the eastern part of the country, Phoenix was nearly eighty degrees. Jack jettisoned his jacket and flannel shirt. Being in just a T-shirt felt good.

Anna's mood seemed to have lightened. Her brow was crinkle-free, and her hair bounced about her shoulders as she walked.

They checked in at the security officer's station, and Jack let Anna do the talking. She used one of her aliases.

Anna followed the direction Mr. Sewell had given her, and she asked for the Regional Director of the CDC. "We're here to see Dr. Montoya. I believe she's expecting us. Yes, Stacey Adams."

As they waited for Dr. Montoya, Jack's palms grew sweaty. He was excited to see if Erika and Ian were with Dr. Randall. He would even be glad to see Tex, but the roiling of his stomach was more than just the excited expectation of seeing his friends. He had difficulty hiding his feelings, especially from Erika and Ian. He had tried to hide his growing desire to know Anna better, even from himself, but he knew Erika would see through any charade he attempted. He kept imagining the glare on Erika's face when she found out that while she had been on an alien planet by herself, he was spending twenty-four hours a day with Anna.

Not soon enough, the elevator dinged, and a petite, dark-haired woman of at least middle years stepped into the lobby. She held out her hand to Anna. "You must be Ms. Adams."

Anna took her hand and smiled. "Yes, but please, call me Stacey."

Dr. Montoya gave her a slight wink and nodded. She then turned her eyes to Jack and held out her hand to him. "And you are Mr. Harper?"

Jack quickly wiped his hand on his jeans and shook her hand. "Nice to meet you."

Dr. Montoya gave them a warm smile. "Please, come with me. Let me introduce you to my team."

Her team? Sewell had only mentioned Dr. Randall. *Can it be?* Jack's heart hammered away.

They went to the fourteenth and uppermost floor of the building. Jack wondered if Dr. Randall enjoyed being aboveground for a change. Plentiful Arizona sunshine poured in through floor-to-ceiling windows.

The halls were painted a blue so light it was nearly gray and were well lit with fluorescent lights that reflected off the highly polished blue linoleum floor. The building was too warm for Jack's taste, as if the heat was on even though the day called for air conditioning. Jack wished he was wearing shorts and flip-flops instead of jeans and heavy black work boots.

Dr. Montoya used a key card to gain entry to another hallway to their left. They zigzagged a few more times and finally arrived at a laboratory. It was filled with tables full of large microscopes, computers, and other machines and equipment Jack couldn't identify.

Jack recognized a familiar face at one of the computers. Ian stared at the screen, engrossed in something. His hair was longer than Jack had ever seen it, but the length suited him. His cheeks were hollow and his frame overly thin.

Ian barely looked up when they entered. At first, he just took notice of Dr. Montoya, but then his eyes caught Jack's, and he lit up. "Jack!"

Ian was up and away from the desk, his arms around Jack in a hug before they had fully entered the room. They hugged like two old friends that hadn't seen each other in years, and that's what it felt like.

Ian tousled Jack's hair. "What happened to you?"

"I was tired of being a blond," Jack said and winked. "Whaddya think?"

Ian put a finger to his chin and scrunched up his face. "I don't know. While I do prefer brunettes, blond worked on you." He smiled warmly. "You look good, Jack. Damned good to see you." As he stared at Jack, the smile faded, and his eyes filled with tears.

Jack let out a nervous laugh. "You look like someone died."

Ian looked away and wiped at his face. He clapped a hand on Jack's shoulder and forced a wan smile. "I'm here for you."

Before Jack could ask Ian what he meant by that, Dr. Randall strode quickly toward them, beaming. "Jack Wilson, you made it. And Anna. My goodness, what a beautiful young woman. Why, the last time I saw you, well, you were just a sprout. Look at you." He gave Anna a hug, and she stiffly hugged him back.

"Yes, look at her," Ian said. His voice was low, and he shot Jack an impish smile.

Dr. Randall had had the appearance of a crazy hermit the last time Jack had seen him. Now, though, he looked like a respectable old professor. His face was cleanly shaven, save for sideburns that were a bit too long and thick to be in style. His glasses were clean and repaired and sat evenly on his nose rather than crookedly. His clothes were fresh, his body bathed, and his hair trimmed and combed.

While Jack wanted to catch up with Ian, he couldn't take one more minute without knowing if Erika was with them. "Is Erika here?"

Ian shook his head.

The roiling in Jack's stomach churned harder. "Oh no. Please don't tell me—"

Dr. Randall clapped him on the back. "She made it back with us and survived the virus, so don't worry about that."

Virus? "Can I see her?"

"She's not here," Ian said.

"She went back to Ajo?"

Ian let out a low breath. "Oh dear, you don't know about the virus, do you?"

"Ian, what the hell's going on?" Jack's palms were sweaty once again, and the old, familiar feeling of his gut falling to the floor was back.

Ian knew his friend well. "Calm down, Jack. Erika is fine. She's with Tex, and they're on their way to New Mexico." Ian checked his watch. "Probably there by now, I suppose."

Ian's words were meant to comfort him, but Jack didn't feel comforted. Erika had taken off with Tex—to New Mexico. Not only was she alone with a guy that Jack considered the most dangerous person he'd ever met, but she hadn't waited for him. She hadn't even tried to contact him when she got back to Earth.

He felt as though he'd been punched in the gut. *I wasted time feeling guilty that I'd dared have thoughts about Anna.*

Ian seemed to read Jack's mind. "Don't be angry at her. You don't understand the situation. Tex needed to get out of that place. I was really sick. Dr. Randall was too. There was no one else to get Tex away from the Makers."

Jack would have to discuss the issue later with Ian in private. Ian made excuses for Erika, but the problem wasn't just that she'd helped Tex. Ever since she laid eyes on the guy, she seemed lost to Jack, as though she'd do anything for that alien guy—risk her life, even—for a person she hardly knew. *I wonder if she'd do that for me?*

Jack kept the subject off Erika for the time being. "So what's this about a virus?"

Dr. Montoya gave a nervous cough. "Yes, well, there's much to say about that. How about I fill Jack in on that in my office while Dr. Randall... You can talk with Anna about the work you'll need her to help you with here."

Dr. Montoya led Jack by the arm to an office tucked into the back corner of the large lab. Instead of sitting behind the desk, she sat in a white molded-plastic chair across from the desk and gestured for Jack to sit as well.

"What I'm about to tell you is classified information. I'm not supposed to tell anyone. Seeing as how you were at A.H.D.N.A. and you've seen hybrids and the alien ship, I figure I'm not going to be telling you anything that will rock your worldview more than it already has been." She gave him a wan smile.

Jack was impatient for information and didn't respond.

She coughed lightly again. "About a month ago, there was an outbreak of a pernicious virus. We now know that the virus was seeded into the population by the aliens we Earthlings refer to as the Roswell Greys. But we have learned from Dr. Randall that they refer to themselves as Conexus."

"Why would they do that?"

"That is an excellent question. And we likely would not know the answer if it weren't for the fact that Dr. Randall and your friends ended up in their world and learned the truth. They intended for the majority of the human population to die from the virus."

"So they could take over this planet?"

Dr. Montoya shook her head. "Not exactly." She took a deep breath. "It's a bit more complicated than that." She eyed Jack. "Have you heard the reports of the war in Europe?"

Jack nodded. "But it's not what it seems, is it?"

"No, it's not. It's an alien attack, but not by the Greys."

Jack hit his knee. "I knew it!"

"Don't be too happy that you were right. Not about this, anyway." She looked at him gravely. "There's a lot more that Dr. Randall and I or even your friend Ian can tell you about all of that. But I don't want to get off track of the virus because this pertains to you."

Jack sighed with impatience. "Spit it out, already."

Dr. Montoya wrung her hands. "When the virus first hit—it spreads so very quickly—we had no way to fight it. Have you seen anyone with it yet?"

Jack shook his head. "I've been in New York. And driving here."

"There have been many casualties."

Her lips moved, but the words were like a far-off mumbling in his ears. She said something about first deaths and mentioned his mom's name. Her hand was on his, her eyes warm and glistening.

"I'm so sorry, Jack."

Jack had been overly warm before in the stifling, still air of the lab. But now he was shivering with cold. Blackness played at the edges of his vision, and despite his chill, his neck was covered in sweat. A wave of nausea hit him, and he swallowed to prevent himself from upchucking on this Dr. Montoya whom he had just met.

"Are you okay? Do you need to lie down?"

Jack couldn't speak. If he did, he'd likely vomit. He forced a slow nod.

Dr. Montoya helped him up and led him by the arm to another office that had a pleather couch in it. He lay on the small sofa, thankful for the cool upholstery against his hot cheek.

"You just rest here. I'll get you some cool water."

Dr. Montoya brought him a paper cup of water, and he drank it in one drink. It helped push the bile back down his gullet.

"Do you want to talk to anyone?"

He shook his head.

"I understand." Dr. Montoya turned off the harsh overhead fluorescents. "Rest here as long as you'd like." She closed the door quietly behind her.

Jack lay on the lumpy couch, his feet hanging over the side. He wanted to cry, but tears did not come. He wanted to scream, but his throat was too dry to speak. He wanted to run, but he had nowhere to go.

In an instant, his world had been obliterated. An invader so tiny one could only see it with a microscope had murdered his mother and taken from him the one thing that mattered to him more than anything else. If a person had killed her, he could at least have mustered the ambition to find the son of a bitch and wrestle the life from him. Instead, a silent marauder had taken her, too small to have its ass kicked.

But if the Greys—these so-called Conexus—had created the virus, he could have his vengeance on them. As he lay there with his face stuck to the fake leather, he fantasized about wrapping his hands around the scrawny necks of Tex's so-called "cousins" and watching life ebb from their big, black, terrible eyes. Tears came to his eyes. In the span of less than six months, he had gone from a neohippy peacenik to a potential murderer. *Once you've killed a man, I suppose the idea comes more easily.*

Finally, the tears spilled over the dam, and he cried for the loss of his beloved mother and friend. He cried because she had died without him being there with her. He wept because while she lay sick and dying, he had killed people. He cried for the loss of his mother and friend as well as for the loss of his former self. A terrible knot of hatred that he'd once held toward Commander Sturgis redoubled. If she hadn't taken them to A.H.D.N.A. in the first place, he would have been home. *I would have been there for her when she died.* The thought made his throat tighten.

Of course if he had been home, then he likely would have been infected as well. If Sturgis hadn't compelled Jack, Ian, and Erika to A.H.D.N.A. that night, they might all have died.

Sturgis's actions had forced him to become a soldier, something he had never wanted. The war these so-called Conexus had started took whatever had been left of his youthful innocence. He was alone in a world that suddenly felt harsher than he had ever imagined it could be.

Jack had no idea what to do next. Even if Ajo wasn't quarantined, he couldn't imagine ever going back to it. He would forever associate the place with the pain of knowing his mom died there alone.

Anna, you may be stuck with me for a while longer. Joining her quest to take down the Croft family would at least give him an outlet for the unwelcome rage growing within him.

Niyol and Kai's house was even smaller than Dana's cabin. A living room connected to a galley kitchen and eating area, a single bedroom, and a bathroom.

Aunt Dana and Niyol had carried Tex into the cottage and laid him on a small couch by a heating stove. The warm house smelled of burning piñon pine. The wood stove filled the air with a faint smoky haze, but Erika didn't mind.

Niyol and Kai worked quickly to remove Tex's shirt while Niyol peppered Erika with questions. Since having met Tex in the desert, her life had been one of subterfuge and survival. Answering questions honestly felt strange to her. She still worried what Dana would do with the information that the Makers wanted her and Tex, but she knew Niyol would have no chance of helping Tex if she lied. She would have to deal with Aunt Dana later.

Niyol didn't seem fazed in the slightest to learn that Tex was a hybrid being, genetically engineered from both human and alien DNA. While they spoke, his hands slowly worked from Tex's scalp to his face, down his neck and arm, then back up to his chest, down the other arm, and back. Tex lay as still as a stone and gave no indication that he had any awareness of Niyol's touch. If she didn't know better, she'd think he was dead.

Niyol's eyes were closed as he felt Tex with his age-gnarled fingers. He didn't seem to be listening to her, but he must have been because he followed up each question with another.

Niyol opened his eyes briefly when she told him how the Conexus had taken a piece of Tex's liver, a kidney, and part of a lung. He closed his eyes slowly, shook his head, and moved his fingers to those regions of Tex's body as though he could feel something that wasn't visible to Erika.

Kai stood by and watched Niyol work, her face an impassive mask. Erika had no idea what the woman was thinking about having a human-alien hybrid being lying on her couch, life ebbing from him. If she considered Erika's story a pile of crap, she didn't say so or even look askance at her.

Niyol stopped asking questions. His knees creaked as he rose from the floor. "He has told me what medicine he needs."

Tex had never been able to communicate with humans telepathically, but maybe Niyol was gifted with the ability to speak to Tex on a wavelength where Erika had never been able to go.

"He spoke to you?" Erika asked. "You mean telepathically?"

Niyol shook his head. "Not like that. His body spoke to me. Our bodies are wise. Much wiser than our heads." Niyol thumped his chest lightly with two fingers. "Wise in here."

"What does he need? I'll help—just tell me what to do. I'll get anything you need—"

Niyol grabbed Erika gently by the shoulders. "Calm yourself. You have done what you can. He needs herbs and sweat."

Erika had never participated in a sweat lodge ceremony, but she had heard about them, and she knew that moist heat was an integral part. The heat was a fine idea, but moisture...

She shook her head, her eyes wide. "No. You can't do that."

Niyol's eyes, once warm and kindly, grew dark and stormy. He likely wasn't used to having someone, particularly an outsider, question his guidance. "You know what medicine he needs? Then you don't need me." He turned to walk away from her.

She wanted to argue that bringing him to Niyol hadn't been her idea. That had been all Dana. She opted not to argue with the one person among them who might have been able to help Tex, though.

"Wait," she said. "I meant no offense."

Niyol stopped. His eyes had softened, but only a little. Impatience played at his eyes.

Erika continued. "He's not like us. He takes water in through his skin. If he gets too much moisture, it weakens him. He may even die. He's so frail right now, even a moist room may kill him."

Niyol nodded once to Kai. She quickly left the house, a cold breeze immediately sucking the heat out of the room.

Niyol grabbed a blanket from the back of the recliner and motioned for Dana to help him. They wrapped Tex in the blanket, his face peeking out. He looked like a burrito. Niyol knelt and hoisted Tex up in his arms and groaned under the weight of him.

"Steel is forged in fire. Diamonds form from heat and pressure," Niyol said.

Tex wasn't made of metal, though. He was no lump of carbon. He was flesh and bone and blood, and in that moment, he was more fragile than an eggshell.

Niyol didn't wait for a response or argue the point further. Dana opened the door for him as he carried Tex through the small portal.

Erika followed Niyol out into the cold night. He turned, and his breath was visible in the air as he spoke.

"This is a journey he must take without you."

Aunt Dana caught Erika's hand and held her back. "Stay here with me. There's nothing more you can do for him now. Trust in Niyol."

Erika had no reason not to trust Niyol, but hope and trust were in rare supply for her those days, and she'd only just met him. She knew nothing about him. She allowed Dana to hold her back, though the reason might have been more from her desire not to sit and watch Tex die than from obedience to Niyol's command. The memory of holding her mom's hand as she took her last breath drifted into her mind, and she mentally batted it away before it brought tears.

She watched Niyol's back for a few seconds as he walked toward a small round hut with a domed top. Dana pulled at Erika, and she allowed her aunt to guide her back into the small house.

They'd left the door ajar, and the cottage had become chilled. Dana wordlessly motioned for Erika to lie on the couch. Her teeth chattered as Dana wrapped her in thick woolen blankets.

"There is nothing you can do for him now. The medicine he needs will take a while. Maybe days," Kai said.

Erika bolted upright. "Days? But—"

"It is late." Kai handed Dana a small cup made of glazed pottery. "Something to help her rest."

Dana held the cup to Erika's lips. "Drink."

Erika had not been mothered in a long time. She hardly remembered what it felt like. Dana smoothed Erika's hair off of her forehead as Erika sipped the warm, slightly bitter tea.

Dana's fingers were frigid from the cold, but her touch still soothed. "Sleep. You've done what you can. Time to let someone else worry for a while." Soft lips grazed Erika's forehead.

Erika's shoulders relaxed and released weeks of tension she hadn't realized she'd been holding. The crease in her brow uncrinkled. She had assumed it had become permanent. The wood stove warmed the small room up quickly, and the coziness coupled with the sleeping tea worked their magic. Before she had the chance to think about what to do next, she drifted off to a deep sleep.

Jack stayed in Dr. Montoya's office until he'd cried himself out. Then he pulled himself together and sauntered back to the heart of the lab. He didn't know what he was going to do next. Ever since they'd met Tex in the desert, his overarching goal had been simply to go home, but he no longer had a home to go back to.

Things had been strained with Anna, but as soon as she saw him, she wrapped him in a hug. Her tears made a wet spot on his T-shirt. They now had something in common—a horrible thing, to be sure—but they were now in a club together of people who had lost their parents. He stroked her back and coaxed the tears from her that she'd pent up since seeing her dad get killed.

Ian sauntered over. He put a hand on Jack's shoulder. "You okay?"

Jack wiped a tear. He thought he was cried out for the time being, but as soon as Anna began crying, his tears flowed again. "No. But I will be."

"What can I do?" Ian asked.

"Put me to work." Jack meant it. Empty time on his hands was the last thing he needed.

Ian nodded and gave him a small smile. "I can do that."

Jack primarily spent his time being a lab assistant to the lab assistant helping Anna help Dr. Randall with his gene-therapy work. He and Anna eased back into the companionship they'd had in New York. She seemed to understand his need to keep his mind off of what had happened to his mom. She kept him occupied most of his waking hours, and he was glad of it.

On their tenth day in Phoenix, Dr. Randall announced they had succeeded in creating a gene therapy that he hoped would work. He was prepared to inject Alecto, but Anna put on the brakes.

"Did you even ask her if she wants it?"

Dr. Randall's blank expression was the answer.

"Look, treat her like you would a human patient because, you know, she is part human. Tell her the risks and the benefits. Informed consent," Anna said.

Jack nodded, his heart swelling with affection for her. Though she was nothing like Erika, they both shared a compassion for others. That was something he admired about each of them.

Dr. Randall fidgeted with his glasses. "Perhaps that is why I did not become a medical doctor, Anna. I am no good with bedside manner."

Anna rubbed his forearm gently. "It's okay. I didn't mean to scold. It's just that my mission was to free her from Croft. And the way she's been treated throughout the years... Well, we need to put an end to it."

Dr. Randall nodded. "I completely agree. I will... I'll do my best."

Jack and Anna found Alecto where they'd last seen her. She had spent most of her time in the small apartment she shared with Anna, Jack, and Ian. She had never watched TV before and sat with her eyes glued to the screen for hours as if sucking up a lifetime of mediocre sitcoms and made-for-television movies in just a week.

Jack was flabbergasted that she was content to remain holed up in an apartment all day, the blinds closed and draperies drawn, when she could have been out exploring the world. Unlike her half-brother Tex, though, Alecto seemed to enjoy the darkness and comfort of enclosed spaces. She was the least social person Jack had ever met, even including Thomas.

Anna forced her out of the apartment and to the lab, where she sat in the small, cluttered staff kitchen. She had a knit cap over her bulbous head, which was further camouflaged by the hood of her jacket. She wore a pair of dark owl-eyed sunglasses, black pants, and sneakers. She could almost pass for human, though she looked a bit like a late-elementary schoolchild playing dress-up with her mom's sunglasses.

She was not reading a book or paper, and she didn't stare at a phone or tablet screen. She sat with her knees to her chest, her arms wrapped around them, staring off at some unseen point.

Anna sat across the table from her, and Jack took a seat between them. Alecto did not acknowledge their presence.

Anna reached an arm across the table and gently touched Alecto's arm. "Alecto, we need to speak with you. It's about the procedure Dr. Randall would like to perform on you today."

She unwound her arms from around her legs. She removed her sunglasses and blinked her eyes a few times as though they were adjusting to the bright light of the fluorescents.

"You want me to turn the lights off?" Jack asked.

She shook her head. When she spoke, her voice was hoarse from disuse. "I need to get used to the light if I'm to live in this world." She didn't sound very happy at the prospect.

"I want to make sure you're okay with this and that you understand what's going to happen," Anna said.

"Do I have a choice?" Her voice was flat and matter-of-fact, without a hint of regret or sarcasm or bitterness.

"You do have a choice," Jack said.

Anna nodded. "You could remain as you are. You'd still be vulnerable to attacks by water and weakened by humidity. But it is your choice."

Alecto blinked her huge eyes, looked at both of them, then said, "You do not understand. Commander Sturgis created this cure for me. It is her directive that I undergo this change. I must do this. There is no choice."

Anna began to protest, but Alecto put up her hand and said simply, "Silence."

Though no force or anger existed behind Alecto's words, Anna complied.

"I do not expect humans to understand. I am not like you, Anna. I was not born into a world of freedom. My Conexus genes crave order. Structure. I need command. I will do this, and I do not need to contemplate whether it is good or bad for me—only that my commander wills it. That is all."

She did not wait for further protests from Anna or argument from Jack. She stood, put her glasses back on, and said, "Take me to Dr. Randall. I am ready."

Jack walked on one side and Anna on the other as they led her to the room in the lab where Anna and Dr. Randall had worked on the gene therapy. Dr. Randall had placed a stool beside one of the high tables. He had a steel tray there with two needles filled with liquid, a few cotton balls, and some flexible bandages.

Dr. Randall wore a wide smile and greeted her warmly. "Alecto, you are looking good. I think the time out of the cave has served you well."

She did not reply.

Dr. Randall nervously adjusted his glasses. "Yes, very well then. Please, have a seat here, and we will begin."

Alecto took the seat, her back rigid and her posture perfect.

"I'll need you to remove the sweatshirt so I can give the injections."

As Alecto unzipped the hoodie and removed it, Anna said, "Remember, doc. Informed consent."

After their conversation with Alecto in the kitchen, Jack figured the idea of informed consent pointless. Clearly, the young woman would drink cyanide-laced Kool-Aid if Commander Sturgis told her to.

Dr. Randall did his best to inform the patient even though doing so would make no difference. "There will be two injections, one in each arm. I will not lie. It will likely hurt, and the liquid may burn as it enters your veins."

Alecto showed no outward sign of understanding or emotion.

He coughed nervously. "After that, well, the truth is I do not know what will happen. This is, of course, a wholly unique situation, never been done before. But if other gene therapies are any indication, you may feel nauseous, even vomit for a day or so. You may feel weak and have stomachaches. You may run a fever."

Dr. Randall continued for nearly three minutes listing all the potential side effects she might suffer through. Alecto stoically listened, though Anna and Jack both shifted anxiously on their feet. The cure seemed potentially worse than the disease. That point seemed especially clear when Dr. Randall cited the last of the possible effects.

"And last but surely not least, it could kill you."

Even that did not cause Alecto to change expression.

"Are you sure you want to do this?" Jack asked. He wasn't sure that, if he had to make the choice, he would choose to undergo a risky, untried therapy. She was about to put something in her system that would rewrite her genetic code.

Alecto nodded her large head.

Dr. Randall again pushed his glasses up his nose. "Yes, well, unless you have any questions then, we will proceed."

He lifted the first needle and was moving it toward her arm when she grabbed his arm with her other hand. The movement was so quick the action was nearly a blur.

"I have just one question, Dr. Randall."

He stammered. "Yes, um, anything. What do you want to know?"

"Did Commander Sturgis order that this procedure be done?" She let loose his hand, and he put the needle down to his side.

"Well, since she was removed from command of A.H.D.N.A., I mean officially, Dr. Sturgis is no longer a commander, so she has no authority over you or anybody, really."

The answer made her brow furrow, the first sign of emotion Jack had seen from her since he first met her.

"If she does not command me, then who does?"

Dr. Randall put the needle back on the tray. He coughed lightly again and hesitated. "Well currently, I would say that no one is in command. You are—"

Alecto's face, normally as devoid of emotion as cold, hard stone, contorted with pain. Her mouth was twisted in agony, her eyes narrowed as though fighting back tears.

Anna rubbed her bare arm to comfort her, and Dr. Randall stood with his mouth open like a fish sucking in air. Alecto's eyes darted wildly, and she pulled her knees to her chest. She was getting ready to go into one of her trances.

Jack blurted out, "He's wrong, Alecto. Commander Sturgis is still in command." He didn't know what made him say it, but it had the immediate effect of pulling Alecto back from the brink of what may have been a mental crisis.

"Explain," she said.

Jack thumbed through his mind, trying to find an answer that would appease her, and he came up with something that may have even been plausible. "You were created as part of the H.A.L.F. program, right?"

"Of course," she said.

"Okay, so that was funded with taxpayer dollars. And this Croft guy, he seems to think he's in charge of you, but he's not even a US citizen. And since he had Commander Sturgis unlawfully imprisoned, any paper saying she was stripped of command is invalid. Therefore, she is still your commander."

Alecto sat quietly for a moment, her head cocked to one side. Finally, she asked, "And did Commander Sturgis order this procedure?"

Dr. Randall fidgeted with the buttons on his shirt. "Well, *order*, I don't know if you can say—"

Anna interrupted. "She did, Dr. Randall. When I spoke to Sewell—who, by the way, has been acting supervisor of A.H.D.N.A. in her absence—anyway, he said—and these are his exact words—'Commander Sturgis has given me notes on a gene therapy that she created to cure Alecto and Tex of their water vulnerability. She said to synthesize it as quickly as possible and administer it to Alecto as soon as you can.'"

Alecto apparently heard what she needed to hear. "Then do not delay, Dr. Randall. Inject me as commanded."

Jack felt a bit guilty about manipulating her, but she had seemed to come unhinged at the thought of having no one to give her orders. Clearly, Commander Sturgis intended her to get the therapy, and Alecto seemed comforted to know she was still getting orders from someone. Alecto and Tex were as distinct from one another as Anna was different from Thomas.

Dr. Randall let out a sigh and quickly set about injecting the medicine into Alecto's vein. She winced only slightly as he poked the needle in. She let out a small moan of pain as the liquid burned its way into her system.

When he had injected both needles, Dr. Randall said, "I suggest you take her back to the apartment now and have her rest. Someone should be with her twenty-four, seven, understand? Do not leave her alone, and at the first sign of any trouble, contact me immediately."

Jack attempted to help her up from the stool, but she shrugged off his help. She rose on steady legs and walked of her own accord to the elevators.

Back at the apartment, Jack and Anna began Alecto Watch. At first, no ill effects appeared. Alecto took up residence on the couch again, engrossed in a reality TV show. But a couple hours after the injection, Alecto complained of an odd sensation she had never felt before. Before they could inquire further, she promptly upchucked all over the wooden floor.

She looked aghast at what she had done, as though her vomit was a hairy bit of moldy cheese someone had scraped out of the back of the refrigerator and thrown onto the floor.

"Have you never vomited before?" Anna asked as she knelt to clean it up with paper towels.

Fortunately, Alecto had not eaten before the procedure. The vomitus was mainly liquid.

Alecto shook her head. "I am cold now. Very cold." She shivered and wrapped her arms around herself.

"You should lie down. I'll get you covers," Jack said.

She allowed his help that time as he led her to the bedroom she shared with Anna. Jack piled two more blankets on her, and when she still complained of being cold, he ran to the nearest drug store and bought an electric blanket to add even more warmth.

Anna called Dr. Randall and explained the situation. He said they could do nothing but give her comfort and wait it out. He hoped the discomfort would pass within forty-eight hours.

Alecto slept fitfully and occasionally mumbled about being cold. Anna stroked her bald head as she shook with fever. Jack kept her sick bucket clean and watched her through the night so Anna could get rest.

Jack had nodded off sometime in the middle of the second night. He awoke to the eerie sensation that he was being watched. He opened his eyes slowly. They were still bleary with sleep. Hazy, soft first-morning light filtered into the room through the gauzy curtains. A silhouette sat upright on the bed in front of him.

Alecto's black eyes stared back at him. "I require... water."

Jack rubbed the sleep from his eyes with the palms of his hands. "Not sure I heard you right." He yawned. "Did you just ask for water?"

She nodded.

"You mean to drink?"

"Yes."

Jack pushed himself up from the chair and fetched Alecto a tall glass of cool water. In all the time he'd been around her, Jack had never seen Alecto drink anything. She had told him she got the liquid her body needed from the food she ate and by absorbing moisture from the air.

By the time he got back to the room, Anna was sitting upright in her bed, yawning.

Jack handed Alecto the glass. "You may want to drink this—"

She took the glass and downed the water in one long gulp.

"I was going to say slowly."

She handed the empty glass back to him. "More."

Anna yawned as she threw off the covers. "No, I think Jack is right. You should take it slow. We need to wait to see what effect that water you just drank will have on your system."

"More water, Jack," Alecto said. When he didn't make a move to fill her glass, she looked up at him and blinked her wide eyes, her lips drawn into what may have been a sad frown. "Please. My lips and throat are—what is the word?"

"Parched," Jack said. He could believe it as her voice was hoarse and sounded as if she'd just swallowed gravel. "How about a half a glass?"

"Maybe we should call Dr. Randall before we give her any more water," Anna said.

"Please," Alecto said. Her voice was small and hoarse and pleading.

"You call Dr. Randall. But I can't let her go thirsty while we wait for him," Jack said. He handed Alecto a half-full glass of water. "Drink it more slowly this time, okay?"

She nodded and took just a sip. She closed her eyes, and her face relaxed. Her lips curled up in a small smile, and she appeared to be savoring the cool liquid as it ran down her throat.

"Are you feeling any ill effects?" Anna asked.

Alecto blinked her eyes slowly a few times then opened them and smiled more widely. "I always wondered what water would taste like. It is... it is good, is it not?"

"That it is," Jack said. As her glass was empty again, he took it from her. "How do you feel?"

Alecto cocked her head to one side, her eyes staring off toward nothing that Anna or Jack could see. She was quiet and still for a moment, but abruptly announced, "I suffer no ill effects from the water. I am cured."

Jack chuckled. "It's great that you're feeling well, but I think Dr. Randall will want to run some tests before he pronounces you cured."

"Now you can't be controlled by Croft anymore," Anna said.

"Or by Commander Sturgis," Jack said. He recalled the ease with which Alecto had attacked Erika and Tex in Apthartos. Jack shuddered at the idea of an Alecto unfettered by a vulnerability to humidity. Now, nothing would stop her if she decided to turn on any of them.

Alecto rose from the bed. "I want to cleanse myself with water."

"You mean shower?" Jack asked.

"Yes. A shower."

"No. I'm putting my foot down," Anna said. "Drinking water is one thing. Your body is replenishing the liquid it lost during your illness. But standing under a blast of water is another thing. If your skin still draws water in, you could drown in a matter of minutes."

Alecto pushed past Anna on the way to the bathroom.

Anna ran after her. "Alecto, stop!"

Alecto stripped out of her clothes, unconcerned with modesty. She left a trail of clothing behind her but stopped by the tub, staring at the closed shower curtain.

Jack wanted to look away from her naked body. Watching someone disrobe in front of people was awkward as hell, and staring seemed impolite, but stare he did. He couldn't pull his eyes away.

Her body looked human yet not quite. Her ribs were clearly visible, as was each nodule of her vertebrae. Her skin was pulled taut over her frame. She was gaunt yet well muscled. Her thighs were tightly wound cords of muscle, and her calves were also well formed. Her breasts were buds, barely there but enough to distinguish her from being male.

Anna stepped between Alecto and the shower curtain. "I cannot allow you to do this. Not without Dr. Randall present. At least wait for him to get here to monitor you. Okay?"

Alecto did not immediately answer but finally nodded in acquiescence. Jack found a robe and threw it over her shoulders. The modesty was more for their benefit than hers.

Dr. Randall took less than half an hour to arrive. His face was flushed with excitement at the news that she'd drunk nearly two full glasses of water with no apparent ill effects.

He stared at Alecto, wrapped in the robe and sitting on the sofa. He scratched his chin then pushed his glasses up his nose. "Fascinating."

"She wants to take a shower," Jack said. He wasn't sure Dr. Randall remembered that was why they had called him over.

"Yes, well, I think you should," he said. "We can't know if you are cured until we try it out."

"Shouldn't she maybe dip her feet in first? Take it slow?" Jack asked.

"If she drank that much water and has suffered no ill effects, I think we can skip straight to a shower," Dr. Randall said.

Alecto did not hesitate. She stood and let the robe fall away. Tex had done the same thing on Bell Rock—just dropped trouser in front of all of them. Jack didn't think he could ever get used to people just peeling their clothes off whenever and wherever they wanted.

Anna ran the water until it was warm and helped Alecto step into the tub. With the shower curtain pulled, Jack no longer saw Alecto's face. The only sound was that of the water pinging against the porcelain tub.

The peaceful water sounds were interrupted by a guttural scream, like an injured animal yowling.

Dr. Randall had been standing just outside the bathroom door, but he ran to the shower and threw aside the curtain.

From the sound, Jack expected Alecto to be in a heap on the floor of the shower, her body limp and near lifeless. Instead, she stood tall with her arms outstretched to her sides, her face upturned, taking the force of the shower directly.

Dr. Randall turned off the water and threw a towel around her shoulders. "Do not worry. We'll get you dried out and—"

Alecto's lips were upturned in the first genuine smile Jack had ever seen on her face. "Water is... good."

Jack let out the breath he'd been holding, relieved her guttural scream was from happiness instead of pain.

He helped her out of the shower, and Anna threw another towel over her head. Anna and Dr. Randall rubbed the water off her as she stood still, her eyes shining bright, wetness twinkling at the corners.

Alecto still wore a broad smile, and her eyes were focused on a distant horizon none of them could see. "Nothing will stop me now."

14

ERIKA

Erika had fallen onto Niyol and Kai's couch and slept for nearly fifteen hours. When she woke, the house was quiet, the only sound the crackle of a fire in the wood-burning stove. Her head felt full of cobwebs, and her mouth was as dry as cotton. *That was some tea.*

She tiptoed down the hall of the small house, searching for Dana. The kitchen, two small bedrooms, and bath were empty.

Erika stepped outside into a clear, cool late-autumn day. Tents had sprouted around the house, and people sat on lawn chairs around a small bonfire. They all appeared to be Native American, though Erika didn't know if they were from the same tribe as Niyol and Kai. Dogs chased each other or napped quietly on the ground by the fire. Despite a crowd of at least a dozen people, the morning was nearly silent, save for the pop and hiss of the fire and panting of dogs.

A few people looked up when they heard her, but mostly they stared into the fire. Erika was thankful that no one descended on her and hounded her to tell her story.

Dana was sitting by the fire with the strangers. She motioned for Erika to come sit by her.

Erika pulled an empty chair next to her aunt. "How is he? Have you heard anything?"

Dana shook her head. "Kai says to be patient. Niyol will send one of the men out of the lodge with news when there is any."

Erika stared at the sweat lodge for a while, willing Niyol to emerge with a healthy Tex. The small building's door of layers of thick woolen blankets remained closed. It sat there silently, offering no answers.

She took up vigil with the rest of them. She watched flames eat a log. They rendered the wood to ashes in less time than was necessary to bake a cake. Someone handed her a warm piece of fry bread covered in pinto beans. She ate it in half a dozen bites.

Kai pulled up a chair next to Erika. The smell of wood smoke wafted off Kai's hair and thick multicolored woven wool jacket.

"How is he?" Erika asked.

Kai poked the fire with a long stick, and sparks spiraled up and disappeared into the sky. She didn't look directly at Erika and said only, "He still lives."

Though she would have liked more specific information about Tex's condition, the starkly honest answer comforted Erika.

Erika pulled around herself the jean jacket Dana had lent her, wrapping her arms around her middle in an attempt to stay warm. She quietly observed a few men enter the domed hogan where Niyol had taken Tex. A few minutes later, a few other men exited. They were bare chested, their faces red and wet with sweat. Their faces revealed nothing. They grabbed their shirts off a wooden rack hung to the outside of the hogan and soon blended into the crowd. Women put stones into the fire to heat up and took hot ones to the hogan to keep it warm.

Erika approached a stooped, elderly woman with silver hair. "I'll take the stones."

The woman's eyes were warm and kindly. "No. You are not part of the medicine."

"But I... He's my..." *What is he exactly to me?*

To call him a friend seemed somehow less than a full explanation of what he had come to mean to her, yet he was neither family nor her lover.

"When I was young, probably about your age," the woman said, "I had a young man. My mother used to say we were practically joined at the hip. More like locked at the lips." Her laugh was a dry cackle.

The elderly woman's laugh was infectious, and Erika couldn't help but smile.

"We're not—"

"He got sick. Everyone thought he would die." The mirth was gone from her face. "I wanted to be with him powerful bad. But the wise one told the men to keep me out."

"What did you do?"

"Oh, my anger!" The woman's eyes blazed as she recalled the feeling. "'You can't keep me out!' I yelled. But the wise one came out and said to me, 'His love for you distracts him from the work of healing he has to do. If you are there, he will worry for you instead of thinking on himself.'"

Erika wanted to protest further, to tell the woman that she and Tex were not in a relationship like that, that he wasn't her boyfriend and hadn't professed any kind of love for her. She didn't argue, though, because on some level, what the woman said felt true. The elderly woman resumed her slow walk to the hogan with the warm stones.

People cooked and ate. Dogs played and slept. New people came while others left. All was done in a reverent quietness that seemed impossible for a crowd that numbered at least two dozen.

People had quiet conversations around the fire. None included Erika. She tried to listen to the quiet whispering, to hear if they had more information about Tex than had been shared with her, but the people talked quietly and often in a language Erika didn't understand.

Dana had left the fire but returned with two Styrofoam cups of hot, black coffee. Erika wasn't much of a coffee drinker, but she allowed it to warm her hands.

She whispered to Dana. "I'm trying to hear if they're talking about Tex, but I can't understand what they're saying. Do you know anything other than 'he's alive'?"

Dana took a sip of her coffee. "I understand only a little, but they're talking about the end of the fourth world."

Erika nearly spat out the sip of coffee she'd just taken. "End of the world?" *That doesn't sound good.* "What does that have to do with Tex?"

"I don't think it's necessarily a bad thing. They think he may be part of a prophecy. There's supposed to be a new sky god that will usher in the new age—the fifth world."

Erika chortled. The idea that Tex was some kind of savior made her snicker. She'd seen him kill effortlessly, and he seemed to have little regard for human life in general. She believed he could learn to appreciate the value of life—in time—but being humane seemed to have been engineered and trained out of him.

She nearly blurted out her thoughts on the subject but stopped herself. Dana didn't know about Tex's powers or about his training to be a skilled killer.

Aunt Dana frowned at Erika. "Don't scoff at others' beliefs." She threw the last bit of her coffee out on the parched ground. "Be respectful. These people are helping him—and you."

Erika wiped the smirk from her face. "I'm not laughing at them. It's just... Well, if you knew Tex like I do, I don't think you'd believe he's messiah material."

Dana shook her head. "I didn't say *I* believe that. Personally, I think he's bad news."

Heat rose in Erika's cheeks. "What are you saying?"

"I'm saying that when he gets well, you should send him on his way. I think he's no good for you. You're clearly infatuated with him, so you don't see the truth."

"Truth? Oh, enlighten me." Erika's voice was no longer a whisper.

Aunt Dana looked around to see if people were staring then moved in a bit closer to Erika and spoke even more quietly. "Erika, look at him. And look at yourself. You've been on the run from something, and this young man—or whatever he is—has pulled you into it. If you stay connected to him, you'll meet a bad end. I can feel it."

Erika didn't bother keeping her voice down. "How dare you."

Dana's eyes flashed anger. "Keep your voice down," she hissed. "This is a sacred time. Show respect or leave."

Erika's skin prickled. "Maybe you need to respect me. You abandoned me—"

Dana shook her head. "You know now that's not true. Your mom didn't give you the cards, letters, and presents. And I had no number for you—"

Erika held up her hand and spoke quietly through gritted teeth. "You knew where I lived."

Dana fell quiet.

"You gave up the right to have a say about what I do or who I'm with when you crapped out on me as my family, not that you probably had much to say in the matter anyway."

"You're still a minor, Erika. And as your only living relative in the US, I'm your guardian now, and—"

Erika laughed out loud, drawing attention again. "Don't even." She spat out the words with as much poison as she could muster. "I'll be eighteen in a few months."

"Half a year is more than a few months."

Erika rose from her chair. "Take care of your own life, and don't even think about trying to control mine."

She walked away before Dana could argue. A few rust-colored dogs followed her as if she had a steak strapped to her back. She was glad for the quiet company of the animals. She wanted to seethe in silence.

The day turned into night, yet Niyol and Tex remained in the hogan. Erika asked men who left the sweat lodge how Tex was, and all said the same thing that Kai had said: "He still lives."

What had been refreshing truth the first time became irritating then downright infuriating. "Alive like 'clinging to life' alive or alive like 'improving and there's hope' alive?" she wanted to ask. She didn't push it, though. She was in unknown territory, a world where she was unschooled in the customs and language. She didn't want to offend and put Tex's chances for survival at risk.

For two days, Erika helped around the makeshift camp as best she could. She carried firewood to the bonfire, pitched tents, and carried food to people. On the second day, Aunt Dana had to get back to her forest-service job.

"Come with me. You need a break," Dana said.

"My place is here. For now, anyway."

Dana shook her head, donned her forest-service hat and got into the truck. "I've got to check on my house after work, but I'll be back tonight. Get some rest, Erika." Dana's eyes were soft, and she gave Erika a smile.

Erika forced herself to smile back, not wanting to feud with her aunt. "I'll try."

Dana wasn't back before Erika finally decided to give in to sleep. After the first night, Erika had given up her spot on the couch to Kai's elderly mother. Erika made her way to a tent and pulled a sleeping bag up to her ears. The ground was cold and hard beneath her. She'd gotten somewhat used to sleeping on a floor, so that wasn't the issue with getting to sleep. Her mind flitted back and forth from loneliness to worry and fear. She missed Ian's quick wit and Jack's easy banter. She even missed the strange and often tense conversations she had with Tex.

She found that her mind dwelled on Tex more than on anyone or anything else. She was sick with worry for him, of course, but she also found herself fantasizing about him in a way she had never done with anyone else before. She imagined him strong and well, as he had been when she first met him. She wanted to spend time with him without people chasing them or being in danger. *What would he be like if he could just be himself?* Also, she longed to show him more of the world than the inside of a car or house. She wondered what would he think about snow and if he wanted to see the ocean even if he couldn't get in it.

She drifted off to a fitful sleep and dreamed.

In her dream, the sun was low in the sky. The canyon walls glowed vibrant pink and orange. She found a tall tree and decided to rest beneath it and watch the sunset. *I thought it was morning, not night.* Erika put aside her confusion and gazed peacefully at nature's light show. She couldn't remember the last time she'd watched the sun rise or set.

"I wish Tex was here."

15
TEX

A dry, thin finger stroked Tex's cheek. The Regina's voice, raspy and low, whispered in his ear. "You will make us strong again." Her odor—the smell of rotten fruit and peat—clung to his nostrils.

He thought his eyes were open, but he floated in darkness, vast and endless. The Regina was around him, inside him, everywhere and all consuming.

Tex kicked his legs and flailed his arms, trying to beat her away and off of him. She was there, her face mere inches from him, her purple lips curled in a sinister smile. She faded into nothing but then reappeared behind him, her voice piercing his mind, the Conexus speaking all at once, the all-too-familiar buzz of their collective voices droning on and on, the pain a railroad spike through his skull.

"You dream," a male voice said.

That was not the Regina's voice, but it was not his own either. Yet another voice had been added to his already crowded mind.

Flames licked at his insides, yet he shivered with nearly unendurable cold. His lungs ached and felt full of fluid. *I am drowning. Again.*

"Please, no!" Tex screamed. Well, he tried to yell, but he knew the words had not left his mouth. He was paralyzed, unable to move even the muscles of his jaw to speak. He was with the Conexus again. *No, that cannot be.*

"Please, no water," he said with his mind. "I will drown."

The Regina's putrid odor drifted away, replaced by a new scent. A sweet yet slightly acrid aroma wafted to him. It was smoky yet clean. The smell carried him away from the dream of the Conexus.

Something gentle touched his hand, warm and pleasing. The same voice he had heard before, low and melodious, said, "Follow the sacred smoke. Follow the sound of my voice."

"Who are you?"

Again, he felt a gentle tug at his hand. "I am your guide on this spirit journey."

The touch was gone, the warmth gone with it. He followed the sound of the voice and the trail of smoke as it became thicker and more pungent. He was surrounded by fog, the world around him milky gray and cold.

"I do not believe in spirit," Tex said.

The male voice chuckled softly. "That does not matter. Even if you do not believe in spirit, it believes in you. Come to me. Follow my voice."

The darkness dissipated. Tex's vision was blurry, but he walked toward a horizon, fuzzy and indistinct but visible. A figure shimmered before him like a mirage on a hot day.

Tex quickened his pace. He knew he should be frightened, but for some reason he was not. He wanted to figure out who had infiltrated his mind. The mirage took form, Tex's eyes less bleary. A small man stood before him, his skin weathered with age, his long, white-streaked black hair pulled back in a smooth, salt-and-pepper tail. The man stood on a sage-covered red-soil mesa. He did not smile at Tex, but he did not frown either. The man's expression was wholly free of judgment, peaceful yet curious. It was a look Tex had never experienced before.

The bright-blue midday sky was dotted with puffy clouds. The air was pleasantly cool, but the sun was warm on his face and bare shoulders. Tex looked down and saw he wore only pants, his emaciated chest and bony feet bare. *I do not remember taking off my shirt and shoes.*

"Is this real?" Tex asked.

"As real as it needs to be."

"Where is Erika? Is she—"

"She rests." The man walked away from him. He stopped after a few paces, looked back, and gestured for Tex to follow.

Tex spun and looked behind him. They were surrounded by endless mesa in all directions. Having no clue where he was or what to do, Tex followed the man.

They walked for what felt like many minutes. No matter how quickly Tex walked, the man was always a few paces ahead of him.

The path narrowed and twisted and turned as they went down a hill and into a valley formed by high rust-red rocky canyon walls.

In a small clearing at the base of the canyon stood a small cottage made of weathered wood. The man opened its door and waved for Tex to follow.

Tex stepped through the door. He expected a warm, inviting cabin much like Aunt Dana's, but it was dark inside, with no warm hearth or smell of cooking food or warm lights. The room was cold, stone, and gray.

The place was empty and dark except for a smooth white stone table that had erupted from the ground. The only illumination was a bright white cone of light that spilled over the table from overhead.

A tiny, fragile-looking gray-skinned creature lay on the table. Its ribs were clearly visible, its face all gaunt shadows.

Tex edged closer. All the Greys had looked identical to him, but still, maybe he would somehow be able to distinguish it from the others.

He was only a foot away from the table, so close he could touch the being lying there if he wanted to. A metal clamp was affixed to the back of the creature's head. A puddle of blood had dried on the table below the poor thing's head. A plastic tube snaked from the blackness of the ceiling and went into the creature's head, held there by the metal clamp.

Tex got closer still and gasped when he looked down into the creature's face. He, Tex, was on the table. He was the thin, nearly unrecognizable Grey, lying like a specimen on the cold stone slab.

"No," he whispered. "It cannot be. I... I escaped." He could still be in the Conexus collective, and all that he thought had happened—the battle in the pool room, the death of Xenos, the escape from the Makers—it all could have been a dream. "Is this the past? Or am I still locked into the collective mind of the Conexus?"

The man who had led him through the door stood across from him now. Pityingly, he too looked down at the pathetic creature on the table. "What does your heart tell you?"

Tex had never been asked to speak from the fictional place humans sometimes referred to as "the heart." He was not sure he knew what the man meant. Somehow, though, the strange yet comforting smell of the smoke drew him to a place within himself that he had never been aware of.

"This is my past. I am in a waking dream."

The man nodded. "This is how your friends found you."

As Tex stared at the alien version of himself, covered in angry and festering wounds, he wished he could rescue himself from the place.

The man's voice, deep and low, resonated in his chest. "Walk in their shoes. What would you have done?"

"I would have pulled me away from this place." The ache in his head intensified, and the uncontrollable shivering returned. He felt as though he was bathing in ice yet had swallowed an inferno. "I am not much better off now than I was then, am I?"

"Your physical body lingers at the door to death," the man said.

Tex saw a thin filament out of the corner of his eye and noticed it was connected to his body. The strange thread shimmered and looked frayed, near to breaking.

"I am not ready to die. Dr. Randall. Erika... they need me."

"Many need you."

The words reminded him of the things Commander Sturgis had told him his whole life. He had hated her for determining his fate before he was even born. He had been created to be a weapon, a warrior to fight for people he did not know in a war he never understood, but no one had ever asked him if he wanted the job.

"Perhaps choice is an illusion," the man said. He had a pipe in his hand and took a long draw from it. Rings of smoke billowed in the air around him, his dark eyes clear and bold. They seemed to see right into the very center of Tex's being. "Illusion or no, what choice would you make now?"

Tex was not sure of what options he had. He was sure of nothing. He knew only that he wished to see Erika again and that he wanted to live if for no reason than to save her from dying at the hands of the aliens currently plundering Europe.

"You care for this woman?" The man handed the pipe to Tex.

He had never smoked before, but he took the pipe and drew the smoke deep into his damaged lungs. It was an inopportune thing to do, given that his lungs were already compromised, but the smoke did not burn or hurt. It filled him with warmth and eased the pain in his head.

"I do." As Tex tried to focus on Erika, spikes of pain reared in his brain, and his head felt as if it would split open.

His hands flew to his head, and he pressed against his skull as though he could stop his head from shattering into a jigsaw puzzle. A strangled cry escaped his lips, and he knew the sound existed not only in the dream world but also in the material world that his body inhabited.

Strong arms wrapped around him and cradled his shivering body. A coolness grew at his temples and feet. The air was still, but he felt a low rumble, steady and rhythmic. Drums pounded a rhythm in time with his heart.

The whole Earth pulsed at the same speed, a gentle *thrump, thrump, thrump*. A chant rose. Male voices sang in unison, strong and low, melodic and hypnotizing. The sound was melancholy. *Is it a death song?*

Tex sank deeper still into the gentle arms that held him. The spike of pain was gone though his head still ached. He allowed himself to be rocked and carried away on the wave of the beat of the drums.

"Go to her," the man said. "She will be your guide now."

"I cannot," Tex said. "I am broken. Fractured. I cannot show this to her. I cannot let her see me this way."

"She has already seen all of you yet remains at your side. Trust in her. She will help you choose, and when your choice is made, the fracture will heal."

"How can I go to her? I cannot move."

The man did not answer, but the drums beat more loudly, their pace quickening. Tex sank into the rhythm. Deeper and deeper he went, into the heart of the Earth, the waiting arms of the Great Mother. Young sapling branches with new shoots of green cradled him. A thick canopy of forest leaves and bark surrounded him, gentle shafts of dappled sunlight peeking through here and there. This place was mostly dark and warm and quiet, save for the insistent thrum of the drums and the beat of the Great Mother's heart.

"Go to her," the man said, though his voice sounded far off.

Tex did not know how to find Erika in that realm of dreams and smoke. He recalled his times with her, from first seeing her in the desert, Joe's prisoner, to watching her as she helped him dump Gary's lifeless body into a watering trough. From the first moment he'd seen her to the last, he was intrigued by her nature, so foreign to him, so unlike his own. He tried to understand her, yet each time he thought he had figured her out, she showed him something new, and she was an enigma once more.

The drums called him, and he sank even further. He was in a cocoon of branches, swaying gently as a leaf caught by a breeze.

He remembered the moment Erika had pulled him to safety in A.H.D.N.A. She had held him, and her heart beat against his back, her body warm, gentle yet unyielding against him. Her heartbeat from his memory melded with the steady rhythm of the drums and the beat of the Great Mother's heart. One beat. One song.

"Tex?" she called.

"Erika!" He was suddenly running |through a brightly lit white hallway. He opened door after door, but each room was dark and empty.

"Tex!" she yelled.

The corridor seemed endless. For every door he opened, two more sprang into existence.

A voice—the man's voice—from far off said, "Follow the rhythm."

Tex stopped, his heart hammering wildly in his chest. It beat out of time with the drums, but as he calmed himself, he got back in sync with the cadence of the Earth's thrum. "Erika?" he called again and listened.

"I'm here," she said.

Her voice was louder, the beating stronger.

He went toward the voice as they called back and forth to each other. The endless hall disappeared, and he was once again on the mesa. The sun was no longer high overhead but low in the sky. The heat that had threatened to immolate him from the inside out was gone, chills returning.

A lone house sat at the edge of the mesa, its two windows like bright yellow eyes winking at him in the dusk.

"Erika?"

"Come to me," she whispered.

He opened the door of the tiny house. He hesitated, his feet as though in quicksand, his breathing ragged. The last time he'd followed the man into a house, it turned out to be a cave of nightmares.

The light inside was warm and inviting, though. Heat poured from within.

"I am here," she said.

Tex stepped across the threshold, and as soon as he did, the house was gone.

Erika sat with her back against the thick trunk of a tall tree. She stared toward the western sky, ablaze with brilliant orange, purple, and azure, the sunset painting the canyon walls. She turned toward him, her smiling face lit pink by the sky. She waved him over.

His legs were like lead. He tried to run quickly, but every step was an eternity. Her smile never wavered, and he was glad of that as it was the only thing allowing him to keep his legs moving.

He finally reached her and sat across from her. He wanted to look into her eyes, to know if she was really there or another illusion planted into his mind by someone—or something—beyond his control.

Erika's brown eyes were rimmed in red and shot through with tiny blood vessels. A yellow splotch of a faded bruise surrounded the right eye, and a pink scar marred her upper lip, the remnant of the injury she had received the night he'd first met her.

Tex reached out slowly and gingerly touched her cheek. His fingers shook as he made contact. "Erika?"

She smiled and put her hands on top of his. She sighed lightly, closed her eyes, and kissed the inside of his hand. A single tear escaped her eye. "I thought... I thought you were gone."

"No," he said. His other hand found her hair, and he smoothed a stray strand back from her face, his fingers trembling. "Not yet, anyway."

She opened her eyes and stared into his. "Don't go." She moved closer, her lips mere inches from his own. "Don't leave me," she whispered. Her warm breath was a fluttery kiss against his cold skin.

Shivers ran the length of his spine. He wanted to kiss her, but he had never kissed a woman before. He didn't want to ruin their closeness with an awful kiss. Instead of kissing her, he pulled her hair free of the band that held it in a ponytail. A long, thick cascade of black hair fell around her face, and he caught a bunch of it in his hand.

"I am very ill." He caressed her hair, which was soft and silky in his fingers. "I have lost so much of myself. I am... fractured."

Erika took his hands in hers and held them. "Maybe you're not lost so much as never found."

Her statement was at once confusing and yet the most sensible thing anyone had ever said to him. "Find myself?"

"Maybe it's a choice, Tex. Who do you want to be?"

Images flooded his mind. He was killing the attendant when he was a child, then he was strangling the life out of a snake and the man called Nacho. He dispassionately noted the death of Gary, his latest victim. "*You are a weapon*," Commander Sturgis had said. That was a phrase drilled into his mind, over and over. A phrase repeated often enough becomes a truth, even if it is initially unwanted and unbelieved.

Erika kissed his open palm, sending a chill up his spine. "You're more than a weapon," she said.

He felt as though she was as much inside his mind as he was inside hers. Warmth spread up his arm and through his limbs and finally settled in his loins. The images of death were replaced with memories of Dr. Randall, Ian, Erika, and even Jack Wilson. All had shown him kindness that he likely did not deserve. Even Dr. Dolan had given his life in the end to help Tex escape A.H.D.N.A.

"I need help to become the man I want to be," he said.

His fingers traced the outline of her face. They were so close that he felt heat radiating from her.

"So let me help you," she said.

Erika leaned even closer. Her lips—soft, warm, and yielding—were on his. He did not know what to do, so he was still, his eyes open, his hands at his sides.

Erika took one of his hands and put it on her back.

"I do not know—I've never—"

"Follow my lead," she said, her voice husky.

Her lips were again on his, and that time, he kissed her back. Their lips still touching, his hand at her back, he pulled her into him. Her heart beat against his chest, a steady *thrum, thrum, thrum* in sync with the drums and the Great Mother. The beat was in her—of her. Her arms flew to his neck and drew him into her. There was no beginning or end—only the two made one in a never-ending embrace, a kiss that melded day to night and man to woman.

His lungs burned and ached as cells reproduced and divided and repaired. New alveoli stretched their way this way and that and filled the empty space in his chest with new lung. A part of him wanted to seek out an answer to how growing a new lung was possible, but Erika's warm embrace and the deep, resonant *thrum, thrum, thrum* drew his mind away from questions. He was with her, and she was all that mattered.

Erika kissed his cheeks, her lips a tiny flutter at his neck and collarbone. He sought her neck, nuzzling her hair. She smelled of soap and sweat and smoke from the fire. He drank it in, her pale skin smooth and cool against his lips as her fingers ran through his hair, twisting the wavy locks in her fingers.

Liquid fire burned through every capillary in his body. He felt not the flame of Conexus torture but the heat his body was producing as it repaired the missing pieces of him. His head swam, dizzy from the sensation of her lips on his, her body warm and soft against his own.

Memories flooded his mind—not of torture and death, but of sitting on Dr. Randall's lap when he was a child as Dr. Randall read him a story about a family of rabbits, of a kindly aide walking slowly back from the testing lab so Tex could spend a bit more time away from the sedating high humidity of his quarters.

Synapses repaired, and neurons connected. His head throbbed, but the memories kept coming, of standing on Bell Rock, naked, cold, and aware that Erika stood behind him and saw him. He had wondered what she thought of him.

"I was curious."

Her mind was in his. Or she existed only in his mind. He could not be sure. Her lips were on his again, her hands seemingly everywhere.

His mind and body were becoming whole again. No, for the first time. He made his choice, and he became the being that he had always wanted to be.

As his mind repaired, the fractures were no more, and in that instant, he knew what he had to do. He knew what he had to become.

His hands roamed over her face, memorizing every feature. He picked her up in one easy motion. She was light in his suddenly strong arms, her body soft against his firm chest. He placed her gently on a bed of soft green grass he hadn't recalled being there before. That didn't matter. All that mattered was her body beneath his, their minds intertwined, her thoughts only of him, not of Jack.

He explored every inch of her, from armpits to toes. His lips lightly caressed her forehead, the crook of her elbow, her knees. They were interlocked for what seemed like hours yet might have been only minutes. They explored each other so wholly and completely that he could have identified her body from seeing only a few inches of her.

Afterward, she curled into the crook of his arm and rested her head on his chest. Exhausted, she dozed on him. Tex was not tired. His time with Erika left him exhilarated, but he was content to watch her sleep, trying to emblazon the moment into his mind. He felt he would likely need those memories to carry him through what was to come. He left her to sleep in peace, blissfully unaware of the full extent of the danger of the outside world that would soon creep in on them.

Tex unwound Erika's arms from around his waist and laid her sleeping body down gently to rest on the soft ground. He took a moment to drink in the beauty of her—the curve of her waist and rise of her hip, the cleft where her collarbone met her shoulder and the soft plumpness of her breasts as they gently rose and fell with her breath.

He kissed her gently one last time and reveled at the soft moan of pleasure that escaped her lips.

"My love," he whispered in her ear. The words felt good to him. They felt true.

"I love you," she said softly.

He knew it to be true. His heart beat in time with hers, their bodies in rhythm with the Great Mother, the cosmic rhythm of the universe.

Tex left her there in a pleasant dream. He left the soft grass. He followed the scent of the smoke and followed it back to his body, which still lay in the hogan. He hovered over it and was pleased with what he saw.

At once, he was one with his body again, the dream world a memory. His eyes fluttered open. The hogan was dark and filled with thick smoke. Tex pushed himself up to sitting. His head no longer swam.

Niyol's voice was hoarse. "It is done." He handed the pipe to another man and rose.

Tex rose too. The sweat on his naked chest evaporated almost instantly as he left the darkness and warmth of the sweat lodge. The drums had stopped, but the air was not quiet.

The morning sun was bright and hurt his eyes after days in the small dark hut. Outside the hogan, dogs barked and men shouted. In an instant, the dream world was a hazy memory. Worry for Erika filled him.

He reached out to her with his mind, but she did not answer. Their telepathic communication—if it had been real—was severed.

He pushed through the flaps of carpet that served as a door. He had to find Erika.

In Erika's dream, she was filled with a peaceful joy she had never known. She rested in Tex's arms, her head on his firm, bare chest. His body heat seeped into her and warded off the cold of the hard ground beneath them.

In the next instant, Tex was gone. The warmth that had suffused her vanished as well, leaving her with a bone-chilling void that reminded her of how she had felt when she'd been taken aboard the Conexus ship.

Her eyes flew open. She was alone in the tent. The sunset by the tree, kissing Tex—that had all been a dream. She was dressed in three layers and cocooned in the sleeping bag, but still the cold made her shiver.

The experience had been so real that she thought for sure he had been with her. Before her eyes, as they kissed, he had changed. His eyes had gone from black to glimmering glacial-blue pools. His body filled out, and his face morphed into a more human-looking one.

That wasn't real, though. Surely it had been just a dream. *A fantasy I didn't know I wanted.* She blushed at the recollection of his lips on hers.

The blush gave way to guilt. Even if it had been only a dream, she'd allowed herself to kiss Tex without a thought about Jack. *Why do I feel guilty? It wasn't even real.* Besides, she and Jack had been in the friend zone.

Howling and barking dogs interrupted the confusing tension of her thoughts. Outside the tent, people were talking loudly, no longer keeping their voices down in a reverent respect. Her usual morning grogginess was gone instantly. *Tex.*

She shimmied out of the bag, threw her shoes on, and unzipped the tent flap to peek her head out.

The sun was only just peering over the horizon, but the makeshift camp was full of commotion. Dogs ran and barked. People exited the many tents. Still others were already out. They talked to each other and gestured toward the hogan.

Erika pulled herself the rest of the way out of the tent. Dust flew into the air as a line of cars made their way up the dirt lane leading to Niyol and Kai's refuge. The lead car was a sheriff's SUV, but just behind it was an all-black Hummer. The driver of the Hummer wore a black Makers uniform, and the other men inside appeared to be dressed in black as well. People darted about Niyol and Kai's property as both men with the sheriff's department and Makers men disembarked from the newly arrived cars.

The passenger seat of the Hummer was occupied by none other than her Aunt Dana. Erika tried to meet Dana's eyes, but Aunt Dana kept her gaze averted. She did not appear to be in distress. Dana spoke calmly to the man who had driven the Hummer and pointed toward the sweat lodge. She still wore her pistol in her waist holder and was still in uniform. There were no visible bruises or injuries to evidence a struggle.

Erika's fear that the black-clad men had captured Aunt Dana gave way to the realization of betrayal. She swallowed hard to keep herself from dumping the contents of her stomach onto the ground. As much as she wanted to have it out with Dana right then, that would have to wait.

Erika ran toward the hogan. *I have to protect him.* Even after three days and nights of healing, Erika imagined Tex was still too weak to do much to help himself. She made it no farther than the edge of the bonfire when she stopped dead in her tracks.

Niyol and half a dozen men were standing just outside the hogan. They surrounded Tex, so she couldn't see him fully, but he was there in the center of their human shield, and the transformation she'd seen him undergo in her dream was not merely the hazy mist of the dream world. He was indeed changed.

She could explain neither how he had been remade into a new man by three days in a healing ceremony nor how she had known that in her dream. It was true, though. His new face, while by all accounts more human, was in its perfection perhaps more otherworldly than the one he'd had before.

The sun rising behind him made his billowy, shoulder-length white-gold hair glow about his head. Nearly all the time Erika had spent with Tex had been in the dark recesses of a dank, underground world. She had rarely seen him in daylight. The full effect of his unnatural beauty caught her off guard, and she gasped.

Erika edged closer and peered between a squat woman on her left and a tall, thin woman on her right. They were staring too, their eyes riveted on the young man that had been in the hogan with their kin for three days. One of the women whispered, "Bodaway," and the other repeated the word.

Soon, a low chant rose in the crowd: "Bodaway, Bodaway, Bodaway," they repeated.

Behind them, men poured out of the cars and trucks. Their boots crunched on the gravel around the house. The dogs barked, but at the policemen and Makers, not at Tex.

Tex's eyes were open, and they were still large but no longer black mirrors. Like the others, she could not help but stare into his eyes like two glacial pools. His lips were pulled up into a small, relaxed smile. His face was entirely smooth, without a wrinkle or frown line. His body was erect but not taut. Despite the din of the dogs and crunching gravel and people shouting, Tex stood as calmly as though he was alone in a peaceful forest.

A middle-aged, clean-shaven man with dark, closely cut hair stepped forward. He was tall, probably just over six feet, with wide shoulders and a trim waist. He was dressed in a desert-tan sheriff's uniform and held a rifle across his body. He pushed past women a few yards away from Erika. Three men in all-black Makers uniforms were right behind him. Aunt Dana was directly behind them.

Erika glared at Dana, but her aunt didn't seem to notice. Dana avoided Niyol's eyes as well and stared at Tex.

"Niyol, we don't want to make trouble. But there's a warrant for that one behind you. Hand him over, and we'll be on our way," the sheriff said.

Niyol did not yield. "He is dighin, Sheriff Armijo. We will not let you take him."

Sheriff Armijo stepped closer. "Come on, Niyol. He's not dighin. He's a felon. Mr. Smith here is with the feds, and they've got multiple warrants for him." The sheriff indicated the lead man in the Makers uniform with a slight nod of his head.

The mention of warrants made Erika's stomach lurch again. She pulled herself behind the large woman standing beside her. If warrants were really out for Tex, then warrants were likely out for her as well. She had, after all, shot a man during their escape from the school.

"You are on Apache land, Sheriff, and this man seeks asylum. Our tribe grants it to him. We don't acknowledge your federal warrants, sir."

A low murmur rose from the police officers that had mingled into the crowd and effectively surrounded Niyol, Tex, and the other men circled around Tex. Erika wished she had a pistol. Her eyes roamed the ground immediately around her, and she grabbed a long, thick stick that someone had used to stir the fire. It wasn't much, but it felt good to have something in her hand.

"You're respected in the community, Niyol, but you don't have the authority of the tribal government to grant asylum to that... thing."

"No," a woman said, "but we do."

Six men and women stepped forward out of the crowd of onlookers. They stood between Niyol and the police, their arms across their chests, their faces set and stern.

"The stranger has been named. He is Bodaway, and he is dighin. Under the US Constitution, international law, federal treaties, and tribal law, you cannot take him," the woman said.

Sheriff Armijo wiped his forehead with the back of his hand and shook his head. "Now, they have a warrant. You can't use treaties and such to give haven to someone wanted for murder."

The men surrounding Tex drew toward each other even more tightly. Tex could hardly be seen behind them.

Mr. Smith let out a sigh loud enough for all to hear. "I don't have time for this. Use the cannons!" he yelled.

Sheriff Armijo's voice rose to protest, but it was no use. In a flurry of activity, the three men clad in all black and some in blue police uniforms, armed with what looked like small rocket launchers, opened fire and let loose a torrent of water. Their intended target was Tex, but the tribal elders took the brunt of the water attack.

Erika screamed, "No!"

The powerful jets of water knocked the tribal government officials down, then Niyol went down as well. Erika and the women near her surged forward, acting on a unified instinct to help. Kai was among them, and she ran to help Niyol.

Erika had made it a few steps, intent on wrapping herself around Tex to prevent him from being drowned, but he didn't need help.

Tex stood tall, unharmed, and as dry as the desert in summer. His face was serene. His arms were outstretched, the muscles taut. He had gathered the water sprayed at him into a large, luminous ball that hovered in the air above him.

Kai helped Niyol to his feet and threw a woolen blanket around him. He was sopping wet but uninjured. All stepped away from Tex, and he stood alone on the small hill, the water above him shimmering like a jewel in the morning's first light.

While the others backed away from him, Erika moved forward. Her eyes were locked on his. He was the same man that she had held, kissed, and caressed in her dream, yet she did not know him. Her Tex had eyes that were devoid of light and revealed no emotion.

This man's eyes blazed with feeling, though. He gazed at her, and she felt, from only his look, a depth of love for her that she had never felt before, not even from her parents. His entire countenance emitted peace, contentment, and love.

Her Tex had always looked like a string strung too tightly and likely to break if yanked on too hard, but this man's body was anything but fragile. His outstretched arms revealed taut, muscular biceps, and his naked stomach was rippled and toned. His skin had turned the color of burnished alabaster and so smooth it seemed molded from plastic.

His head and eyes were still overly large, but with the rest of him filled out, his unusually large eyes were strikingly beautiful, no longer bordering on monstrous. He had the air of a Raphaelite angel.

"Bodaway," she whispered.

Tex's attention was entirely on her for a moment, and in that brief time, she felt as though they were alone. The sounds of dogs barking, people yelling, and water pouring from the water cannons disappeared. He smiled at her. Always before, Tex's attempts to smile had made his face look forced into an unnatural position, but that smile was genuine and beautiful. His face shone with feeling that made him look as though he was lit from within. Though his lips didn't move, she heard his voice plainly.

"It will be okay," he said. "I will be okay."

The surreal beauty and serenity of the moment was broken by Aunt Dana's voice rising high and shrill. "Erika! Step away from him. They don't want you, only that one." She stood beside Sheriff Armijo, one hand on the pistol in the holster at her waist.

"How could you?" Erika yelled. Bitter, hot tears played at her eyes.

She and her aunt had spatted, and yes, both sides had hurt feelings. She had been angry with Dana for her harsh words about Tex, but Erika had figured that when Dana came back, they'd work it out. Family sticks together, no matter how asinine you think the other person has been. But some betrayals are unforgiveable.

"I had no choice," Dana said. Her voice cracked and trembled with unspent tears. "They tracked you to me. Showed up at my work. You're on the FBI's wanted list, Erika. And they promised to exonerate you if I showed them where it was."

Erika shook her head and sighed loudly. She had not figured on her Aunt Dana being so naïve. "I thought I could trust you. I guess I was wrong."

Erika ignored her aunt's plea and walked the few steps more to stand beside Tex, still gripping the large stick in her right hand. Her voice rang out loud and true in the crisp morning air. "These men in black uniforms are not what—who—they say they are. They do not work for the US government. They're part of a corrupt organization that has infiltrated our democracy and uses government resources for its own purposes. If you let them take us, we will not get a trial. They will not let Bodaway or I live. In fact, they'll probably kill all of you too, simply because you've seen too much."

Another ripple of murmurs ran through the crowd, and many people nodded. They didn't need much convincing that people descending on them in uniforms would go badly for them.

Mr. Smith's voice rose above Erika's. "Do not be fooled by its parlor tricks. This... thing... is a cop killer, plain and simple." He raised a shaky finger and pointed at Tex as though he needed to clarify who he was talking about. "He pointed at Erika too. "As is she. Both are fugitives of the law."

Smith took a few more steps toward Tex and Erika. "Young lady, the Makers have no beef with you. But you have aided and abetted a murderer. Now, step aside, and I promise that you will be dealt with fairly by the law."

"Wait," Aunt Dana said. "Mr. Smith, you promised she'd go free if I brought you to the creature." She tried to push toward Erika, but two men in Makers uniforms held her back.

Only seconds before, bile had risen in her throat at the idea of Dana's betrayal, but now the urge to protect Dana came on strong. She was mad at Dana, but that didn't mean she wanted anything bad to happen to her aunt. Erika took a step and raised her stick, ready to defend Dana.

Tex gently grabbed her wrist. "Do not worry for her," he whispered. "I will not let them harm her."

Erika stood down, but her heart was still racing. Sweat covered her forehead despite the chilly air.

Smith ignored Aunt Dana. He wore a smirk as he spoke to Tex. "You're wasting time, 9. Come with us peacefully, and they can go back to their lives."

Tex didn't budge from his spot, but the large ball of shimmering water exploded in a fierce torrent that rained down on the men surrounding him. It wasn't enough to knock them over, but it disoriented them for a moment.

"Fire," Smith said.

The acrid smell and thunder of gunfire filled the air. Uniformed men shot pistols and rifles at Erika and Tex.

Chaos surrounded them. Niyol and the others that had nursed Tex screamed and ran, seeking shelter from the bullets. Dana lunged forward and yelled, "No!" Her face was twisted in pain and shock.

Erika's body reacted before her mind comprehended what was happening. Her instinct was to run and hide from the bullets being fired at her, but Tex again closed a hand around her wrist, this time more forcefully. He glanced at her, and his face was still serene. She closed her eyes and braced for the ripping heat of pain to tear through her as she tried to figure out why Tex would force her to remain in the line of fire. He could heal a gunshot wound, maybe even two, but she doubted he could save her if she was filled with bullet holes. He definitely couldn't save her if he was dead.

Pain did not come, though. The loud thunder of gunfire dwindled then subsided entirely. She opened a slit in one eye. She was alive. Tex was standing as still as a mannequin. Neither of them had a scratch on them.

The bullets—every last one of them—hung in the air as if someone had pressed the pause button.

The crowded makeshift camp turned battlefield was wholly still. Erika wasn't sure anyone even breathed in that moment. Despite the men having emptied their magazines of bullets, not a single person had been injured. Tex and Erika still stood.

Mr. Smith reached to his gun belt and was in the middle of loading a new magazine when he fell to the ground, his face contorted in pain. He cried a high-pitched scream as his eyes rolled back in his head, his face red and the veins in his neck bulging.

Tex's voice was low and calm. It boomed in the morning air. "As you can see, I am not like you." He walked toward Smith, and as he did, the crowd collectively drew back from him a few steps.

Tex continued. "I can take the life of this man if I wish to. I can take the lives of all of you simultaneously if I so desire it." The bullets that had hung in the air plinked to the ground. Several people gasped. He stood over Smith, the man's black uniform now covered in mud as he writhed on the ground.

Tex released his telekinetic hold on the man, and Smith lay in a heap as he gasped for air, sweat beading on his forehead, his face still red.

Tex's voice was low. "It is true that I have killed men."

Murmurs rose from the crowd.

Smith rubbed at his throat. When he spoke, his voice was raspy. "As I said. A murderer."

"Is it murder if done in self-defense? Or defense of another?" Tex threw a glance over his shoulder at Erika. Though spoken as a question, his voice carried an authority that left no doubt what the answer should be. "Niyol, Kai—the Diné—took me in. They helped me find my way. To see the truth that has been kept from me."

Smith snickered. "How wonderful. The teenage mutant went on a vision quest." Smith rose and dusted himself off the best he could. "He's nothing more than a rogue soldier. And he needs to be put down." Smith had apparently gotten that magazine loaded. He fired his pistol.

Smith had not shot at Tex, though. His bullet landed in Niyol's chest. The old man slumped to the muddy soil, his hand over his heart, where a stain of red bloomed.

Kai and a few others screamed. Erika ran to Niyol's side. Kai knelt beside him, and Erika pushed her hand to his chest to try to slow the loss of blood.

Smith shouted for all to hear. "You can end this, 9. I'll shoot one after the other of these people until you come with me."

"No, you won't." The sound of a bullet entering the chamber of a gun clicked behind Smith's head. Aunt Dana held her pistol to his skull. "Tell them to stand down, or—"

"Hedges, kill her." Smith did not lower his weapon.

Erika's hand was covered in Niyol's hot, sticky blood. Tears welled in her eyes as she shouted, "No!"

Erika was unclear on whom Smith was talking to, but no one shot Aunt Dana. Instead, Sheriff Armijo cracked the butt of his rifle into the back of the head of one of the Makers men, and several of the blue-clad officers turned their guns on the black-uniformed men rather than on Tex.

Sheriff Armijo turned his rifle on Smith. "Mr. Smith, I don't care if your orders come from the President, we're not going to stand by and watch you shoot civilians. Someone call for an ambulance and see what you can do for Niyol."

Tex said calmly, "There is no need. I will heal him." He walked serenely in his preternatural way to Niyol's collapsed body and smiled warmly at Kai, who had cradled Niyol to her body. Tex gently took Erika's shaking hand from Niyol's chest, smiled reassuringly at her, and turned Niyol outward. Kai's eyes were wide with fright, and she gripped Niyol to her.

Erika's voice came out shaky. "I have seen him save a life before." She wiped a tear with the back of her nonbloody hand. The new name they had given Tex felt strange to her, but she used it anyway. "Bodaway is the only one that can save him now. Do not be afraid."

Erika's words, coupled with Tex's calm, peaceful countenance, must have reassured Kai. Her face relaxed, and she loosened her grip on Niyol's limp body.

Tex closed his eyes and hovered his hands over the old man's abdomen and chest. He placed one hand on Niyol's chest and the other on the man's forehead. The crowd stood quietly, guns still pointed at the men dressed in black, all eyes on Tex.

His thin fingers worked slowly in a circular pattern. They picked up speed and soon wound clockwise around Niyol's body, knitting a tight circle around the red spot on Niyol's chest. Tex's fingers were a blur. Erika's eyes were fixed on Niyol's chest, her breath caught in her throat, as the glinting metal of the bullet appeared beneath Tex's fingers. After a few more minutes, he held up the bullet that had been lodged in the man's chest. He allowed it to plink to the ground and turned his attention back to his healing, his face the picture of concentration.

After a few minutes more, Niyol coughed and opened his eyes. He stared up into Tex's face. At first, he blinked and looked confused, but after a few seconds, his lips curled into an easy smile, and he nodded slowly at Tex. "Dighin."

The local people cried out his new name softly. "Bodaway." A few knelt, and others made the sign of the cross. One man held a rosary in his hand and mumbled prayers. The word "dighin" was repeated.

Erika had implored Tex not to kill people—to search for a way other than being a weapon. She had never expected him to become a demigod.

Tex gently lifted Niyol to his feet, but Niyol and Kai too knelt before him, their hands clasped in a position of prayer at their chests. Their faces were wet with tears, their eyes bright with the light of love.

Sheriff Armijo did not kneel or pray, but he addressed Tex. "Who are you, really?"

"I am Bodaway, and I have come to save the human race."

Tex put one hand gently to Niyol's head and the other on Kai's. "You do not need to kneel before me. I am no god."

In the dream state of the sweat ceremony, Tex's change in appearance had felt right. Erika seemed to like Jack's appearance, so he altered his own features to be more like Jack's. Once he had figured out how to grow a new lung, changes to his face and body were simple. Besides, a more human appearance would make traveling through their world easier.

Garnering human adulation had not been his goal. His new appearance and display of his abilities had them staring at him with reverence on their faces as though he was a demigod. Their looks of awe and their kneeling posture unnerved him.

Smith's voice rang out. "Don't be fools, people. He's an alien, not a messiah. He admitted that he's a killer. He's responsible for at least a dozen deaths in two states."

Tex had not counted how many people he had killed, but he thought Smith was exaggerating the numbers.

Erika strode toward him as Kai and Niyol rose. Her eyes were wide, and her heart beat wildly. The scent of her adrenaline permeated the air. *Is she afraid of me now?* If she was, he found it odd that she should be more fearful of him now that he was not killing people than before, when he had been a threat to the lives of so many.

Afraid of him or not, she stood by his side. "There isn't enough time to tell the whole story of how he came to be here," Erika said. "What Smith says is partly true. My friend here—who you now call Bodaway—is part alien. But he's part human as well. And we came from the future."

The kneeling people did not stand up, but the ones mumbling prayers stopped, and all listened to her. Erika's Aunt Dana had eyed him suspiciously since she'd first met him. The new information made her face turn ashen and her mouth gape. Her eyes darted between Erika and Tex as though she was trying to determine if what Erika said was true.

Erika continued. "Our world is in grave danger. What's happening in Europe is not a terrorist attack as you've been told."

Again, the crowd grew louder with talk amongst themselves.

Erika held up her hand for silence. "Europe has been attacked by aliens." She put her hand on Tex's shoulder. "This man is the only one who has the knowledge that can save us from being destroyed."

Smith laughed out loud. "Alien invasion?" His eyes were wide, his voice incredulous. "Just listen to what she says. This creature is the spawn of Satan, not a savior from the future." He pointed a thin finger at Erika. "And her?" He spat the words out as if they tasted awful. "She is the devil's minion. She was with him every step of the way as he slaughtered your brothers in blue. In fact, we suspect she may have pulled the trigger a few times herself."

Erika's fingers, still on Tex's shoulder, tensed.

Tex's mind twitched with a desire to terminate the man. Killing was, after all, what he had been created and trained to do. Cutting off the man's air supply was instinctual, but if he wanted to keep the trust of Niyol and his family and tribe, and to gain the trust of the law-enforcement officers, he needed to show restraint. "I have had nearly enough of this Smith fellow," Tex whispered to Erika.

"A savior shows mercy," she whispered back, her voice laden with sarcasm.

Tex had no desire to be the savior of these people. In fact, he still teetered in indecision about whether he wanted to help them at all, but in order to give Erika a chance at survival, he had to assist them as well. He had no indecisiveness about his desire to help Erika.

He stepped toward Smith, and the man's face lost its perpetual sneer of disapproval. Smith tried to step back, but the sheriff and Aunt Dana hemmed him in.

"Back off, creature," Smith said.

Tex was at Smith's side in a few quick strides, his legs a blur as he moved. Tex smoothly took the gun from Smith's trembling hands and tossed it to the ground. He placed his hands on either side of the man's head and tried something he had never attempted before.

"What's he doing?" one of the men in black shouted. "Don't let him kill Smith."

Erika said, "He's not going to kill him. He's just calming him down."

Tex dropped the protective shield he had worn about himself ever since the Makers men had appeared. Maintaining the shield took a great amount of energy, and he needed all of his concentration on Smith's thoughts and memories. Because the force field was invisible, he hoped the Makers still believed he had it around him and would not waste their bullets.

Smith's mind was like a filing cabinet with the doors flung open, its contents strewn everywhere. His thoughts flitted from the command given to "bring the rogue hybrid down by whatever means necessary" to memories of running into a bombed-out building, bloody bodies covered in dust strewn about the floor. A vision of the man's wife and his secret loathing of her but adoration of his young daughter flitted into the man's conscious thoughts. That was followed by Smith's feeling that he was not worthy of the little girl's love. He had done many things for which he felt deep shame.

Tex knew all that and more in less than a minute. The man was more deserving of pity than ire. Smith's face twisted with pain. Tex knew well the agony the man was in because he had felt it every time the Conexus infiltrated his mind against his will.

Tex had never before attempted to rewrite a person's circuitry. He was not confident that he could, but he gave it a go. He interfaced even more deeply with Smith. With each memory of his time with the Makers organization, from recruitment until the last order from his supervisor in Phoenix, Tex overlaid the memory with a new story. The word "hybrid" was replaced with words like "protector" or "valuable asset." Tex deleted any reference to killing Tex and replaced it with words such as "defend" and "obey."

Smith whimpered.

Erika called out to Tex, "Stop. You're hurting him."

Tex pulled himself from the man's mind and caught Smith before he fell to the ground. He wasn't sure that rewriting the man's memories was better than simply killing him. Tex had violated the man. He knew what that felt like, too. The Regina had violated him in a similar way.

But if he was to gain the trust of the humans around him—and he needed their trust—then he could not kill Smith or any of the other men. If he was to prevent the alien enemies, the M'Uktah, from annihilating the human population and prevent the humans from ending life on the planet in a failed attempt at protecting themselves, all would need to work together.

Smith's eyes were bleary as though from waking. He blinked rapidly and looked up at Tex. His eyes were wide and wet with tears. "You are... you're the one." His voice was a hushed whisper and full of awe.

Tex merely nodded and took his hands from the man. Tex had no time to feed the mythology and adulation that the humans created around him, seemingly growing with each second. His mind was on shutting down the intragalactic highway the M'Uktah used to get to Earth. "I need to go to a place that I believe is near here. There is an area in the desert with many large radio telescopes. Do you know the place of which I speak?"

Smith nodded, but it was the sheriff who answered. "The Very Large Array. The VLA. That's what you're talking about."

"How far is it from here?" Tex asked.

The sheriff scratched at his beard. "Sixty, maybe seventy miles, I suppose."

"Good. You will take me there."

WILLIAM CROFT

The elevator opened onto the Croft penthouse vestibule, which was empty save for one man in a black uniform sitting at a lone desk. The uniformed guard stood when he saw William in the open door of the elevator.

"Sir Croft." He stood at attention and saluted William.

Croft ignored the guard and pushed open the glass doors to his penthouse apartment overlooking Central Park. He had not told Lizzy or the penthouse staff he was coming, so they were not expecting him. He assumed the possibility that Lizzy would not be there at all or that he would find her hidden away in her suite, nursing her wounded ego after his ass-chewing lecture over the phone.

He did not have to search for her, though. Lizzy was on the creamy marble floor on her hands and knees, her long hair a cascade of brown covering her face as she scoured bloodstains with a scrub brush. She dipped the brush into a bucket of sudsy water and went back to the floor flecked with red.

William walked quietly toward her and stood on the damp marble she had just washed. "You can take the girl out of the slums, but you cannot make her into a lady. Pygmalion was a fantasy."

Lizzy stared up at him, her eyes rimmed in red, and her mouth set in a frown. "I thought you would be impressed, Father, that I am cleaning up my own mess rather than relying on servants. Isn't that what you always say? 'Handle your own messes, Lizzy.'"

He kicked the bucket, sending water and soap spilling across the shining floor. "And is this how you handle messes? By blowing the brains out of our allies? By creating a colossal disaster, the likes of which not even your idiot brother Evers achieved?"

Seeing her on her hands and knees like a housekeeper made his blood boil. Lizzy was his daughter by his beloved mistress, Carolina. He had allowed Carolina to raise the child as a commoner rather than taking Lizzy into his home to be raised by his late wife. Lizzy had not grown up in a world of mansions and penthouses, of private jets and chauffeured limousines to school. Not until year ten of her education had he brought her into the world of the Makers.

She had proven herself the brightest and most loyal of his three children. He personally groomed her to be the heir apparent, to take his place as the head of the Inner Circle of the Makers someday. Bending knee to floor was beneath their station even if she was cleaning up the blood she had spilled.

He hissed at her, "Get up."

She stood, her hands tightly balled fists at her side. Her chin was up, her face defiant. Her strong will was both an asset to him and a liability. While her brothers lacked the backbone to make the hard decisions sometimes required of a leader of the Makers, Lizzy had no difficulty doing the hard things, but her decisions were often rash with youth and inexperience. Also, she was all too willing to take a life in order to please him. This time she had taken the wrong life, and no matter what either of them did, she could never make that right.

"It is not my fault, Father. Anna and Thomas—"

His bony knuckles made contact with her jaw, whipping her head to the side as he backhanded her. A red mark bloomed on her face, but to her credit, she neither cried out nor moved away. Lizzy simply glared up at him with brown eyes so dark with anger that they looked black.

"Do not blame others for your failings."

"I don't know why you're so angry. I took care of that boil in your side, Robert Sturgis."

William pulled back his hand, ready to strike her again, but he did not let the second blow fall. His anger was so great he feared that if he let loose and struck her he might break her jaw. His voice was a low, seething whisper. "Do not speak to me of Robert Sturgis ever again. He was an asset to our organization that cannot be replaced."

"Should I have taken out Anna instead?" Her voice lilted with a mocking tone. "Pretty, pretty Anna. She's not so beautiful now, Father. But knowing Anna, she'll make eye patches and ugly face scars become fashion trends."

He shook his head. "We are the Makers, Lizzy, not the mafia. Your work was sloppy, and the petty jealousy is trashy and beneath you. That is not how the Makers do things."

"Daddy, please do tell me how we do things." She put her finger to her chin and pretended to think hard. "Oh, I know. We make an unnecessarily complicated plan, trust the wrong people, then have it fail spectacularly, just like this whole hybrid thing has."

His hand again flew to her face. Blood trickled from her nose, but she stood tall, her face still held in a insolent mask.

William's face was inches from hers. "You know nothing." His voice was low. "Anna Sturgis was genetically engineered to be perfect, you idiot. You didn't think that any one person could naturally be that beautiful and intelligent and physically strong without a bit of help. Even we of the blood could not naturally produce such a specimen as her." His voice now boomed. "And you nearly killed her."

While William's father had masterminded the plan for the Makers to occupy an underground city to survive the M'Uktah attack, William had seen the potential for the Makers to use their time below ground to give humanity a boost down the evolutionary highway. Anna and Thomas had been genetically engineered to be smarter, stronger, and more attractive than even the upper echelon of the population. Though something had clearly gone wrong with Thomas, Anna had proven to be all he had hoped for. Between Sturgis's cloning techniques, perfected through her work in the H.A.L.F. program, and genetic material from Anna, the Makers would be able to create a small army of superhumans ready to repopulate the world once the M'Uktah purged the population.

Lizzy's petulant stare turned to a sheepish wonderment. "I... I did not know."

William threw up his hands. "Of course you did not know. Because I did not share that with you." He wiped his face again with his handkerchief. "You know so very little, Lizzy. Do not forget that. You are a pup. And you will not live to become the alpha dog if you don't learn your place."

He leaned closer again and glowered down at her. He kept his voice calm. He had discovered that sometimes, cool serenity was more effective than yelling for putting fear into people. "You will do as I say when I say it, or you will find yourself sharing a hole in the ground with your late brother. Do you understand me?"

Lizzy swallowed. All defiance had evaporated out of her. When she spoke, her voice cracked. "I do understand, Father."

He hoped that she did. Perhaps having her mother raise her as a commoner had been a mistake. She had an unnecessarily large need to please him, coupled with an overall lack of grace and propriety. The whole purpose of William's plan was to preserve and indeed enhance the refinement and poise of those of the blood. The Makers and all his efforts meant nothing if they were no better than the common rabble.

William neatly folded his handkerchief and placed it back in his inside coat pocket. "Clean yourself up, and pack. We leave for Arizona in the morning."

Lizzy opened her mouth as if to ask a question but closed it. William left her standing in the puddle of water, her knees still wet from scrubbing the floor.

He opened the double doors to his spacious suite and was pleased to find it immaculately clean. The morning paper was on his desk, along with a pot of warm water, tea, and lemon wedges with the seeds removed for his morning ritual of drinking warm lemon water. *At least the butler here can get things right.*

He was tired from the journey and sat heavily in the chair. He loosened his tie and poured the warm water before he noticed someone sitting on one of the armchairs in the alcove of windows overlooking the park.

She sat with her legs crossed, her hands resting on the arms of the chair. "You look like hell," Hannah Sturgis said.

He did not doubt that he did, but the same could not be said of Hannah. Anna's DNA might have been genetically engineered, but she got her beauty from nature's engineering. Though in her late-middle years, Hannah was as strikingly beautiful as she had been in her youth. She wore her blond hair long, and not a hint of gray was in it. Hannah's eyes were the blue of a clear summer day in the high mountains. Her skin was smooth, with only the barest hint of laugh lines. Her legs were long and well toned. Her high cheeks and aquiline nose looked as though a master sculptor had chiseled them, tasked with recreating the loveliness of a Greek goddess.

With anyone else, William would have played a coy game of cat and mouse, of one-upmanship and rapier wit until the other person tired of it and left him to his thoughts.

She, however, was his beloved cousin Hannah. Though she was seven years younger than he, they had been the closest of friends in childhood. They shared a bond of secrets that only the close ties of family can provide.

He went to her without words, fell to his knees at her feet, wrapped his arms around her waist, and buried his head in her lap and wept. "Please do not blame me. I did not ask her to kill him."

At first, Hannah remained stiff, her hands still gripping the arms of the chair. After a few moments, though, she stroked his hair. "She is not fit to replace you, Wills. You know that, don't you?"

He did not look at her—he could not look at her—but he mumbled, "Yes."

"Look at me," Hannah said. It was a command, not a request.

William lifted his head. He had not cried in years and was unused to bleary, puffy eyes.

Her cheeks were also wet with tears. He wiped them away with his thumb. His touch was as gentle with Hannah as it had been harsh with Lizzy.

"I am so entirely sorry," he whispered.

"You should be," Hannah said. Her voice was not bitter or sarcastic. The sheer matter-of-fact coldness and truth of the statement made him wince with guilt.

"He was my friend too, Hannah. I will miss him as well." He knew that would not sway her anger or blame, but he said it anyway.

She took a deep breath as if to calm herself and hold in her tears. "The worst part—" She put a hand to her mouth as her voice cracked with emotion. Hannah sucked in another breath and began again. "The worst part is that Anna and Thomas no longer have the chance to reconcile with him. With Robert dead, he can no longer make things right with them."

"He would not have had need to 'make things right' if Thomas had stayed the bloody hell out of things."

Her hand was quick, and his reflexes were slow from lack of sleep. Her hand met the flesh of his face. He might not have stopped her even if he had been able to, though. He deserved the pain.

"You do not get to blame my children for being the intelligent, inquisitive people that they were engineered to be. And after all you've put Thomas through..." Her voice was a low hiss. "Do not ever speak to me of him again."

They locked eyes. His eyes pled with her to end their spat. Hers bore back into his with the pent-up anger she had harbored for years over his attempts to eliminate Thomas from the Makers stock. While William had never disputed that Thomas was extraordinarily gifted in mathematics and computer engineering, he was emotionally unstable. Thomas was hardly the pinnacle of perfection that William could clone and thus was useless to the Makers and the ultimate plan.

He could do nothing—offer nothing—to end her ire, and he desperately wanted to have Hannah on his side. William had lost both his sons and wife. Robert, his closest ally, was dead, and Lizzy, though of the blood, was young and inexperienced. He could not share the burdens of his station with her as he could with Hannah. His cousin understood him, perhaps as no other ever had.

He offered the only thing he had left to give her. "I promise you, my beloved, that I will not harm Anna."

Her eyes softened, but only a bit. Her jaw was still clenched.

"Or Thomas," he added. Though Thomas's genetic material could not be harvested, he remained a potential asset to the Makers. Thomas was worth two or three of the ordinary computer geniuses that William kept on the payroll.

Hannah stroked his hair again and gave him a small smile. "Swear it. By the blood."

"I swear it. By the blood. If I or any of my kin harm those you hold dear, my life and the life of my kin are forfeit."

She kissed the top of his head. "I accept your oath." Her smile quickly vanished. "Get them underground, Wills. Protect them as you would protect Lizzy."

His fingers traced an imaginary circle on her thigh. "I will do my best, but it will be difficult to save those who do not want to be saved. Least of all by me. I am the enemy, you know."

She put her hands on his face and turned it up toward her. Hannah's eyes twinkled with unspilled tears, her brow creased with dismay. "You must do more than your best. They are the future we prepared for—them... and Lizzy. Do whatever you must, but get them to Apthartos. In time, they will understand."

William had tapped their communications long enough to know that both Anna and Thomas considered him pure evil. No way would he ever be able to convince them otherwise. *But she could.*

"You must come with me. They will listen to their mother."

Hannah shook her head vigorously. "No. Lizzy poisoned it. She told them I sent Robert over to meet his death. I was out shopping." Fresh tears sprang to her eyes, and she dabbed at the corners with the heels of her hands. Her face twisted into a sarcastic smile. "I am a cliché. Out shopping, completely unaware of the danger my children were in and that Robert marched into. He kept it from me. And now I am *persona non grata* to my own children. I am their enemy now as much as you are."

William took her hands in his. "You will tell them the truth. Better yet, Lizzy will be made to tell the truth, to set the record straight. We are, after all, a family. They must be made to see this, to understand that all has been done for their benefit."

Hannah again shook her head. "No. It no longer matters what they think of me. Get to Arizona, Wills, and get them underground." She kissed the top of his head, and William rose. Her eyes flitted to the table next to the chair.

The round side table next to Hannah's chair held a crystal lamp, a small round vase with an arrangement of fresh, pale-pink roses and lavender peonies, a cup of tea that looked untouched and was likely cold, and a small empty brown vial. He picked it up, unscrewed the black cap, and sniffed. The odor was acrid and made his nose wrinkle.

Hannah picked up the cup, raised it in the air and said, "Salute," before she drained it in one gulp.

It happened in one swift action before William's brain had processed the truth he smelled in that tiny, empty vial. Hannah's body convulsed. Pink foam tinged her lips as her eyes rolled back in her head.

He grabbed her in his arms before she hit the floor. William scooped up her petite body and carried her to his bed. He placed her there gently, her body still wracked with spasms. He pushed the intercom and called the head of security.

"Get to my room. Quickly. And bring medical equipment. My cousin has drunk poison."

He was back at her side as swiftly as his feet would take him, but in the time it took him to walk from the wall to the bedside, her body was still. Her eyes were open and glazed, fixed at a point on the ceiling. Her skin was already two shades paler from death.

He again fell to his knees at her side and took her lifeless hand in his. He closed her eyes with his other hand and shook with grief and anger.

In his younger years, his outbursts of anger usually ended in someone's death, but his past was littered with the corpses of both enemies and ones he had cared for. He was sitting beside the dead body of one of the few he had ever truly loved. His instinct was to lash out and make someone pay.

He had promised her he would not take the life of either Anna or Thomas, though. That was an oath made on the blood, and such oaths lived beyond the life of those either making or receiving them.

By the time the door swung open, William had collected himself and stood quietly beside the bed. His face was composed and dry, with not a hint of the tears he had shed. To an outsider, he would appear to be looking down on the body of a complete stranger.

"You are too late," he said calmly. "She died of a stroke. Such things run in her family." He looked at the new head of security, a replacement necessitated by the shooting spree that had taken the life of the man who had previously held the job. "Do you take my meaning, Mister...?"

"Jacobs, Sir Croft. And yes, sir, I understand. I will ensure that enough C-notes find their way to the coroner's pocket to guarantee the correct cause of death on the certificate."

Croft nodded once. "See that you do."

Hannah was well loved in society circles both in the States and abroad. It would not do for people to think she had met her end in such a base way.

Jacobs nodded. "Understood, Sir Croft."

William's voice was deep and back to its usual authoritative air. "Good. I reward reliable people, Jacobs. And unreliable people... Well..."

William looked down at Hannah's still body. Jacobs coughed nervously and shuffled his feet.

"You can count on me. I will not let you down, Sir Croft. That death certificate will have stroke as the cause of death even if I have to break into the office and write it up myself."

Croft clapped the man on one shoulder with more force than was necessary. "That is what I like to hear. Get to work on it then, Jacobs. I have work to do, and I want this body out of here."

Jacobs nearly ran from the room, leaving William standing still beside Hannah's lifeless body. He was relieved to have the underling gone so that he could drop the mask of indifference and authority.

He bent and kissed her cold forehead for the last time. "Goodbye, my beloved Hannah. I will honor you by keeping my promise. Your children will be safely in Apthartos by the end of the week."

Erika had no idea what Tex had done to Smith, but the man had gone from calling Tex devil spawn to defending him.

"Stand down," Smith ordered. "We are mistaken. We must get this man to the VLA."

The Makers men exchanged skeptical looks with each other. A few still stared at Tex in awe, but most wore skepticism on their faces.

One of the Makers men spoke up. "He brainwashed Smith."

The other black-clad men nodded.

Smith was quick to defend himself. "There is no brainwashing. I have been given—" Smith coughed and looked as though he was choking back tears. "I have been given a great gift. To see the future." His eyes were far off for a moment, as if he saw something on the horizon that no one else could see. He abruptly pulled his attention back to his men. "You can do what you want, but I for one will do everything I can to get this guy where he says he needs to go."

Another man in a black uniform stepped closer to Smith and Tex. "No, Smith, you've been played. He's a killer."

Aunt Dana's voice rose over the increasing tide of voices. "If he was a killer, you'd all be dead by now."

Erika was still seething at Dana for bringing the Makers to their doorstep, but she was glad to hear her aunt finally defending Tex.

The uniformed men squabbled and quickly split into two factions. The sheriff, his men, and the local police, along with Smith, urged in favor of a police escort for Tex to the VLA. The rest of the Makers men were prepared to go back to Phoenix and inform the "top brass" that the "creature" was still at large and where he was going.

Erika whispered to Tex. "You can't let these Makers guys leave. If they know where you're going, they'll just tell Croft, and he'll send even more after you."

Tex raised an eyebrow. "Are you suggesting I terminate them?"

Erika wasn't sure what she was suggesting. She was never in favor of bloodshed, but she knew allowing the Makers to leave and go back to Phoenix would be a mistake. "I'm not saying to kill them. But they can't be free to run back to Croft, either."

Tex eyes glazed a bit, and he looked as though a part of him had left the scene entirely. After a few seconds, he said, "You are correct. Perhaps the sheriff can be of assistance to us." Tex's voice rose above the din. "Sheriff. Your assistance is required."

Sheriff Armijo walked to them. Aunt Dana followed and gave Erika a sheepish smile. Erika glared rather than smiling back at her. Dana cast her eyes down and avoided Erika's withering look.

As Tex spoke, Sheriff Armijo stared at him in awe. Erika had little doubt the sheriff would do anything Tex asked of him after he'd seen the "miracle" of Tex deflecting a rain of bullets and saving a man's life using nothing more than his hands.

"Sheriff, I need you to hold these men in your jail. You are not to allow them access to phones or computers. I do not have time right now to explain to you in detail why they are a clear and present danger, but trust me when I say that they are."

Sheriff Armijo nodded. "I will do as you request." The sheriff and a few of his men cuffed all the men in Makers uniforms and shoved them into the sheriff department's SUVs.

Even Smith was handcuffed and placed into the back of Sheriff Armijo's vehicle. "I will not act against you, Bodaway," Smith said. He still looked as though he'd sucked helium or something. He looked way too happy for a guy in handcuffs headed to a jail cell.

What did Tex do to him?

Niyol, Kai, and the tribal leaders gathered around Tex. They reached their hands toward him, and he touched each of them in turn while Erika and Aunt Dana stood back.

The female tribal leader who had spoken out on Tex's behalf said, "We will come with you, Bodaway. You may yet meet with resistance as you travel the path of peaceful resolution. We can assist you in your journey."

Erika thought that was a good idea. So far, she had often felt as though she and Tex were fighting an uphill battle for the protection of the planet, with only Ian and Dr. Randall to assist them. Adding more voices couldn't hurt. *Who can say what we'll find at the VLA?*

Tex took the woman's hands in his, looked down into her deep brown eyes, and shook his head. "I will not allow any more danger to come to any of you on my behalf."

All at once, half a dozen voices rose in protest, chief among them Niyol's. The old man's skin had good color, and his eyes were bright. His bloody, muddy clothes were the only evidence that he had been shot.

Erika considered raising a protest, too. She had no idea what they'd find at the VLA. Having more allies with them would be good. She was tired of feeling that everything rested on the shoulders of only two people.

Tex smiled warmly but shook his head again. He held up a hand as a request for silence. "We have much work to do, and not all of it will be accomplished at the VLA. Niyol, you shared the sweat visions with me. You know what is coming."

Niyol's face turned grim. He nodded.

"Your people need you here. Spread the word. Make sure the people know the truth, and prepare to protect yourselves."

Tex stood with them for a few minutes. They were all silent, their eyes closed, as were Tex's. They looked as though they were praying together, but that was an unlikely thing for Tex to do. At last, he opened his eyes, turned, and headed back to the vehicles.

Tex got into the front seat of Aunt Dana's truck. Erika squeezed into the small seat in back.

"You will take us to the VLA," he said as Dana got behind the wheel.

To Erika's surprise, Aunt Dana said only, "Okay."

They drove on a two-lane road that twisted through mountains and snow and finally descended into a desert valley. The going was slow. Driving the sixty miles between the reservation and the VLA took them close to two hours.

The Very Large Array sprawled its way through a barren valley that sat like a bowl surrounded by mountains. The valley looked as if it had been created with a giant scoop, leaving a tawny sea of sand and rock. The white satellite dishes sprang up like giant otherworldly mushrooms. The bright white of the telescopes was a stark contrast against the cloudless, jewel-blue New Mexico sky. When they had been at a higher elevation and looked down into the valley, the radio telescope dishes appeared rather small. As they got closer, though, she realized they soared several stories high.

Aunt Dana drove in silence, and Erika and Tex remained quiet as well. Erika saw only Tex's back, but he was quite still. She figured he had pulled into himself as he often did to meditate and rest. His deep meditations seemed to help him revive more than sleep or food did for most people.

Erika wished she could have talked to him instead of sitting quietly. She had so many questions for him. *What had happened during his sweat? Why had his appearance been altered so dramatically? And what they had done with each other—was it a dream? Or real? Of course it wasn't real.* She wished it had been, though. With Tex taking on the status of demigod, she thought it less likely than ever that she would get to know what it was like to touch him for real.

Erika didn't even know why they were going to the VLA or what Tex hoped to accomplish there. As they approached, she thought they might never find out.

A makeshift fencing structure similar to the one that had been placed around her school was erected around the perimeter of the small grouping of buildings that was the center of operations of the VLA. Four guards wearing desert camo and carrying rifles stood by a metal gate. The guard on the driver's side held up his hand for Aunt Dana to stop.

One of them approached the driver's window. "The VLA is closed to civilians until further notice." He searched the inside of the SUV as he spoke. After he'd glanced into the back, his eyes came back to Tex in the front seat and rested there.

"I'm Forest Service, sir," Aunt Dana said. "Not civilian, and I'm here on official business. Now, stand aside. It is urgent that I speak to the head of operations of this facility."

Erika was impressed with how even and authoritative Aunt Dana's voice was, but she couldn't imagine what kind of bullshit story

Dana would have to come up with to qualify as "official business" of the Forest Service at the VLA.

The guard's face remained stoic as he replied, "You'll need to call him or send an e-mail, ma'am. Facility's closed. Turn it around."

Aunt Dana's voice got pitchier. "This kind of sensitive conversation cannot simply be sent over the Internet or phone wires."

The guard was unmoved.

Erika edged to the front of her seat and leaned forward, her head poking over the front seat. She was about to intervene, but Aunt Dana cleared her throat and tried again.

"Dammit, man, this is a matter of national security. Now, get your butt on the radio and get someone down here with authority so I can talk to them, or guard duty's about the best detail you'll ever hope for."

The guard's jaw twitched, the only outward sign of annoyance, but his voice had an edge to it when he spoke again. He leaned closer, his close-set hazel eyes boring into Dana's. "Are you threatening me?"

Aunt Dana leaned her face closer, their noses inches apart, their eyes locked in a mutually disdainful glare.

Tex interrupted their standoff. His voice was deep as usual but firm.

"You are correct. Ms. Holt, on behalf of the Forest Service, lacks authority with your superiors to cause you any serious setback in your military career."

Erika thought Aunt Dana, idle though the threat had been, might have been making some headway. Erika glared at Tex, but he seemed not to notice it.

The guard pulled his attention away from Aunt Dana and bent his head slightly to see into the car. "What are you talking about?"

Tex took his oversized brilliant-blue eyes from the spot in front of him and fixed them on the military guard. "Oh, I was simply agreeing with your thinking on the matter."

In the silence that filled the gap after Tex spoke, Erika heard the guard swallow. All eyes were on Tex. His face shifted. His nose shortened. His cheeks caved in, forming dark hollows. His chin receded to a mere nub below his lips. His skin went from a smooth alabaster to a gray nearly as dark as the skin of the Conexus beings.

Tex's eyes lost their color and reverted to the black pools of emptiness of his natural-born state.

Tex soon wore the face he'd had when she met him. It was familiar to her and had never frightened her, but the abrupt change was such a contrast that it forced her to see how gaunt and sad Tex's original face looked.

The change took less than a minute, but in that brief span of time, the guard's face went from its stoic smugness to looking as though he had just walked out of a crypt filled with ghosts. The man stuttered, "What the? Who...? Holy..."

Tex's voice retained the same low, firm tone, but since he looked more alien than human, it somehow seemed more ominous. "Aliens have invaded the planet. I am part alien, and I have information that may help your government defend this country against the invaders. There are powerful forces that would have me silenced because while your family dies a gruesome death, these men and women stand to profit from your loss."

The guard's face went slack, and his eyes rolled up in his head, his mouth hanging open. It was the same look that Smith had had when Tex had placed his hands on the man's head and appeared to be doing something to the guy. The guard's face contorted with pain, his eyes filled with tears.

Erika was ready to intervene and ask Tex to stop, but the guard said, "No, not my little Macy."

"I want to help Macy. But I must meet with the scientists that operate this machinery in order to do that. You will help me, yes?"

The man wiped at the tears that had sprung to his eyes and nodded vigorously. He shouted to the other guards, "Official business! They're cleared to go in." He motioned for the others to open the gates.

The other men did not lower their weapons or open the gate, though. "Is he on the list, John?" one of them asked.

"Emergency. Screw the list. I'm ranking, and I say open the damned gate and let 'em in."

Another of the guards said, "But we've got orders, and if we go against orders—"

"I'll take any heat on this. Now open 'em!" John shouted.

The two guards on either side of the locking mechanism shrugged, but apparently getting a new order overruled prior orders for them so long as someone was willing to take any blame. They unlocked the gate and manually pulled it back to allow the vehicles through.

Aunt Dana's eyes were still glued to Tex, as were Erika's. As they watched, his face quickly morphed back to the more human appearance he'd created for himself during the sweat ceremony. He was nearly angelic again, his gray skin now rosy-tinged alabaster, his eyes crystal blue, and his features so classically human as to be nearly inhuman.

"That's damned unnerving. I do hope you don't plan on making that a regular thing," Aunt Dana said. She put the truck into gear and rolled forward. "Which of those faces is your true one?"

Tex responded in a matter-of-fact tone. "They both are. Now, drive please, Dana. Time is our enemy, and we have wasted enough of it."

As Aunt Dana drove over the gravel drive, a series of guards used hand motions to urge her on toward the next guard, and finally one steered her to a place to park. It was a makeshift parking lot with sage-green desert plants beaten down by cars driving over them. At least thirty vehicles were parked there. While most had emblems on the doors denoting US Air Force, a car with a NASA emblem was there also, as well as some civilian cars.

The NASA vehicle intrigued Tex. He had planned to see whoever was normally in charge of operations at the VLA, but if he was to alter the timeline that led to the Conexus future, perhaps he needed to veer from the course his logic suggested he take.

As they disembarked, a man in desert camo addressed Aunt Dana. "Guard shack was a bit vague about who exactly you were here to see."

Aunt Dana's aura of confidence that she had feigned to get past the guard shack had worn off. Tex feared she'd falter.

He reached out to the mind of the man asking them who they wanted to see. He searched for a name to go with the nondescript white car from NASA. The man's face scrunched up, and he rubbed at his temples. Tex took only seconds to retrieve what he needed from the man's mind. He released his telepathic connection, and the man looked dazed and confused by what had just happened.

"We are here to see Dr. Susan Lewis," Tex said.

The military man nodded. "*All* of you need to see Dr. Lewis?"

Tex stepped toward the guard. "In fact, only I need to see Dr. Lewis."

Erika hurriedly stepped around the car and stood beside Tex. "And me." She frowned at Tex.

Tex hadn't excluded Erika because he didn't want her with him. After the sweat ceremony, he knew one thing more than he knew any other—that he wanted to be with Erika.

But he also wanted to spare her pain and discomfort. Back in the forest after they'd taken care of Gary, he'd told her only a partial truth. He was worried that what he had to tell Dr. Lewis would prove difficult for Erika to hear.

Her hands were on her hips, her feet planted, her upturned face determined. She was so adorable when she was mad at him, which seemed to be most of the time. Her defiant stance made him smile, which had the effect of making her face scrunch up into an even angrier look. If they had not been standing in a crowd of onlookers waiting for Tex to tell them what to do, he would have liked to kiss the frown off her face.

He settled for appeasing Erika by giving in instead. "Yes, and Ms. Holt as well."

"Wait a minute. I didn't drive you all the way down here and put my neck on the line to be dealt out," Aunt Dana said.

Tex drew in a breath and threw up his hands in concession. "Fine, you too. You may want to be more mindful in the future about what you ask for, though."

The VLA facility was not large. As far as Tex could see, only three buildings were there, arranged in a nearly U shape with gravel and rogue bunches of spiky grass between. The buildings were not new, but they weren't old either. The red brick seemed somehow out of place in the desert, which as far as he had seen, was dominated by stucco-and-plaster architecture.

They were led through a door at the far end of the building and into a bright room lit by overhead fluorescents and a bank of windows facing west with the blinds open to let in ample light. The room was filled with desks covered by computer equipment and stacks of books and papers. Tall filing cabinets and swivel chairs were crammed into nearly every remaining inch, leaving a few narrow walkways for people to fit through. The room buzzed with discussion from people huddled around a grouping of screens and monitors.

He didn't need extraordinary hearing to know they were in a heated conversation. Voices rose each above the other as they appeared to argue over the meaning of "the signal" and disagreement over whether the government knew more than they were letting on.

The guard coughed loudly to get their attention. When the din quieted and all eyes were on him, he announced, "Dr. Lewis, there are some people here to see you."

The people huddled around the computer screens looked up. As their eyes fell on Tex, the buzzing chatter ceased.

A woman's voice came from the back of the room, not from the crowd that had been quarrelling. "I told everyone I was not to be disturbed. I'm very busy and don't have time to give tours or talk about a Mars mission with reporters."

Dr. Lewis didn't look in their direction as she spoke. Her long, straight blond hair streaked with strands of white was pulled back in a ponytail. Her eyes were riveted to a screen as she typed furiously on a keyboard.

"They're not reporters, ma'am."

Dr. Lewis threw up her hands, stood, and shoved her rolling chair back from the desk with a quick kick. She stormed toward them, strands of pale hair flapping by her ears as she walked.

She stood just a few feet from the guard, her arms across her chest. She quickly glanced at Aunt Dana and Erika, but her eyes lingered a few extra seconds on Tex.

The guard whispered, "The guard house let them through because one of them is... Well, ma'am, he's not human." The military guard shot Tex a furtive look then as if trying to decide for himself if what his colleague had told him was true or not.

Dr. Lewis's clear blue eyes were rimmed in red and bloodshot, giving her the appearance of someone who needed sleep. Her face was smooth, and besides the barest hint of crow's feet around her eyes, she looked too young to have advanced to a high position at NASA.

A few of the other people behind the desks made their way toward Tex, Erika, and Aunt Dana.

Dr. Lewis's eyes homed in on Tex as though the other two he'd arrived with were not there. She seemed to inspect him as if trying to see the alien within him but coming away empty-handed. Her brow creased, and her lips turned down in a frown.

"He does not look like the reports. Not nearly large enough. No, not by a long shot. And he looks far too human." She turned her attention to the military guy. "Look, you all know that I was adamantly opposed to your mucky-mucks militarizing this civilian-operated facility and taking control. But dammit, if you're going to be here, at least do your damned jobs. All I've asked is that you leave me alone to do my work, and now you let this guy in based on his word that he's an alien." She gestured toward Tex as if the military man had not seen him already.

With humans, many words seemed necessary to achieve the communication he had become accustomed to having instantaneously with the Conexus. He had never found conveying ideas to humans very easy in the first place. So much was mistranslated, and they relied so very much on gestures and facial expressions. Tex had found that visuals seemed to work well and cut through much of the clunkiness of human speech.

He contorted his face once again into its nearly original form. He accentuated the Conexus aspect of himself for effect. It had taken considerable energy the first time he had ordered his cells to rearrange themselves into a new pattern. The process caused a throbbing ache, and his skin tingled. Each morph took less energy than the last, though, and while morphing his features was still painful, he forced himself to ignore the discomfort.

Erika took his hand in hers. She seemed to have a way of knowing when he was in pain. Her touch comforted him, and the pain lessened.

Dr. Lewis's jaw dropped open, and the angry crease in her brow vanished. The entire crowd of people stopped talking or moving. The room was utterly silent save for the gentle whir of computer cooling motors and the low but persistent hum of the fluorescent lights.

Dr. Lewis got out only a few words. "Son-of-a..."

Tex had gotten used to the new pattern of his face and found he had to exert significant effort to hold the shape of a Conexus face. He let the pattern reform back to the one he'd assumed after his sweat-lodge experience. He held out his hand to Dr. Lewis. "I have been called by several names. But you may call me Tex."

Dr. Lewis absentmindedly took his hand. Her eyes were still riveted to his face, her mouth still slightly agape. "You're really... I mean you're not—"

Tex smiled at her. "I am many things. But that is of no matter right now. We have much to discuss, Dr. Lewis, and not much time." He quickly scanned her mind for evidence that she was linked in any way to the Makers. He found no thoughts of the Makers and decided she was trustworthy, at least unless she did something to prove otherwise. "Is there somewhere that we may speak more privately?"

When he let loose her hand, she stood there for a few seconds without responding.

"Dr. Lewis?" Tex pressed.

She shook her head and swept some stray strands of hair behind her ear. "Forgive me. Yes, yes. Upstairs. Follow me."

Tex had no problem keeping up with her agile speed as they climbed concrete stairs that led to a second floor of offices. The place smelled of aged paper and harsh cleaning fluid. Erika and Aunt Dana trudged behind him.

Dr. Lewis led them into a cramped room that looked like a computer graveyard. Dingy, aged-tan machines were there in various stages of being torn apart. Tex didn't know if they had foraged them for parts or tried to repair them but gave up. Old keyboards were strewn about, as were computer mice and what seemed like miles of wire.

Plunked in the middle of this disarray was a plastic table with a top made to look like wood, surrounded by several plastic chairs. Dr. Lewis sat on one of the chairs and gestured for the others to sit. "Best I can do in this situation."

Erika closed the door behind them and was the last to take a seat. "After all the places we've been, this is just fine," she said.

"Why did you ask for me?"

Tex considered using his telepathic powers to simply command Dr. Lewis to do as he needed. That way, he could continue to spare Erika the harsh truth as well, but he had used his newly discovered ability very little. He had no idea what permanent damage it might do to humans, and he needed Dr. Lewis's mind at full capacity. Besides, she seemed far too intelligent and strong-willed to be easily manipulated, even by him.

He decided to follow his first instinct, which was to tell her the truth. "I need someone I can trust. I believe I can trust you."

"You can, but trust me with what?"

Tex folded his hands on the table and looked at her evenly. "What do you know about what has happened in Europe?"

Dr. Lewis stated the events as though reading a transcript from the news accounts they had heard on the radio, but she did not look him in the eye.

"That's all bullshit," Erika said.

Tex held up his hand to her, and to his surprise, she merely folded her arms across her chest and leaned back in her chair, defiance written on her face, but her mouth remained shut.

Dr. Lewis's eyebrows rose, and she appeared ready to argue, but Tex spoke before any fireworks started between the women.

"We know that the events in Europe are due to an alien attack, not due to terrorists, and clearly that's why you and the military are here at the VLA."

Dr. Lewis attempted to work her face into a stoic mask. "I can neither confirm nor deny anything that you said."

Tex had assumed that once she saw his ability to shape-shift his appearance, she would cut the... *What was it Erika said?* "Bullshit" was her word. It was a good word for the situation. Tex took a breath and recalled the wisdom he had received from Niyol in the sweat. *"Patience, Bodaway."*

"We do not have time to play games. The survival of the human species is at stake, and the people giving orders are going to make all the wrong choices if we do not intervene."

Dr. Lewis remained silent, but her attention was fixed on Tex.

He sighed out his impatience. "Perhaps once you understand that I know at least as much as you about the situation and possibly a good bit more, you will relax from the rules dictated to you from your chain of command and be more helpful."

Her eyes softened a bit, but her lips remained pressed closed.

"The European attack is not from terrorists but instead from an alien species. Of course, you knew that, otherwise you would not be here. My supposition is that the signal from their ship was detected by the instruments here at the VLA when their ship entered the outer solar system and that a team was assembled here shortly after. That means that certain persons within the federal government knew that aliens were on their way long before the attacks in Europe. But that information was not shared with the world, was it?"

Aunt Dana had been sitting quietly, but she thrust herself forward in her chair. "Is this true?"

Erika let out a loud breath. "Just look at her face. Of course it's true." She shook her head, and her voice dripped with disgust. "Protectionist crap."

Dr. Lewis's jaw had gone rigid, and she blinked rapidly.

Tex waved his hand in the air. "But that's no matter now. Let me tell you a few things you may not know. These invading aliens refer to themselves as the M'Uktah."

Dr. Lewis's eyes grew wide. "How do you know that?" She quickly closed her lips again as if to keep herself from saying anything else that would reveal more than she should.

Tex did not answer her question. "They come from a planet on the far side of our galaxy and traveled through a conduit of warped space which they call a Mocht Bogha."

Dr. Lewis stood and visibly trembled. "Look, I don't know who you are or how you know these things, but somehow you've breached the highest levels of national security and—"

Tex remained seated, his face placid, his body still, yet an invisible force pushed Dr. Lewis into her seat and pinned her there. Her arms were immobilized at her sides. Tex's face morphed once again into the shape and color of a Conexus, his eyes as black as night.

He had infiltrated nothing. All the knowledge he had about the M'Uktah came from the Conexus archives, but explaining all that to Dr. Lewis would take more time than he had.

She likely did not even see him move, but within the span of time it takes to blink an eye, Tex was at her side, glowering down at her with his ebony eyes.

"The M'Uktah will use that galactic highway to send ship after ship here, Dr. Lewis. What we're dealing with now is but the first round, meant to subdue and disarm. They're readying us for colonization, doctor. First come the hunters. Next, the farmers will come to prepare humans for continued harvesting."

Her face wrinkled in horror and revulsion. Tears sprang to the corners of her eyes, though Tex was not sure if it was because she was frightened of him and what he might do to her or in terror over what he told her.

"We are simply a food source for them, you see. And a plentiful one at that. Despite the US government's attempt at protectionist zeal, the US will fare little better than Europe. And after a million or so have lost their lives and it appears that all hope of winning is lost, our government will use its weapon of last resort."

Dr. Lewis's eyes widened. She sniffed and whispered, "Nuclear?"

In an instant, Tex was back in his seat, his hands folded on the table again, and his face stoic and morphed back to its more human form. He nodded. "It will succeed in destroying M'Uktah ships. But the number and extent of bombings required, coupled with counterstrikes made in retaliation, will lead to the large-scale destruction of the ecosystem of this planet. Allowed to continue on its present course, this planet will be doomed within a year. And the only survivors will be the elites, hand-picked by the leader of the Makers, to live in an underground world paid for by the US taxpayers."

Dr. Lewis shook her head. "But none of this has happened. How do you know this?" She shook her head more vigorously. "Listen to me. I sound like a fool." Her voice hardened again. "There is no such thing as a crystal ball. I don't know who you are or what your game is, but I won't be played by you." She made a move to get up, apparently forgetting about the invisible restraints that held her. She yanked and pulled with her arms and legs, but she remained in her chair as if glued there.

Aunt Dana shifted with discomfort in her plastic seat, making it squeak.

Erika sighed loudly. Apparently, she was done with sitting quietly. "Look, lady, he could have gone to anyone, but for some reason he chose you. He could go back to living underground and tell you all to screw yourselves. But he's here trying to do the right thing, so cut the crap and listen. Just because your science hasn't gotten there yet doesn't mean it's impossible. I was in the future with him. And with Dr. William Randall."

Dr. Lewis turned her full attention to Erika. "Dr. Randall? *The* William Randall of A.H.D.N.A.?"

"One and the same," Erika said.

"He is my father," Tex said.

Dr. Lewis blinked. "Your father?" She shook her head again. "I didn't know—but wait, how is that possible? You're—"

"Half human," Tex said. "Dr. Randall contributed DNA and was the lead scientist of the project that created me."

Erika cut in. "You can contact Dr. Randall if you want. He will confirm all that Tex is saying and vouch for him. But do it quickly because time is wasting."

Tex had not wanted to involve Dr. Randall further in anything he did. His feelings about Dr. Randall were still confused. The old man had been like a father to him, but he had also kept Tex as a captive all those years. Tex shot Erika a glare, but she ignored it.

Erika continued. "He is currently working with Dr. Montoya at the CDC in Phoenix."

"With Dr. Montoya? Then he must be working on—"

"The virus. Yes, it was instigated by the Conexus, also known as the Greys," Tex said. Though he was not happy about Dr. Randall getting back into his life, he had to admit that perhaps Erika was right to suggest Dr. Lewis contact him. Dr. Randall lent authority to their statements.

Dr. Lewis attempted to move but was stymied by the invisible cords that bound her. "I won't bolt. You've convinced me that I at least need to learn more before I decide what to do. Will you release me so I can contact Dr. Randall to see if your story checks out?"

In the instant he thought it, the bindings were removed. Dr. Lewis's shoulders dropped as she let out a big breath. Relief washed over her face. She pulled her phone out of her pants pocket and dialed but looked frustrated.

"His prior phone number is not a working number." Skepticism had worked its way back into her voice.

"How long has it been since you talked to him?" Erika asked.

Dr. Lewis put her phone on the table. "Years, I suppose."

Erika snatched the phone up. "I told you, he's with Dr. Montoya at the Phoenix CDC." She swiped and tapped until she had the number pulled up and dialed. Erika listened until she heard a voice then handed the phone back to Dr. Lewis.

Dr. Lewis stammered, "Yes, well, I'm not sure you can help me, but um, I'm uh—well, I'm looking for Dr. William Randall. Do you have anyone by that name there? Working with Dr. Montoya?" She listened for a few seconds, then her eyebrows rose. "You'll connect me? Thank you."

Tex heard only one side of the ensuing conversation, but Dr. Randall was clearly confirming the story Tex had given her. Her face continued to soften, her jaw becoming less rigid as she spoke to him.

Tex had wanted to convince Dr. Lewis to help him and achieve his mission on his own—to feel like a man, not a boy. He hated that he needed Dr. Randall and Erika to make things happen.

"That's a good question, and one I had not gotten to yet," Dr. Lewis said. "As you can imagine, I was trying to get my head around his story." She tittered then said, "Let me ask him." She put her hand over the phone and said, "He wants to know why you're here and what help you think I can give you?"

Tex took the phone from her and spoke to Dr. Randall. "I need your assistance to convince the scientists here to align the telescope array so that I can travel to the planet of the Architects of the galactic gateway being used by the M'Uktah to travel here. I aim to ask the Architects for their help to shut it down."

Dr. Lewis's face turned ashen, her eyes wide. Erika was quiet, but Tex felt her heart racing and smelled sweat pouring from her. Aunt Dana sat back in her chair and listened quietly as Tex laid out to Dr. Randall the entire plan and the likely issues they would face, getting it to happen.

After a few minutes, he hung up the phone. "He says he'll be here as soon as he can."

Dr. Lewis was quiet for a few seconds, and when she spoke, her voice was shaky. "What do you need me to do?"

"I need you to convince whoever is in command here to align the dishes to my specifications. And I need the Arecibo dish aligned as well. Oh, and I need them to flood the great pyramid in Giza with water."

Dr. Lewis tittered nervously. "Anything else?" Clearly, she had meant it sarcastically, but Tex answered anyway.

"No. That will be sufficient. And we must hurry, Dr. Lewis. Before someone orders a nuclear strike."

Dr. Lewis's sarcastic smile disappeared.

21
JACK

Jack stood in Dr. Randall's makeshift lab at the CDC and wound electrode wires onto a hard plastic storage board. After two days of putting Alecto through test after test, Dr. Randall had officially pronounced her cured from her vulnerability to water.

Anna was finishing typing data they had collected into the computer. "I wonder if it will work as well for Tex?"

Alecto hopped off the table. The electrode Jack had been trying to gently peel off ripped off and left a glue stain on her collarbone.

"You will cure my brother too?" Her voice quavered.

Jack didn't know if excitement or fear was in her voice.

Dr. Randall nodded. "That's the plan."

Ian had been preparing slides for Ben and Dr. Montoya, but he ran into the small lab where they were working. "Dr. Randall, you have a call. It's Tex."

"Speak of the devil," Jack said.

Dr. Randall's fingers froze, an electrode stuck in mid-peel, half on and half off Alecto's upper chest. Alecto's eyes grew wider, and her lips curved into a frown.

Jack's chest tightened though he wasn't sure why. He was with Anna now. What Tex and Erika did wasn't his business.

Dr. Randall finally unfroze himself. He peeled the electrode off and handed it to Jack. "I must take this call."

Jack nodded and stepped into the spot where Dr. Randall had been. He continued to peel electrodes off and wind them for storage.

By the time Dr. Randall returned, Alecto was finally free of wires. Jack used cotton gauze damp with an alcohol solution to gently wipe the spots where the electrodes had been attached, to remove the remnants of adhesive from Alecto's skin. He had never thought of working in a medical or research field, but he had enjoyed helping

Alecto over the past few days. He was satisfied knowing he had played at least a small part in helping her to live a more normal life.

Dr. Randall's face was drawn and even more ashen than usual. He walked slowly, and his lips moved as though he was talking to himself.

Alecto, normally dense about human emotions, immediately sensed something was amiss in Dr. Randall's world. "Is 9—is my brother in danger?"

Dr. Randall turned his head toward her slowly and looked at her for a few seconds almost as though trying to remember who she was and why he was there. He shook his head. "No. Not any more than usual, anyway. No, Tex is fine. In fact, he may be better than fine." His look was far off and preoccupied.

Anna took Dr. Randall's hands in hers. "What did Tex say?"

"That he needs my help." He cast his gaze downward at Anna and smiled wanly. "And he apologized for how he spoke to me before he left Arizona."

Alecto snorted. "Of course he did. He wants something of you."

The venom in her voice was unmistakable. Jack didn't have siblings, but he was pretty sure Alecto had a serious case of sibling rivalry with Tex. Jack agreed with Alecto's note of caution, though. He considered Tex a dangerous person with a penchant for manipulation as great perhaps as Tex's "mother," Commander Sturgis.

"Alecto's right, doc. You should be careful in your dealings with him," Jack said.

Anna shot a glare at Jack, though he had no idea what he'd said or done to justify the look.

"Focus, people," Anna said. "Can't you see he's shaken up? Clearly, that call was more than just an apology."

"You are exactly right," Dr. Randall said. His eyes were far off again, and he mumbled. "It's not possible, but he says it is. It's crazy... It can't be, but is it? I suppose it's theoretically possible if you have all the signals triangulated and the frequencies matching precisely, but—"

Ian clapped Dr. Randall on the back. "Doc, stop rambling. What are you talking about?"

Dr. Randall stopped mumbling and ran a hand through his gray hair. "Tex wants to activate and triangulate electromagnetic energy in three locations on Earth so that he can hitch a ride on the energy waves and travel to a planet many light-years away in our galaxy."

No one responded. Jack could almost hear the brains of the others trying to wrap their gray matter around what Dr. Randall had just said and make sense of it.

Jack didn't tax himself over it. He didn't want to waste his mental energy on figuring out the "how." He was only concerned with one thing. "Why would he want to do that?"

Dr. Randall stared blankly at Jack, blinked a few times, then said, "To meet with the architects."

Jack rolled his eyes. "Sure. The architects. Makes perfect sense."

Dr. Randall nodded. "Yes. You understand!"

Jack took a deep breath. "No, I don't. How about explaining it in plain English without metaphor?"

Dr. Randall pushed his glasses up his nose. "He wants to have a chat with the architects of the intergalactic highway these alien invaders are using to come to Earth." Dr. Randall smiled, and when he spoke again, his voice was filled with pride. "My boy wants to find a way to shut it down."

Alecto crossed her arms and looked for all the world like a petulant child. Jack figured she wasn't a fan of her brother getting all the attention.

"What does he need your help with?" Anna asked. "Electromagnetism, radio waves, and stuff—that's not exactly your area of expertise."

"True," Dr. Randall said, "but I speak the language of science, and I know a lot of people both in the scientific community and within government. Apparently, he is at the VLA in New Mexico and is working with a Dr. Lewis from NASA. But he says they are having quite a bit of trouble cutting through bureaucracy and convincing military brass to allow them the resources to move forward."

Ian pulled a chair out from under a desk and sat backward on it. "And he thinks *you* can help with that?"

"Well, I have worked off the books and black budget for over thirty years. I know a thing or two about getting things done by going through back-door channels." He took his glasses off and rubbed his eyes. "But who we really need for this is Commander Sturgis. She is frankly much better suited to the task than I."

"But we don't even know where she is," Anna said. "Sewell refuses to tell me her location. He fears Alecto and I will go to her if we know where she is."

"I will go to her," Alecto said.

Jack believed Alecto would and decided Sewell had best keep the info from them. Alecto was growing more independent each day, but if she went to Commander Sturgis, she'd likely revert back to the machinelike automaton she had once been.

Ben poked his head around the door frame. "Oh, there you all are." His messy hair looked as though he'd raked his fingers through it, and his eyes were bloodshot behind his thick glasses. His hands were in the pockets of his white lab coat. "Whatchya doin' all huddled together in here?"

Ian's face brightened at the sight of Ben. "Hiding from you," he teased.

Ben looked astonished for a moment. Then, realizing it was a joke, he laughed nervously.

Dr. Randall placed his glasses back on his face. "Well, I best shove off. Any of you youngsters willing to volunteer to drive an old man through the desert to the VLA?"

Jack had driven nearly three thousand miles, almost single-handedly getting them from New York to Phoenix. He didn't even want to get in a car, and he wasn't thrilled at the prospect of seeing Erika and Tex. If they were together, and he assumed they were, he wasn't sure he could be civil toward the guy that he blamed for putting Erika in danger.

No one volunteered, and an uncomfortable quiet permeated the room.

Alecto broke the silence. "I will go."

Dr. Randall shook his head. "No, you can't."

When she balled her fists at her side and began to argue, Dr. Randall put up a hand. "Your place is here for now. Rest and recover your strength."

"I am rested. I can take care of myself, you know," Alecto protested.

Jack was ready to back her up. He'd seen her more than able to hold her own.

Dr. Randall gently placed his hands on her shoulders. "You will have plenty of opportunity to fight, young lady." His eyes teared up. "There will be much to fight in the weeks to come. Stand down for now, Alecto. When the time comes, we need you with us and not holed up in a dank government lab somewhere. You've had enough of that." He looked around at them. "We all have."

"Where you going?" Ben asked quietly.

"I've been summoned by someone at NASA to the VLA."

"Oh," he said. "If you need a ride, I could take you, I guess."

"No, Ben. Dr. Montoya needs you here," Ian said. He rose from the chair he'd been on and turned it back around.

Ben took Ian's hand in his. "She does need me. We're just about ready to upload her findings to the main office. Ian, why don't you take Dr. Randall?" He put his hand on Ian's cheek and kissed him softly. "You've worked so hard. Time away from all this may do you some good."

"I would like to see Erika again," Ian said. "She's probably a disaster without me."

Jack chuckled. "Probably true." A flood of memories of the three of them spending time together came to him. Ian and Erika were more like twins than friends and had been close long before they knew Jack. They needed each other in a way that Jack would never quite understand. Erika was likely an emotional wreck without Ian by her side, especially given that her mom had died recently. Also, if not for having Ben near him twenty-four seven, Ian would have been a mopey mess without Erika there.

Dr. Randall shook Ian's hand and clapped him on the back with his other hand. "Great, my chauffeur. Get your stuff together. We should leave immediately."

Ben hugged Ian and kissed him again, a bit longer that time. "I should head back to the lab." He took a few steps toward the door and looked back at Ian. "Come find me before you go."

As Ben disappeared down the hall, Ian looked as though he would cry. Jack knew the feeling of saying goodbye. He ached for the way Ian had to be feeling.

Dr. Randall turned his attention back to Anna and Jack. "The two of you are responsible for Alecto until I get back. I know it's a lot of responsibility to lay on you, but—"

"Doc, I think we've got this," Jack said. "We did rescue her from Croft and got her safely to Arizona, remember?"

Anna turned her attention to Alecto. "Besides, she hardly needs a babysitter. She's not a child."

Alecto stood a bit taller, her arms still across her chest. She forced a wan smile and nodded once to Anna.

Within a few hours, Ian had said goodbye to Ben, and he and Dr. Randall were on their way to New Mexico. Ian promised to text Jack when they got there and to keep in touch.

Jack caught his arm before he got into the car. "Tell her... Let her know—"

"That you're okay. Oh, and that you're falling in love with a beautiful, highly intelligent, über-rich older woman?"

"Love? What are you talking about? We're just friends."

Ian rolled his eyes. "Come on, Jack. I've got eyes. It's okay. She's definitely hot—if you're into girls, that is." His lips curled into an impish smile.

"How about leave Anna out of it. Just let Erika know I'm okay and that I hope she is too."

Ian gave Jack a quick hug then got into the driver's seat. "It'll be okay, Jack. You'll see. Things like this have a way of working themselves out."

Jack watched the dark silver-gray sedan pull away and drive off into traffic, headed east. Until the night they met Tex, Jack had never thought about the possibility that he'd never see someone again when they left.

His mom was gone, though. Most of the people in his town were gone, and Erika was as good as gone, at least to him.

Anna took his hand in hers. "You'll see him again."

"I hope so." He smiled down at her. Her hand was small and warm. He wanted to kiss her, but by the time he was nearly ready to lean in, she let his hand go and headed back to the building.

In the elevator on the way up to the lab, Jack said, "We've finally got a bit of free time. Why don't we blow off work this afternoon and do something fun?"

She glanced up at him, her long hair partially covering her injured eye. "What did you have in mind?" Her voice was a soft purr.

Come on, Jack. She's practically giving you a written invitation.

"Oh, I don't know. Maybe a movie."

The sultry look was gone. He wasn't sure what she'd wanted him to say, but apparently sitting in a theater wasn't the right answer.

"I'll take a rain check on that. Besides, I should check on Thomas. With Dr. Randall gone, I need to make sure he's got food in his place and look after him."

The bell dinged, signaling they were on their floor. The elevator door opened, and Thomas stood only a few feet away.

Thomas's face was slick with sweat as though he had run there. His beard was scraggly and needed a trim. His eyes were wild and rimmed in red. "Good, you're back. I've got to talk to you." He pulled Anna by the hand and yanked her along behind him as he walked to a small office.

Jack followed even though Thomas hadn't indicated the conversation would include him, but Thomas didn't ask him to leave when he closed the door behind them.

Anna sat cross-legged on the light-blue pleather couch. "What's up?"

Thomas ran his shaky fingers through his greasy hair. It was still short but was getting shaggy and needed a trim that would likely not happen unless Anna took the time to cut it herself. "I know I shouldn't have done it—know it'll likely end up bad for me—but I had to monitor. Gotta know what's going on." Thomas paced as he talked.

Jack had been standing just beside the door, his arms across his chest, leaning against the wall. Anna rolled her eyes and took a deep breath. She was just about to get up, but Jack held up his hand in an I've-got-this motion. He stood in Thomas's pacing path, forcing him to stop.

"Slow down, and tell us what you came to say. Who did you monitor?"

Thomas raised his eyes from the floor and looked into Jack's. "The Crofts."

Jack let out a loud breath. "Oh boy."

Anna untangled her legs and bolted off the couch. "Thomas, what did you do now?"

"Listening. Hacking. Tracking. Same as always."

Anna put her fingers to her temples, closed her eyes, and let out a loud breath. "Tell me you didn't get caught."

"I don't think so. Not yet, anyway. But he's here. They're here."

"Who?" Jack asked.

"Both," Thomas said. "The old man and Lizzy. Their private jet landed at Sky Harbor less than an hour ago. And they've got men on the move."

"What are they doing in Arizona?" Anna asked, but she wasn't asking it of Thomas. Her eyes were intently focused at a spot on the floor, and her brow was crinkled. That was her thinking face.

"In these communications you intercepted, did they say what his plans are?" Jack asked.

"You don't expect a guy like that to write a detailed memo, do you? I know it's his plane because of the call sign. I monitor communications for that, and I got a positive ping. And I know he's got men moving because I traced his phone to a local Phoenix number. I hacked that phone and intercepted a text message that said, 'All men move out. Code Alpha Henry Delta Nancy Alpha.'"

Anna nearly screamed it. "A.H.D.N.A." She grabbed Thomas's arms excitedly. "They're on their way to A.H.D.N.A." She kissed his cheek. "Great work."

Thomas smiled at her. "Thanks. I was worried you'd be mad."

She put on a fake frown. "Well you did put yourself in harm's way again, and that makes me unhappy." The mock frown disappeared and was replaced with a genuinely large smile. "But you learned where Aunt Lilly is, and that's worth the risk, I think."

"Wait a minute," Jack said. "I thought he was talking about Croft?"

Anna nodded. "Oh, he is. But why do you think Croft is in Arizona? The man hates to be anywhere but London. He barely tolerates New York. What would bring him here? And specifically A.H.D.N.A.?"

Neither Thomas nor Jack answered.

Anna threw up her hands. "Think, guys." When they were still silent, she groaned as if they were being unbearably dense. "Thomas, he let you get that information. Don't you see? He wants us to go to A.H.D.N.A. because that's where Aunt Lilly is. It's a trap to snag Alecto back."

"I don't know why he wants her so badly. I mean, it's clear that she's not going to side with him. Lizzy couldn't break her," Jack said.

Anna put a finger on her chin and thought for a few seconds. "Croft is the ultimate in conceited, Jack. He probably thinks it was just that Lizzy didn't do a good job. You know, like let me show you how it's done. He's probably livid that your friends hijacked the antivirus. And with the alien attacks in Europe, he's running out of time for his long-game plan. The hybrids were supposed to be his insurance policy for survival. I bet with the attacks in Europe, he's crapping his pants. He wants Alecto by his side to protect him."

"And he still thinks he can control her with water," Jack said.

Anna's face got even more animated. "Ha, I'm going to love seeing the look on his smug face when they hit her with water cannons and she just laughs at him."

"You don't plan on going down there, do you?" Jack asked. He'd spent more time in the creepy A.H.D.N.A. cave than he needed in a lifetime.

"Hell yeah, I'm going down there. And if Lizzy's there too..." Anna's small hands were balled fists at her sides, but she still wore a smile. Her right eye still wore the ugly scar slashed across it, which Lizzy had given her, the iris still milky white. "Alecto and I owe that bitch some payback."

Dr. Lewis had shown Erika and Aunt Dana to a room and Tex to a separate one in the dormitory-like sleeping quarters of the easternmost building on the grounds. Dr. Lewis then excused herself so that she could work on setting up the meeting with the military commander in charge of VLA operations as Tex had requested. Erika leaned against the doorframe of Tex's small room while he looked out the sole window.

Her arms were across her chest, her fingers nervously tapping her arms. He was standing so calmly that she wanted to shake him. "You've known about our future—about nuclear Armageddon— since when? Since we left the Conexus? And you didn't tell me?"

He did not turn to face her.

"So is it that you think I'm too stupid? A mere human. Am I so unworthy of talking to?"

His head dipped slightly, but he still had his back to her.

Erika moved a few paces into the room and stomped her foot. "Dammit, look at me."

Tex turned to face her, and she looked into the familiar black eyes surrounded by purplish-gray skin. His angelic features were gone once more. "What do you want me to say?"

She sucked in a breath and let it out slowly. His alien features seemed to frighten others, but to Erika, they had always made him look smaller and more vulnerable. The edge in her voice was gone. "Why did you keep it from me?"

He looked down at the ground. "I do not know exactly. Perhaps the time never seemed right to—"

"Tell me we're all going to die."

His eyes met hers. "I need you to know—to understand—that everything I do, all that I will do, I do it to protect you."

"What do you mean all that you will do?"

Tex rubbed his temples. "I apologize, Erika. I know that you have many questions. But I am fatigued. I need to regain my strength. Please, allow me to rest. We can speak of this later." He fell onto the bed, curled himself into a ball and was gone to her without another word.

Erika didn't know what to do with herself. She had been in survival mode for months. Her next move had been dictated by immediate necessity and survival. She finally had a moment to relax and think about what she would do next, and her heart was racing with the fear she'd pushed aside for weeks in order to get through the day.

She sat on her small bed, her knees to her chest, and realized she had no idea what she should do. She could go back to Aunt Dana's house and try to make a life there, but she was still sore at Dana. Trust had been torn, and the rip wasn't repaired yet.

And what if Tex still needs me? She didn't relish the idea of sitting around with nothing to do, though, waiting to be needed. Dr. Randall was on his way. *Maybe he'll have a job for me?* The thought of seeing the old man again brightened her mood.

That evening, she and Tex sat at a small round table in a break room filled with vending machines, a microwave, and a musty-smelling refrigerator. The military had set up a makeshift mess hall, but Tex preferred to dine on frozen dinners and avoid the stares of others. Erika couldn't blame him. They stuck out like a sore thumb on the campus, fitting in with neither the military personnel nor the scientists.

She attempted to draw more information out of him about what exactly he planned to do.

"Patience," he replied. "You'll learn more at the meeting with all the rest."

"All the rest? So I'm just lumped in with the military guys?" *Is that what he thinks of me? I'm just like everybody else?* Even as she thought it, she knew it was wrong. He had come to her in his sweat-lodge dream. He had sought her out, not anybody else.

Tex sighed and closed his eyes. He opened them again and said, "No. That is not what I meant. It is only that once you know what I must do, you may try to talk me out of it. And I may let you."

He picked up his half-eaten, sodium-laden dinner and threw it in the trash, leaving Erika still sitting at the table, staring after him. She scurried to throw out her trash and caught up to him as he headed out into the quad area between the buildings.

Tex had stopped on a gravel path and was staring at a car that drove toward them, kicking up dust. Ian parked the midsize sedan beside the building that housed the dorm-like temporary living quarters. The sun was setting, and the wind sweeping across the low desert valley was chilly.

As soon as Ian was out the car, Erika grabbed him in a bear hug. The sight of Ian, healthy and in a significantly improved condition, made her happier than she'd been in months. He was still too thin, but she had no doubt he would eventually be back to normal.

Ian hugged her tightly. When they separated, his eyes were filled with tears. He tucked a few stray hairs behind her ear. "Looks like you've managed okay without me. But dang, girl, when's the last time you bathed?" Ian pinched his nose shut with his fingers then flashed the impish smile that Erika had missed so much it hurt.

Erika had been too busy worrying about how they were going to prevent nuclear Armageddon to shower. She lightly punched Ian's shoulder and returned the smile rather than blurting out the grave fears occupying all of her mental energy. They would talk about the dire situation later.

Tex stood beside her and said nothing. Dr. Randall approached, his mouth open in awe, his eyes wide and unbelieving.

Erika had forgotten that neither of them had been there to witness Tex's transformation. Ian turned his attention to Tex, and his mouth also opened in astonishment, his eyes wide with wonder.

"Tex?" Dr. Randall said. "Is that really you?"

Tex nodded. "It is."

"But... how?" Dr. Randall asked. "And why?"

"A long story, Dr. Randall, and one we do not have time for at this moment. We must hurry to the conference room in the main operations building. Dr. Lewis has gathered the military personnel and scientists we require to help us get this project off the ground."

While they waited for Dr. Randall to arrive, Dr. Lewis had worked feverishly to arrange a meeting between Tex and the general that had taken command of and militarized the VLA, the officers under him, and the scientists that had worked at and been in charge of the VLA for years. Gathering the relevant military personnel and scientists for a meeting had seemed simple to Erika. They were, after all, all on the grounds.

Apparently, doing it was not that easy, though. The military personnel were busy planning a war in the air and the sea and on land. The general groused at giving Tex and Erika even fifteen minutes of his time as he was not convinced that an option other than armed conflict existed. The scientists were also dismissive of Tex's request, not because they had anything to plan so much as they thought it was pure fantasy, not science. The lead astronomer at the VLA, Dr. Fisher, was appalled that Dr. Lewis from NASA was going along with it. While neither side agreed with Tex, they also did not agree with each other on what should be done. The tensions on the grounds of the VLA were running high.

Dr. Randall pulled his jaw back up from the floor. "Yes, yes, of course. Lead the way."

Their shoes crunched on gravel as they walked the fifty or so yards to another, larger building in the U-shaped compound. Tex opened the door, and the din of arguing voices filled the air.

"We need to face facts," a man said. "We've lost Europe already. Our men are getting mowed down. Time to nuke Europe and preserve what's left."

"You can't just nuke the continent," Dr. Fisher said.

"The hell we can't," Brigadier General Hays said. His green uniform was immaculately ironed, and his left chest was covered with colorful pins of rank and honor. "This is about preserving American lives, Dr. Fisher. I doubt you'll be so damned principled when these M'Uktah barbarians land on American soil and start ripping people to shreds over here." His bright-blue eyes were pulled together, forcing a deep furrow between his brows. His square jaw was set, his thin lips pulled back and down into a derisive look. "We can deploy nuclear on foreign soil and end the invasion before they reach North America. Yes, Europe will be a shambles. But we're talking about saving the rest of the world."

A chorus of voices rose in assent, and someone yelled, "Nuke the bastards!"

Erika still wanted to vomit at the thought of the death she, Ian, Jack, and Tex seen around them in Apthartos. The idea that possibly billions would perish in a nuclear war made bile rise to her throat. She had not seen the invaders. The idea of them was an abstraction to her. But like most people, she had seen photos and movies about the aftermath of Hiroshima and Nagasaki. She knew what nuclear war looked like, and she wanted no part of it.

The scientists' voices rose in a chorus of opposition, all speaking at once. Finally, Dr. Fisher yelled for silence. "What we're saying is you should at least try diplomacy. Work with these invaders toward a treaty, and if one cannot be reached, you should be giving humanitarian aid and sending ground troops and air support to Europe, not a nuclear bomb. If you bomb Europe, you'll wipe out some M'Uktah, yes. But you'll also kill millions of innocent people and destroy the environment. Bombing of the magnitude you're talking about will affect the entire planetary ecosystem."

Erika moved farther into the room. "That's right!"

Her voice was drowned in a sea of everyone speaking at once, though. The room was soon filled with a cacophony of voices in which no one truly heard another.

Dr. Lewis stepped forward and added her voice, high and loud to the mix. "Shut it!"

To Erika's surprise, they did shut it. All eyes turned to Dr. Lewis's diminutive form.

"There is another option. It is out of the box, but it may be a way that we can avoid the nuclear option and will lead to the least amount of bloodshed."

Dr. Lewis motioned Tex to step forward. All in the room stared at him, and some shifted uncomfortably in their seats. Though Tex again looked nearly human, his appearance was so otherworldly in its perfection that it made some antsy.

Tex's voice was low and clear. "For any of you who do not yet know, my name is Tex, and I am a human-alien hybrid."

The crowd murmured, and most looked at him with complete surprise, but General Hays's stare remained fixed, even, and unflustered by what Tex said.

"I have been to the future. Your future." He waved his arm across the room to indicate all the people sitting, their eyes riveted to him. "I know how this ends. It is not pleasant."

The room was so utterly silent that Erika doubted anyone was even breathing. She realized she wasn't and took a deep breath, silently cheering Tex on.

Tex turned his attention to the side of the large conference room where the military officers were sitting. "If you employ your nuclear options, it will lead to the destruction of this world."

General Hays interrupted. "We won't employ nuclear on American soil. In fact, the President has already made it clear that he will not deploy any nuclear capabilities in North America. We've run the simulations. A half-dozen strategically detonated nukes in Europe will take out those invaders and, yes, destroy some cities of Europe." He looked around the room. "But it will not 'destroy' the world. The President and the joint chiefs are putting Americans first. If we survive this, we'll be here to help rebuild Europe. If these invaders take us out too, then we're all lost."

People talked amongst themselves again and ignored Tex as he tried to speak again. Erika tried her best whistle between the teeth, but no one even noticed it.

Tex's jaw tensed, and his hands balled into fists at his sides. Erika knew he was trying his hardest to be a more peaceful person, but they were surely trying his patience to the breaking point with their refusal to hear him out.

The ground quaked slightly, and pens and cups on the conference tables clattered. Erika put her hand on Tex's shoulder to lend him some calmness.

The shaking stopped. The room had become quiet. Someone said it was a small earthquake, but Erika knew that had been the beginnings of a Texquake.

Dr. Randall stepped forward and coughed to clear his throat. "Some of you know me—others do not. I am Dr. Randall, former head of the A.H.D.N.A. program and the H.A.L.F. project and long-time consultant to General Bardsley." Dr. Randall looked at General Hays when he said the last bit.

Hays's look remained stoic.

Dr. Randall continued. "I have worked as a military consultant on above–top secret weapons programs for over forty years. And I, too, have seen our future."

Though Dr. Randall more often than not appeared to be a myopic, introverted scientist with underdeveloped people skills, he had the ability to turn on a more political side of himself when he chose to. He had more of a knack for it than he admitted. All eyes were on him, rapt with attention.

He looked at the side of the room where the scientists sat together. "We cannot negotiate a treaty with a species whose language we do not understand. It could take months, even years, to learn their language. We do not have months. Also, these M'Uktah are here not for land or mineral resources. It is not a matter of negotiating who gets the larger slice of the pie."

Dr. Fisher interrupted. "Then what do they want?"

Dr. Randall was matter-of-fact. "To slay us like a herd of elk and carry our carcasses back to their planet in the refrigerated hull of their ship."

The scientists murmured amongst themselves. Dr. Fisher looked gobsmacked by Dr. Randall's blunt statement.

Dr. Randall ignored the scientists again and turned his attention back to the military chiefs. "In at least one timeline, we utilized our nuclear capability. It did not end well. You seem to be forgetting, General Hays, that the United States is not the only country with nuclear capability. We are not clear how it came about in the Conexus timeline, but we do know that for some reason, there were nuclear strikes worldwide. These strikes beat back the M'Uktah threat, but in the end, the planet was not habitable. Life—the life that led to the twisted creatures known as the Conexus—happened underground in a world destroyed by nuclear war."

Dr. Randall pulled himself up to his full height and straightened his glasses. "There is another alternative. It is not one that existed in the Conexus timeline." Dr. Randall put his hand on Tex's shoulder. "This young man did not exist in their history, and he is the key. He has a plan to shut down the galactic highway the M'Uktah used to get here, to strand the ships that are already here and prevent new ones from coming through the gate. I suggest you listen to him. I've seen the alternative, and I guarantee you this"—he pointed around the room—"none of you will survive it."

A few people coughed nervously or shifted restlessly. When Tex began again, he had their attention. He detailed how he needed the cooperation of the personnel at the VLA and needed to use the large array as well as the Arecibo array in Puerto Rico. He had their undivided attention until he got to the part about obtaining the cooperation of the Egyptian government to flood the great pyramid of Giza.

General Hays banged his fist on the table. "Stop right there." He stood, put his hat on, and grabbed the papers he had spread in front of him. "I don't have any more time for nonsense. I've got a country to defend." He pointed a thin finger at Tex. "I don't know what you're trying to pull, but it won't work. This facility will support the authorized operations of the US military as directed by our Commander in Chief. It needs to be at the ready for whatever they need us to do, and that does not include science-fiction projects for teenagers." General Hays directed his gaze at Dr. Fisher. "Do I make myself clear?"

Dr. Fisher returned his glare with a cool stare.

General Hays stormed from the room. The rest of the military folks followed without being asked. Tex stood still and emotionless as they watched the General leave.

The scientists did not vacate. Dr. Fisher turned her attention to Dr. Randall. "Please, Dr. Randall. Help us understand what Tex wants to do."

Erika sat to one side and listened as intently as everyone else did as Tex calmly laid out the specifics of his plan. People occasionally threw out questions, which he easily and dispassionately answered. They seemed to understand the answers given as they all scribbled madly on notepads, trying to keep up with all that he said.

The formulas and scientific terms were far beyond her grasp. She got especially lost when he talked about why he needed them to flood the great pyramid.

"Explain again what the water will do?" asked Dr. Lewis.

Erika was glad to see she wasn't the only one that didn't understand. Even Drs. Fisher and Lewis nodded and waited expectantly for his answer.

Tex went into a lengthy explanation of the mechanism for using the internal structure of the pyramid to create what he called a maser, or microwave laser. "The grand gallery will need twenty-seven Helmholtz resonators, but once installed, the gallery is a perfect resonator, pushing the hydrogen into the collimator then into the King's chamber, which will focus a beam with microwave energy hitting the ionosphere."

He seemed to have lost most of them before he even got to the word Helmholtz. No one was writing anything down by the end.

Tex pushed his palms together, bowed his head, and took a deep breath. "You are following me, aren't you? It is quite simple, really."

The scientists still stared at him blankly.

"This has never been done before," Erika said. She put a hand on his and spoke to him quietly. "We all want to understand. Explain it to them."

He unclenched his hands. "With sufficient quantities of hydrochloric acid, zinc, and plain water, we can create a high-energy maser. It will act as a plasma channel, pulling energy directly into the pyramid. The pyramid was built to resonate at the exact frequency required to match the resonant frequency of the home planet of the architects of the Mocht Bogha. Once the pyramid resonates at that frequency, the Arecibo dish will be used to collect the signal. The Arecibo dish will amplify the signal and send it to the VLA. The radio dishes here will be aligned to the coordinates dictated by the resonant frequency, which I will match so that I can travel to the planet of the Architects."

Dr. Fisher shook his head. "I'm sorry. I'm with you until you get to the part about ancient architects and traveling on what? A photon, basically. Is that what you're saying?"

Tex cocked his head in thought for a few seconds then said, "Yes. I believe that is one way you could think about it."

Murmurs rose from the crowd. They talked amongst themselves and shook their heads. *He's losing them.*

Dr. Randall whispered in Tex's ear, and Tex whispered back. Erika couldn't hear them and suspected that, even if she could, she wouldn't understand what they were saying.

Dr. Fisher spoke again. "It's not that we don't want to help you. You know that we're in agreement with you that bombing Europe is not the way to go. But we just—well, you're talking science fiction, Dr. Randall. We can't risk our professional reputations to follow this fool's errand to its logical conclusion. Not when so many lives are at stake."

Erika shot to her feet. "Professional reputations?" She sneered in disgust as she looked across the table at their faces. "There are aliens ripping the throats out of countless people right now, as we speak. And you're worrying about your reputation." She spat the words out as though they tasted terrible to her.

Erika stood behind and between Tex and Dr. Randall and put a hand on a shoulder of each of them. "The three of us traveled to the future. That's science fiction too, isn't it?"

None of them answered, but a few shifted in their chairs.

"And this man is part alien. That's science fiction, too." She flung her hands in the air. "Hell, aliens are pouring out of a rift in the space-time continuum and attacking our planet. Are you going to tell me that's fiction as well?"

Erika walked to a chalkboard that covered nearly an entire wall. It was plastered with aerial and ground photos from satellites and other intelligence gathering, showing the devastation that the M'Uktah had already wreaked in Europe. She pointed at a particularly gruesome photo of two huge creatures bending over human bodies, their mechanized jaws unhinged, razor-sharp metal teeth tearing into flesh. An involuntary shudder ran up her spine. She plucked the photo from the board and flung it onto the table. "Is this also fiction?"

Dr. Lewis had been silent, but she broke her silence. "I for one will not sit idly by and watch as they destroy us."

Erika wasn't sure if by "they" Dr. Lewis meant the M'Uktah or the government forces, but the doctor continued without clarification.

"We—all of us in this room—pursued science as a career because we want to know the truth. We seek answers to profound questions. Some of those answers are out there. Other answers sit right here in this room." She gestured toward Tex. "We've wondered if we're alone. The answer is clearly 'no.'" She smiled warmly at Tex. "But if we're to survive this first meeting with another species, we'll have to work together, and not only with each other, but with scientists around the world."

Murmurs of assent rose from the others around her.

"This is not an issue for one country. We're talking about preservation of our species. And it will fall to us, the scientists, to make it happen."

A few people cheered. Dr. Fisher kept his mouth shut and let Dr. Lewis finish.

She held up her hands for silence. "One last thing. I've checked his math. What the young man says is theoretically possible. So I say, while the generals plan a war, let's put Tex's plan into action and send him to the stars. He just may succeed before the nukes fly."

Dr. Randall clapped Tex on the back. "Looks like you're going to become an astronaut."

Tex sat stoically, showing neither excitement nor fear.

All the scientists, including Dr. Fisher, stood and clapped for him. Dr. Randall rose and joined in the cheer.

Erika imagined Tex succeeding and disappearing before her eyes. She did not clap. She almost wished she had not intervened to help him. *What have I done?*

23
JACK

Anna wiped down equipment and stowed instruments in the lab. Jack knew that fire in her eyes. He didn't think talking her out of her plan to go to A.H.D.N.A. was likely, but he tried it anyway.

"I know you want to make sure Lizzy gets what's coming to her."

"Damned right." Anna chucked into a trashcan a wad of tape that had held electrodes to Alecto's body.

"But you're walking into a trap. You know that, right?"

Alecto levitated a microscope, which Anna had just covered, back into a closet. Anna didn't stop to remark on it, as though hovering microscopes were totally normal.

"The great game, Jack. Cat and mouse. Croft thinks he's the cat," Anna said.

"He thinks that 'cause he is," Thomas said. He stood in the doorway, his arms tucked in his armpits.

Jack slapped his thigh. "Exactly. Talk sense into her, Thomas. Tell her she can't go down there."

Anna stopped what she was doing long enough to turn an intense glare on Jack. "Watch my back then, Jack Wilson." She turned her attention on Thomas. "Get hold of Mr. Sewell. We need schematics for A.H.D.N.A. and directions and coordinates for the tunnel entrance Tex used to escape."

Thomas didn't move.

Anna blew out a breath, making a stray hair blow up. "Fine. I'll do it myself." She attempted to push past Thomas.

He grabbed her gently by the shoulders. "Hold on. I'll do it." His eyelashes glistened. "It's just..." He lifted the butterfly pendant hanging on a chain around her neck. "I can't lose you."

Anna's voice, normally filled with patience when she spoke to Thomas, was shrill. "We've been through this. You're not going to

170

lose me. I'm not going down there unarmed. And I'll have Alecto with me. Right?"

Alecto stood with her hands on her slim waist, her lips set and thin. "Affirmative. I will terminate anyone that attempts to harm Anna Sturgis."

Alecto spoke as if reading from a script she'd memorized. Alecto had been like Anna's guard dog. That should have comforted Jack, but it didn't. He tried to see Alecto through Anna's eyes, but his vision was clouded by the memory of how Alecto had hurled Erika into a wall and nearly killed Tex.

Thomas turned to leave.

"Where are you going?" Anna called to him.

"To do what you asked."

Anna began to leave as well and gestured for Alecto to follow her. She was miffed at Jack—that much was clear.

Jack wasn't about to give in on the argument just to put a cease-fire to the hostilities, though. He'd vowed to himself never to go back to that place, and too much was at stake to fling themselves into A.H.D.N.A. without a small army of backup.

He followed Anna to the office where she had stowed her purse. "Stop. Please, let's talk this through."

She stopped and waited for him to catch up to her. "What do we need to talk through? You only want to talk me out of it."

"Well, yes, but—"

She continued walking.

Jack groaned. *Why is it always so difficult?* "At least tell me your plan for how the two of you are going to combat a small militia? 'Cause if the guards at the penthouse were any indication, he's going to have a small army down there."

She stopped again and looked him in the eye. "One carcass at a time until I put a bullet in William Croft's head, just like Lizzy did to my dad."

The cold determination on her face chilled Jack to the marrow. "But you've never been inside the place. It's like a maze down there. Blind corners. Many ways to die."

"No, I haven't been there. But she has." Anna indicated Alecto with a flick of her head, and her expression warmed. "And you have."

The statement was an invitation—no, a plea. Jack knew what his response would be. He'd known before the conversation even started.

He briefly imagined wrapping an arm around her waist and drawing her to him. He'd kiss her deeply until he felt her body relax against him. He let the moment pass, again unable to risk her rejection. "Of course I'm not letting you go down there alone. What do you need me to do?"

Her face lit up in a smile, and she blushed. She had an answer ready, indicating she'd already thought about it. "I'm putting you on weapons detail."

Jack was fine with being in charge of ensuring they were well armed. The only problem was he didn't know where to start. He took the elevator down to Dr. Montoya's office and hoped she had a resource or could at least point him in the right direction to obtain the weapons and armor they needed.

The elevator pinged, and Jack stepped off into a brightly lit linoleum-floored corridor, identical to every other floor in the building. The walls were a pale, peachy, 1960s brick with offices running down the hall on both sides.

The time was after five, and the offices were empty, the lights turned off. A soft pink glow filled the corridor, streaming in from the office windows. Dr. Montoya's office was the last one on the left. Jack hoped she hadn't already left for the day.

Before he hit the door, he knew something wasn't right when he heard someone ransacking the place. Papers were being thrown about, and desk drawers rattled.

Jack wished for the gun he'd been carrying while in the Croft penthouse, but he was unarmed. Jack pressed himself to the wall and tiptoed toward the door.

He took a deep breath to steady himself then peeked around the doorjamb. He expected to find one of the Makers goons, dressed in black, ransacking the office.

Instead, he found Dr. Montoya. Her hair had broken free of its smooth, sleekly groomed ponytail at the back of her head. Her eyes were wide, her mouth open and pulled back. She was rifling through the contents of one of her desk drawers and mumbling to herself.

Jack stepped into the door opening. "What's up?"

She visibly jumped, put her hand to her chest, and sighed. "Oh, Jack. You startled me."

"I can see that." Jack looked around the room, trying to make sense of the mess she'd made. "Lose something?"

She stopped her frantic fingers rifling through some papers. "Yes."

For as neat as Dr. Montoya's appearance was, her office had been a disaster even before she went on a pillaging rampage of her own stuff. Even the day before when he'd been there, it had been strewn with piles of papers intermixed with large medical volumes and a lone, sickly, spindly avocado plant that sat atop a filing cabinet and strained toward the light of the window. Jack figured she was looking for a thumb drive, which certainly would have been like looking for a needle in a haystack.

"What are you looking for?"

Dr. Montoya sat back in her chair, took off her glasses, and wiped her eyes. "It's missing, Jack. All of it, gone." She rubbed at her temples.

Jack hadn't known the woman long, but she had struck him as a solid person, not prone to crying jags or irrational fits of worry. *This is about more than a lost thumb drive.*

He figured he didn't really want to know the answer, but he asked the question anyway. "What's missing?"

She put her glasses back on and coughed. Her voice quavered when she answered. "The antivirus and..." She indicated the mess in the room with a sweeping gesture of her hand. "And all my notebooks with notes about it."

Jack nodded toward the computer. "But you've published stuff on it, right? You put it in the database already? Got it backed up and all that?"

Tears spilled down her cheeks. "We had everything on a local server. I didn't want to announce a cure until we were certain—until we'd tested and retested to be sure. I was going to upload all of my research to D.C. tomorrow. The server has been wiped. All computers here scrubbed. Someone knew exactly where it was and exactly how to delete it permanently."

Jack didn't bother flicking the papers off of the chair across from Dr. Montoya before he sat down. The papers crunched beneath him. "But who... I mean, hardly anybody here even knows what it is you're working on. Only you, Dr. Randall, Ian, Anna, and I."

Dr. Montoya grabbed a tissue from a dusty box on her desk and blew her nose. "You forgot one."

Jack wracked his brain. "Ben?"

She nodded. "He was busy in the lab this morning when I left for an all-day meeting on the other side of town. I asked him to take a look at my report and notes to check for errors. He was the last to have his hands on the antivirus—the last that logged into my computer. When I came back late this afternoon, he was already gone."

Jack's stomach lurched at the thought that Ben could be behind the missing antivirus. *This will break Ian's heart.*

"Why would he do this?" she asked. "Who is he really working for?"

She might have meant the questions to be rhetorical, but Jack had a pretty good idea of the answers. "He's working for Croft."

Dr. Montoya blew her nose again. It was red and her eyes puffy from crying. "Croft? The same man that Dr. Randall said wanted to take that strange young man away from the virus outbreak unit in Ajo?"

"One and the same. I'm not sure I fully understand how the two things are related. But what I've learned so far in this mess is that anytime something smells rotten, Croft's got his mitts all over it." Jack stood to leave. He'd come down to discuss weapons, but Dr. Montoya already had her hands full. "If it's any consolation, we're going Croft-hunting tomorrow. With any luck, we'll find the missing antivirus, too."

"You said 'we.' You mean you and Anna?" Her voice was shrill with worry.

Jack nodded. "And Alecto."

"Well, that's something, but you can't mean to go up against this man, just the three of you. I mean, down in Ajo, there were dozens of those Makers men roaming around."

"Yep, that sounds like them."

When she said it, the whole thing sounded like a suicide mission, but then, she hadn't seen Alecto in action. Jack figured Alecto was worth at least a dozen men, maybe more.

Dr. Montoya rose from her desk. "I'm useless here tonight, and I'm guessing you need help."

"Well, since you asked. Have any idea where we get firearms and ammo for our three-person militia?"

Dr. Montoya put her arm through Jack's and walked with him to the elevators. "What made you think I would know anything about guns?"

Jack shrugged. "Don't know. Just a hunch, I guess."

She pushed the number to go one floor up to the lab. "You've got good instincts, Jack. Follow your gut."

"So you can help us?"

She smiled. "Leave the armory to me."

The sky was still full dark outside the window of Tex's room at the VLA. With Dr. Lewis and her assistant in the small room with him, they barely had room to turn around. They helped Tex shimmy into the insulating long-underwear layer of his space suit. Having someone help him into gear and fussing over him brought to his mind his days at A.H.D.N.A. In some respects, the experiences were little different. He was still an experiment, but this time he was going to an unknown planet. His every breath would be measured and analyzed. When he got back—if he got back—they'd no doubt want to pick his brain and prod his body for information about the journey. *Only this time, it is by your choice, Bodaway.*

Drs. Lewis, Fisher, and Randall along with the other scientists at the VLA had worked tirelessly for a solid week to get things ready for Tex's journey. Dr. Fisher had managed to get Arecibo on board fairly quickly. Egypt was another matter. The Great Pyramid was their greatest treasure, and Tex's plan was likely to irreparably damage it. Dr. Randall did his best to urge their cooperation, but the M'Uktah truly pushed Egypt to action. The invasion was spreading, and the Egyptian government saw the writing on the wall. They finally acquiesced with the plan and committed the resources needed.

Dr. Lewis had engineered a state-of-the-art biosuit that Tex would be the first astronaut to wear. Gone was the bulky white air-filled suit of the early days of human space travel that had made astronauts look as if they were wrapped in a white helium-filled balloon. Dr. Lewis's suit utilized smart fibers and integrated circuitry to apply the steady pressure needed to survive space.

The assistant strapped a unit onto his back that looked like a large backpack. It contained two oxygen tanks as well as other equipment.

Dr. Lewis helped the assistant get the pack strapped onto Tex's back. "Depending on a person's metabolism, there are twelve to sixteen hours of oxygen in these two tanks. Because we haven't had a chance to run you through simulations, I have no idea whether your metabolism runs high or low. Let's be conservative and assume twelve hours." She fastened the last strap to hold the unit onto his backpack unit, which she referred to as the PLSS.

"I can alter my metabolism," Tex said.

She stared at him as if trying to figure out if he was joking or being earnest. His kept his face a stoic mask.

"Well, that may be. And if you can slow your breathing, you'll have a bit of cushion, then. But I'm still going under the assumption of twelve hours at most. So this is important. As soon as you get there, synchronize your watch. It's there, on the computer screen embedded in the left arm of the suit." She lifted his arm gently and tapped the screen.

A display came on and flashed the time and date in bright green digital numbers. After a few seconds, the display changed to a screen with several icons. One was labeled "Comm," another "Stat," and the third "Anal."

Tex knew what the first abbreviation meant but was unsure, even with icons, what the second meant. He wasn't sure he wanted to know what the third term referred to. "What do these stand for?"

"Oh, yeah, I keep forgetting this is all new to you." Dr. Lewis smiled briefly. "A tiny screen without much room, so we had to abbreviate. 'Stat' stands for 'status,' and it refers to the status of your suit and life-support systems. If your onboard computer detects any flaws in your suit or if your oxygen is running low, for example, it will alert you by flashing red and telling you what's wrong. If you tap that icon, it will give you the current status. Go ahead. Try it."

Tex did as she suggested, and a display showed a diagram of his suit and reported all systems at one hundred percent. "Useful," he said.

Dr. Lewis nodded. "Very. Wearing this gear is like carrying the conditions of our planet with you. And seeing as how you're adapted to this planet and we don't know what you're stepping into, it's very important that your mini Earth functions exactly as needed to keep you alive."

"And this last abbreviation?" The third abbreviation had an icon of what appeared to be a graph under it.

Dr. Lewis smiled and covered her mouth to hold in a laugh. "Oh, that one. A little joke, I suppose, by smarty-pants engineers. That means 'analyze.' You tap that when you want your onboard computer to analyze the environment outside of the suit."

"A weather app?"

"Well, yes, I suppose, but more than just temperature, barometric pressure, and humidity. It will also analyze the composition of the air outside the suit as well as inside the suit. That way, you know if the air is compatible to breathe or not."

"You're saying that if I get there and the computer says I can breathe the air, that I can take the helmet off?"

Dr. Lewis did not hesitate when she said, "No. Don't do that."

"But if the air is safe to breathe—"

"Air quality is only one part of the puzzle. The helmet also protects you, especially your eyes, from harmful radiation and flying dust and debris. You'll be there by yourself, without the possibility of medical assistance. For your protection, keep the whole suit on for the duration—that includes the helmet."

Tex didn't like the idea of having a glorified fishbowl on his head. Though the suit was not bulky, it fit like a full-body neoprene glove. It kept the astronaut safe in space by applying pressure throughout the body. Tex felt as though he'd been wrapped like a mummy, and the boots were heavy on his feet. Though he was stronger than he'd ever been and in peak condition, the whole thing still weighed him down. His movements were much slower than he was used to. He attempted to walk across the room with preternatural speed but managed only a fast walk.

Panic seized him. *Does this suit somehow nullify my telekinetic abilities?* Tex searched the room for a small object to test his powers. He raised the T-shirt he had taken off and hovered it in the air briefly. A sigh of relief escaped his lips.

Dr. Lewis stared at the shirt with wide eyes. When Tex released it back onto the bed, she smiled at him in wonder. "Amazing. I would like to learn more about how you do that."

"Perhaps when I get back." He forced a wan smile. "But I have a job to do now."

"Yes, of course." Dr. Lewis brought her attention back to Tex. "We'll monitor your vitals constantly."

Tex walked back to where she stood. "If you can receive a transmission."

Dr. Lewis nodded once. "True."

"Let us assume—to be conservative, as you suggested—that we will not be able to communicate with each other. I will not be able to signal my readiness to return. How will I—"

"Get back?"

Tex nodded. He tried not to think of the possibility of never returning because when he considered the odds, he realized they were not good. *If I acknowledge the realistic chance of my success, no one will let me go.* "Not much point in me going if I never return. Then you would miss out on the information needed to quash this M'Uktah threat." A hint of sarcasm had seeped into his tone.

Dr. Lewis caught his eye. "You're cynical about humans, aren't you?"

Tex tugged at his left glove, trying to get it to be less bunchy at the tips of his fingers. "Perhaps I have reason to be."

Her lips turned down into a frown. "I can only imagine." From the dour look on her face, she seemed to be imagining it, in fact. She ran a hand through her pale white-gold hair, adjusted her glasses, and forced a drawn smile. "I want you to return, and not just to study you. I enjoy your company."

Tex believed her. He formed the opinion without the need to read her mind. He was learning to size people up the way Erika and other humans did.

"We will keep the dishes aligned in the same pattern until you return, our assumption being that you will return the same way you went."

"Please ensure they stay aligned, Dr. Lewis. If the gate closes, there will be no hope of my return." If Tex was stuck on an alien planet, he might survive there. For all he knew, he could end up in a place more hospitable to him than Earth. If he did not return, though, he feared Erika would have little hope to survive.

Dr. Lewis's face was grim. "Then failure of the gates to remain open isn't an option, is it?" She tried to smile at him, but his lack of mirth in response made her smile fade quickly.

———————

Tex walked between Dr. Lewis and several technicians as he made his way through the hallways of the dormitory and into the cold late-night November air. The courtyard was empty, and they walked as quietly and quickly as they could to avoid unwanted attention from military personnel. Drs. Lewis and Fisher were, after all, violating the direct orders of General Hays by helping Tex and Dr. Randall.

A jeep waited for him. The techs helped him get in, and they drove over the rocky terrain and dusty soil of the high desert to the center of the array of radio telescope dishes.

From afar, the dishes looked small, so he was surprised to find himself dwarfed by them as he stood on the ground and looked up at one. The brilliant whiteness of the radio dish was like a giant ghost in the black of the night. Stars dotted the sky, and the Milky Way hinted at the galaxies that lay beyond his own. *I'm going there.* The realization was both thrilling and chilling at the same time.

"This way," a scientist said.

Tex followed the man to where a small crowd had gathered. The spot was in the center of the top of the Y shape the dishes had been arranged in. Tex didn't recognize most of the faces, but he knew one of them in an instant.

Erika stood in the center, her arms wrapped around herself for warmth, a hoodie over her head. His heart quickened at the sight of her.

People chattered in his ear about protocols and what he was supposed to do and what to do if this happened or that happened. Their voices were an annoying hum in his ears.

Erika smiled at him.

"What do you think?" he asked.

"It makes you look... larger," she said. Her cheeks were flushed red.

He was close to her—close enough to smell the soap she'd bathed with and the coffee she'd drunk, close enough to feel the warmth rise from her body and to hear the beating of her heart.

With his boots on, he was a few inches taller than her, and she had to crane her neck upward to look into his face.

"It kills me that I can't come with you," she said.

"I wish I could have you by my side, as well." He drank in the color of her eyes, the same hue as the brownies they'd shared the day before; the rosy pink of her lips; and the curve of her neck, the paleness of her skin the color of shells. The journey was full of unknowns, the chief of which was whether he would ever return and, if he did, whether he would be too late. He figured he had slim odds of ever seeing her again. *This moment will have to last me a lifetime.*

With that thought, he did what he had previously lacked the courage to do. He bent his head, put his hand at the small of her back, and drew her to him as his lips met hers. He practically felt the crowd watching him, but Tex did not care. He held a universe in his arms, the whole world at his lips.

Tex had often imagined what kissing Erika would be like. They had shared that marvelous dream, which had been as close to reality as he thought he would ever get with her.

Never in his imagination, though, could he have conjured the sensation that coursed through him. Her aroma was all around him, intoxicating and maddening at the same time. Her lips were soft yet insistent, moist but not wet. Her breath was in him, and his was in her, and as she pressed against him, her warmth seeped into him.

His loins tightened, and his breathing became ragged. He wanted to hold her like that for the rest of time and to know her as fully as any man had ever known a woman.

But Dr. Lewis's gentle cough reminded him that then was not the time. Duty pressed on his shoulders as if gravity had suddenly doubled.

He withdrew his lips from hers and felt as though all the warmth he had ever known had been sucked out of him. Her eyes had been closed, but they fluttered open yet languid. Her lips were still parted, and though she looked like she wanted to speak, she said nothing.

Tex remained silent as well, allowing their kiss to be the final word between them. *For now.*

The lead scientist told everyone to clear out, and they scurried away.

Dr. Lewis was the last to leave the area. "Good luck," she whispered. She kissed him lightly on the cheek then helped him get his helmet on and fastened. Then she, too, walked away, leaving him entirely alone on a spot in the center of the array marked with a fluorescent green X.

The helmet muffled sounds, but he could have heard them clearly if he'd wanted. He decided, though, to save his energy and focus instead on the task at hand. He would need to be more focused than he had ever been if the plan was to work.

As he attempted to meditate, doubt played at the fringes of his mind. He had convinced those scientists to put themselves at risk to support a plan based on implanted memories he had received in the future from a race that had intended to kill at least three-quarters of the population. *What if the Conexus history I accessed in their future world was merely myth?* The flicker of doubt pulled him from his meditation. *What if all of this is simply a fantasy I created because I want so badly to save her?*

Something was nagging at him, though. Perhaps it was what humans called intuition. This mission felt right to him, and he focused on that. He stretched out his arms and tilted his head up toward the starry sky. The arid, high-desert air had been good for him. His synapses fired without obstruction. The conditions would never be better.

Tex closed his eyes and signaled his readiness with a thumbs-up. He withdrew then into a deep meditation. He no longer fretted over whether they had gotten the Arecibo dish aligned properly or whether the north-south shafts of the Great Pyramid had the required chemicals flowing through them to create the reaction required.

Tex focused on his breath and followed it down to an awareness of his body then to his cells. He was simultaneously cognizant of every one of his cells and was in direct communication with them. At the cellular level, he became aware of electromagnetic waves pulsing through him from the telescope array. His cells vibrated. That merest hint of movement was subtle at first, but the small vibration grew into an oscillation that was at once disorienting but also created a pleasant, tingly sensation throughout his body.

He focused even more deeply, down to the atomic level, where the oscillation was a thunderous earthquake. His atoms threatened to rip away from each other and scatter, but they resisted. Pain like a million white-hot pokers tore at him, and he was aware on some level that he screamed in agony.

With great effort, he pulled his attention away from the pain. He refocused on the wave pulse. It was there, moving through his physical body, yes, but also touching his consciousness. If all had gone as he had directed, the radio dishes had aligned the waveform to the proper destination.

The feeling of ripping and splitting was replaced by immense pressure, as though he was being compressed down, squashed and smashed until he was no more than the size of a pinhead.

Physical sensation ceased entirely. He was aware only of being aware. He was everywhere yet nowhere. The feeling was neither pleasant nor unpleasant. He simply was, yet he was not.

Before he had the opportunity to grapple with that existential conundrum, sensation returned to his body, and he was slammed with great force. He felt as though his very being was forced back into his body, or quite possibly, his body was thrown hard against the ground. Either way, searing knives of pain throbbed in his legs.

He blinked and, upon doing so, became aware that he once again had eyes and could see. His vision was blurry, the clear plastic of his helmet facemask covered in dust. He tried to see beyond the plastic of his helmet but saw only sand—no emerald-green spires of glass or wide boulevards of pink marble and gleaming stone as he had envisioned, based on the ancient history archives of the Conexus.

He was splayed like a specimen ready for dissection. Tex tried to push himself up to standing, but the pain that shot through him revealed that both his legs were broken.

Tex lay in the sand, nearly blind due to the dusty helmet and completely incapacitated by the fractured bones. The dust that smeared his helmet was the same color as the dust that had covered the ground he'd stood on at the VLA. *I didn't go anywhere.* Though he had failed utterly, his only consolation was that he'd soon be with Erika again. *At least until the M'Uktah eat us all.*

25
JACK

After trudging for nearly an hour through desert scrub, Jack, Anna, and Alecto made it to the hidden entrance to A.H.D.N.A. Their packs were heavy with body armor, weapons, and rappelling equipment. Despite the chill of a cloudy, late-autumn day, Jack's back was wet with sweat.

"We'll be tired before we get there," he said.

Anna and Alecto breathed heavily behind him.

Thomas had made a half-hearted demand that he come with them. When Jack explained that they would need to climb in complete darkness down a tunnel that extended for nearly a mile, he'd decided to stay behind and monitor things from his computers.

Jack was glad of it. Thomas was at his best behind a screen, his fingers clicking a keyboard. Jack needed to focus on keeping Anna safe. He didn't relish the idea of having to watch out for Thomas as well.

Sewell's directions and coordinates had led them easily to the hole in the rock that led to the tunnel entrance to A.H.D.N.A. It was the same route Tex had used to escape on that fateful night Jack had met him in the desert.

They rummaged through their packs and donned the rappelling harnesses. Jack and Anna put on caving helmets equipped with halogen lights. Alecto could see in the dark as well as any night-dwelling cave creature and had no need for the lamp.

"I'll go first," Jack said. He squeezed through the rocks. It was a tight fit, and the rough sandstone scraped up his shoulder.

He emerged on the other side and found himself in a small cave. No lights, doors, or other evidence of a manmade structure were below, only a gaping hole no more than five feet around. Anyone unlucky enough to find the cave would likely fall to their death if not paying close attention to the surroundings.

"Okay, step on through, but be careful. The tunnel entrance is just on the other side of the opening. A step too far, and it'll be like skydiving in the dark without a parachute."

Jack had done some rock climbing over the years, but he hadn't used the equipment in over a year. He'd practiced tying knots a few times before they packed their gear.

He hooked a carabiner onto Alecto's harness. "You'll need to go down first. Sewell said there's a ladder made of iron rods pounded into the rock. Clip yourself onto the ladder as you make your way down." He demonstrated the way the clips opened and closed. "You'll be tied to Anna, and the same rope will be tied to me."

Alecto cocked her head to the side. "If I fall, will that not pull you both down with me?"

"The idea is that if you lose your footing, we'll keep you from falling to your death."

Alecto simply stared off for a few seconds then said, "Yes. I understand."

"Once you've gone down a rung, reclip yourself. Then Anna will go down a rung, clip herself, then I will do the same."

"This is going to take forever if we have to unclip, step, clip and wait for the other two to do the same," Anna said.

Jack tested the knot holding the rope to Anna's carabiner. They were so close that her body heat warmed him. He looked into her deep blue eyes. Her lips were parted slightly, her cheeks flushed. He pressed closer, their lips nearly touching. "Better to take it slow than end up sorry."

She stepped back from him. "Then let's get going before I change my mind," Anna said.

Another lost opportunity.

Alecto sat in the dirt at the edge of the hole. She gingerly knelt over the edge and clipped herself to the first rung. She clung onto the dirt and slowly eased herself over. "I have found the first foothold." She unclipped herself, stepped down another rung, and clipped onto the next rung just as Jack had told her to. "Anna, you may proceed."

Anna sat at the side of the tunnel as Alecto had done. She looked down as if trying to see the bottom. "The first step's a bitch."

"You're tied to me. I won't let you fall," Jack said.

She looked back at him and gave a weak smile.

He watched her helmeted head disappear over the side and was relieved to hear her clip onto the metal rail.

Anna called up to him, "Your turn."

He looked over the precipice of the giant black hole leading down to nowhere and wished he hadn't. Even with the headlamp, he could see only about five feet downward. After that was a black void.

He sat near the edge and eased himself closer to the abyss. He bent and clipped himself to the first rung then swung his legs out and down to the next one down. His heart leapt into his throat as his legs hit air and searched for the metal rung. He let out a breath of relief when he found it. He had taken only one step, but his forehead was already covered in slick sweat.

The three progressed slowly downward. Jack got into a rhythm. Unclip, step, clip, and repeat. He didn't look down. He focused on the foothold below him and the stone wall in front of him.

They continued downward for close to an hour, with hardly a word between them. Each was focused on stepping carefully. Still, nothing but a dark void was below them. Jack tried not to think about that. He focused on counting to one hundred steps. When he finished, he would start again.

He lost count of how many hundreds he'd done. He was on step number forty-two when the rope around his waist jerked. Anna's scream pierced the silence of the black hole. He gripped the rung with both hands and tightened his muscles, willing himself not to fall.

Anna swung below him, her body weight tugging at his waist. Her scream ended, replaced with a silence more unsettling than the scream.

Jack hoped she hadn't passed out. "Anna?"

Her voice trembled. "I can't get back to the wall."

Jack let out a relieved breath that she was conscious. "Don't panic. I'll pull you back."

That was easier said than done. Anna was a trim person, but she was dead weight, swinging and pulling against Jack. He tensed his legs, held tightly with his left hand, and pulled on the rope with his right. Sweat poured from his forehead into his eyes, and his shoulder muscles burned as he hoisted Anna up with one arm.

Her helmet came into view. Seeing her gave him the extra jolt of strength he needed to pull her up next to him. "Grab on."

Her thin fingers trembled as she gripped the iron handhold with both hands. Her body quaked as he wrapped his aching right arm around her.

"You're all right," he whispered.

"Is Anna safe?" Alecto asked. Her voice echoed off the stone walls of the tunnel.

Even with the halogen lamp on his head, Jack couldn't see Alecto below them. Her voice was disembodied as if coming from the void itself.

"She's okay," Jack called back. "Just shaken up. We'll need to rest here for a few minutes."

If Anna could press any more closely into him, she would be a second skin. Jack clipped her to the rung with him, his body wrapped around hers. Even though her back was to him, he felt her heart hammering. She trembled against him.

His lips found her ear, and he whispered, "You're safe now." He nuzzled her hair and kissed her neck softly.

Anna shuddered. She turned her face up to him.

He sought her lips and kissed her softly. She did not shrink back from him as he'd feared she would. Anna pressed even closer to him and kissed him back. He squeezed her gently in his arms, making a warm cocoon for her trembling body.

"Don't let me go," she whispered.

He smiled down into her glistening eyes. "I fear, Miss Sturgis, that you are stuck with me."

She answered with a light kiss then snuggled her back into him as she tried to regain the strength in her legs to keep going.

Kissing a girl had never felt so natural to Jack, even with Erika. Anna's body snuggled against his felt so right. She fit there perfectly, as if they were a matched pair that had been separated but reunited. Though they were clinging to a stone wall, their situation precarious, Jack was filled with a joy he'd never felt before—and a renewed sense of purpose.

They stayed pasted to the wall until Anna's trembling subsided and her legs were no longer like noodles. His shoulder and arm muscles throbbed, and his legs ached from the effort of holding onto the thin metal rungs keeping them from falling into the abyss.

Once Jack felt Anna's breathing return to a normal pace, he said, "We should keep moving."

"I don't think I can go on." Anna's voice was hoarse. Her face was still plastered against the wall and her quaking body curled into Jack.

Jack squeezed her tightly to himself. "Well, you have two choices, love. It's down or up. Either way, we can't stay here. Do you want to abort this mission?"

Anna was quiet. Finally she said, "No."

He squeezed her again before taking his arm from around her. He unclipped her from the wall. "A step at a time. Don't look down. Clip on, and remember: I've got you." He kissed her forehead.

She took a deep breath. Her still-trembling fingers let go, and she stepped down. Jack released another deep breath of relief when he heard her clip on.

They continued downward. Unclip, step, clip, repeat—over and over, for what felt like hours.

The change was subtle. The dry air became moister. The faint smell of iron in the rock was replaced by the odor of dirt. The change spurred them on, and the pace quickened.

"I see something," Alecto called up.

"What is it?" Jack asked.

"Light."

His heart quickened with anticipation, but he recalled what he'd learned from his rock-climbing instructor: most mistakes are made near the end. "We're nearly there, then. Stay focused."

Unclip, step, clip, repeat—again and again. Light seeped into the darkness from below. It was a barely there faint yellow that grew brighter with each step.

"I see the ground," Anna said. Her voice was excited and exhausted at the same time.

A few steps later, Alecto called up, "I have reached the bottom." Her voice was more animated than Jack had ever heard from her.

Jack's feet finally hit solid ground. His legs were like spaghetti. His shoulders and back ached as though he'd been beaten by a baseball bat.

Anna was bent down, her hands on her knees. She wiped away tears and snot with the back of her hand.

Jack unclipped the rope and stepped out of his harness. "You okay?"

She rose up and smiled so widely her face looked as if it would crack. "I don't think I've ever been happier in my life."

Even Alecto's lips were upturned in the semblance of a smile.

They sipped water, ate protein bars, and gave their muscles time to stop quaking from the effort of traversing the tunnel. They switched their rappelling harnesses for weapon belts, each tucking a pistol into a shoulder harness, with a rifle across the back.

"This way," Jack said. He headed to the right, following the path lit by dim yellow lights embedded into the rock ceiling.

The women followed behind him, their feet crunching lightly on the gravelly dirt path. Jack held his rifle at the ready, mentally preparing himself for whatever he'd find at the end of the tunnel and the entrance to A.H.D.N.A.

26
U'VOL

U'Vol Vree had taken the first kill in the new M'Uktah hunting grounds on the planet K'Sarhi. After he lifted the still-beating heart of his prey into the air for all Vree to see, they swiftly fanned out across the esplanade and hunted with vigor. Nearly four years had passed since he had hunted, and his bloodlust ran high. He quickly took down three more Sarhi and ate their hearts before he was sated. Within minutes, Sarhi bodies were strewn everywhere.

The Sarhi panicked and attempted to flee the wide-open area in which the *Wa'Nar* had landed. They screamed as they ran, headed toward the streets that led to the park. The Vree chased them, killing many before they made it out of the area. When the park was nothing but carcasses, U'Vol gave the order to continue their advance.

U'Vol initiated a communication to the piloting crew aboard the *Wa'Nar.*

The lead pilot, Tu'Rhen, answered him promptly. "Yes, Captain."

"Send the game dressing and packing crews out immediately. There are abundant fresh kill for them to attend to."

"Yes, Captain. I will dispatch them straightaway."

"Advise them to be vigilant, Tu'Rhen. This K'Sarhi is unlike any world we have hunted before. These Sarhi were easily dispatched, but their warrior forces may be on their way."

On board every Vree hunting expedition were a crew of Vree'Sho, the ranchers and farmers of the Vree class. They were well versed in methods to clean, dress, and prepare the fresh kills for storage and export. They would get the fresh meat quickly to the freezer compartments aboard the *Wa'Nar* before it spoiled.

U'Vol was at the back edge of the Vree advance. He looked back at the Wa'Nar before he exited the open-air plaza to enter the fray in the streets. The Vree'Sho crew was already exiting the *Wa'Nar* and busy at work preparing the carcasses for travel.

U'Vol left the plaza and entered a wide boulevard, now empty save for dozens of dead Sarhi. His men were further ahead and had fanned out in several directions down side streets radiating from the central boulevard.

Through his cerebral implant, U'Vol simultaneously monitored multiple communication channels. A loud, thunderous explosion of gunfire erupted at the same time as his comm link crackled with reports of the first encounter of Sarhi counter-aggression.

U'Vol was on all fours within seconds, the krindor electronics coupled with his genetically engineered body allowing his spine to undulate and his limbs to move as a canine's. He headed down a street to the east and stopped when he saw a mass of bodies ahead.

He analyzed the scene with the computer-assisted eyes in his helmet. The throng contained at least twenty Sarhi, but they were not as vulnerable as the first they had encountered in the park. These Sarhi wore primitive body armor. The armor was surely made to protect against Sarhi weapons, but the M'Uktah would have no trouble ripping through it. The graphene and drosh metals used to construct the krindors and the mechanized claws could cut through every material they had ever encountered. He watched as his men did just that. The Vree claws sliced open the chests of the Sarhi prey as if their primitive armor was no more than a thin layer of silk.

The armored Sarhi also held weapons in their hands. Some were short metal objects while others were long, but all seemed to work on the same principle. A primitive firing mechanism caused a small explosion that shot a metal pellet at the intended victim. M'Uktah had used such weapons in their distant past, but once they discovered how to control and manipulate plasma and manufacture advanced metals, the gunpowder weapon had become obsolete.

U'Vol watched as the Sarhi warriors stood their ground, firing round after round upon the M'Uktah hunters, but the bullets did not penetrate the krindor armor. U'Vol's heart soared with pride in both his Vree as well as the M'Uktah scientists who had worked to improve the krindors since the Kreelan uprising. The Sarhi warriors fell one by one while he had not lost a single Vree.

U'Vol had to admit, though, that the Sarhi fought bravely even if their primitive technologies meant they were woefully underpowered.

The Sarhi stood their ground. As the Vree advanced further into the city, they encountered new waves of Sarhi warriors. *These Sarhi are worthy adversaries, unlike the craven Navimbi.*

U'Vol had an incoming message from Tu'Nai at the front lines. "Look at this," the message read. Once U'Vol acknowledged the message, his optical interface synced live with what Tu'Nai was seeing. The Sarhi had moved large metal vehicles into the streets. As U'Vol watched, the Sarhi fired a weapon that protruded from the front of the large box of a vehicle. The large weapon appeared to be simply a bigger version of the small, handheld ones that operated on a gunpowder method, but the punch was significantly larger. Two M'Uktah were down.

"Are they dead?" U'Vol asked Tu'Nai.

"No, just injured, my Captain. But we will need medical and reinforcements in this area if we are to advance further."

U'Vol immediately relayed the information to the crew of the *Wa'Nar*, along with the order for a medical team and additional Vree to assist in Tu'Nai's quadrant.

Typically, during the first hunt in new hunting grounds, U'Vol would take the first kill then hunt at the edges of the fray for a few hours before returning to the landing ship. He would monitor the hunt from the landing ship until the meat storage was full, then he would return with his crew to the *Dra'Knar*. Fresh crews would be sent to the planet to hunt, day after day, until the holds of the *Dra'Knar* were full. It was a very large ship, thus the hunt could conceivably last for months.

This K'Sarhi planet was not typical, though. Even the Kreelan had not the sort of advanced technology and firepower that the Sarhi had. Instead of making his way back to the *Wa'Nar*, he decided to stay with the hunt.

Eponia's worried words came back to him. *"There is bad fortune for you in the scryr's tea leaves."* He had laughed off her fears. U'Vol had never taken the cryptic warnings of so-called seers seriously. The scryrs were frauds, telling womenfolk what they wanted to hear. After all, how could tea leaves reveal his future?

Then why do all of my senses warn me?

U'Vol batted the nagging worry out of his mind the way he swatted down a Sarhi who came at him with a sharp knife. He tore through the Sarhi's body as though it was little more than an underripe fruit. He left it for the cleanup crew as he made his way to the front lines. The M'Uktah would take this city. He would see to it.

27
JACK

Jack, Anna, and Alecto walked about two hundred yards and found a small opening in the rock at the end of the tunnel. It was no more than three feet tall and even less wide. Jack hoped he would fit through. Tex had come that way, but he was of a smaller build than Jack.

"I'll go through first," Jack said. He got belly down on the gravel floor of the cave and shimmied through, using his elbows to pull himself.

The place smelled like a dank basement. After only a few feet into the opening, warmer, moist air hit his face.

"What do you see?" Anna asked. She was on her belly too, her head poking into the small entryway.

Jack switched on his headlamp and scanned the area. "Well, it looks like an empty cabinet."

"That's odd."

He laughed. "For this place? Not the strangest thing you're likely to see."

Jack knocked on the wood panels in front of him. After a few hard raps, one finally swung open. Warm, moist air rushed into the small cabinet. The room into which he peered was mostly dark, but low-watt bluish-white lights lit the floor and ceiling perimeter. He turned off his headlamp so that his eyes could adjust to the dim light.

"I don't see or hear anyone. I'm going in," he said. When he reached the edge of the cabinet, he toppled down about six inches onto a dusty concrete floor. The room he fell into was quiet, the only sound a low hum that sounded like the buzz of fluorescent lights. Jack instinctively pulled the rifle from his back and moved slowly and quietly a few steps into the room. He neither heard nor saw movement. He bent down to the opening. "It's clear. Come on through."

The walls of the room were filled with floor-to-ceiling cabinets and a couple sinks. Anna tumbled onto the floor behind him. Jack moved ahead slowly and found row after row of what looked like smooth, rectangular black-topped lab tables. Lighted cabinets were in the center of the room, and Jack headed that way.

Anna sidled up next to him, her rifle drawn as well. "What is that?"

"I don't know." Jack hadn't heard Alecto come through the opening. He looked behind and was startled when Alecto moved past him. She walked so quickly and quietly, an invisible force seemed to pull her forward.

Jack and Anna followed her to the illuminated cabinets. His eyes had grown accustomed to dim light during the journey through the dark tunnel. Looking at the glass cabinets lit by bright white halogen bulbs hurt his eyes.

Alecto stood by the first case and stared. Her back was straight and rigid. She blinked rapidly but continued to stare into the case.

Inside was a glass cylinder filled with dingy yellow liquid, and floating in the liquid was a small being no more than six inches long, its dead eyes eternally open and black as night. It was a fetus, and if it had been a bit more mature when it died, it would have been nearly identical to Tex. A placard sitting on the glass shelf read, "H.A.L.F. 6."

On the shelf next to the H.A.L.F. 6 was another glass canister, larger than the first. It contained another dead creature with its eyes closed. It was larger than the first, but its limbs were too short to be normal, its hands curled into two stumps without fingers. Both its head and chest were cleaved in the center. The placard next to that one read, "H.A.L.F. 7."

Alecto moved slowly from cabinet to cabinet. She silently took in the eerie spectacle of the failed attempts to create a hybrid which came before her.

Anna put a hand on Jack's shoulder. "This is so—"

"Creepy," Jack said.

"I was going to say disturbing. But creepy works, too. Why would they keep these?"

Jack had no answer. He couldn't comprehend anyone working to create what was intended to be essentially a slave race to be used as the creators saw fit. He wondered if those tiny beings had suffered before they died. *And did they die naturally, or did Sturgis order them killed?*

Alecto stopped at the last cabinet and stared into it at a container larger than any of the others. What appeared to be a full-term baby rather than a fetus floated in the yellow liquid. It was fully formed and looked normal—at least, as normal as any human-alien hybrid looked. It had no obvious deformities and was of a size to be viable. As Jack inspected it more closely, he saw something wrong with its head.

"What is that? On its head."

Alecto moved even closer to the case and looked where Jack was pointing. She blinked her huge black eyes a few times as she cocked her head to the side and examined the dead hybrid. Her voice was its usual monotone. "That is a gunshot wound."

The placard beside the specimen read, "H.A.L.F. 11."

Anna stood on the other side of Alecto. "Aren't you number ten?"

Alecto nodded. "It is—was—my sister." Her eyes were riveted to the dead black eyes of the baby sister she would never know.

Anna touched her arm. "Come. Let's leave here."

Alecto allowed Anna to lead her away from the gruesome scene. Jack followed closely behind. They passed more rows of lab tables. A red light to his left caught Jack's eyes. He recognized it from his previous time at A.H.D.N.A.

"There's a keycard scanner over there," he said. "That means there's a door."

"Be ready. We don't know what we'll find on the other side," Anna said.

Suddenly, Jack was hearing only his own footsteps, not the footfalls of Anna and Alecto. He looked back, and Alecto was standing as still as a stone, her eyes distant.

"What is it?" Jack asked.

Anna shrugged.

"Commander Sturgis," Alecto said. Her voice was low and sounded far off. "She is here."

"We know she's at A.H.D.N.A.," Anna said. "That's one of the reasons we came down here."

Alecto darted away from them.

"We walked through this whole room," Jack said. "If she's in here, she's hiding herself well."

Alecto ignored him. She arrived at the far right wall and stopped. Her hands moved frantically up, down and across the wall, feeling and searching for something.

Jack ran to her. "What are you doing?"

She opened her mouth to answer, but before she got any words out, her hands flew to her head. Her eyes pinched shut, and a high-pitched cry escaped her lips.

Anna was at her side. "What is it?" When Alecto did not answer, Anna looked at Jack. "What happened to her?"

"I have no idea. One minute she was feeling along the wall with her fingers, the next she was like this."

The way she grimaced and held her head reminded Jack of how Tex had looked when he'd been contacted by the Conexus on their trip to Sedona. Ian had told them the Conexus were effectively stranded in their future now, unable to travel back in time since Erika, Ian, and the rest stole their time-travel machine.

"It can't be..." he said.

"Can't be what?" Anna asked, panicked.

"Alecto, are the Conexus trying to talk to you?" Jack asked.

Her eyes squinted open slightly, and she looked at him. Her words were clipped and low. "Not... Conexus." She groaned. "They call to me." She rubbed her bald temples. "Not all at once!" she screamed. Alecto flung her hands into Jack's chest and stared up into his eyes. "Make it stop. Please."

Jack was taken aback by the pain on Alecto's face. His throat was dry and tight. When he spoke, his voice was hoarse. "You were searching for something?"

Alecto nodded, and her voice rasped. "Behind the wall." Her hands flew to her head again as though she was attempting to squeeze the pain out. "I feel them."

Jack and Anna searched the wall as Alecto had. They opened cabinets and felt inside, searching for another hole in the wall or false panel.

Anna shouted, "I found something!" She was on her hands and knees halfway inside a cabinet. She knocked and beat at the wooden paneling. It finally splintered. "Jack, come give this a kick. You should be able to break it open."

Anna moved aside, and Jack kicked at the brittle wood at the back of the cabinet. He aimed for the spot where Anna had broken through. On the third kick, the wood shattered into pieces. A reddish-orange light spilled into the room through the cracked wood. Jack pulled at it until he widened the opening enough to fit through.

"Definitely something on the other side," he said. Jack again got onto his stomach and squeezed through the narrow hole he had made.

The room he'd just come from was brightly lit in comparison to the narrow stone corridor he crept into. It was much like the hall, cut into stone that had led from the tunnel entrance to the lab, but this hall was barely one person wide, and the lights embedded in the low rock ceiling were an orange-red rather than yellow.

Jack peered into the darkness but saw nothing. He stood as still as he could, straining to hear footfalls or other evidence of movement. He heard only his own breathing.

He knelt and called back through the opening. "Come on through."

He had his rifle at the ready as he cautiously stepped forward. The passageway was so narrow that his shoulders scraped the rock as he walked.

Alecto and Anna made it through. Alecto still gripped at her head and grimaced, but she kept moving forward.

"They are near," she said.

"Who are the 'they' you're talking about?" Jack asked. His muscles tensed at the thought that he was going to soon meet a band of Croft's mercenary forces. *Or worse yet, what if Sturgis has more hybrids that we didn't know about?*

Alecto only groaned with pain in response to his question.

After about twenty yards, the narrow hall widened slightly and then dead-ended into what looked like a solid rock wall.

"Looks like we've run out of path," Jack said.

Anna squeezed in beside him. "Why would there be a hallway to here if it's a dead end?"

Alecto took her hands from her head and forced herself between them. Able to see far better than they could in the dim light, she homed in on an indentation in the wall and pressed. A small door opened in the wall, and a mechanism jutted out with a place to swipe a keycard and a small keypad.

"We don't have a keycard," Jack said.

Alecto ignored him. She put one thin hand on the keypad, her eyes closed tightly. Her lips were set in a thin line, and her head was covered in a thin film of sweat. After about a minute, a slit appeared in the wall and opened inward.

Alecto didn't wait for Jack or Anna to make sure the room was clear of enemies. She surged forward with preternatural speed into another room cut into the bedrock.

That room was much smaller than the outer room where they'd seen the preserved H.A.L.F.s. It was dark and smelled of stone and iron. Row after row of starkly white cylinders about four feet high with blue lids filled the room. Each lid had a flexible stainless-steel tube coming out of it and going to the next cylinder.

"What are these?" Jack whispered.

"They look like cryogenic containment systems," Anna said.

Jack quietly moved close to one and inspected it more fully. It had no writing or label and looked a lot like the propane gas cylinders he used on his barbeque grill, only larger.

"They know me," Alecto said. She stood next to one of the cryo cylinders, her hand resting on it. Her eyes were wide, and she looked far off again.

Anna moved silently and stood between them. "Is your pain gone?"

"Mostly," Alecto said.

"You said 'they' know you. What's inside of these?" Jack asked.

Her stare had been far off, but she focused on Jack and Anna, her voice matter-of-fact. "They are my sisters." She reached out and touched her other hand to the cryo container on her left. "Thousands of sisters."

28
TEX

Tex was certain he had failed to leave the VLA. He lay in the dust and waited for Dr. Lewis and her crew to arrive and take him back to the dorm. The seconds turned to minutes, but he heard no footsteps. In fact, when he reached out with his senses, he heard nothing but the sound of whistling wind.

He took a deep breath, mustered his courage, and groaned loudly as he pushed himself up to sitting. He wiped his helmet the best he could with his dirty gloves, which helped only marginally. His gloves were as dusty as the helmet, and wiping only seemed to spread the dust around, not remove it, but at least he could see the mini computer screen embedded in the left sleeve of his spacesuit. He tapped it as Dr. Lewis had shown him, but the screen remained blank.

Tex was not one for cursing, but he let one fly as he tried to push down the feelings of panic. "Breathe," he said aloud.

He tapped the screen again, and the display flashed on then off quickly.

He let out another, more emphatic curse.

No one had come to help him, which meant he was not at the VLA. He had indeed gone somewhere. *But where?*

He had not given much stock to the idea that the comm link would work, but at that moment, he wanted nothing more than to hear Erika's voice. Tex was not one to lose his head. He generally remained calm in the face of danger, even when others were losing their minds. That was what he had been trained for, what he had been made for.

He lay there like a helpless newborn, though, with two broken legs and less than twelve hours of oxygen. His chest tightened, and his throat was dry.

Commander Sturgis's voice came to his mind. *"You are a wonder, 9. Don't ever forget that. You can do what others cannot.*

You are unique in all the world. Heal yourself, and get up out of that dirt."

Commander Sturgis—or his imaginary version of her—was right. Healing would take precious energy needed for the return trip, but he had no choice. With two broken legs, he was going nowhere.

Tex mended his broken bones, but the task took valuable time—and oxygen—he couldn't afford. The panic had caused his heart to race and his breathing to become ragged. *So much for slowing down my metabolism.* He figured he had probably burned up an hour or two of oxygen simply by mending his wounds.

Once his bones were repaired, he stood at last. Tex surveyed the horizon from his new vantage point, but the scenery had changed little. In every direction was the same expanse of endless, dusky-coral-colored sand and orange sky. Seeing where land ended and sky began was difficult. The wind was strong and whipped the sand into dunes and drifts.

He was possibly still on Earth. His home planet had sand dunes. He had never, though, seen photographs showing a sky as orange-red as the one he now saw. He sensed no life-forms in any direction. Even in the most remote places he had been on Earth, he always sensed at least the heartbeats of insects. *I do not think I am on Earth any longer.*

Tired of standing like a fly caught in a spider's web, Tex walked. His legs were wobbly, and they felt heavy as he trudged through the sand.

He had no map or GPS. He didn't have a landmark to march toward. Because the Conexus archives described great cities on the home planet of the Architects, made of glass with boulevards of creamy marble, Tex had assumed he would land in such a city. He presumed that when he appeared out of thin air in a populated area, he would be surrounded by people and taken to leaders who knew about the galactic highway, but his plans were like the sands blowing aimlessly in the wind. He saw no great city of gleaming glass, and no denizens of the harsh sandy planet greeted him.

The sun was high overhead, so he presumed the time was midday, but he had no way of knowing how long a day lasted on that unknown planet.

His legs ached, and his feet felt like they were burdened with lead weights. *Perhaps the gravity is stronger on this planet than on Earth.* He certainly felt heavier. Walking through sand and up and down dunes was slow going. He kept his head down so the lip of his visor shaded his sensitive eyes.

He occasionally looked up and around. Every time, he saw the exact same thing he had seen countless times before—sand. He saw no evidence of life.

He stopped at the top of a dune and sucked on the tube that supplied water from his life-support backpack. One of the nuisances of his self-induced therapy that made him less vulnerable to humidity and water was the new requirement that his body had for hydration. He now experienced thirst, a sensation previously entirely unknown to him.

As Tex sucked down the lukewarm water, a glint in the sand caught his eye. He rubbed his face shield, trying to wipe away the smudges of dirt. He blinked and looked again, sure he had seen a mirage.

It was there again, though. Something was on the horizon, just beyond a vast sea of dunes indistinguishable from the sea of dunes he had already crossed. Judging by how much ground he had covered and his current pace, he figured reaching the strange glint in the sand would likely take at least another Earth-time hour.

He set off toward the glimmer. He had no idea what it was, but at least it was something different from the endless dunes he had already trudged over. His steps were faster though not as swift as he would have liked. Despite the biosuit's climate control, he was getting hot. A thin film of sweat covered his forehead and neck.

He trudged toward the shining object for what seemed like hours, each drift the same as the last. The only thing keeping him from lying down on a dune and waiting for the sands to claim him was the hope that shone from that solitary blinking beacon, somewhere ahead of him.

The sun overhead remained high, as though the planet had stopped spinning and he was in perpetual high noon. Stepping forward was like moving a sack of bricks with only a wet noodle for leverage. The oxygen tanks on his back had felt like nothing when he first began but were now like hauling a car strapped to his back.

He walked in a large valley between two high dunes. The sand was harder there and less slippery to walk on. When he began the ascent up the next dune, he made the mistake of looking up and seeing just how far the dune stretched toward the hazy, dusty-red sky. That made him want to stop, but he reminded himself why he was there and kept going.

He panted hard as he reached the top of the dune and nearly collapsed into the hot sand, but he didn't dare sit. He was afraid the sands would swallow him, and he doubted he had the strength to dig himself out. He settled for resting his palms on his knees as he tried to calm his breath to a normal respiration. He rose and sucked more water, hoping that neither his oxygen nor his water would run out just yet. He tapped the screen of the computer embedded into the left arm of his suit. It flickered. He tapped again, harder. The second time, it didn't even flicker. He wanted to rip the little screen out and throw it as far as he could into the dunes, but that would only cause a massive failure in the integrity of the suit and put him in danger, so he settled for cursing at it instead.

He looked up. The mere glimmer he'd seen several miles back was revealed to be a spire of faceted, emerald-green glass. It jutted out of the sand and rose high into the air. It was the first sign of civilization he had seen, and the color and shape matched the visions imparted to him by the Conexus.

The vision was true. I am here.

Tex's heart raced with both anticipation and fatigue. He wanted to run toward the glimmering spire like a child chasing after a wayward balloon. He tried, but his legs were too tired, his boots too heavy, the sand too thick. He settled for walking, but his spirits soared.

After nearly another hour of slogging through the sand, he reached the spire. All the way, he hoped it was only the first sign of the outer edges of what would be a whole city.

As he approached, though, he saw no additional buildings—only one large, triangular spire cut in flawless facets out of solid glass the color of a light emerald. The effect of the facets shining in the sun made the spire look as though it was lit from within. He saw no signs of life either around or inside the spire. *But it had to be built by someone.* The thought energized him to keep searching for the Architects.

Tex circumnavigated the beacon, hoping to find a sign—some symbol or marking—to indicate which way he should proceed. But the glass was smooth and without symbols or writing. It was about thirty paces around and towered at least forty feet into the air above him. It looked as though more of it could possibly be below the shifting sands.

As beautiful as the spire was, it was a disappointment to Tex. It was no more a clue to his bearing or how he should proceed than the infinite grains of sand he was surrounded by.

Hot, tired, hungry, and defeated, Tex leaned against the shaded side of the spire and took a draw of water. The liquid was warm now, nearly hot, yet it still felt good in his parched mouth. A part of his brain worried that the water was warm. It was supposed to be chilled by a special cooling system built into the suit, but that worry was like an annoying gnat buzzing at his ear. His focus on finding the Architects overrode the concern about the warm water. *I'll puzzle over that later.*

The sands shifted beneath his feet, and the ground rumbled. *Great, a damned earthquake.* Tex steadied himself against the spire, hoping he would not be tossed to the ground again.

The sands jostled and slid under him. Tex clung to the spire as the land across from him rose, sand flying, the ground rumbling.

Seeing through the nearly worthless scratched helmet shield was hard, but an object appeared to be rising from the sands about twenty feet away from him. Tex didn't dare take his hands from the spire, for fear he'd be flung wildly and buried beneath the sand.

Finally, the quaking ceased, and the sands settled.

Tex wiped madly at his helmet and wished he could take it off and kick it away like a football. *Damned useless thing.*

Before him was a glass pyramid no more than twenty feet tall and wide. It too was made of the same green glass as the spire. It was also cut with facets that made it glisten in the sun.

Tex gingerly stepped away from the spire and toward the pyramid. Though the pyramid was made of glass, it was solid and thick. He could not see all the way through it to the other side, nor could he see through to the interior. No darkened shapes were visible inside to indicate people or mechanisms within.

Again, no markings, etched symbols, or writing were apparent. Tex felt the pyramid's glass through his gloves and wished he could pitch those as well so he could use his bare fingers. Without access to his onboard computer, he had no way of knowing if removing his gloves for even a few minutes would be safe, so he kept them on.

As he moved his hands along the glass toward the center of the side of the pyramid facing the spire, the glass changed. It did not open, exactly, nor did it melt or break. It simply morphed itself somehow. It was solid one moment, and the next, a small doorway appeared.

Tex peered inside the opening. It appeared to go nowhere, yet it was a door. The idea of putting himself inside the tiny vestibule gave him pause. It had not been there seconds before and led nowhere. It could easily close in on him as soon as he was inside, encasing him in the thick glass like an insect in amber.

But what other choice do I have? I cannot very well remain planted here in the sand forever. He had no way of knowing how much time had elapsed, but his oxygen supply would not last forever.

He stepped a toe over the threshold, and when nothing untoward happened, he took a full step in and then another. As he did, the sand shifted again to reveal a flight of stairs. They descended downward into utter darkness.

Tex had to muster courage to step into a glass wall that could enshroud him for eternity, but stepping into the dark unknown took an even larger leap of faith. He tried to reach out to the world around him to sense bioelectrical energy from sentient beings, but his internal radar reported nothing. For all he knew, the planet was dead and the spire and pyramid were machines continuing to operate even though the people who constructed them were long dead.

No answers were in the kilometers of sand covering the surface, though. If he was to learn anything that could help them defeat the M'Uktah, he had to go below.

Down into the deep. Back into the dark underground, a place he'd vowed that he would never go again when he left the world of the Conexus.

Jack stared at the cryo containers in the dark, hidden cave of A.H.D.N.A. and nearly stopped breathing. He wished he had something to hold onto as Alecto's words, "thousands of sisters," echoed in the chambers of his mind. The memory of Alecto nearly killing Erika was as fresh as though it had happened the day before. The thought of thousands of Alectos chilled him to his core. His mouth was as dry as dirt in the summer desert.

Jack moved forward, deeper into the room filled with cryo canisters holding the embryos of what could become thousands of powerful hybrid beings. His throat hurt as he tried to swallow. His palms were sweaty as he gripped his gun more tightly.

A spot of bright light appeared ahead, and he forced himself to walk toward it. Anna walked in the aisle to the right of him, a row of white cryo canisters between them. She held her gun at the ready, too, her lips pulled into a thin line.

Jack had thought that the nightmarish parade of hybrid horrors in the outer room was the creepiest thing he would ever see.

He was wrong.

The frozen embryos were only part of the story. At the end of the rows of cryo chambers were at least half a dozen machines as large as refrigerators. Each apparatus had a white-enamel-and-stainless-steel oval base about three feet in diameter. Each base had a computer touchscreen affixed to the front on an extendable metal arm. Two stainless-steel tubes came out of each base and snaked up to an ovoid glass container filled with viscous blue-tinted liquid.

Inside each glass ovoid was a hybrid baby. Their skin was gray. Their limbs were thinner than a human baby's and their heads far larger. All of them had their eyes closed, but the eyes were nearly twice the size of a human eye. Like both Tex and Alecto, their noses and ears were tiny afterthoughts on their enormous heads.

Low, persistent pumping and swooshing sounds emanated from the machines.

Jack stared at the tiny beings floating peacefully in the artificial wombs. Anna stood across from him and stared as well.

Jack nearly pissed his pants when someone said, "What are you doing here?"

Commander Sturgis's voice was shrill with anger. She walked briskly toward him with an electronic tablet in her hand. Her hair was pulled tightly into an impeccable twist at the back of her head. She wore no makeup, and her skin seemed more wrinkled and sallow than he remembered it. She had traded her navy-blue suit for a white lab coat and dark slacks.

She glared with narrowed eyes in his direction. He was sure she was going to strike him, but she approached then pushed right past him.

Alecto's voice was a full octave higher than usual. "I am following orders, Commander."

"I ordered you to stay away. By coming down here, you have put my entire clone operation in jeopardy." Sturgis's voice was pitchy. "Croft has Makers mercenary forces searching for me. You've likely left a bread-crumb trail leading them to me."

Alecto's voice was small, her eyes downcast. "I am sorry, Commander."

"They couldn't have followed us because none of them saw us." Anna squeezed between two womb machines and interjected herself between Sturgis and Jack. "By the way, I'm happy to see you too, Aunt Lilly." Her voice was firm, the sarcasm evident. Clearly, she was not afraid of her aunt the way Alecto was.

Sturgis's anger gave way to a weak smile. She hugged Anna lightly. Anna lifted one arm from her gun to give a half-hearted hug back.

"Don't be harsh with Alecto. You ordered her to protect me. Since I insisted on coming down here—well, what was she supposed to do then?"

Sturgis's face became a bit less pinched. She tucked some of Anna's stray hair behind her ear. "I'm sorry you lost your father.

Robert and I had our differences, but he was my brother, and I loved him."

Anna wiped a tear with the back of her hand.

Sturgis lightly touched the pink scar slashed across Anna's brow. "Lizzy gave you this?"

Anna nodded.

Sturgis's lips pursed, and her eyes darkened.

Jack wanted to wrap Anna in a hug. He figured that wouldn't go over well with Sturgis, so he opted for leaning closer to Anna so that he was subtly touching her.

"Mr. Wilson, it seems that you have beaten all the odds and survived a meeting with the Croft family." Her steely eyes bored into him as if she could read his every thought.

Jack shifted uneasily. He wanted to say something clever. He wished he had the gift of snarky comebacks as Ian and Erika did. All he could get to come out of his mouth was, "Yes, ma'am."

Sturgis's thin lips pursed. "Sewell took it upon himself to involve you in something you should never have been a party to."

Jack found his tongue. "I think you did that when you kidnapped us in Sedona." *Erika would be proud.*

She scowled at him.

Before Sturgis had the chance to erupt, Anna said, "Jack saved my life more than once." She took his hand in hers.

He wasn't sure that a public display of affection in front of her psycho Aunt Lilly was the best idea, but if Anna could be bold about it, he could be too. He squeezed her hand in his.

Sturgis noticed the handholding and rolled her eyes.

"Problem?" Anna asked.

"If you want to throw your future away on a boy that's beneath you, I won't interfere. I've given up being part of trying to control what happens in my family. My work is everything to me now."

Her intentionally demeaning dig at him should have offended Jack, but he was too busy being glad that Sturgis wasn't going to try to off him because he was with her niece.

Sturgis's tablet sounded an alarm. She glanced down at it. "You must excuse me. It is time to make my rounds."

She pushed past them and stopped at the first artificial womb machine. She pulled the computer touchscreen up to a readable position then tapped the screen. A page of graphs, numbers, and other data appeared.

Anna interrupted her. "These babies are human-Conexus hybrids?"

Sturgis didn't look up as she used the tablet to take a photo of the computer screen. "Yes."

Alecto moved forward and entered the conversation. She asked the question that Jack wanted answered. "But why?"

Sturgis had her back to them but turned. "Years ago, I was given a mandate to create a hybrid army."

Anna said, "We know about your orders. But now, you know that the army was supposed to be for the benefit of Croft and the Makers, not the people. You're not going to give him what he wants, are you?"

Sturgis tittered. "Of course not. Don't be daft." She touched a graph on the computer screen and entered a command on the touchscreen keyboard. "I'm done with Croft. These hybrids will be used for their intended purpose."

"What's that?" Jack asked.

"To preserve humanity."

Jack let out a dry laugh. "Then you better shoot 'em up with some growth stimulation hormone or something 'cause by the time they're old enough to walk, humanity might already be history."

Sturgis stopped typing. Her voice was soft. "I have developed technology decades ahead of what's going on up there. But still I may be too late."

She swiped left on the screen, and it went dark. She pushed the screen gently back down to its storage position and moved quickly to the next womb machine.

"You are not too late." Alecto's voice was quiet but did not quaver. "I am here. And 9 is helping too."

Sturgis turned to them and forced a small smile that crinkled the skin around her eyes. "9 has special gifts—that is true. If he has decided to help, then perhaps there is hope."

Sturgis's comment ignored Alecto's prodigious abilities. Jack felt a pang of sadness for Alecto. The poor girl wanted only to please Sturgis, but even though Sturgis had hunted Tex like an animal to be put back in its cage, she openly preferred him to Alecto. Jack could understand Alecto's seemingly confused feelings about Tex. One minute, she seemed to want to be his sister, but at other times, the sibling rivalry was evident.

Sturgis continued her work as she spoke. "I assume you did not come all the way here for a family reunion."

"Actually, that's exactly what I came for," Anna said. She fingered the pistol in the holster at her side. "Lizzy and I have unfinished business."

Sturgis glanced up at her. "An eye for an eye? Isn't that a bit archaic for you?"

"She killed my father. Thomas would be dead now if it weren't for Alecto's healing. And Croft turned my own mother against us."

Sturgis interrupted Anna's rant. "Why do you think your mother is against you?"

"My mom is the one who called Lizzy and let her know Dad was coming over to the penthouse. Lizzy was ready for him when he walked in."

Sturgis gave a wry chuckle. "And you trust what Lizzy tells you?"

Anna shifted her feet. "It seemed credible. My mom is a Croft, after all."

Sturgis's eyes were soft. "You know, I was never a fan of your mom. I thought it was a terrible idea for Robert to marry her. My mother was behind it, like some kind of medieval consolidation of royal bloodlines or something." Sturgis's lip curled up in a sneer. "But I'll say this about your mom. Hannah is an honorable woman. She keeps to her word. That's not something I can say about Lizzy. So you've come all this way for payback?"

Anna pointed at her damaged eye. Her voice had a steely edge Jack had never heard before. "The scars you can see are nothing compared to the ones you can't."

Jack rubbed Anna's back. "This is more than a revenge mission, though. Croft had a mole at the CDC. The guy stole the Conexus antivirus and all of the work Drs. Randall and Montoya had done on synthesizing a stable antivirus."

Jack's statement got Sturgis's attention. "That I did not know. We can't allow him to get away with that."

"No, we can't," Jack said.

Sturgis narrowed her eyes at him then smiled. "You're starting to grow on me, Mr. Wilson."

Jack was relieved that she no longer wanted him dead, but he still wished he was a few states away from her. The woman creeped him out.

Anna squeezed his hand. "We need to eliminate the Croft threat once and for all and get that antivirus back into Dr. Montoya's hands."

"We could use your help," Jack said. "If I recall correctly, this place is full of blind corners, traps for the unwary. And with only three of us against a small army—"

"We need an advantage," Anna said.

Sturgis steepled her fingers beneath her chin. "No one knows this place better than me." She pushed the computer screen she had been working on down and away. "There are secrets to A.H.D.N.A. that only I know. I'll give you the advantage you need to prevail."

U'Vol ran on all fours toward the front lines of the M'Uktah assault on the Sarhi city. His heart thrummed, but his mind raced even faster. Never before had he experienced being underpowered during a hunt, and never before had scouting reports so inadequately described the situation they would find at new hunting grounds.

These Sarhi were far more advanced—and clever—than the reports revealed. *At least the reports I was given.* U'Vol had to allow that thought. That was an entirely new idea to him—that he, the captain of the *Dra'Knar*, would be kept in the dark about valuable information—but the idea bloomed in his mind like the blossom of the kiknari flower on lush Ghapta. It was, in fact, the only thing that made any sense. *But why would anyone keep from me details about how adaptable these creatures are and how formidable their defensive capabilities?*

And so we must adapt as well.

He contacted Tu'Rhen, commander of the pilot crew aboard the *Wa'Nar.* "Relay this message to the *Dra'Knar.* I want armored vehicles down here now. Tell him to send the *Rik'Nar* down with all of the armored transport and as many Vree as he can pack into it. Report back to me at once with the estimated time of arrival. They should land at these coordinates." The computer embedded in his brain synchronized with his krindor and merged U'Vol's coordinates into the message he sent to Tu'Rhen.

"Yes, Captain." Tu'Rhen blinked off.

U'Vol's optical interface was quiet for a few minutes at least. His thighs burned, and his back ached, but he pushed the pain signals aside. He had no time for it. He ran through the empty streets of the Sarhi city. Here and there, Sarhi bodies were strewn about, bloody but lifeless, waiting for the Vree'Sho crew to catch up to the hunt. Fortunately, the temperature cooperated with them. K'Sarhi was still bathed in darkness, and the air was cold. The meat would not rot in the warming rays of K'Sarhi's star before it could be cleaned and dressed for transport.

He came across a few Sarhi that were ravaged but still alive. He quickly put them out of their misery. He logged a notation to chastise the Vree crew that had hunted that area. Leaving prey mortally wounded but alive was against Vree regulation—and certainly against their hunter ethics. The sloppy work made his anger rise.

His ire gave way to nagging concern, though, when he found the first body of a fallen Vree. The man was still ensconced in his krindor. U'Vol inspected the body but remained confused as to what could fell a Vree hunter still wearing his krindor. The graphene-and-drosh armor was impenetrable by nearly any method the engineers had ever tested. Fueled by the bioelectrical energy of the Vree wearing it, the krindor bonded to the wearer and became like a second skin, powered by the user's bioelectric energy and operated by his brain the same way his organic body was.

U'Vol was not much for religion, but he had a strong connection to Doj'Madi as all Vree did. He said a prayer to Doj'Madi for his fallen Vree crewmember then moved on.

He had not gone far when he found another of his crew. That man's head had been shot into a bloody, mangled mess, the face unrecognizable. The man's helmet had been blown off and lay a few leg spans away.

U'Vol had never considered before that the helmet they all wore posed a potential vulnerability. But they had never faced a species with gunpowder, either. The Sarhi who killed this Vree had made a very lucky shot through the open mouth of the helmet's hinging jaw. The bullet pierced the flesh of the fallen Vree hunter and took him down.

Though U'Vol was concerned about the vulnerability that posed to all the Vree, a Sarhi would have to be an excellent marksman to hit such a small hole while moving and being hunted by a Vree. Clearly, it was possible, though, as the dead mate before him proved.

U'Vol placed his fingertips on the Vree's eyes and pushed them closed. He prayed to Doj'Madi to guide the dead hunter's light body to the eternal hunting grounds to be with his ancestors and brothers of the hunt.

As he rose, he caught sight of a body in the distance. Its pale, nearly bone-white skin shone in the midday sun. It was a stark contrast to the black pavement on which it lay.

U'Vol ran to it. The dead was one of his own. The Vree's large body lay entirely naked, stripped of both his helmet and krindor. The Vree lay diagonally beside a dead Sarhi, its size dwarfing the adult Sarhi body and making it look like a child. He searched the area for the missing krindor and helmet of the fallen Vree, but it was nowhere to be seen. The Sarhi warriors had taken it.

His interface flashed yellow, indicating an incoming message on a secure channel only he had access to. He blinked once slowly to allow the message through.

"Captain, Tu'Vagh reports there are no armored vehicles aboard the *Dra'Knar*. Repeat. No armored transport to send down, sir."

He felt as though the K'Sarhi ground shifted beneath him. Heat rose to his face, and his ears filled with the whooshing sound of pumping blood. If he had not been kneeling, he might have fallen over.

U'Vol had specifically ordered twenty armored transport vehicles for this expedition. He recalled how the Council of U had denied his request for twenty, citing financial reasons, but they had approved half what he'd requested. He wanted ten anyway but knew that if he requested ten, they'd give him only five. Early on, U'Baht, his mentor and friend, had taught U'Vol that was how the Council and politics on Uktah worked.

U'Vol had never thrown up in his life and had rarely known the feeling of a queasy stomach, but that news coupled with the sorely lacking accuracy of the scouting reports threatened to make him dump the contents of his stomach on the ground.

Nausea was quickly supplanted with perfect rage. "Banch-nagging spurl-chucking grash phister." He hurled the string of some of the most crass expletives the M'Uktah knew across the uplink. It was vulgar enough to make even a battle-hardened Vree blush, but he cared not who heard him. He wished only that Tu'Vagh had been on the receiving end of his tirade rather than the pilot of the *Wa'Nar*.

Tu'Vagh, his first officer on the *Dra'Knar*, was responsible for checking the manifest before each trip. Part of his job was ensuring that everything that was supposed to be on board was and that anything not required was put off before they left. Tu'Vagh was responsible for the error that the armored transports were not aboard the *Dra'Knar*.

A chill began at his navel and ran up his spine, freezing him to his marrow. *Sabotage.*

What if my expedition was never meant to be successful? He rolled the idea around in his head, piecing together all that he could remember of the preparation for and argument in the Council of U about the hunt. *Perhaps some planned for me never to return?*

Doj'Owa's eyes—yellow, cold, and glaring—flashed into his mind. She had hated him as long as he could remember, though he had never been sure why. He recalled her smugness toward him at the last meeting of the Council of U, her callous disregard of his concerns over the safety and advisedness of the expedition.

As he searched his memories, another chill shook him to his core. Doj'Owa had been the one to argue strongly in favor of advancing Tu'Vagh to first mate aboard the *Dra'Knar*. Tu'Vagh had been on the short list for the job, but he was not U'Vol's first choice. The fellow had always seemed overly ambitious for U'Vol's taste. Most Vree showed zero concern for politics and even less inclination to care about political battles. Tu'Vagh was the rare exception to the rule, which had made U'Vol uneasy. Tu'Vagh had apparently shown a greater than usual generosity to the Temple of Doj'Madi. That had won him Doj'Owa's favor.

She handpicked him to be a saboteur of this mission. It was a wild accusation, but with the facts before him, it was also wildly plausible.

Tu'Rhen made no comment about U'Vol's vulgar language and continued, "Tu'Vagh asked me to convey his deepest apologies and beg forgiveness of his captain. He takes full responsibility and awaits judgment upon your return."

"Yes, well, judgment he shall have. Though I doubt he will be so happy to have it when the time comes."

"Captain, there is something else that needs your attention. On the large continent across the ocean to your west—the one the Sarhi call North America—we detected a massive surge of radio waves emitted from a single source."

"Is it a weapon?"

"I conferred with the science officers aboard the *Dra'Knar*, sir. They do not believe it is a weapon. There was a substantial burst that lasted only a few minutes, then it was gone."

"Was this burst directed at the *Dra'Knar*?"

"No, sir."

"And it happened only the one time?"

"Yes, sir. But the transmission was off the charts, Captain. We've never seen anything like it before. I thought you may want to send a crew down from the *Dra'Knar* to check it out."

U'Vol agreed that it was worrisome. A massive energy spike consolidated in one location was never a good sign.

"We need all ground crews aboard the *Dra'Knar* to join the front here. We are far from ready to begin battle on another front." He could not spare even a small portion of his crew already on the ground. "I will investigate this power surge myself. Ready the light travel module. Prepare coordinates to open a gate. Do your best to get me as close as possible to where this radio transmission occurred."

"But sir, I mean no disrespect, sir, but—"

"We have no time to stand on ceremony or concern ourselves with petty offense. Spit it out, man."

"Sir, what if the Sarhi have set a trap, Captain? Perhaps they sent the transmission solely to lure Vree there to investigate. There could be thousands of Sarhi waiting for you. You could wait for the second landing party and take a team of men with you."

Tu'Rhen was making good points. "Did Tu'Vagh tell you how long until the second party arrives?"

A moment of silence passed. "A half rotation of K'Sarhi."

U'Vol laughed a dull, sardonic laugh. "Of course."

"Sir?"

Tu'Vagh knew how desperately they needed additional ground support. U'Vol's request for armored transport made that more than clear. Fresh crews should have been able to arrive in less than half a rotation. Tu'Vagh was purposefully delaying sending crew to the surface.

U'Vol's stomach roiled again. He nearly wished a hole would open in the K'Sarhi ground and swallow him and get it done with. Tu'Vagh was his first officer. He had always trusted the crew under him with his life, but he no longer trusted Tu'Vagh. *And if I cannot trust my First, who can I trust?*

He kept those thoughts to himself. "Just be sure to have the light module powered and ready for me. I am on my way."

U'Vol blinked off his connection with Tu'Rhen. As he picked up speed on his way back to the *Wa'Nar*, he switched his comm to a private, encrypted channel and contacted Tu'Nai.

Tu'Nai had been U'Vol's choice to be his first mate on this voyage. They had served together during the Kreelan uprising and through the battle formed a blood bond of respect and trust. But U'Vol's request had been overridden by the politics that sometimes played a role in shuffling personnel. He had not thought much of it at the time. It was not without precedent that the son of a favored benefactor or wealthy patron was moved up the food chain. If Doj'Owa was in fact the one behind these gross errors in preparation for this expedition, she had played her hand well. Tu'Nai would never have allowed them to leave Uktah without armored transports aboard.

Tu'Nai was on the secure comm link. "Captain?"

"I must leave the landing party, Tu'Nai. You are hereby in command of the land-based forces. Reinforcements will arrive in a half rotation of K'Sarhi."

"Are you going back to the ship, Captain?"

"No. I must investigate a situation an ocean away from here." U'Vol jumped easily over a large, abandoned Sarhi vehicle in his path. He did not stop running as he spoke. "This mission is compromised, Tu'Nai. All Vree on the ground are at risk so long as I remain part of the landing party."

"Captain—"

"It's just the two of us on this channel, Tu'Nai. Speak freely."

"U'Vol, remember the First Canon of Vree? Stay with your brothers. Never separate from the pack."

U'Vol's throat tightened. Tu'Nai's words brought with them a complex tableau of memories laden with emotion. They reminded him of his father, who had first taught him Vree Canon. *Stay with the herd, my son, or risk becoming the hunted rather than the hunter.* The First Canon had been repeated throughout his Vree training. It was hammered home to him when he saw a Vree brother brutally gored by a thukna on his very first hunting expedition. In essence, 'stay with the pack' was at the core of what it meant to be Vree. Separating from the pack was akin to saying, "I am no longer Vree." It was not something he did lightly.

"Tu'Nai, that may be First Canon for all Vree. But captains learn another lesson. Sacrifice, brother. A Captain knows when he must put his own life on the line if it means protecting his crew. Now is such a time for me."

The circuit was quiet.

"I am uploading to you on this secure channel all facts and conjectures I have on the allegation of sabotage of the K'Sarhi hunting expedition by the first officer aboard the *Dra'Knar*. If you make it back to Uktah, see that it gets to Vrath. Promise me this, my brother."

"You have my solemn oath. By Doj'Madi and all the life she brings, I swear I will do this for you."

"And Tu'Nai... should you return and not I, tell my wives and children... tell Eponia—"

"I will tell them that you died with honor in service to your family and all of Uktah. I will tell them that there never was—nor will there be—a finer example of all that it means to be Vree."

U'Vol's throat tightened again, and he swallowed hard. "Thank you, my brother."

By the time they finished their conversation and the upload of information from U'Vol directly to Tu'Nai, he was back at the *Wa'Nar*. He signed off of his communication and tried not to think about Tu'Nai not making it back home. He also pushed aside speculation about what was happening on Uktah. He was certain that someone—or multiple someones—wanted him gone. They had gone to great lengths to ensure it, but going down that rodent hole would get him nowhere in his present circumstances and serve only to draw his attention away from what he needed to focus on.

Through the uplink, he signaled Tu'Rhen of his approach. The doors opened, and the ramp unfurled. He bounded up the ramp. Tu'Rhen was waiting for him at the top.

"Coordinates have been input into the Valo'Kar as you requested, Captain."

U'Vol entered the elevator and rode up with Tu'Rhen to the highest floor of the ship. Command central for the ship was on one end, the Bogha creator on the other.

M'Uktah lore was filled with speculation about the origins of the Mocht Bogha, the vortex of warped space that allowed the M'Uktah to travel across interstellar space. Some M'Uktah scholars argued that the Mocht Bogha occurred naturally. The fact that the vortex was near enough to Uktah to be useful was a welcome coincidence. The clerics urged that it was not coincidence. The Mocht Bogha had been placed near Uktah by the almighty Doj for the M'Uktah to use. The clerics and true believers always found in nature plenty of reason to argue for the superiority of their species and to place themselves above others they encountered. The clerics asked, "Why was the Mocht Bogha only found near our home and not others?" Surely, that was a sign that it was there by design, not happenstance, they argued.

Whether the Mocht Bogha had occurred naturally or had been placed within easy reach of the M'Uktah by the almighty Doj, the M'Uktah learned much about it over the millennia. Just a few dozen years before, the blink of an eye for M'Uktah, engineers finally grasped the principles enough to create mini gateways using the same principles as the enormous Mocht Bogha.

The *Wa'Nar* had the technology on board to warp space around a small module large enough for only one Vree. The module, a Valo'Kar, was necessary only as a protection for the Vree. Warped space caused massive variances in gravity. Anyone traveling through it would feel squeezed and pressed one second, pulled and torn the next. Ears popped, and eyes bulged. It was a highly unpleasant experience. The capsule sought to minimize the effects of the gravitational variances, making for smooth, painless travel.

U'Vol stopped only long enough to drink thirstily and eat several slices of dried phlegering, his favorite fowl. He stepped into the shiny, smooth opaline ovoid module.

While nearly every other craft or vehicle the Vree used was made of ebony drosh or graphene, the Valo'Kar were constructed of an exceedingly rare material manufactured in small quantities. It was called vrana and had been discovered less than a century before by an intrepid scientist searching for a moldable material that could withstand the rigors of a Bogha portal. Vrana was fabricated from a mixture of silicone, titanium, and the rare mineral verisha. Verisha was so uncommon that it had been found only on Kree. Not only was it the key to the incredible plasticity yet strength of vrana, it also imparted the opalescent quality that made vrana beautiful.

U'Vol checked the coordinates on the small control panel embedded in the wall of the Valo'Kar. "You cross-checked these yourself, U'Rheng?"

"Yes, Captain. It should land you in the western third of the continent, in an area that is arid and semimountainous. I referenced data mined from the Sarhi satellite reconnaissance of their own planet. This should land you in a flat basin area with sparse vegetation. Not good for the hunt, Captain."

U'Vol was glad to know U'Rheng had taken the step to verify any information he'd gotten from Tu'Vagh. "Good work, U'Rheng. I will uplink when I arrive."

He tapped the smooth wall of the module, and rows of pale-blue lights came on. He pressed an icon, and the door closed smoothly. "Initiating Bogha generator."

"All systems report stable to proceed, Captain."

U'Vol pressed another icon, and the giant magnets embedded in the *Wa'Nar* both above and below the Valo'Kar became energized by plasma bursts. The Valo'Kar shook like a large egg wobbling on a table. The lights inside the module blinked off while the cabin outside the module was filled with intense white light. The deck outside was filled with the ear-piercing, high-pitched whine of the energized magnets reaching max status, but the Valo'Kar's noise-reduction technology kept it virtually silent inside. U'Vol closed his eyes and tried not to dwell on the reality of being pressed into a quantum vacuum and jolted into an area of compressed space. An alarm would sound when he arrived at his coordinates—it was extremely loud, to jolt a traveler back to consciousness if he passed out on the voyage, a fairly common occurrence.

U'Vol stood upright as no one could sit or lie down in a Valo'Kar. He kept his eyes closed and took a deep breath. He had no idea what he would face in the desert of the western continent. He focused his mind and mentally prepared for battle.

I will not go down without a fight. I am Vree, like my father before me. 'Tis better to die in battle than sitting on my banch.

Eponia would not have agreed. He was glad she was not there to witness what would come next.

U'Vol forced his thoughts away from his home and the delightful laughter of his children. He did not allow himself to dwell on Shree'Ka's swollen belly and whether she was carrying a son or daughter that he would never meet. Most of all, he denied himself memories of Eponia's lithe body next to his.

He focused solely on preparation for battle and ramped himself up until bloodlust ran hot in his veins. He almost pitied the forsaken Sarhi that had the misfortune to meet him when he exited the Valo'Kar.

Erika stood on the sandy ground of the VLA and stared at the spot where Tex had stood mere seconds before. He'd been whole and material and solid. Then he was a shadow of himself, then not there at all.

For a few seconds, all who had witnessed him disappear seemed to collectively hold their breath. Their moment of shocked silence was followed by a loud whoop of excitement.

Erika turned, and someone hoisted her into the air. The scientists hugged each other, their faces wearing broad smiles.

She would have liked to feel the joy they were experiencing. They made someone disappear. For them, it probably hadn't yet occurred that they didn't quite know where he had gone.

Or if he would ever return.

For Erika, though, that was the only question that mattered.

Ian knocked his elbow into her arm. "Ready to head back?"

Despite the warm morning sun, Erika was chilled to the bone. "No."

"Staring at the spot isn't going to make him reappear."

She shielded her eyes from the sunlight and looked up at Ian. She plastered on a small smile. "It might."

He rolled his eyes and sighed. "*Stubborn* doesn't begin to describe you."

"How about *persistent?*"

"No."

"*Tenacious?*"

He shook his head. "I was thinking more along the lines of *obnoxious.*"

Erika flicked her leg up and kicked him lightly in the backside.

"Well, you can stand out here until the buzzards start trying to pluck at you, but I'm going back to bed." He yawned and walked away.

"Ian," Erika called out to him. "Can you bring me—"

"Blankets and some food? Already planned on it."

Ian took his time about it but eventually brought her some supplies for her vigil. Erika wrapped the thick blanket Ian brought around her shoulders and sat in the dust. She'd been there for nearly four hours, and her stomach growled. The pancake and banana Ian had brought her in the morning had worn off long before.

Feet shuffled through the dusty ground behind her. She looked back and was surprised to see Aunt Dana headed her way with a messenger bag slung across her body.

Dana kicked a stone out of the way and flopped down on the ground next to Erika. "I figured you were hungry." She took the bag off and rifled inside. She plucked a square, foil-wrapped parcel out and handed it to Erika.

The foil reminded her of the material Tex's space suit had been made of. The silver square of food was warm and felt good in her cold hands.

"You going to play with it or eat it?"

Erika glared at her sideways. "My hands are cold." She unwrapped the package and was happier than she should have been to find a double-decker grilled cheese sandwich inside. The bread was golden with butter and more soft than crispy, just the way Erika liked it. Orange-yellow cheese oozed out the sides. Even a small packet of yellow mustard was there. Erika wasted no time opening the packet and squirting some on the bite she intended to take first. The gooey sandwich was like magic. It warmed her and lifted her spirits.

"This is exactly what I wanted. And cooked just the way I like it. Thank you."

"I remember, you know. It wasn't that long ago you were a little squirt, running around the cottage, getting into everything. You may be grown up, but you're never too old to want the food from your childhood. Especially when things suck."

Erika downed half the sandwich in three bites.

"You're eating like you're feral."

Erika felt a bit feral. Her life had become an hour-by-hour struggle to survive.

Dana rummaged in the pack and took out a bottle of water. She placed it on the ground between them and dug in the pack again.

That time, she pulled out a black metal device that looked like a thick, long flashlight. She handed it to Erika.

"What's this?"

"A Taser."

Erika guffawed. "For what? Rabid ground squirrels?"

Aunt Dana didn't laugh. "That's military grade. More advanced than civilians can buy. Heck, it's better than what most cops get."

Erika didn't know the first thing about Tasers, so the comparison was lost on her. She stared at Dana blankly. "And? Why did you trudge all the way out here to bring me this?" She gestured with her hand at the empty desert around them. "Not like a high-crime neighborhood."

Dana's brow furrowed, and her lips were set in a thin line. "I overheard some of the marines talking. They said recon in France had recovered armor worn by those aliens. Said they were analyzing it for weaknesses and found one."

Erika waved her hand for Dana to continue.

"Apparently, bioelectric energy powers their armor. They think if we disrupt the bioelectric energy, we can make 'em vulnerable."

Erika put the Taser on the ground. "Okay, good to know. I'll keep that in mind the next time I see an alien out here." Erika finished off the sandwich and crumpled the foil into a tight silver ball.

"Can you cut it with being flippant about everything I say to you?" Dana took a pistol from the shoulder harness under her jacket. "Here. Take this too."

Erika took the pistol, seeing as how Dana was unlikely to leave until she was well armed. She plopped it down in the dust next to the Taser. "Where'd you get this stuff? I thought they confiscated your gun. They took mine."

Dana looked around as if checking to make sure they were truly alone. "I pinched these."

"*You* stole weapons from the US military?"

Dana shrugged and smiled at her.

Erika laughed. "I never thought I'd see the day when one of the Holts broke the law like that." Her dad's family was a long succession of folks working in law enforcement in some form or another. The family had sort of a running joke that, during a natural disaster, the Holts would use the crosswalk rather than jaywalk.

Dana smiled and joined the laugh but quickly brought it back down. "I'm sorry, Erika. For what I did back there at Niyol's. I didn't know who they were. Hell, I didn't understand what Tex was. You know... All I wanted to do—all I care about—is protecting you. I'll do anything to keep you safe. You know that, don't you?"

Erika mulled her words over. The fact was that she had no reason to doubt they were true. She picked up the now-dusty gun and shoved it into her back waistband. She put the Taser on her lap and covered herself back up with the blanket. She didn't know why Dana felt so compelled to give her those things when the predator aliens were an ocean and a continent away, but she was glad to know that at least one person on the planet was looking out for her.

"Thanks," she said. She looked over at Dana and gave her a genuine smile. "We're okay."

A tear welled in Dana's eye, and she looked relieved. She put her hand on Erika's leg and squeezed. "I'd tell you not to stay out here all night, but I know you're not going to listen to me. I'll make sure to get you a sleeping bag and some warmer clothes before the sun goes down."

Dana rose and dusted her butt.

"Thanks. For everything," Erika said.

Dana smiled and walked away, her feet kicking up dust as she left.

Erika resumed her vigil of staring at the empty spot in the dusty desert where Tex had once stood.

Tex was thankful for the light mounted on the helmet of his space suit. He was also glad he had not indulged his whim and kicked the helmet to the sands. He flicked the helmet light's switch and peered down the stairs. Sand blew about the top few steps, but farther down, they appeared to be relatively clean of sand or debris.

What are you waiting for?

He stepped slowly and lightly onto the first step. Then he paused, waiting to see if the stairs shifted or moved, but the step was stable beneath him, so he went down another step.

The farther down he got, the darker it became. At the top of the stairs, the way had been lighted by the bright sunlight filtering in through the glass of the pyramid, but the sunlight was gobbled by the darkness. No lights of any kind lined the stairs.

Tex's helmet-mounted light cast a fairly wide beam, but he could still see no more than three or four feet on either side of himself and no more than five feet in front of him. The stairs were wide, for no matter where his beam of light landed, all he could see were steps made of what appeared to be a swirly cream-and-light-pink marble. Outside, even with his helmet on, he had heard the whistling of the whipping winds, but here, he heard nothing.

He counted the stairs, and as he neared one hundred, a diffuse light appeared ahead of him. It shone on the last few steps and revealed a landing.

A sliver of dim sunlight came from high above. *A glass ceiling.*

The stairs ended at a wide plaza that extended in every direction as far as the low light allowed him to see. Tex ventured forward in the direction of the sun shafts. Though he sensed no life forms, he continued to hope that he could find the Architects.

As he walked deeper into the black void, other breaks of light came from above to reveal wide boulevards of the same pink-tinged marble of the stairs. The boulevards were lined with tall buildings made of the same green-tinged glass and creamy marble.

They were unlike any buildings Tex had ever seen. The facades were ornately carved with swirling patterns that resembled curling cloud wisps or twirling branches and leaves. Others had markings etched into the marble but in a language or symbology Tex did not understand. The boulevards branched this way and that. Tex paused and took it all in. He stood in the heart of the city that the Conexus had shown him in their shared consciousness. If the sands above had not blown over the glass ceiling covering the whole of the city, it would in fact be a gleaming city of green and pink and gold.

He spoke out loud. "It must have been beautiful once." His voice echoed off of the empty stone and glass.

His throat tightened, and his eyes filled with tears. If the planet was dead, that meant his planet would die as well.

He recalled the visions he had received from the Conexus—Earth, as lifeless as the planet on which he was standing, ravaged by disease; nuclear war landing the deathblow. He knew that future could be prevented, but only if he had the help of the architects of the gateway that had brought the predators to Earth's doorstep.

Hope drained from him. He wanted to lie on the dusty stairway and sob. He had come to find answers from the architects of that grand city and of the highway between the star systems, but the throne of the gods was empty. His trip had been for naught. He'd go back to Earth, if he could get back, and have to face them all with no more answers than he had before.

"It was once beautiful beyond compare."

Tex's heart leapt to his throat. Sweat beaded on his forehead again. He was used to hearing voices other than his own inside his head. That was how the Conexus had communicated with him. Yet he was feeling no painful buzzing or discomfort. The voice was clear and distinct.

"Who are you?" He reached out with his preternatural senses but sensed neither bioelectrical nor mechanical energies.

"We are that which you seek."

His heart pounded even harder. "Where are you?"

"At the center and deeper still."

That sounded like a riddle, the kind of thing he might have once taken joy in deciphering, but the endless sands above him had sapped his patience. Fear of being unable to breathe shattered his concentration.

"You need not worry for air. You can remove your breathing apparatus. You will find the environment suitable to your biological unit."

Tex's life experience had engendered in him a cynicism greater than his limited number of years warranted. He wasn't about to subject himself to the potential of nearly instantaneous death by trusting the disembodied voice of an unrevealed source.

"We must gain your trust. We understand. Come to us, our son. You have many questions. We have answers. Meet your ancient ancestors. The Elosians welcome you to your ancestral home."

33
JACK

Sturgis quickly finished making her rounds to check on each of the hybrid fetuses incubating in the artificial wombs. She then led Jack, Anna, and Alecto into yet another narrow passage dug into the rock.

The tunnel was chilly and dark. Ceiling-mounted lights cast some illumination, but they were spaced farther apart than in the first underground shaft they'd walked through. The path twisted this way and that. They passed by a few small holes cut into the rock much like the one they'd used to enter Sturgis's hidden lab.

Sturgis set a brisk pace. She occasionally called over her shoulder, admonishing them to keep up. Jack brought up the rear of their group. The farther they walked, the lower the rock ceiling and the narrower the tunnel. Staying with the others became difficult for Jack because he had to duck and slant sideways at times to make it through the chiseled rock.

After about half an hour, the tunnel ended in a wide room. Like the passageway, it was primitive. The walls were exposed rock marked up from the boring equipment used to create the cave. However, the far wall was covered in conduits, computer screens, digital readouts, lighted panels, and dials. The wall of machinery was at least ten feet high and more than twenty feet long.

"What's that?" Anna asked.

Sturgis stared up at it. "This is the heart and lungs of A.H.D.N.A. and Apthartos."

Jack took in the vast apparatus of interconnected conduits and what looked like on/off valves like the one outside his house for turning the water on and off for the whole house. "This is the master control for the humidity system?"

"It controls that and more," Sturgis said.

"I am no longer vulnerable to water," Alecto said. "The cure that you designed for me was successful." There was obvious pride in her voice.

Sturgis favored her with a small smile. "Ah, so Dr. Randall was able to decipher my notes. Good. The Crofts may be unaware of the change in your functionality. Use that to your advantage. But I can give you a few more advantages as well."

Sturgis walked briskly to a small desk in a dark corner. She pulled a clear plastic earpiece wired to a small black box no larger than a cell phone out of a drawer and handed it to Anna. "Wear this. It's a secure channel."

Anna put in the earpiece, fed the wire down her shirt, and hooked the receiver to the ammo belt at her waist.

A channel to Sturgis was not Jack's priority. "I hope you've got a map too." He had walked the halls of A.H.D.N.A. a few times, but each time, he'd gone a different way. The place was a maze, and he had no idea how to get to the underground city.

Sturgis's voice was full of impatience. "Alecto knows the way."

Alecto did not agree, but she also did not disagree. She remained still and silent, her huge black eyes fixed on Sturgis.

"How many men do you think Croft has down here?" Anna asked.

"I'm not certain. Assume many, and hope it's few. But with stealth and Alecto, you may have a chance of making it to Croft, regardless of their numbers."

Jack didn't like the sound of their odds. "Where do you think we'll find Croft?"

"He is, if nothing else, a supreme coward. I lay odds that he's holed up in the house built for him. It's in the furthest corner of Apthartos. But as I said, he's had armed patrols roaming the halls, looking for me. You're likely to run into them before you even get to Apthartos."

Jack had already witnessed one carnage in Apthartos. He didn't want to be a casualty in another or, worse, lose Anna. "Have you got anything useful to tell us? Like tips on how to infiltrate Croft's underground Alamo? Or are you just going to wig us out?"

Sturgis glared at him. "Croft is brilliant in many ways. But he's also predictable. That's why I always beat him at chess when we were kids." A small smile crept to her lips.

Jack and Anna listened intently as Sturgis laid out her plan for how to get to Croft. They asked questions and fine-tuned the plan while Alecto sat quietly and listened. They went over the timing and key details several times to ensure that everyone was on the same page.

After about the third time Sturgis tried to run through it, Jack found it psyching him out more than helping. "I think we're as ready as we're going to be." He checked the magazine of his pistol, replaced it, and shoved the gun back into his shoulder holster. "Locked and loaded. Let's get going."

"Agreed," Alecto said, the first thing she'd said in over an hour.

Only Anna hesitated. It was odd for her to be the one holding back.

Though Jack was unsure what emotion was playing at Anna's eyes, Sturgis seemed to understand. Her eyes softened, and she hugged Anna loosely, careful of the ammo belt slung across Anna's body. She loosed her hug and held Anna by the shoulders. "You are a Sturgis. You can do this." She lightly kissed Anna's forehead. "Your father would be proud of you. He wanted to stand up to Croft. Did you know that?"

Anna sniffled. "No, I didn't."

Jack knew Sturgis was a skilled liar and manipulator, so what she told Anna could have been complete BS, but her words lifted Anna's spirits, so Jack chose not to question Sturgis's statement.

Sturgis released her grip on Anna. "Now go. Retrieve that antiviral. Many people are counting on us."

Anna nodded and wiped her cheek.

Jack was at the doorway. He looked into the dimly lit hall but saw no signs of Croft's men. Anna and Alecto were at his heels.

"And Anna," Sturgis called.

Anna stopped and looked back.

"An eye for an eye," Sturgis said.

———————————————

Alecto led them through the maze of corridors from the farthest reaches of A.H.D.N.A. toward Apthartos. The pistol she wore looked oversized on her tiny waist. She'd chosen not to carry a rifle too.

Chances were that with her telekinetic weapon, guns were overkill for her anyway.

Jack and Anna had both donned Kevlar body armor. They tried to find something small enough for Alecto, but nothing Sturgis had in her weapons cache was small enough for Alecto's child-sized torso.

They walked quickly. Despite their attempt to be stealthy, their footsteps echoed off the concrete floor and cinder-block walls. Alecto was in the lead and about to turn a corner to head east, but she pulled herself back and flat against the wall. She held her finger to her lips and motioned them to get against the wall as well. She cocked her head and was still as a statue. After a few seconds, she whispered in a voice so faint Jack had to strain to hear it, "Three. All males."

Jack's heart amped up to double time. He knew he wasn't going to make it out of A.H.D.N.A. alive without more blood on his hands, but he didn't relish killing. He took a deep breath and readied himself to round the corner and open fire. A loud thud made him hesitate.

Alecto's eyes were closed, her hand outstretched.

A man said, "What the…? Jamison?"

Another voice screamed in agony but only briefly. Another thud.

Jack moved forward to round the corner, but Alecto pushed him back with one arm.

Someone moaned in pain. His voice rasped, "Stop. Please."

Alecto did not stop, though. A sheen of sweat covered her bald head, and her outstretched fingers trembled, but she persisted. Within seconds, the man stopped moaning. Jack heard a third thud as the man's body hit the ground.

Alecto's whole body shook. She slowly opened her eyes. Her voice was soft and hoarse. "They are… terminated." She wiped the sweat from her brow with her sleeve.

Jack moved cautiously around the corner. Three men lay on the ground. Their eyes were open and glassy, their arms and legs askew. Two of them had blood trickling from their noses. The third had pink froth around his lips.

Jack motioned the all clear. They stepped over the bodies and moved down the corridor.

Alecto took point again. She was even paler than usual.

"Do you need a break?" Jack asked.

"Negative."

"But you look tired," Anna said. "Maybe you should rest a few minutes."

Alecto continued to walk briskly, her eyes forward, her spine erect. "Keep moving," she commanded.

"Hey, Alecto... thanks," Jack said.

Alecto kept walking but tossed a look back at him over her shoulder. "For what?"

"For taking those guys out. You spared me some bullets. And blood spatter."

Anna rolled her eyes and shot him a disgusted look.

"What?" Jask asked.

Alecto continued walking.

If Ian had said that, it would have at least made them smile. Jack didn't have Ian's gift for lightening the mood. Remembering Ian made him miss his friend. *I wonder what's going on in New Mexico?*

They soon encountered another patrol. Alecto had taken out the first three men they'd encountered in less than two minutes total. Those guys hadn't even known what hit them.

The next encounter was not as easy, though. After Alecto took out one man, the other two rounded the corner, guns drawn.

Fortunately, Jack's trigger finger acted more quickly than his brain. Instinct forced him to fire his rifle. The first bullet missed by a mile and blasted chunks of concrete off the wall ahead of them. The second bullet grazed the man's shoulder. Dazed, he didn't get his shot off before Jack's third bullet knocked him to the ground.

The third man limped toward them, his gun up and pointed in their general direction. "Come with me, and Sir Croft will spare your friend here." The man spoke to Anna and indicated Jack as her friend with a slight nod of his head.

As soon as the words were out of his mouth, he dropped his weapon and fell to his knees. His hands were at his temples, his mouth open as if to scream, but no sound came out. His eyes were squished shut, his face pinched in agony. "Please... make it stop." He opened his eyes slightly, tears filling them. "Please," he said to Anna.

Anna's face was contorted with pain as well. Tears spilled down her cheeks. She looked away, and the man fell the rest of the way to the ground. He kicked and writhed for a few seconds more until he finally lay still.

Jack wished he had looked away as Anna had. The man's agony was seared into his brain, part of the collective memories of this ghastly episode in his life.

He put a hand on Anna's shoulder. "Are you sure you want to continue?" Waging a cyber war against Croft was one thing, hacking and infiltrating his servers and phones, but killing was an ugly business. Jack hated how comfortable the rifle felt in his arms, how easily he had pulled the trigger and mowed a man down, but he would put down a thousand more men if it meant Anna would never have to feel the guilt, shame, and sadness he would know for the rest of his life.

She swiped a sleeve across her face and sniffled. She turned to Jack, her eyes a turbulent storm. "Don't ask me that again. Now, let's go." She was careful not to look down as she stepped over another mass of bodies.

Alecto followed.

They had two more encounters that played out similarly to the last, but terminating each man took Alecto twice as long as the last to finish the job.

Alecto's trembling hand was outstretched, her bald head covered in beads of sweat, as the last man writhed on the ground and held his head, screaming for mercy.

Jack had had enough. "Stop," he said.

To his surprise, Alecto did as he asked.

Jack stood over the man and looked down into the guy's teary, puffy red eyes. Jack pulled out his pistol and aimed at the man's head. "You have two choices. Renounce Croft and pledge to help us take him down, or die."

The man's mouth went from being twisted in agony to forcing a derisive smile. He choked as he tried to talk, but finally got out, "You plan to kill Sir Croft?" He chuckled, and it came out as a pathetic croak. His smile faded when he noticed no one else was laughing with him. "You're serious?"

Jack nodded.

"Looks like I'm going to die either way."

Jack flicked his head toward Alecto. "She has single-handedly taken out close to a dozen of his men in the last thirty minutes. I'll take our odds." When he said it out loud, he began to believe it.

The man sat up, and Jack's stomach lurched. "Stay where you are." His palms were slippery with sweat, but he managed to keep his gun trained on the guy.

The Makers guard held up his hands and stood. "My name's Michael Donovan, but people call me Mick. I'll switch sides. What the hell. I'm only in it for the money anyway, and I hadn't planned on dying today. I'll pledge to help you as long as you swear on your mother's life that that thing won't attack me again." He pointed a shaky finger at Alecto.

"My mother's dead," Jack said. His throat tightened, and he swallowed to keep tears away. He indicated Alecto with his head. "And her name is Alecto. She'll leave you be as long as you stay loyal." He got into Mick's face. "But you make a move that puts either of them in danger, I'll kill you myself."

Mick nodded. "Sure. I get it. But you know you don't need to worry about anyone killing the girls, right?"

"What do you mean?" Anna asked.

Mick put his hands down to his sides. "We got orders to bring you both in alive. That's why you've burned through our guys—I mean Croft's men—so easily. We was hamstrung by our orders not to harm the two girls." He turned his eyes on Jack. "Sorry, bud, but you're not so lucky. You're a marked man."

Jack shrugged. "I've gotten used to it."

Anna stepped closer to Mick. "Why does Croft want *me* taken alive?"

Mick shook his head. "Don't know. I'm a grunt, ma'am. A guy like me is hired for one thing. Follow orders without question, and shoot whoever they tell me to shoot. The less I know, the better. Like, take your situation. You got me on your side now. You tell me shoot Croft, I'll shoot him. Don't matter if he was the one giving me orders this morning."

Anna's lip was curled up in a disgusted sneer. Her hands were balled in tight fists at her sides, and she looked up into his eyes. Her voice was low. "Then let me make this very easy for you, Mr.

Mercenary. Our mission is to take William Croft out of this world. You help us, and you live. You even flinch in the direction of giving him aid, and you die. Are we clear?"

Mick gave her a curt nod, his face wearing a sneer.

Jack had the urge to smack the sneer off of the guy's face with the blunt end of his rifle.

Anna eased back from him. "Let's get going, then."

Alecto pushed onward with Mick on her heels. Jack continued to bring up the rear and watch their backs. As he watched Anna's head bob in front of him, he thought about how he hoped to never be on her bad side.

As they walked, Anna and Jack peppered Mick with questions about Croft's location and the extent of the defenses he had already installed around him. Anna tried also to get intel about the stolen antivirus, but Mick said he knew nothing about it. He was less than helpful, but the reason was hard to say, whether because he was withholding information or because he truly knew little.

The only thing remotely useful that he gave them was that two patrols were dispatched twice a day to search A.H.D.N.A. to try to find Sturgis. "One of those patrols radioed that they had heard something and were going to check it out. When they didn't answer the radio call, more patrols were sent out."

"Is Lizzy in charge of the patrols?"

Mick said, "Lizzy? I don't know who you're talking about."

It seemed unlikely that the guy wouldn't know who Lizzy was. Jack let the statement go, but it gave Jack another reason to be wary of the guy.

Alecto turned a corner, and they entered a wide hallway. Jack recognized the place. It was a junction he'd been in before. One corridor led to the lab where he'd nearly died by lethal injection. Another hall led to the administrative offices and the heart of A.H.D.N.A. The hall to the left led to the jail cells where Jack had been a prisoner, and ahead of them down a wide hallway were the double doors that led to Apthartos.

"We're nearly there," Jack said.

"Good. Once we're through the doors, we'll—" Anna said.

The double doors opened, and when they were only halfway, water cannons unloaded on them. The men wielding them, dressed in black Makers guard uniforms, aimed at Alecto, but the water sprayed over Jack, Anna, and Mick as well.

Alecto stood planted and pulled up to her full height, her hands on her hips in defiance.

A woman's voice yelled out in a British accent, "Take her down!" Lizzy Croft stood in the center of a throng of half a dozen men. Her brown eyes were wide and dark with fury.

When Jack had first seen Lizzy in Apthartos, she had worn a businesslike skirt and blouse with high heels and immaculate hair and makeup. Her high heels were gone now. She was dressed in all-black military-style pants, boots, and long-sleeved shirt over which she wore body armor. Her long, chestnut-colored hair was pulled behind her head in a neat ponytail. Her forehead crinkled, and her lips pursed as the water had no ill effect on Alecto.

"Have your dogs stand down so we can talk," Anna said. Her voice was calm, her face smooth and unfazed by seeing Lizzy.

"Talk?" Lizzy tittered. She watched and became angrier by the second as she saw that the water cannons had no ill effects on Alecto. She finally yelled, "Stop! Save it."

The men turned off the water cannons. Jack was soaked and chilled by the cool underground air.

"We have nothing to talk about," Lizzy said. Her lip curled into a derisive sneer as she looked Anna up and down. "Little Miss Perfect. I used to envy you, but now I know the truth. I almost pity you. Almost."

"Truth about what?" Anna asked.

An unsettling grin came to Lizzy's lips. "You'll find out. Now, time for you and the thing to come along like good girls. Father is waiting for you. Say goodbye, Mr. Wilson."

When the Conexus had spoken to Tex telepathically, it made his head feel as if it was being split open, but the voice he'd just heard in his mind did not cause an agonizing buzz or dizziness. *Maybe I'm going mad.* He also considered the possibility that he was running out of oxygen and his mind was starved for the chemical element that sustained it.

Even if he was going mad or suffering from hypoxia, he answered the voice that had referred to itself as Elosian. "Where are you? Show yourself to me."

His voice had more edge to it than he had intended, but he didn't regret it. He was too hot, tired, and frustrated to care if he offended. *Perhaps I was not the best choice to be a diplomat for humanity with a new species.*

The voice repeated its prior direction. "At the center and deeper still. Come to us, Bodaway."

Tex had been walking, albeit more slowly than he would have liked, but he stopped then, stunned to stillness. They—whoever "they" were—had just referred to him by name. That was the name he was given after his journey of the sweat, but it was still his name.

He tried to rub his temples, forgetting that his hands were wrapped in gloves and his face stuck in a plastic bubble. *I am going mad. I am talking to myself.*

"Reach out to us. Feel our presence. Continue your journey, Bodaway. To the center and deeper still."

He decided to follow the command of the mysterious voice. He had no choice. He could do that or lie down in the dust and wait for death to claim him. That option did hold some appeal for him. He was tired beyond what he had ever experienced—tired of searching, tired of running, of trying to escape.

The memory of Erika's lips on his flitted into his mind. He could nearly smell her citrusy sweat-and-soap aroma. *If I die, I am no help to her.*

Tex made one leaden foot move in front of the other. At that point, his only fuel was the promise of answers. *"Reach out to us,"* the voice had said. Tex closed his eyes, took a few calming breaths, and moved his attention inward. His mind raced with question and worry. Reaching a place of inner calm was more difficult than he had ever found it. He was finally able to focus his attention on the core of his being.

At last, he was aware on a level removed from the material world. At first, he sensed nothing other than the beating of his heart and movement of air through his lungs. He focused deeper still, and after a few minutes, he became aware of what seemed like a second heartbeat. It was faint, like an echo of his own. The second beat came from outside of himself, though. As he concentrated, it became less a beat and more of an awareness of a wave pulse.

The pulse was slow, but it was there. He mentally chastised himself for not noticing it before. It was the sort of thing he should have been aware of, had he not been so focused on the needs of his body in that place.

Somehow, he was able to pick up the pace of his walking. He moved into the dark void ahead of him. Diffuse light trickled down from above but did little to dissipate the darkness.

"That is it. Come to us."

Tex kept his attention deep and removed from the physical. His preternatural speed returned, his feet no longer mired by sand dunes. The only light came from the helmet lamp. Even with his better-than-human night vision, he saw no more than five feet ahead of him at a time.

"You do not need to see to discover," the voice said.

Though the headlamp was nearly useless, he kept it on anyway. It was a comfort that he clung to as he made his way farther and deeper into the blackness.

His foot found air, and he wobbled as he nearly tumbled down a wide set of stairs that he had not seen. *"Deeper still,"* the voice had said. Tex waited at the top of the stairs and allowed his racing heart and wobbly legs to settle. Once his legs were steady, he stepped down, then down again, step after step, deep down into a pitch-black void.

He moved based purely on faith that he was going to see or experience something worthwhile, but his heart fluttered with panic. Deeper and deeper still, the stairs spiraled down and down. He counted until he hit one hundred then stopped counting. He didn't want to know.

Finally, the stairs ended. He moved forward cautiously, his feet skimming along the surface gingerly, hoping not to find another set of stairs.

The low, constant thrum was stronger there than it had been above. He sensed the wave pulsing through him then with his human senses rather than only noticing it in the void of pure consciousness.

He shone his helmet light down and saw he was walking on stone. It had been smoothed and appeared worn by the ages, but it was not the slick, colorful marble of the city above. He still saw no lights. His vision remained limited to only a few meters in any direction.

Each step on the stone floor echoed loudly. He felt as though he was walking into a forbidden sanctuary.

After twenty paces or so, he came to a wall. It was not made of the pink or coral-colored marble of the city above. He reached out and touched it. The wall was made of smooth glass. The light from his helmet glinted off the glass but was unable to penetrate through to reveal anything within. *It must be thick.*

"You are nearly there, our son. Step inside."

He would have gladly stepped inside if he could find a door. As with the green pyramid on the planet's surface, though, as he walked along the edge of the glass structure, he found only meter after meter of smooth green glass.

He turned a sharp corner, and his hands slid along the glass as he walked the edge. He searched for a mechanism or lever, a handle or a button, but as with the pyramid above, an opening suddenly appeared.

Tex cleared the glass threshold and walked pace after pace down a corridor made of glass. The thrum of the wave vibration that had been a low beat in his belly grew in intensity and rattled his chest.

Something shifted beneath his feet. The subtle rattle of his chest boomed like a cannon firing. Tex braced himself by placing a hand on either side of the narrow glass corridor. The thunderous roar of engines filled the space. A mechanical beast groaned as if angry after being awoken from hibernation. After so many hours in nearly total silence, the sound of machines was nearly deafening but also like sweet music to his ears.

The structure he was in vibrated so much that his vision blurred. He felt as though the entire ground beneath his feet and the walls he was pushing against moved with him.

Light spilled from above and dispelled the darkness. At first, the movement was barely perceptible, but he was rising, and the light grew brighter. Tex looked up and had to shield his eyes as he had become accustomed to the darkness.

The light revealed what had been shrouded in darkness below. He was in a glass structure that rose from the cavernous depths into the bright light of the alien planet.

The higher it rose, the more the light caught at the facets of the glass and revealed the structure. Tex was near the outside edge of the building, in a corridor cut diagonally toward the center. Glass towered over him, glimmering green and silvery in the bright light. His eyes watered and burned from the brightness.

The quaking had stopped, but the glass building continued to ascend. He braced against the glass walls and continued walking. *"At the center,"* the voice had said.

The great glass building groaned to a halt. He looked back through the corridor he'd walked, back toward the outer edge of the structure. He was deep enough into the building that nothing but green glass was all around.

The deep cuts and planes of the glass reflected the intense daylight. The entire structure seemed lit from within by the faceted glass.

The hallway ended, and Tex stepped into a large, perfectly square open space. He stepped slowly into the cavernous room and peered around. The walls sloped upward to a point. He was in a pyramid, and based on the size of the room and the length of corridor he had walked, it was huge, perhaps the size of a city block.

The floor and walls of the central room were made of smooth glass, with no furniture and no decoration.

He wasn't sure what he had expected to find, but an empty room wasn't it. Tex sank to his knees and let exhaustion take him. His eyes were bleary from weariness and a misting of tears that sprang there.

"Rise, Bodaway," a voice said.

He glanced up and thought he saw a shimmering image of Erika holding her hand out to him. "Erika?"

She smiled, and her lips moved. He thought he heard her say, "Take off your helmet, Tex."

But Dr. Lewis... Didn't she say something about the helmet? What was it she said?

His vision was dark around the edges. His sight wavered like shimmering heat on the pavement, but Erika was there, her hand out to him, her voice beckoning.

"Your suit is out of oxygen, and you're suffocating. This room has air that you can breathe. Take the helmet off."

Attaching the helmet had taken two people. He fumbled at the closures with shaky fingers as though grasping a grain of rice with boxing gloves on. He twisted and turned, unsure if he was making the screws tighter or loosening them.

Finally, he got the fasteners free, and the entire helmet pushed back off of his head. He gasped in the air, half expecting it to take what was left of his life.

His lungs burned as oxygen filled them. He gulped the air greedily, like a dying man drinking water from a desert oasis.

He fell the rest of the way to the smooth floor, lying on his back and breathing deeply. The air was fresh and clean, not dank, as he had expected. Also, the room must have been pressurized because he hadn't exploded.

As his cells refueled their oxygen supply, his head cleared. He was lying in a room entirely silent save for the sound of his breathing. He realized that he had imagined the voice just as he had imagined Erika. *But it directed me here, didn't it?*

As if reading his thoughts, a clear, deep male voice spoke. "Rise, son."

The sudden sound startled him, and he was on his feet nearly immediately.

"Who are you? Where are you? Show yourself."

The room had been filled with light filtering through the layers of glass, but it darkened as though invisible shades were pulled over the glass.

The walls and ceiling then filled with lights moving and whizzing around and around the walls at a dizzying speed. All the many-colored lights came together in a single point hovering a few feet in front of Tex. It was a tiny spot no larger than a speck of sand, but it cast a glow that nearly filled the space.

"We are the Elosians, the ancient ancestors of your species." As the voice continued, the point of light pulsed brighter then dimmer, a bit larger then smaller.

"You're beings made of light?"

"This light projection is merely our way of giving you something to focus on. We are pure consciousness and without form. But perhaps you would prefer this?"

In an instant, the single point of light disappeared. The space in front of Tex shifted. He squinted and blinked.

A male figure materialized out of the empty air in front of him. The humanoid man stood at least three feet taller than Tex. The man's broad chest was bare, the brown skin smooth and rippling with well-defined muscles. His head was large, his forehead and jaw wide, his eyes set deep and far apart. The man's head was bald on the right, but a long, sleek black braid of hair hung on the left. Around his neck was a thick golden collar, set with coral and turquoise jewels, that matched the golden belt around his slim waist. His lower torso and legs were covered with a silver-white skirt flowing in a shimmery wave of fabric that seemed to move slightly in a nonexistent breeze.

Though his size was formidable, the most striking aspect of the man was his eyes, larger than human eyes though not nearly as large as Conexus eyes. The color was unlike anything Tex had ever seen, though. They were nearly white, flecked through with gold. Tex didn't think the eyes were actually glowing, but the white color in contrast to the man's dark skin made his eyes appear to cast light out.

Tex's mouth hung open. He had so many questions, so much he wanted to ask and to say, but the man's form towered over him, making Tex feel small and befuddled.

The man's lips curled upward into a smile. "Perhaps this form is better. This figure is Cynothian. He was on the Council of Elot, the ruling body of Elosia." The man's lips moved, but the sound seemed to come from everywhere, not just out of the man's face.

"Where is he now? Is he dead? Is this a projection or... What is it?"

Cynothian threw back his head and let out a thunderous laugh that rumbled in Tex's chest. "Ah, our star child. We had nearly forgotten how impatient humans are."

Irritation rattled Tex. Cynothian had not only laughed at him but also called him human.

"But I'm not human. Not entirely, anyway. I am from Earth, but I was created in a lab with both human DNA as well as DNA from another species, the Conexus. They are from Earth's future so technically human—in a way—but definitely evolved far enough into the future to be a wholly new species."

Cynothian laughed again. His voice echoed throughout the cavernous space.

"I did not risk my life to be here simply so I could be laughed at. Earth is in trouble. The situation is rather dire. And seeing as how you are the architects of the galactic highway the M'Uktah are using to come to our planet to destroy us, I had hoped you would come to Earth and help us destroy the gate they're using."

Cynothian stopped laughing. He shook his head, his eyes closed. "Many mistakes."

"What mistakes? I'm running out of time. Are you the Architects or not?"

Cynothian opened his eyes, and the room was again brighter. "Architects? Yes. We like that term as far as we understand it. The builders. The creators—but of more than a warp in space-time used for many millennia for galactic travel."

Tex wasn't interested in the marvels of their engineering. "You're great builders. I have seen that, but what I need to know is how can we prevent the M'Uktah from coming to Earth? Can you shut the galactic gateway down on their end? Or destroy it on our end?"

Cynothian's eyes grew wide, and his brows furrowed with anger. "You seek answers, yet you listen not. You have wisdom beyond that which most humans achieve, but you are young yet. You fail to grasp the larger picture that has been shown to you."

Tex was typically interested in wisdom, but he was focused solely on his visions of Erika being mowed down by one of the monsters with the hinging jaws set with razor-sharp teeth. He could nearly smell her blood as the animal sank its jaws into her throat. The mental picture haunted his days and nights alike and was swimming before his mind's eye.

Cynothian's face relaxed, and he took on the countenance of compassion. "Please relax, Bodaway. Time is not your enemy. Fear is. Focus your attention on us. We have the answers that you seek. You will leave here with the information you require. Be still, star child. The gods would have a word with you."

Jack stood at the gateway to Apthartos with half a dozen guns trained on him. Lizzy Croft wore a smug smile as though she was looking forward to watching Jack's blood stain the floor.

A gun nudged Jack's back. He realized too late he'd made the rookie mistake of allowing the mercenary to get behind him.

"I'd like the honor of taking this one out for you, Lady Croft," Mick said.

Anna stepped in front of Jack. That wouldn't keep Mick from pumping some bullets into him from behind, but Jack appreciated the gesture.

"I won't allow you to kill Jack." Anna sounded calm and assured. "You'll take all of us, including Jack, to see your father."

Jack admired Anna's attempt to do some Jedi mind trickery on Lizzy, but he doubted it would work. Lizzy was not the type to be intimidated.

"Oh, I will?" Lizzy asked, mocking. "Or you'll what? Bat your long eyelashes at me or flip your hair?" She laughed. "You're pathetic. What my father sees in your genes, I'll never know." She thrust her chin upward haughtily as her lips pulled back into a thin, angry line.

Anna eased her rifle up and pointed its red laser dot at Lizzy's chest. "I'll kill you now and worry about killing your dad later."

The men surrounding Lizzy didn't know where to aim their weapons. Half of them stayed on Jack, but the other half shuffled and pointed their weapons at Anna instead.

The gunpoint was uncomfortable at the small of his back. At eight against three, Jack knew they couldn't win a shoot-out, even with Alecto's help.

Jack slowly reached for the radio device on Anna's belt and tapped the call button three times.

"He's reaching for something," one of the men said.

Jack quickly put his hands in the air. "I was scratching an itch. See? Nothing in my hands."

Lizzy let out a loud sigh. "I tire of this game, cousin. There's a gun at your boyfriend's back. You may have found a way to get the thing there to resist water, but a few bullets will end her anyway. Don't think that just because my father favors you that—"

The lights blinked out, leaving them in darkness. Sturgis had gotten the predetermined radio signal and cut the lights in A.H.D.N.A.

Jack spun quickly, taking advantage of the momentary confusion. He tried to grab for Mick's gun but caught only air.

A few seconds later, red lights embedded in the ceiling blinked, and an alarm wailed as the A.H.D.N.A. lockdown sequence commenced. Metal screeched and groaned as gates rolled out of the ceiling, cutting off the hall in which they stood from A.H.D.N.A.

The scene was lit by an eerie red glow as the lights blinked on. After a few seconds, the lights pulsed off, and everyone was again in the dark. When the lights came on again, Lizzy's eyes were wide, the smug confidence gone. Anna stood with her gun still aimed at Lizzy, seemingly oblivious to everything else. Mick found Jack again with his aim, his eyes locked onto Jack's form.

The red lights blinked off again. As darkness engulfed them, Jack bolted to his right and pushed Anna to the left. The large hall echoed with gunfire. Jack got down on one knee and pulled his pistol from its holster. The scene lit up again in a red glow.

Two bodies were down. One was a black-clad Makers guard. The other was the mercenary named Mick.

Alecto's eyes were closed, her hand outstretched, looking very vulnerable standing in the open. The only reason she wasn't dead already was because Croft had ordered them not to kill her. *But how long will that last when she's knocking them down like bowling pins?*

Movement caught Jack's attention out of the corner of his eye. Lizzy fumbled with the gun holster at her waist and finally got the pistol free.

The red lights flickered out again, leaving them in darkness.

Jack moved as quickly as he could. Two more bodies thumped onto the ground, and he hoped one of them was Lizzy.

He was so close to Anna that he felt her breath on the back of his neck.

"Move," she whispered. "You're blocking my shot."

The red glow lit the corridor.

A deafening explosion filled the hall as the hammer of Lizzy's gun hit the pin, igniting a chain reaction that sent a bullet whizzing through the air at him at the speed of sound. The impact of the bullet hitting his chest knocked him to the ground.

Anna sounded as if she was yelling to him through water. "No!"

The sounds of his beating heart and rushing blood filled Jack's ears. Air was forced from his lungs.

Jack's head spun. His chest burned, and pain shot through his upper arms and back. The dim red lights pulsed off again, leaving them momentarily in the dark. His vision blurred and narrowed. Darkness played at the edges of his vision. He was in danger of losing consciousness.

He blinked and sucked in a deep breath of the dank recycled air. He forced his aching arm to feel under the Kevlar vest for blood. He was bruised and maybe had a cracked rib or two, but his hand was dry—no blood.

The red lights blinked on again as Jack forced himself up to his knees then staggered to standing. Anna's eyes were filled with tears, but she smiled widely at him as he stood on wobbly legs.

He turned to face Lizzy, his body still a human shield in front of Anna. "You can send a hundred bullets at her. I'm going to take every one of them," he said.

"You want a hundred bullets? Ask and you shall receive. Take him out," Lizzy commanded.

Jack wished he'd thought through his smack talk before saying it.

"Without lights, we risk shooting her," one of the men said.

Lizzy threw up her hands and yanked a rifle out of the hands of the man next to her. Then the lights went out again. "I'll do it myself. I'll tell him she got in the way. Oops, I accidentally killed your pet fa—" She gasped for air.

The red glow came back. Lizzy dropped the rifle. Her hands were at her throat, trying to pry away invisible cords wrapped around her neck. Her eyes bulged.

Alecto's hand was trembling, her large eyes focused solely on Lizzy.

Lizzy writhed on the floor, choking and gasping.

Anna screamed, "Don't torture her!"

Alecto cocked her head to one side and let her hand fall.

Lizzy Croft's head whipped sharply to the side. The cracking sound of the bones in her neck breaking echoed off the stone walls. She fell to the ground like a puppet whose strings had been cut. Her face was plastered to the cold, gray concrete floor of A.H.D.N.A. much as Robert Sturgis's dead face had lain on the marble floor of the Croft penthouse when Lizzy had shot him.

Jack had almost looked forward to Lizzy's death. She had caused Anna, Alecto, and Thomas untold agony. Her glassy dead eyes staring up at them gave him no satisfaction. The stench of death permeating the corridor made his stomach lurch.

The red lights blinked off and on. Off and on. Only three Makers guards still stood, huddled around Lizzy's lifeless body.

Jack wanted to offer them an out, but the last time he'd done that, he ended up with a gun in his back. Mick had proven more loyal to the Crofts than Jack had expected.

He didn't spend more time dwelling on the choice. Without the antivirus, Ian's entire family might die. Everyone he knew was in danger, including Anna and himself.

He unloaded round after round from his semiautomatic until the three men were as dead as Lizzy. "Radio Sturgis. Let her know we're on our way to Croft." Jack stepped among the dead bodies and avoided looking into the faces of the men he'd killed as he took Anna's hand and marched toward the doors leading to Apthartos.

The first star was visible over the horizon to the north, suspended in a deep-azure sky hung like a curtain atop a rim of orange. The night was beautiful, but Erika was in no mood to appreciate nature's splendor. Her butt was numb from sitting on the hard ground all day, her eyelids heavy with the kind of tired that came from being bored. She wanted to be there for Tex when he came back, but she had to admit, if only to herself, that she wasn't sure she'd make it through a night in the desert.

A cool wind whipped the blanket and nearly ripped it from her. She clutched it more tightly about herself and shivered.

Behind her, the air crackled with electricity. *There are no power wires out here.*

She grabbed the Taser from her lap and was on her feet in an instant. The woolen blanket fell from her shoulders, and cold air stole what little heat she'd built up inside the blanket cocoon.

Her hands shook as she pulled the pistol from her back waistband while she turned toward the crackling sound. Less than twenty yards away, a ball of purple-and-white electricity lit up the dusky sky. Electricity arced and sputtered in a spherical ring, as if thrown off by a Tesla coil. The arcing currents were so bright that she couldn't see whether any mechanism was within the sphere of light causing the anomaly.

She backed slowly away but couldn't take her eyes off of it. The light was so bright she had to squint to protect her eyes. The sphere of electrical current was beautiful and scary at the same time.

The ground around the radio dish was sparsely vegetated, but the few small dry shrubs and grasses nearby caught fire. Smoke filled the air around the electrical sphere and further obscured what might lie inside.

That the anomaly was appearing where Tex had vanished into thin air caused hope to well inside her. He had assumed he would get back to Earth the way he left it, but perhaps the Architects, as he called the distant aliens, had an advanced machine. *Can it be?* She stopped backing away, her feet rooted.

"Tex!" she cried.

No answer came.

The electrical current fizzled and buzzed. As suddenly as it had appeared, the sphere of electricity vanished, leaving behind a patch of scorched and smoking earth. As the wind cleared the smoke, an iridescent egg-shaped orb was revealed.

Erika moved slowly toward it. She lowered her gun and Taser but kept them in her hands. She was nearly certain Tex had returned safely to Earth. She wanted desperately for it to be him, but she approached cautiously, in case the orb was not what she hoped it was.

The smoke shifted ever so slightly, and she saw movement. The small brush fires had nearly exhausted their fuel and burned low. The sun was almost completely set, leaving her in near darkness. The orb glistened white, but everything around it was silhouette and shadow.

She heard a faint whoosh and stood perfectly still and quiet. Her eyes were wide, her ears alert. Sweat beaded on her brow, and she wiped it so the salty liquid wouldn't sting her eyes and obscure her vision. Her heart thrummed in her chest, and she took a deep breath, trying to calm herself. Footsteps sounded.

The hairs on the back of her neck stood on end. She couldn't see what had come out of the pod, but her instincts told her it wasn't Tex. Her armpits were wet, and her knees felt like limp noodles.

Rocks crunched beneath feet. Two eyes glowed orange-red and came at her.

She raised her gun and Taser nearly simultaneously. Whatever had come out of the white orb was huge. The shadowy figure towered over the desert floor. At first, it moved somewhat slowly, but it picked up speed.

Her brain finally caught up to her instincts. *Run, idiot.*

Erika bolted toward the buildings of the VLA. The distance to the nearest one was close to half a kilometer. She didn't look back.

The lights of the VLA compound seemed to bounce in the distance as she sprinted toward them.

The thing behind her, whatever it was, was still there. It did not pant or snarl. The only sound it made was the crunch and snap of dried branches giving way beneath its feet as it chased her.

She pushed her legs to run faster than she'd ever run before. Still, the behemoth creature gained on her.

The thing made a low, eerie sound as if its voice was filtering through a mechanized voice modulator. If it was attempting to speak to her, she did not understand it. The language was all clicks, squeaks, and guttural noises, complete gibberish to her ears.

Her panic swelled at the hollow, tinny sound of its voice. Her thighs burned, and her chest ached. She pushed her legs to pump faster. The lights of the buildings got closer. *Why hasn't anyone come out here yet?* She figured the creature's pod-shaped ship should have shown up on military radar, but the VLA compound was quiet and still. She was alone with the monster hunting her like a rabbit.

The creature howled at her. It spoke again, low and menacing, which was still nothing but frightening noise to Erika.

It stopped speaking, and a motor whirred. Branches snapped and popped beneath her feet as she trampled everything in her path. She tried to listen to what was going on behind her over the rush of blood in her ears and her loud panting to catch her breath. She heard two sets of footsteps instead of just one.

Sure she would see two of the monstrous machines, she tossed a look over her shoulder but saw nothing. Erika chanced another look back. That time, she saw its glowing eyes—only two eyes, not four—and they were lower to the ground.

She was losing steam, her legs wobbly with fatigue. Her arms ached from pumping vigorously, urging herself forward.

With another look backward, she saw the M'Uktah hunter on all fours, running like a giant wolf. What little light there was glinted off shiny metal fangs. It had sleek black fur running from its head down its back, and centered in its head were two round, glowing orange-red eyes.

She'd seen enough of the thing. Erika planted her eyes forward and pumped her arms. She was still a good quarter kilometer from the VLA buildings. *Run, dammit, run.*

She sensed herself falling and tried to right herself but was too late. She was going down. *Don't fall on the gun.*

She tucked her shoulder and did her best to roll to one side as she hit the sunbaked earth. She landed on her left shoulder in a crusty sagebrush bush. It cradled her fall somewhat, but the dry, spindly branches caught at her as if the thing was alive and holding her down, trapping her like quarry for the predator hunting her.

She tried to scramble to her feet, but the hulking beast loomed over her. Even in the nearly total darkness, its glowing eyes cast enough light for her to see what had been chasing her.

The creature was black from head to toe. Its wide head looked much like a wolf's, with pointed ears on top of its head, wide-set, large almond-shaped eyes and a snout. The wolflike head was made of metal, though, and smelled of iron and steel. The M'Uktah hunter's chest was as wide as two men. Her eyes were drawn to the silvery glint of its razor-sharp teeth bearing down on her.

Its mouth was open, and it made the horrid, tinny sound again. She didn't know if the thing was trying to talk to her or sing a song. Its language was unlike any she'd heard before.

It bent lower, its body nearly touching hers. Its huge hands were on the ground on either side of her, effectively pinning her to the spot where she'd fallen.

Her hand throbbed from landing on it while gripping the Taser. *The Taser.*

She pressed the end of it against the hulking beast and pressed the button. Shimmering arcs of electricity danced at the tip of the Taser and, to her surprise, corkscrewed up the creature's chest as though conducted by its body armor. For a brief instant, the body armor disassembled slightly, revealing what looked like pale skin beneath.

Erika shot the current again, sending it to the creature's chest. That time, the tasing jolted the creature slightly. It growled through its mechanized mouth, and a chill ran up Erika's spine.

She fired the Taser again and watched the creature's midsection. The armor there looked to be made of hundreds of tiny black rectangular insects that scrambled this way and that, with tiny arcs of electricity buzzing between them.

Erika pulled the trigger of the pistol in her right hand. The gun fired directly at the creature at close range but didn't seem to faze it. She fired again. The beast flinched but did not let up. Its armor began to reform. She tried to tase it again, but nothing happened. The Taser had lost charge. She dropped it to the ground and put her left hand on the grip of the gun to steady it as best she could with her quaking arms.

One of the creature's arms rose into the air. Claws of steel shot from the tips of its fingers. Its arm swung toward her, ready to rip the still-beating heart from her chest.

A sliver of pale skin caught her eye. The armor had not fully reformed yet. She fired two successive shots, aiming as best she could at the small patch of flesh revealed on the creature's left side. Then she kicked at it with all her might, trying to get the thing away from her as she rolled to her right. Fiery fingers of pain spread across her back, instantly wet with her blood.

The creature howled then went silent. It fell with a loud thud, and the edge of its body landed on her leg, pinning her beneath its hulking form.

Erika tried to yank her leg free, but that was no use. The beast's barrel chest was on top of her.

Her fingers trembled as she pulled the two-way radio from her sweatshirt pocket. She pushed the Talk button. Her voice quavered, and her throat was so dry that speaking was difficult. "Aunt Dana." She let off the button, and the radio squawked.

She heard static then, "Come back."

Erika pushed the button again. "Help. Now. It's got me pinned."

She knew she wasn't making much sense. Getting words out was difficult, let alone sounding sensible.

"Erika, what's happening out there?"

Before Erika had a chance to say anything, a motor whirred, and tires crunched over twigs and bushes.

The radio fell from her hand. Blackness played at the edges of her eyes. She was vaguely aware of men yelling, talking, asking questions.

"Heave it off her!" someone yelled.

She thought that might have been General Hays.

The uncomfortable crushing pressure was gone, then the horrid smell of ammonia was under her nose.

She pushed it away, her nose wrinkled in displeasure. Hands beneath her armpits raised her.

"Can you stand?"

Her legs were shaky, and her head swam. Lights flashed at her, and she covered her eyes with an arm.

Beyond the cone of light shining at her, silhouettes of men with rifles drawn surrounded her, like déjà vu of the time she'd been on Bell Rock with Tex, Ian, and Jack months before, when Sturgis's men circled them.

She raised her quaking arms. "Don't shoot." Tears on her cheeks chilled her. She hadn't realized she'd cried. "It attacked me. I had to kill it to defend myself."

"Get the lights out of her eyes," General Hays said. "And get this thing sedated, strapped down, and back to the compound. I want all the docs we've got on hand to save it so we can interrogate it."

"Yes sir," someone said.

Hays paid no attention to the flurry of activity behind him. His eyes were riveted to Erika. He glanced down at the gun in her hand and the Taser lying like a piece of trash on the ground. "Those are military issue," he said.

She didn't know what to say. She didn't want to get Aunt Dana in trouble, but she couldn't explain why she had them. She settled for a faint nod.

"You took this alien down with just a Taser and a pistol?" His voice was gruff, and his brow crinkled as he glowered at her.

Erika nodded again, still unable to form words. She'd never been at a loss for words before, but then again, she'd never been hunted by an eight-foot-tall wolf-man either.

General Hays's brow relaxed a bit, and he gave her a small smile. "Good work." He turned on his heels and walked away briskly, half a dozen men following him. "Get her medical attention, too," he called over his shoulder.

Someone threw a blanket over her shoulders. She shivered from head to toe.

"Stay with me now," someone said. "Don't go into shock."

Erika thought that advice was a bit late.

The same person who'd thrown the blanket around her shoulders led her to a jeep and helped her inside. She looked back at the scene of her near death. Hoisting the M'Uktah up and into the back of a military truck took half a dozen men. A dozen more were at the orb with a winch, lifting it into a flatbed. Erika had no doubt they'd take the orb to a lab somewhere to analyze the heck out of it. She didn't know what would happen to the alien she'd shot. If it died, she wouldn't feel bad about it. The thing had nearly ripped her heart from her chest. If not for Aunt Dana bringing her those weapons, she'd have been a bloody pile of dead Erika lying lifeless in the desert.

The jeep bounced over rough terrain on the way back to the VLA compound. The jostling cleared away some of the shock caused by extreme fear.

The general wasn't going to leave it at "good job." She knew she'd be interrogated and pumped for details about every last second of the attack. She would cooperate, but she wanted—no, desperately needed—something in return. *Hays has to keep these dishes aligned for Tex to return.*

Her brush with death in the desert that night made their dire reality sink in. If thousands of those things hit the ground running, humanity didn't stand a chance. Tex had been right. Closing down the galactic highway those M'Uktah used to get to them was the only way to prevent the events that, if left unchecked, would lead to the Conexus, and Tex was the only one who knew anything about how the alien highway worked.

Erika looked up as they sped to the VLA compound. The night sky was clear, and the Milky Way was a splatter of white against the blue black.

"Tex, where are you?"

37
JACK

Jack was nearly to the large metal double doors that led to the entryway to Apthartos.

Anna called to him, "Wait. Something's wrong with Alecto."

Alecto was on the ground. She looked as dead as Lizzy.

He moved quickly to her side. Anna knelt, her fingers at Alecto's neck, feeling for a pulse.

"Is she shot?" His heart raced. *Did I accidentally hit her with a stray bullet?*

Anna shook her head. "She's not shot. She just... collapsed."

Jack knelt on the other side of Alecto. Her clothes were stained with sweat. She was as pale as a piece of paper, her bulbous head lolling to one side. Alecto looked as small and vulnerable as she had when Jack rescued her from Croft's penthouse.

He picked up her wrist and let go of it, and her arm dropped to the ground like a limp biscuit. "She probably passed out from exhaustion. She used her powers a lot. I've never seen her snap a neck like that."

Anna's nose wrinkled. She bit her lower lip and rested one hand on Alecto's. "She's so cold." A visible shiver moved through Anna. "What are we going to do? We can't leave her here. And we're not going to get the antivirus from Croft without her help."

When Sturgis had put A.H.D.N.A. into lockdown, massive metal gates came down from the ceiling, shutting them off from the rest of A.H.D.N.A. They were relatively safe from any attack from that direction.

Jack looked back toward the double doors leading to Apthartos. They were closed for the moment, but at any minute, a new group of Makers men could barge in on them.

"Radio your aunt," he said. "She should know what we could do for her."

Anna kept her back to the dead bodies as she tapped a button on the device at her waist and waited. Her eyes looked ahead at nothing as she spoke to Sturgis over the comm.

"Yes. I'm all right." A slight pause. "She's dead." The statement was matter-of-fact. Anna let out a breath of impatience. She cast her gaze at Jack, shook her head, and rolled her eyes. Finally, she said, "We'll have to celebrate later. Right now, we've got issues."

Anna explained the current state of things, including Alecto being unconscious. Jack couldn't hear what Sturgis said, but Anna's brow crinkled, and her eyes became a storm. Anna erupted. "Stop it! I won't listen to you speak about Alecto that way. She's a person, not a machine. She's done her best, and if it wasn't for her, I'd be dead. So unless you have something constructive to add, I'm signing off."

Jack wasn't sure anything was sexier than hearing Anna stand up to the Queen of the Psychos like that.

He reached a hand across Alecto's still body and placed it on Anna's hand. He gave her his best shot at a reassuring smile, and she gave one back.

"Okay, now that I can use." A few seconds later, she rolled her eyes again. "We can talk about all of this later. I'm kind of in the middle of something here. Yes, goodbye. I'll radio again after we've recovered the antivirus and taken care of Croft."

Anna ripped the earpiece out of her ear in frustration. She put her head in her hands and let out a low yowl.

"Talk to me," Jack said.

Anna looked at him through her fingers with red, teary eyes. "My family is so messed up! My aunt's a…"

"Psychopath."

Anna let out a wry laugh. "Probably. Among other things. Why didn't I see it before?"

"Maybe 'cause we tend to see only the best in the people we love. Besides, it wasn't like you'd ever seen her in this underground house built by greed and rampant paranoia. It probably brings out the worst in her."

Anna sighed. "True." She took her rifle off and pulled a small pack from her back. "My Aunt Lilly may be unhinged, but she does know her stuff." She took a small black box the size of an eyeglass case from the pack. "She said Alecto is probably severely dehydrated. She's not used to needing to drink water so hasn't been doing it." Anna took a small white pellet from the box, crushed it between her thumb and finger, and held it under Alecto's nose. "Can you grab a water bottle from your pack?"

Jack did as she asked. At first, Alecto didn't react, but after a few seconds, she wrinkled her barely there nose and pressed her eyes shut even more tightly. She coughed and gagged and pushed Anna's hand away from her nose.

Anna pressed a bottle of water into her hand. "Drink. You're dehydrated."

Alecto tried to hand the water back to Anna, but Anna wouldn't take it. "Listen to me. I talked with Commander Sturgis, and she said to make you drink. You no longer take hydration in through your skin. You have to drink to regain your strength."

It wasn't like Alecto to be defiant with Anna. Jack chalked it up to the effects of her severe dehydration.

Alecto jerked the bottle out of Anna's hand and took a sip.

"You'll need more than that," Jack said.

Alecto shot him a glare that made Jack glad she didn't have laser vision.

Anna's voice was firm. "Drink."

Alecto glared at Anna too but downed the entire bottle. She wiped her mouth and handed the empty bottle to Anna. A bit more color was blooming in her cheeks already.

"What do we do now?" Jack asked.

"Aunt Lilly said to wait about fifteen minutes then have her drink more."

"We don't have that kind of time." Jack eyed the metal doors to Apthartos. "The longer we wait, the more likely that a bunch of Croft's goons will come through that door."

Anna put the empty bottle into her pack and grabbed a full one. "I know. But what's the alternative? We need Alecto."

The petulant look on Alecto's face disappeared. She took the full bottle from Anna and took a long draught. "We will not need to wait that long. My energy is returning to normal parameters." She stood but nearly fell over. Jack and Anna quickly rose, and each took an arm to steady her.

"Not quite right yet," said Anna. "We'll take as much time as you need. I'm not facing Croft without you."

Jack stood guard at the doors to Apthartos. Alecto had curled herself into a tight ball, motionless and utterly quiet. Anna watched over her and chewed her nails. Jack had never seen her do that before.

Each second felt like days. Jack checked his watch, sure they'd been waiting for hours, but less than ten minutes had passed, more than enough time for Jack to think of the many ways their mission could fail. He tried to focus on the goal at hand, retrieving the antivirus. That helped for a few seconds, but he quickly resumed thinking of Anna being gunned down or of losing Alecto in gunfire that she was too depleted to counter.

A few minutes that felt like eternities later, Alecto slowly unwound herself. Anna held out a water bottle for her, and that time, Alecto took it without argument. She drained it and stood, her legs stable beneath her.

"I am ready to proceed," she said.

Anna used the keycard Sturgis had given her and punched an override authorization code into the keypad by the door. The heavy metal doors swung open, and they entered a wide, dark hallway toward Apthartos.

Jack took point, his rifle at the ready. Sturgis had cut the power to Apthartos when she put A.H.D.N.A. on lockdown. The bright-as-day halogen lights were off. The only light for the underground town came from the eerie bluish-green glow of the genetically engineered bioluminescent trees lining the sidewalks and wide boulevards.

Alecto silently brushed past Jack. Her voice was a quiet whisper in his ear. "Allow me. My vision is not impaired by these conditions."

Jack didn't argue. He couldn't see more than a few feet ahead of him.

Even though they walked as quietly as they could down the brick boulevard, every move echoed around the cavernous stone walls that surrounded empty buildings inside the manmade cave. Jack's eyes flitted from side to side as he hoped to see any enemy gunmen before they saw him. He and the girls were like sitting ducks, without cover in the open.

"Head toward the bushes," he said. "Over there."

Alecto moved with preternatural speed to a row of low artificial hedges to the right.

The same place we hid from Sturgis's men before when we were here with Tex.

Anna and Jack knelt beside Alecto, each of them peering over the hedges and behind them for any signs of movement. The entire city was as quiet as a vacuum and as still as stone.

"I don't like this," Jack said. "It's too quiet."

"I know what you mean," Anna said. Her voice was a breathy whisper. "I feel like we're going to step in a snare."

They looked to Alecto for confirmation of their fears or a comforting denial, but she gave neither.

Her head was cocked to one side, her eyes open wide and staring toward an unseen point on the horizon. "Odd."

"What is?" Anna asked.

"I sense no life-forms in this area. There are no men here."

Jack found that hard to believe. Sturgis had made them fear meeting a small army. *Or was that just her paranoia?* "Do you mean in the whole of Apthartos? Or just this central area?"

Alecto blinked slowly. "My ability to sense the bioelectrical energy of life-forms extends no further than a quarter-kilometer radius. Apthartos is more than just this central area. We may meet resistance as we head toward the home of Sir Croft."

Jack believed Alecto, yet his nervous system remained on high alert. His back was drenched with anxiety sweat. "Let's keep going then. I think I know the way."

They rose, but before they got going, Anna put her small hand on Jack's arm. "You okay?"

He wanted to tell her the truth. Hell no, he wasn't okay. The damned place still smelled like blood and vomit and urine. Or maybe that was his imagination bringing back the smells of the dead men he'd seen mowed down here by the Conexus ship. No he wasn't okay being back in the place in which he and his two best friends so nearly lost their lives. He forced a smile to his face. "Yeah, I'm okay."

Anna already knew him well enough to see his response for the bullshit lie that it was. She gave him a knowing smile in return. "Lead on then. We've got your back."

Jack edged around the perimeter of the town square, heading toward the street where they'd found Dr. Randall. "Alecto, if you sense anything at all, let me know right away."

Her voice was low and quiet. "Affirmative."

They stayed in the shadows as they passed the brownstone townhome where Dr. Randall had been a permanent "guest". The door still stood open. The keypad by the door still hung from wires. The wall was black and sooty where Ian had shot at it.

Jack had spent a couple of long days in Dr. Randall's townhouse, waiting for Sewell to spring him from his underground prison. As he remembered the boy that he was then, so frightened of the dark house that he couldn't sleep, he almost laughed out loud at himself. That had been only a few months ago but felt like a lifetime. That Jack Wilson—the one that had a crush on Erika and could think only of spending his time serenading her—was a distant memory. Jack pulled his mind back to Apthartos revisited. *Recover the antivirus.*

They were now in territory Jack had never seen before. Sturgis had shown him where Croft's home was on a map. It had seemed fairly close to Dr. Randall's townhouse, but the underground city was larger than he'd imagined.

They'd gone close to a kilometer when they came upon 'Kensington,' the street they were looking for.

"Aptly named street," Anna said. "Even down here, waiting out the dystopia that he helped create, Croft wants to live like royalty."

Alecto tugged at Jack's arm. "Proceed with caution. I sense humans near us."

Jack stopped and stepped close to a dark townhouse where he was hidden in shadow. Anna and Alecto did the same.

"Do you know how many?"

Alecto tilted her head. "Not many. But Croft is among them."

"How do you know?" Anna asked.

Alecto's lips were a thin line. "I do not know exactly how I know. But I am sure of it. Croft is close to us now."

Jack moved back onto the brick walk lit only by the glowing trees. His eyes had grown more accustomed to the dark. He could now see about as well as he could with a half-moon on a clear night.

The townhomes in this section were larger than the ones near Dr. Randall's home. Instead of tan or red brick, they were constructed of white stones and plaster. The homes on this Kensington Street looked more like they had been lifted from out of London rather than the Bronx of New York. The street was a cul-de-sac, and at the end was a house that stood alone, its symmetrical, white stone two-story façade nearly luminescent in the dark.

It was large enough to fit at least three, possibly four of the other homes on the street. Unlike the dark, brooding houses they had passed, the windows of Croft's house glowed with the welcoming yellow light of incandescent.

"Not trying to hide the fact that he's home," Jack said.

"It's like he's taunting us," Anna said.

Alecto picked up speed and pushed past Jack. "He is unafraid." Her voice became a low, raspy whisper. "Maybe he should be."

Her speed was incredible. Before Jack had the chance to ask her to stay with them, Alecto was nearly to Croft's front door. Jack wanted to call out to her to wait, but he didn't know if snipers lurked in the dark windows of the houses they passed. He and Anna moved toward Alecto but huddled down and stayed pressed into the shadows.

Fortunately Alecto didn't barge through the front door. She stood like a sentinel, waiting for them to catch up.

Jack was winded and his thighs burned from squatting low when they caught up to her. "What's your plan?" He hoped Alecto had one because he was fresh out of ideas.

She gazed at him quizzically. "To kill him, of course."

He resisted the urge to smack his head. "Yes, yes. I know you want payback. Though you may have to arm-wrestle Anna for the honor of taking him out."

Alecto glanced at Anna then back to Jack. "She should not attempt to wrestle me."

Anna let out a soft giggle. "He's joking. I'm not going to fight you over who gets to kill Croft. I know you want to, but if I have a clean shot, I'm going to take it."

"After we get the antivirus," Jack said. He knew that Anna wanted to get that antivirus back into the hands of Dr. Montoya, but he feared that her desire for revenge was taking precedence. It felt like he needed to keep reminding her of their primary mission.

She nodded. "Of course. Jack is right. The antivirus is of utmost importance. If we take out Croft, that's just an added bonus. Besides, I need answers from him. Do you understand, Alecto?"

Alecto stared at the front door.

Jack pressed. "Before we barge in the front door, I need to know that you understand and agree with what Anna said. Antivirus first. Kill Croft after."

Alecto remained motionless, her eyes fixed on that door that stood between her and the man who had masterminded her creation—and life of confinement. "I understand and agree. Now let us proceed before we lose our best opportunity. I am not wearing armor, so I ask that you please create a shield in front of me."

"Tex is able to create a sort of mini protective energy shield around himself. Can you do that?"

"I cannot." The muscles in Alecto's jaw tightened. She thrust her chin out and pulled the pistol from the holster at her waist. She checked the magazine then shoved it back into place. "I pick up the energy signatures of four persons inside."

"Only four? That's a relief," Jack said.

"Do not become complacent. As we have seen, the underground holds secrets. There may be a hidden cave even deeper behind the façade of this house. Croft could have men hiding in such a fashion."

The momentary feeling of relief faded.

Anna moved in front of Alecto. "We'll cover you."

Jack pushed ahead of Anna. He didn't intend to let her take a bullet.

There was no keycard entry at the door as there had been at Dr. Randall's house. The doorknob was polished brass and had an ordinary key mechanism like a typical residential door. He tried the knob, and it clicked open. He gave a head nod, pressed himself against the door and pushed it open.

The entryway glowed pale yellow from the soft light of a gigantic crystal chandelier that hung high. The light flickered off of the highly polished floor of lapis blue and creamy white marble, inlaid in an intricate border of leaves around the outer edges and circles within the border. White Corinthian-style columns rose from the floor, soaring to a ceiling at least thirty feet high. The bases of the columns were edged in gold leaf as were rectangular patterns around the ceiling. Sweeping staircases flanked each side of the room, curving up to a landing that led to a second floor at the far end of the room.

Croft's voice boomed from that direction. "Mr. Wilson, so good of you to pay a call. I do hope you brought Cousin Anna with you."

Jack edged a few more feet into the ornate foyer. Anna pushed up next to him but stayed close at his side. He felt Alecto at his back. She was so small, Croft might not have seen her there.

Croft's salt-and-pepper hair was neatly groomed, his face clean shaven. Jack had expected to find Croft in an expensive suit like he'd worn the first time Jack had seen him in A.H.D.N.A. Instead Croft had donned dark-blue jeans, a close-fitting black T-shirt, and leather driving moccasins. Somehow the clothes made him look smaller and less a threat than Jack had remembered him. Jack reminded himself not to be fooled by appearances. Alecto didn't look like a threat either, but he'd seen her mercilessly render people into lifeless sacks of water.

"You were expecting me?" Anna asked. She was trying to sound strong, but her voice quavered slightly.

"Of course."

"Who told you?"

Croft made his way down the stairs and laughed. "No one had to tell me. I know you, Anna. Better perhaps than you know yourself."

Anna snickered. "Don't flatter yourself."

Croft stood on the last step. His hand rested on the brass finial of the railing, and his eyes rested there for a moment as well. "Your mother sends her regards, by the way." He glanced up at Anna with dark eyes hooded slightly by his prominent brows.

Jack practically felt the heat rise from Anna.

"She was with you? So it's true."

"That your mother set your father against you and Thomas? No. That is not true. That was a foolish lie told by a foolish girl. Who, by the way, I presume is dead, otherwise you would not be here speaking to me."

"You knew we'd kill her?" Jack asked. His own dad had left Jack and his mom high and dry. Asshat father of the year, that one. But Jack couldn't imagine a father so glibly accepting the death of his own child.

"I told her not to kill Anna. So naturally I expected she would attempt it. But I also knew that Alecto would not allow that to happen. You can come out of hiding, my child. It is only Ben, myself, a housekeeper and cook here. But you already knew that, didn't you?"

Alecto squeezed herself between Jack and Anna. Her tiny fists were balled up at her sides, her lips pressed into a thin line.

It threw Jack a bit that Croft was freely admitting that Ben was with him. He'd expected Croft to hide the fact that Ben had stolen the antivirus. *What game is he playing?* Jack was out of his league in the realm of spy vs. spy. He hoped Anna would take the lead in whatever game Croft was playing. She'd had a lot more practice at such things.

Croft stepped off of the last stair slowly. His gait was graceful for a man in his seventies. Though his face had a few deep age lines here and there, his eyes were bright, sharp and focused. His build was slight, but Jack didn't doubt that the man was likely as strong as he was. Jack's muscles tensed, his hands on the gun and ready to fire if necessary as Croft strode toward the center of the room.

"You've done me a great service, Mr. Wilson."

Jack about puked at the thought that he'd helped the douchebag, even if inadvertently. "How's that?"

"You safely delivered to me the two things I prize most in the world." He lifted his arm and gave a wave of it in Anna's direction.

Jack was ready to jump down the guy's throat, but Anna beat him to it.

"We are not possessions." Her voice was a low snarl. "What do you want with me, anyway?"

Croft took a few steps toward them, his eyes intent on Anna. But when he saw both Jack and Anna raise their weapons, he halted his forward movement but showed no fear. "Anna, this city was built for you. Welcome home, my dear. Welcome to the kingdom over which you will one day rule."

Tex's mind had been a bungling confusion of worry and fear. Hungry, tired and recovering from a period of oxygen deprivation, he had lost the ability to remain calmly focused on his task. *Commander Sturgis would be most displeased with me and my performance here.*

After removing his helmet, soothing warmth filled him. It had begun in his core and spread outward though his limbs and finally settled to between and behind his eyes. There it pulsed though not unpleasantly.

His mind was at ease. In fact, he had never felt better. He was alert yet calm. Interested yet focused.

Cynothian's voice was melodious and calm. "Many questions. We have answers. Begin."

Tex started with the first thing that came to mind. "You built this great underground city, but it's now abandoned. What happened here?"

The walls around Tex came alive with moving pictures. At first it was a giant star map with galaxies spread throughout a dark sky. Quickly the image focused in on one galaxy, then to a star system, followed by a single star then a planet. The planet was fairly small in relation to the other neighboring planets, and it was the second from the sun. It was mainly the color of Mars, but there were small oceans of blue and patches of green with small icy-white caps on the ends.

The image paused there for a moment then swiftly blurred and whizzed until it showed a scene of wide boulevards of creamy marble towered over by gleaming buildings of glass and granite. The streets were filled with people who looked very much like Cynothian, both male and female and children too. Their skin was many shades of tan, and their eyes were green, brown, blue and even gold. Their hair was mainly black as night and long and sleek, but there were a few with chestnut-brown hair.

"Elosians existed many millennia before the first of the species known as human walked the Earth." Cynothian watched the moving pictures as Tex did. His eyes drooped with sadness.

The images reflected exactly what Tex had hoped to find on Elosia. But instead he was greeted by sand dunes and an empty underground city. "What happened?"

The images shifted again. Multi-storied greenhouses filled with dried and withered stalks of plants. Dead bodies partially covered by shifting sands.

"Our sun is in its last dance, Bodaway. And Elosia is no more."

"If you're the ones that built the gateway of warped space, then why didn't you use it? You could have colonized a planet."

Cynothian chuckled warmly. "We did, young one. In a manner of speaking."

The images flashed again. A new star system with a fourth planet that looked similar to Elosia then another star system with a fifth planet that was mostly icy but with a band of blue and green at its equator. And a third planet that was familiar. *Earth.*

The focus shifted, and images flew past him in rapid succession. Wolf-like beasts running on all fours. Great winged creatures that resembled eagles but large enough to snatch a small child in its talons. There were animals that swam in oceans and ones that flew or ran.

"Much as a parent achieves a sort of immortality by passing its genetic material on to the next generation, Elosia sought to do the same."

"What are you saying? That you created other species?"

"We merely helped their evolution along. On each planet we found that teemed with life, we sought out the one species that had the most promise of higher-order thinking. Of creativity."

Tex pondered the first animal he had been shown. It was larger than even the largest domesticated dog on Earth. It resembled the mechanized creature now decimating the population of his planet. "The M'Uktah. You made them?"

A rapid succession of images flashed around him. It was like a rapidly moving family album splayed across the walls. Hairy beasts running on all fours in packs, hunting prey. Then a creature that resembled the hairy beast only upright on two legs, its fur replaced by hair, the face with a nose that was less a long snout and more humanoid. The images morphed, and small groupings of huts gave rise to villages and then to a city.

"We guided the evolution both of their bodies and their culture," Cynothian said. "The creatures on Uktah were the first. They took readily to forming society. Their animal ancestors had already mastered a sophisticated social structure with little fighting amongst them. Within M'Uktah culture, there had been relative peace for many thousands of years."

"So long as they keep finding new sources of meat to eat." Tex's voice was filled with the bile he felt whenever he thought about one of those nasty creatures ripping into any of the people he cared about. He'd even hate to see Commander Sturgis taken down in such a manner. If anyone was going to end her, it should be him.

Cynothian's smile vanished. "We recognized our mistake nearly instantly. The original species had an inherent predatory nature that was quite ingrained. Though we counseled and coached the early M'Uktah away from eating flesh and the hunter society, our lessons never seemed to last long. No matter how advanced their technology became, they persisted in their desire for the hunt."

The pyramid walls were filled with images of huge, two-legged beings with long black hair flowing down their backs ripping into the throat of four-legged gazelle-like creatures. The pictures shifted, and the predators now wore biomechanical armor with fearsome helmets complete with razor-sharp teeth. A M'Uktah warrior pounced on a small, two-legged humanoid running through a jungle of green leaves and vines. The humanoid being was not a human. Its face was far wider, its nose shorter, and its skin was a greenish color. Its mouth was open in a scream, its eyes wide with terror as the M'Uktah used its mechanical claws to rip into the being's chest.

Tex's stomach roiled in disgust at the images of carnage. "You just left them to their own devices?"

"You judge us harshly. Perhaps it is no comfort to you that we have judged ourselves for this error as well. The Ulv were not ready to receive the gifts we brought to them. Gifts of advanced evolution and culture and knowledge. They have used it to engender great fear and suffering on the rest of our children."

The admission did little to improve Tex's opinion of these cosmic tinkerers. "You mean to say that these creatures have destroyed your so-called evolved species on other planets?" He shook with anger. "You have to stop them. If you shut down their ability to use the galactic highway, you can prevent them from taking more lives on Earth."

Before Tex could speak again, the images blurred and swirled across the walls of the pyramid. As they slowed, he recognized the white-and-blue planet he called home.

He was shown images of a species that resembled modern chimpanzees. But the creatures were even smaller with head and body proportions that more closely resembled modern humans.

"We found them living in tight groups with an even more sophisticated social structure than the Ulv of Uktah. They had begun to think creatively. They made tools, mixed paints and carried on a form of education one generation to the next through painting onto rocks. When we found your planet, what you call Earth, we believed we had at last found the perfect species to receive the gifts we had to bestow."

Tex watched as people from Cynothian's species, the Elosians, worked in what appeared to be a lab. They wore silvery tunics made of whisper-thin material that barely skimmed their bodies and fell to nearly the floor. Their heads too were covered in elegant, complexly wrapped head coverings that looked a bit like turbans but without the bulk.

Mechanized arms injected what looked like baths of gel auger with pink-tinted material. In another area Elosians inspected several rows of half-shell-shaped glass containers filled with a viscous liquid. Inside were tiny fetuses, no more than four inches long. The fetuses looked nearly human.

The sight reminded Tex of the jars filled with preserved specimens of A.H.D.N.A.'s failed attempts at creating a H.A.L.F. *The ones before me.* It also called to mind the row upon row of Conexus clones that the Regina had shown him. Bile rose in his throat. His head spun.

He wanted to lean on something. He longed for a cool drink of water.

If Cynothian noticed Tex's unease with the knowledge that an alien hand had augmented human evolution, he showed no sign of it. The projected scene continued and showed the results of Elosian genetic tinkering. The creatures they created walked more upright than a chimpanzee or other apes and lost much of their hair. Their foreheads became narrower, but their heads grew larger. Finally they looked like a perfect mix between the chimpanzee cousin and the representative of the Elosians that stood before him now.

And as on Uktah, Tex was shown the evolution of their society from small family groups to tribes to villages and finally to great cities of stone. There were even images of Elosians walking among the people of Earth in a city that must have been in Egypt. They talked freely with the humans, who bowed down to them in the streets.

"How long did you visit Earth?"

"We first came to know your planet well over two hundred thousand Earth years ago."

Tex nearly choked on his own spit. It was a time period impossible for him to truly grasp.

"We seeded the population with our DNA then left and waited. By around 50,000 years ago, humans had made great strides. We visited more frequently then and guided your species toward the development of advanced mathematics and political structure, architecture and rudimentary medicine."

"You were there when the pyramids were built. That's why I could use it to come here."

"Yes. We did not build the structure. Humans did that. But we guided them on how to create such a monumental machine."

"Why did they build it?"

Cynothian turned his eyes to Tex. "So that they could come home."

He said it without the least bit of sarcasm. "Young star child, it was our hope that there would be many before you that would visit their ancestors here. We guided the construction of similar structures on all of the planets we seeded. All were to be conduits to align with Elosia allowing anyone to enter the quanta and come home."

"But I'm the first?"

"And only." Cynothian's face wore a look of utter despair. "It is a sadness that we have had to bear for millennia. All of our machinations for longevity—for immortality—all for naught when our first child eats the others and our last child is bent on annihilating itself."

The pictures vanished. The room was dark and quiet and still. There was only the steady beating of Tex's heart and the low, insistent thrum of the Elosian machine. *Or is the vibration made by their very consciousness?*

Cynothian sighed. "You expect answers from the great architects. You wish for us to smite the M'Uktah and fight your battle for you." He glided closer to Tex so that they were now only a few feet apart. Up close, Tex saw that Cynothian was less corporal than he appeared from a distance. His image wavered.

"You came to a throne room, but the throne is empty, son. The gods you seek—and the answers too—reside within you, not here on a dying planet."

Tex's patience with the galaxy's first mad scientists was as dried up and blown to the wind as the sands whipping against the pyramids exterior walls. Rage welled up within him. It started low in his belly and rose to his chest and finally outward in a scream so loud and ear splitting that it might have knocked Cynothian over if he had in fact been corporeal. Tex's anger-filled shout nearly knocked him to his knees. He shook with fury, his eyes bulged and a trickle of spittle hung at the corner of his mouth. His frustration, fatigue, fear and hunger reduced him to a base animal, eager to strike down the figure that stood before him.

He lashed out like an animal, his more elegant telepathic weapon all but forgotten in a moment of rage. His hand flew to Cynothian's neck, intent on squeezing the life out of the man that towered over him like a giant.

But Tex's hands grasped only air. The image of Cynothian vanished in an instant, and Tex fell to his hands and knees.

Cynothian had teleported himself several feet away and behind Tex. Cynothian coolly, calmly and silently watched Tex's rage-filled tantrum.

Tex's breath was ragged, and his head ached. He finally spoke in halted breaths through gritted teeth. "They spent valuable resources—put all their chips on one number. Me. Their only hope." He wiped sweat from his forehead and massaged his temples. "And you stand there and tell me that there's nothing I can do. That I have to watch them all die?"

Cynothian crossed his arms over his chest. "We said no such thing. You can put an end to the M'Uktah's plans for invasion and thus end the slaughter."

Tex closed his eyes and continued to rub. "When you say 'you', do you mean plural 'you' as in the people of Earth or do you mean 'you' as in me, Tex?"

Cynothian moved even closer, and he touched his fingertip to Tex's chest. Tex had not expected to feel anything. Cynothian was not real after all. But he was startled by the sensation of warmth that filled his chest. It tingled pleasantly.

"You, Bodaway. You are the key."

Cynothian's touch had calmed his racing heart, but his mind was still ragged with anger, fear and worry for Erika and the others he cared about back on Earth. "But how?" His voice cracked.

Cynothian removed his hand, and Tex was instantly colder and wished for the warmth of his touch to return.

"By using the same power that brought you here."

Tex shook his head. "I still don't see. I want to understand, but I just—"

Cynothian put a hand to either side of Tex's head, looked down into his eyes and said simply, "Know this."

The tingly warmth that had filled his chest now filled his skull. His eyes relaxed, and his brow uncreased. His face no longer tensed, and he had the sensation of floating. He thought his eyes were open, and he knew he wasn't dreaming, but he was surrounded by golden light. When he looked down at himself, he was shocked to see that there was no himself to look at. Tex's body was gone, but it did not cause him fear or anxiety. He was simply Bodaway, and on some level he knew that he was now in his natural form and the one he would return to someday.

And in the instant of his acceptance of that truth, he also became aware of the Elosians. He was with them. And not just Cynothian but all of them. They were one collective mind yet many. They spoke to him with one voice, and he understood them easily.

He knew instantly what he must do. He was overwhelmed with the shared anguish this required action caused the Elosians. But in that realm of pure thought they assured him that they accepted the actions he would take.

As he comprehended the method of preventing the M'Uktah's success, he also understood a risk to himself. *This will not be easy.*

"It is a choice, Bodaway. And your choice alone to make."

In that place of comfort and peace, he did not grapple with the decision. Knowledge flowed to him, and he allowed it and catalogued it.

Within the bundle of information fed directly to his mind by a method he did not comprehend, there was a bit that stood out. He was aware of the home planet of the M'Uktah. In his mind's eye, he hovered over an impressive hall built of stone where an old man with hairy knuckles sat on a large, ornately carved wooden seat. A female M'Uktah in a richly embroidered black robe stood, her bright yellow-orange eyes fixed on the old man as she spoke, her arms gesturing wide.

Tex did not know all that was said, but he knew that the old man in the wooden throne liked it not. Other men seated at the long table rapped small stones on the table and howled their support of whatever the woman had said. He could not decipher their language, but one word kept being repeated. U'Vol.

It was a familiar name. But in that place and time of ethereal dream, he was not sure where he had heard the name before. It seemed important, and he wanted to hear more of what the woman with the blazing yellow-orange eyes said and know what happened next.

But his attention was pulled away from that place. He was again in the pyramid in his Tex body. He should have rejoiced, but it somehow felt like a prison, shackled inside a lumbering meat sack.

His vision was bleary and his head full of cobwebs. He blinked to clear his sight, and he searched the room. Cynothian was gone. The pyramid was brighter and grew lighter with each second until he wanted to shelter his eyes from the sun.

A voice boomed, its bass resonating within him. "Wake and remember."

He did not need to be told that he was alone again. The insistent thrum that he had felt was gone. It had comforted him, though he hadn't realized how much that steady, low hum in his chest had tethered him until it was no longer there.

Within the knowledge imparted to him by the Elosians was a methodology for his return trip. The very machine in which he stood was a vast harmonic resonance chamber. His thought could activate it. He saw it now. On Earth he had needed the waves generated by the radio telescopes, but here he had no such need.

He looked around the kingdom of the gods and found it was nothing more than an empty glass room. He stood in the center of the emptiness and activated the wave resonance machine. The photons collected by the faceted glass focused to the point at the very top of the pyramid and fed down into him and through him. The entire pyramid glowed, and he too shimmered with the light as it poured into him. He was hot beyond anything he had experienced before, his skin instantly wet. He wanted to rip the suit off and throw himself in a river of ice water.

He yelled out from the pain, but he didn't move out of the light. That focused beam of pure energy was his ticket back to Earth. His only way to see Erika again. His eyes burned, and even with them closed tightly, the sunlight burned through his lids. It took every ounce of willpower he had not to run back through the maze of corridors out of the pyramid and away from the burning light, but he somehow forced himself to remain planted.

His mind was fixed on what he had to do, despite the physical pain of entering the stream of particles on which he would be carried home. In an instant he felt cool air on his skin and shivered, his face cold from the evaporation of the tears from his cheeks.

35
ERIKA

As Erika suspected, General Hays didn't allow her peace for long after she was attacked by the M'Uktah creature. She was still in the makeshift infirmary on the ground floor of the western-most building of the VLA getting the deepest gash in her back stitched up when he stormed in. She lay on her side and winced as the med tech thrust a needle into her skin and worked surgical thread through.

"Sorry," he said. "I don't have any topical anesthesia. We aren't really prepared for this here."

General Hays didn't seem to notice that she lay there in only a bra. He pulled a stool on wheels over to the table where she lay. "What the hell happened out there?"

His voice was still gruff, but Erika figured that was just how the guy sounded. He didn't seem mad.

Erika had planned to withhold her story until she got assurances that the general would leave the array aligned for Tex. But the details of the attack spilled out of her. It was like she had need to tell it. She shivered with cold, and her lip trembled as she spoke.

The general listened with rapt attention. His eyes never left hers. When she got to the part about tasing the alien, he asked her to repeat what she'd seen twice.

When her story was finished, Erika asked, "Will it live?"

The general's eyes narrowed, and he regarded her for a minute. "Probably. The suckers are damned near invincible. Three gunshot wounds—and good, clean shots, mind you—and the only reason the thing went down was because your last bullet penetrated into the heart."

The med tech tied off the stitches and cut the thread. "You need to leave those in for seven to ten days." He put a gauze bandage over the wound then handed her shirt back. "The back of this is ripped to shreds, but at least it will keep you warm until you get back to your room."

Neither man looked the other way while she dressed. They didn't gawk at her, but it was still awkward. It gave her a small hint at how Tex had been treated all those years living in A.H.D.N.A.

The general rose from the stool. "You should get some sleep. But don't go anywhere. I may have more questions for you tomorrow." He turned to leave.

"General Hays—" Erika's voice came out high and shrill. "You need to keep those telescopes aligned just as they are. We need Tex."

He stopped to listen but kept his face averted from her. "I never authorized the dishes to be aligned in that configuration in the first place."

Erika held up her sweatshirt. The back was a tatter. She pulled it on over her head anyway. "What's done is done. But you know as well as I do, if that gate remains open and more of those things some through—Well, just imagine thousands of those beasts. We don't have enough Tasers, sir."

He looked back at her, and she thought there was the smallest hint of a smile playing at his eyes. "You were brave out there. You'd make a fine soldier."

Erika had never wanted to be a soldier. Heck, she didn't even kill spiders or scorpions that got into the house. She had a catch-and-release policy. Her experience with guns, blood and death made her want it even less.

She shoved her hands in the fleecy front pocket of her sweatshirt and moved toward the general. He was probably close to six foot three and stood high above her. "I don't think you'd want me in your ranks, general. I've got authority issues."

He gave her a wry smile. "The best of us always do." He was through the door in two strides. As he marched down the hallway he called over his shoulder, "You've bought yourself twenty-four hours to get him back, Miss Holt."

Aunt Dana and Ian fussed over her for nearly an hour before Erika literally shoved them out of her room, claiming she was exhausted and needed sleep. It was partly true, but mainly her head ached and she wanted peace.

She dug her last clean T-shirt out of her duffle and scrounged for a sweatshirt that hadn't been shredded by the monster's metal claws. The one she found didn't pass the sniff test, but she didn't care. It was too cold to go without one.

She slept for a few hours in her bed but woke drenched in sweat. She'd dreamed that Tex was calling to her from a swirling vortex, but the general had shifted the position of the telescope array and Tex was stuck, unable to return home. In her dream, he called to her. "Erika!" She reached out to him, but he got sucked away from her.

Erika wiped the tears she'd cried in her dream off her cheeks and slipped from her bed. She quietly padded down the hall, out the door and out into the frigid night to resume her watch for Tex.

She flitted into and out of sleep. The sunbaked ground beneath her was hard and caused whatever part of her body she lay on to go numb. She'd shift onto her side and drowse until the numbness woke her and she'd start the process over again. A few times she ended up on her back and burning pain woke her. The sky to the east had just begun to show baby blue and light pink. She decided to give up on sleep.

She kept her lower half in the sleeping bag and pulled her knees to her chest, making the rest of the bag look like a snakelike appendage. A woven-wool blanket was wrapped around her shoulders, and her jacket hood was draped over her head. From a distance she likely looked like a pile of discarded clothing.

It was nearly full light when Ian came out with a thermos full of hot, black coffee and a napkin containing a pancake wrapped around a link sausage. She was so hungry her stomach felt like it was doubling back on itself, but her vegetarian tendencies caused her nose to wrinkle up at the thought of eating sausage.

"Hey, beggars can't be choosers." Ian shoved the bundle of carbs and meat toward her. "It's turkey sausage, so it's healthy."

She took the bundle as he smirked at her. "I think you enjoy my misery a bit too much." She plucked the sausage out of the pancake, wrapped it in the napkin and devoured the pancake in three bites.

"Torturing you keeps me entertained." He winked at her and rubbed his arms to keep warm. "How's the back?"

"It aches a bit, but it's not the worst pain I've ever had. When Freeman crushed my hand? Now that hurt."

"Jesus, I'd forgotten about that. It seems like a hundred years ago." Ian took a drink of coffee from the thermos he'd brought. "Any sign of Tex?"

Erika had a mouth full of dry pancake. "Do you see him?" She gestured toward the expanse of empty desert beneath the radio telescope where Tex had disappeared.

It had been about twenty-four hours since Tex had vanished into thin air before the eyes of dozens of onlookers. Dr. Lewis had told her that even if he slowed his metabolism, he likely had no more than eighteen hours of breathable air, maybe twenty.

But Erika did not give up on people easily, and she knew Tex better than any of them did. Dr. Lewis had also said that the planet to which he went might have breathable air. She pinned her hope on that thought.

Ian stretched and yawned. "How long do you plan to stay out here?"

Erika wiped her mouth with the back of her hand and washed down the less-than-mediocre food with a swig of warm coffee. "As long as it takes."

Ian laid an icy hand on her thigh. "Erika, at some point you're going to have to accept the truth. He's gone, chica."

It wasn't like Erika hadn't thought the thought. Of course she had. She'd heard Dr. Lewis. She knew the facts. Maybe it was because she'd already lost so much, she wasn't willing to lose any more. Or maybe it was the feeling deep in her gut that he was still alive out there, somewhere. *Or maybe I'm just too damned stubborn to admit defeat.*

Erika wriggled her legs out of the sleeping bag. They'd gotten too warm in the morning sun. "I know you're probably right. But I'm not ready yet to let him go."

Ian wrapped an arm around her shoulder and kissed the top of her head. He pushed her away and held his nose. "Dang, girl, you need to at least take a break from your vigil long enough to shower."

He dropped another napkin-wrapped package on her sleeping bag pile before he left her sitting on the sandy ground. She opened the package and found a half-dozen fresh-baked peanut butter cookies.

"Now we're talking." She downed half of the cookies by the time Ian's form disappeared around the corner of the operations building.

Her eyes had closed and she was just beginning to doze off when the ground beneath her rumbled. *Oh no, not again.* She trembled at the thought of another orb appearing with another alien hunter trying to eat her.

In an instant she was fully alert. She threw off the blanket wrap, was on her feet with the Taser in one hand and a pistol in the other. Erika bristled at how quickly a little earth tremor had made her paranoid mind jump to the conclusion that she needed to defend herself.

There was no ball of electrical current this time. Dust swirled in a mini cyclone under the radio telescope. At first it was no larger than a dog but continued to grow until it blew so hard that she had to cover her eyes with her arm to keep out the dust and tiny rocks and debris.

As suddenly as the mini twister began, it stopped. The dust settled, and the rumbling earth was still, the air silent once again.

Tex lay on the ground. His space suit was so caked in sandy dirt that he blended into the desert soil. Only his wavy white-gold hair revealed him.

Erika shoved the Taser into her jacket pocket and the pistol into her waistband. She ran as quickly as her sore and tired legs would allow. She truly had not entertained the idea that he was dead before now. But he lay motionless, and her heart raced with fear as her eyes filled with tears.

She pulled the two-way radio from a clip at her belt and radioed Dr. Lewis. She screamed into the com. "Hurry! Get medics out here. He's back!"

There was squawking on the other end, but she ignored it. She could never understand what they were saying anyway.

He was face down, and she rolled him toward her. Dr. Lewis had been so adamant with him that he not remove his helmet, but it was gone. Whether he'd ditched it while on the distant planet or lost it in transit, Erika could not say. Tex's face was in its more human form and covered in pale orangey-pink dust. There were tear streaks on his smooth cheeks.

He didn't make a sound when she moved him. Her fingers shook as she tried to find a pulse point to check for a beat. She reached inside the tight collar of his suit and bent to listen for a breath as she felt for a pulse. At first she felt neither breath nor pulse. She trembled all over. Finally she felt a faint beat beneath her fingers.

Erika collapsed over him. Tears of joy and exhaustion traced lines down her dusty cheeks. Tex was alive.

Tex awoke in his quarters with an IV in his arm. Plastic tubing snaked up to a bag full of clear liquid taped with duct tape to the wall behind the headboard of his bed. There were plastic tubes in his nose connected to a portable oxygen tank. He blinked his eyes a few times to clear his bleary vision. He jerked the oxygen tubes from his nose and yanked off the tape holding the IV needle. He took a deep breath, bracing for the pain, and pulled the tiny IV needle from his vein. There was only a small trickle of purply-red blood.

It was dark outside, and the only light came from the hall lights that spilled in from under the door to his room. The digital clock said 2:30. He had no idea if he had been back on Earth for a few hours or weeks, but what he had to tell Dr. Lewis could not wait.

Tex rifled through his duffle bag at the end of his bed. He found a clean T-shirt and pulled it over his head as he slipped on a pair of shoes. He didn't bother to tie the sneakers.

He passed Erika's room and stopped briefly outside the door. He considered letting himself in and curling up next to her. The dream they had shared during his sweat had carried him through his journey to Elosia and back. He wondered if she was as soft and yielding in reality as she had been in his imagination.

His hand was on the knob, but he did not turn it. He pulled his hand back and continued on to Dr. Lewis' room.

He knew that humans valued their privacy and were modest about being seen in various states of undress. He hoped that Dr. Lewis would not be too aghast at the interruption of her sleep, but he was ready for the reprobation.

Tex flung open the door to her room, flipped the light switch and was at her bedside before her eyes were fully open. He stood beside her bed as still as a stone and waited for her to sit up and wake fully.

She blinked and squinted at him while she yawned. Tex handed her the glasses sitting on the stand beside the bed. Dr. Lewis clumsily put the glasses on and blinked again then smiled.

"My, don't you look a hundred times better. I'm glad you're feeling well but kind of wish you'd waited until morning to – "

"The gods have spoken, and I must tell you what they said."

Dr. Lewis' smile faded. She pushed herself up in the bed. "I'm going to need coffee for this."

Tex and Dr. Lewis sat in the small, musty break room. Dr. Lewis clutched a hot cup of coffee in her hands while Tex mustered the patience to wait for her to wake up fully.

Dr. Lewis had wanted to gather all of the scientists and even General Hays for Tex's briefing on his experience on Elosia. Tex had probed her mind and knew that Dr. Lewis wanted to believe that he had actually visited another planet. But she was having a hard time wrapping her head around the possibility even though she had seen him vanish into thin air and reappear on the same sandy soil days later. *If Dr. Lewis only half believes me, the general and his men are unlikely to give it any credence at all.*

He had no proof that it had happened. His helmet cam had recorded hours of video. But the helmet lay now like just another bit of detritus on Elosia, a relic waiting to be found by some future explorer. *Or burnt to a crisp when the sun finally eats the planet.*

Tex implored Dr. Lewis to forego gathering a crowd to hear what he had to say. She said he had been out for nearly twenty-four hours, but he was still weak. He did not have the energy to contend with questions from a dozen people. He again considered waking Erika. She would want to hear about his experience. But he needed to be frank with Dr. Lewis, and what he had to say, he didn't want Erika to hear.

Dr. Lewis was still dressed in her pajamas, her feet in fluffy slippers to ward off the chill that permeated the barracks. She held the coffee like it was life-giving nectar from the heavens.

Tex told her everything in as much detail as he could from the first sight of the alien world to the eerie walk through the abandoned underground city. Her eyes never left his. She asked a few questions but mainly listened intently.

But after nearly an hour of Tex speaking in great detail about his journey over the deserted planet and through the empty city, Dr. Lewis became impatient. "Tex, are you telling me that there was no one? That you did not learn how to close the Mocht Bogha?"

"Oh, no. I know how to close it."

"Cut to the chase. You don't need to tell me about every grain of sand or mote of dust you saw."

"But I thought you would enjoy the details, Dr. Lewis. To share the experience even if vicariously."

She chuckled and sipped her coffee. "Well, yes, ordinarily I would want you to regale me with every second. But we're running out of time, friend. In the brief time you were away, the M'Uktah have killed thousands in Paris. But with the help of NATO forces, including a good deal of our own troops, several of them have been taken out too. Our generals fear that our resistance will only hasten the arrival of even more ships through that portal. We've got to get that gate closed. Now."

"I see." Tex quickly pushed his story ahead to his meeting and conversation with Cynothian. Dr. Lewis appeared to barely breathe as he told her of the truth of human origins as well as their relationship to the M'Uktah.

She didn't seem as shocked as he assumed she would be. She said only, "We're related to them?"

Tex nodded. "But the good news is that I can close the gate. I will need some help from you – and the machines here. But I can do it."

The look of awe mixed with fatigue vanished from Dr. Lewis' face and was replaced with joy. "You can? What do you need me to do?"

"It's quite simple really. In hindsight it seems like I should have figured it out on my own." Tex shook his head. "Anyway, all I need from you is to simply align this array to the exact coordinates in the Kuiper belt where the Mocht Bogha appears."

The smile on Dr. Lewis' face was gone. She threw up her hands. "Oh, is that all?" Her voice was laden with sarcasm.

It truly had seemed like a simple thing to Tex. "Yes. Is that going to be difficult?"

She put her head in her hands and rubbed at her temples. "Dammit, it shouldn't be. But the general cut us off from the controls. He wasn't happy, you see, that I had gone behind his back to orchestrate your travel arrangements to another planet. So I have no ability to align these dishes, nor does Dr. Fisher. Our hands are tied."

Tex rose from the table and stretched his arms over his head. "You concentrate on the science and leave the general to me."

"Yes, you should go to him. I got so wrapped up in your story that I forgot to tell you that General Hays wanted to see you as soon as you regained consciousness. He hopes you can communicate with the creature they captured."

This was a new and surprising detail that Tex had not known.

"One of the M'Uktah is here?"

She sipped her coffee and nodded. "But little good it does us. We have no ability to communicate with him. And he has tried to speak, but our best linguists have no clue what he's saying. Hays wants you to take a crack at speaking with it."

Tex let out a wry laugh. "The general had no use for me before. Now he thinks I have some ability to speak in the language of an alien?"

"Actually, it was your friend Erika's idea. She suggested to Hays that you might be able to communicate with the alien telepathically."

Clever Erika. And perhaps she was right. He had been able to communicate with the Conexus and the Elosians. Maybe he could "speak" with this captured M'Uktah telepathically.

He refocused on aligning the array to the Mocht Bogha. "How much time will you need to get the telescopes aligned?"

Dr. Lewis rubbed her temples more. "Observations. Calculations. Confirmation. Two days, maybe three."

Tex put a hand on her shoulder. "Tomorrow. At dawn."

Dr. Lewis checked her watch. "But that's little more than twenty-four hours. How–"

Tex did not hear the rest of what she had to say. He was already gone.

———————

Tex stood by Dr. Randall's bedside just as he had stood by Dr. Lewis' bed. The old man's mouth was open, and a loud buzzing sound emanated from it.

Being aboveground seemed to agree with the old man. When he had seen Dr. Randall at the school just a few weeks ago before he and Erika escaped, Tex had figured the old guy for dead within days. But even asleep, Dr. Randall looked more alive than he had in years. He was glad of it. His feelings about Dr. Randall had been confused. He had left the world of the Conexus bitter and angry with his creator. But as he stood there looking down on him, Tex was happy to know that Dr. Randall was still in the world.

Tex considered standing there until the old man woke naturally. Many people seemed to have a way of knowing, even in their sleep, when they're being stared at. He wondered if the doctor could sense it.

After waiting a few more minutes, Tex decided he did not have the time for the experiment. He whispered his name. "Dr. Randall?"

The old guy let out a loud snore.

Tex shook his shoulder and said his name again only more loudly this time. "Dr. Randall."

Dr. Randall snorted out a loud snore, and his eyes snapped open. He searched with half-closed eyes, and they finally rested on Tex. A quick smile lit up his face. "Tex, my boy." He sat up and coughed. "Oh, I'm sorry. Old habit. I know you don't like me to call you that." His eyes were downcast, his lips curled into a frown.

"It's okay. Don't worry about it." Tex stepped back from the bed, giving Dr. Randall room to swing his legs over the side. "I have a task for you."

"Anything you need. What can I do for you?"

Tex hesitated briefly, unsure exactly how to put it. Dr. Randall reached for his glasses from the bedside table, put them on and looked up at Tex expectantly through thick glass.

"I want you to contact Mother. The gate must be closed, and I need my sister's help to do it."

Dr. Randall's shoulders sagged, and what little color was in his cheeks drained from them. He wiped his eyes behind his glasses. "I do not think I am the best person to talk to her. Though I helped her with the gene therapy, the last time we saw each other she put me in house arrest."

Tex did not know the full story of their history together. Tex had wondered from time to time if they had been lovers. Or maybe they were merely colleagues that had had a falling out. He did not know, but at this point it was irrelevant. Tex needed Alecto, and if Dr. Randall could not get through to Sturgis' paranoid mind and get her to command Alecto to assist, then no one could.

"You're the only one that can do this. I need you to do this."

Dr. Randall smiled wanly. "You know I cannot refuse you. I never could."

Tex smiled back because he knew it was true.

He left the doctor to take care of his morning routine and work on getting Commander Sturgis to bring Alecto into the heart of a military operation. The thought of working with Alecto brought a mixture of anxious stomach roiling and heart-pounding thrill. She had, after all, twice done her best to kill him. But she was also the only other person on the planet that was of his same species. Regret brought tears to his eyes, but he blinked them away. If things had been different, maybe they could have been like real brother and sister. Perhaps they even could have learned from each other and become friends. But he had no time for might-have-beens. He only hoped now that she would agree to lend the assistance he so desperately needed from her.

Tex sped by Ian's room and Erika's without stopping to speak to either of them, though he very much wanted to. He could withhold the truth of what he had to do from Dr. Lewis and even Dr. Randall. He probably could get through a conversation with Ian and not tip his hand, though he wasn't willing to risk it.

But he knew there was no way he could spend the day with Erika without her knowing that he was withholding information. Though she could not read minds like he could, she had an uncanny ability to ferret out truth like a bloodhound on a scent. And she was especially good at knowing when he lied. If his plan were to work, he would need every ounce of his energy. He had none to spare for confrontation with Erika. His goal was to avoid her for an entire day.

Jack wished he had seen Anna's face when Croft claimed she would one day rule over the warped and empty kingdom he'd created.

"I don't know what you're talking about."

"I grow tired of having guns pointed at me. Come to the sitting room." Croft glanced at his watch. "It's tea time, after all. It will take some getting used to living in the dark." Croft left them staring after him as he walked toward a set of white double doors that were open to a spacious room to their left.

Croft showed them his back. It would be such an easy shot. If Lizzy had done it to Anna's dad, Jack could do it to Croft. *Why is he making himself so vulnerable?* Croft was too smart for that. It felt like a trap. Besides, they needed to get the antivirus first, and they had no idea where it was. Croft could have hidden it in a place they'd never find.

Jack wished he knew what Anna was thinking. She didn't take the shot either.

"Come have tea. Just because the world up top is devolving into chaos doesn't mean we can't behave like civilized people down here." Croft entered the room, the shot now obscured by one of the tall columns.

Jack's stomach chose that moment to growl loudly. "I could go for some tea."

Anna strolled past him but took a moment to roll her eyes at him.

This room was as sumptuously decorated as the foyer. The wall to their left was filled with floor-to-ceiling windows as though the builders expected the room to have a view that it never would. The floors here were wood laid in a parquet pattern. The walls were smooth plaster painted a pale blue accented with white decorative moldings. The coffered ceiling was lit by a row of crystal chandeliers, none quite as large as the one in the entry but still grand.

A central seating arrangement was laid out on a large, hand-tufted rug of rich blue, emerald and yellow. Croft sat in a deep brown leather chair, his legs crossed, his fingers steepled under his chin the way Sturgis sometimes did.

Jack's eyes swept the room. He neither saw nor heard anyone else.

"Please sit." His voice was gracious, as if he was a friend of theirs expecting them for afternoon tea. Croft pressed a button on an intercom sitting on the table beside his chair.

A woman's voice spoke over the com. "Yes, Sir Croft? Would you be wanting your tea now?"

Croft's face tensed, and he slightly rolled his eyes. He was clearly annoyed with the woman on the other end of the com, though Jack had no idea why. She sounded like a pleasant, older British lady.

Croft spoke through nearly gritted teeth in the sort of fake pleasant voice a person uses when trying not to show anger even when livid. "Yes, Dottie, it is 3:00, which means it's tea time. And bring serving for five. We have guests."

"Oh, yes sir," Dottie said. She sounded excited.

It was hard to say how long Croft had had the poor woman cooped up in the strange mansion underground. For all Jack knew, seeing as how Croft's mansion was so far from the town square – or even Dr. Randall's place for that matter – Dottie could have been down there when the alien ship had arrived and probably not even known it.

The sound of footsteps echoing on the marble floor in the entry made Jack jump. Anna had already taken a seat on the tightly upholstered couch diagonally to Croft, but Jack turned toward the door in an instant, his gun drawn. Alecto turned as well, her hand rising into the air, ready to strike.

Ben's lanky frame came into view. His geeky glasses were gone. His chin was shadowed by a few days of facial hair growth, making him look older. He'd exchanged the white lab coat and loose-fitting khakis for a tightly fitted black T-shirt, black jeans and had a gun holster in plain view, a pistol pressed close to his side.

Ben looked menacing without his glasses and dressed in all black. Or maybe he seemed sinister now because Jack knew the guy had made a pact with the devil and put millions of lives in danger.

"Brad, I think you know Anna, Alecto and of course, Mr. Wilson."

Croft using only Jack's last name was getting on his nerves. "I thought your name was Ben. So even your identity was a lie?" Jack shook his head at Brad. "You suggested he go to New Mexico to get him out of the way, not because you were thinking of him. You son-of-a-bitch." Jack was not looking forward to telling Ian the truth. It was going to hurt him more than Jack could imagine.

Brad's easygoing smile was gone. He wore a derisive smirk. "Look, kid, I didn't mean to hurt your friend. He's nice to look at and all. But business is business. If he didn't want to feel the sting, he shouldn't have begun playing with fire."

Jack had never wanted to punch someone more. His hands pumped into fists, and he was about to let loose a punch, but Alecto's thin hand on his arm kept him from swinging.

Brad walked past him and took his smirk with him. He sat in the other leather chair opposite Croft.

Jack didn't want to sit, and he was sure as hell not in the mood for tea anymore. Dottie chose that moment to enter with a cart filled with a three-tiered plate of finger sandwiches and tiny cakes. She brought two pots of tea and enough cups for all of them.

Without being asked, she poured a cup for Croft, dropped in two sugars, squeezed a small wedge of lemon into the cup and handed it to him with a curtsy. You would think she was serving the King of England.

Jack's stomach rumbled again. He decided to give in to his traitorous stomach and eat. They remained quiet, locked in mutual stares of distrust as Dottie doled out a bit of each food item to everyone. If she noticed that all of them save for Croft was packing heat, she didn't say anything about it or even acknowledge the weapons with a flick of her eyes.

After serving the tea and food, Dottie left the room and closed the door behind her. It was a strange thing to do seeing as how the only other person in the whole house was a cook. Anna shot Jack a look out of the corner of her eye. *So she noticed it too.*

Croft's eyes had hardly left Anna. He stared at her now over his teacup. "I deeply regret the errors of my progeny's ways. All of them, so flawed." He set his cup down. "Lizzy's jealousy of your perfect beauty caused her to slash at you, Anna. But even a milky eye hardly diminishes your radiance. In fact, once my medical team gets here, they may well be able to repair the damage and make you whole again. After all, who wants to be ruled by an ugly queen?"

Anna flung her porcelain cup at the floor. The loud crash made all of them jump. "For God's sake, stop saying that. I'm not going to become a surrogate daughter for you and rule by your side over your pathetic kingdom. I've done nothing but try to bring you down. You must know that. What could make you possibly think that I'd help you?"

Croft put his cup down gently on the table beside him. "Because you were born for it. More precisely, engineered for it." He steepled his fingers under his chin again and looked at her intently as though waiting for the meaning of what he'd said to sink in.

Anna's voice was incredulous. "What are you talking about?"

Alecto's stoic voice broke in. "You are like me, Anna. Genetically programmed. Correct?"

"And Sturgis said you weren't the smart one. That's right, Ten."

"My name is Alecto."

Croft acted as though he hadn't heard her. "Ten has the right of it."

Anna rose and faced him, her hands on her hips. She trembled with anger. "Are you telling me that my mother and father aren't really my parents? That I was created in a lab somewhere?"

"Of course Robert and Hannah were your parents. Don't be daft. It was their genetic material we used. Only perfected."

"But what about Thomas? He's my brother, isn't he?" There was panic in her voice.

"Yes, but obviously the process was not perfect. He was a mistake." Croft's eyes grew darker.

Jack's mind was still back on something Croft had said. *'Robert and Hannah were your parents.'* He'd watched her dad get shot and killed. But he thought her mother was alive. He hated to ask the question, but he figured Anna would want to know the truth. "What happened to Anna's mother?"

Croft turned his attention to Jack and narrowed his eyes. "I said nothing about anything happening to her. Why do you ask me this?"

"You referred to her in the past tense."

Anna slowly sat back down. She put a hand out for Jack, and he took it. "You son-of-a-bitch. What did you do to my mother?"

Croft smoothed the legs of his pants and cast his gaze downward. "I did nothing to Hannah." When he looked up again, for a brief moment he looked as though he might cry. "She took her own life, Anna. I would have stopped her if I could. You must believe me when I say that I grieve for her as you will. She was my dearest cousin. And oldest friend."

Anna let out a wry laugh. "You grieve? You can't weep. You feel nothing. How dare you even speak about her as though she was your friend."

"There's so much you don't know. So little that you truly understand. But in time, you'll learn. Your mother and father chose this for you. Planned it for you before you were born. To rule Apthartos is your birthright. Soon there will be others. They're on their way here now, from every corner of the globe. Men and women, the best of the best, chosen to be part of the Makers. And others like you too, Anna. Engineered to be even stronger and more intelligent than their parents. You're one of the chosen ones."

"Chosen for what? To live in a freakin' cave for the rest of our lives?" Anna's voice had gone pitchy. She dug her fingers into Jack's thigh from her anger.

"You will be the mother of a new evolution of humankind, Anna. It's your destiny. I've already chosen your mate. A young man who is your equal in every way. But you've already met him."

Brad put his teacup down on the end table beside his chair. "We'll get along beautifully, I'm sure."

The way Brad's eyes openly roved over Anna's body made Jack come nearly unglued. "You've got to be kidding. This guy? Yesterday he was gay. Now you're saying he's going to be what? King of the underground douchebag brigade? And Anna's husband?"

Croft's voice was impatient. "We have no need here for the trappings and conventions of the world up top. Anna need not marry. But she will be expected to reproduce, and Brad has been matched to her by an algorithm. They are the perfect match to produce the most genetically superior offspring."

Anna was on her feet again. She threw up her hands. "All of this—this waste of taxpayer money—was all for your twisted eugenics experiment?" She let out a nervous laugh. "I don't know why you'd possibly think I would voluntarily be your breeding sow."

Croft gave her a condescending smile. "There is always an easy way and a hard way. Voluntary or involuntary, you will do what is required of you to fill our fine city with perfect Sturgis/Croft babies. And once the virus has run its course and the M'Uktah have culled the herd, so to speak, and left the planet, the Makers descendants will repopulate the Earth with a more perfect version of ourselves."

Jack sprang to his feet. "Over my dead body."

"That can be arranged." Croft gave a small nod of his head to Brad.

Brad had his pistol in his hand before Jack had a finger on his. For the second time in a twenty-four-hour period, a bullet rocketed in Jack's direction.

Jack closed his eyes, braced for the ripping pain of yet another gunshot wound, and prayed that he would die quickly. He didn't want Anna to see him suffer.

Everything happened so quickly. The sound of the hammer hitting the pin. Alecto on her feet, moving with her preternatural speed. Jack trying to duck left to avoid being shot. Alecto standing in front of him, her arms stretched out in front of her.

She's going to take a bullet to protect me?

But the bullet didn't hit her. Neither did the second shot or the third. The casings plinked to the wood floor. Brad unloaded an entire magazine, but not one shot hit any of them.

"I thought you couldn't do that?" Jack whispered.

"Apparently she can," Anna said.

Jack and Anna both stood and grabbed the rifles from their backs. Anna pointed hers at Croft. Jack's was trained on Brad.

Brad reached behind his back for something. Jack wasn't going to wait to see what it was.

"Keep your hands where I can see them," he shouted. "I don't want to kill you, but I will."

Brad ignored Jack's request. He didn't seem intimidated in the slightest. His hands were quick. There was a glint of metal and blades flying at them before Jack had even registered what Brad had retrieved from his back pockets.

"Duck!" Anna shouted.

Alecto did not duck. And her shield did not prevent the blades from reaching her.

She caught each knife with her bare hands.

Brad's face turned ashen. He looked like he was going to puke.

He may have been genetically engineered to be the perfect specimen of humanity, but Alecto was something beyond even him. She held the knives in her hands and deftly flipped them so she held the handles, the blades pointed at Brad.

Croft rose. His voice was shrill. "Enough. You've had your fun, displaying for each other like rams in rutting season." His lip curled up in disgust.

"No, Croft, it is not enough," Alecto said. "You will give us the antivirus and all that you stole from Dr. Montoya. We will then leave here, never to return." She advanced on him, but her backside was exposed to Brad.

Jack kept his rifle pointed at Brad. The guy was still visibly shaken by what he'd seen Alecto do. If his bullets couldn't touch her and she plucked flying knives out of thin air, he didn't stand much of a chance against her.

And he hasn't even seen her snap a person's neck with only a thought.

Croft wore an imperious look on his face. "Or what?"

Brad pushed a new magazine into his pistol.

"Cooperate, and I will spare your life. If you refuse, I'll end you."

"Is that so?"

Croft pushed a button on his intercom station. Sprinklers popped out of the ceiling. Water sprayed and rained down on them. It was cold and smelled of iron and like hard water from a well.

"Now!" Croft yelled.

Alecto stood unyielding, her small body now looming before Croft. The water made reloading Brad's gun a challenge. He cursed as he tried to get the magazine fully loaded. Alecto looked over her shoulder, flicked her arm at him, and the bones in Brad's neck crunched as they snapped.

He fell forward with a loud thud. His head hit the coffee table, and he slumped finally to the floor. His eyes were open, but there was no one home.

Alecto turned her full attention back to Croft. "Your attempts to weaken me will not work. I am no longer vulnerable to water."

Croft's eyes were wide, his mouth agape. "Wha... How?" He plopped down into his chair, shrinking back from Alecto.

"You're surprised?" Anna asked.

"Guess Brad was too busy stealing the antivirus and laying waste to my friend's emotions to pay attention to Dr. Randall's work on the gene therapy for Alecto," Jack said.

The house had been chilly before. The drenching made Jack downright cold.

Alecto didn't seem to notice or mind the cold water. She advanced on Croft, her hand outstretched toward him. "You will give me the location of the antivirus."

Anna screamed, "Don't kill him! I have to question him."

Croft's face relaxed a bit. "Call the creature off, and I will answer your queries."

Anna shook her head, raised her pistol and took a few steps toward him. "You don't get it. You'll never freakin' get it. She's not a creature. We're not your property." Her voice trembled with anger. Tears streamed down her face. She wiped her face on her shoulder but kept her gun trained on Croft. "I'm going to tear down your spider's web. Now tell us where the damned antivirus is, or I'll order Alecto here to torture the crap out of you until you do."

Torture seemed a little dark for Anna, but she'd been pushed to her edge. Croft was so arrogant and defiant though, Jack feared there would be no other way to get him to hand the goods over.

Alecto pressed two thin fingers to Croft's temple. He shrank back from her touch.

"He does not need to speak," she said. "I will obtain the information we need." Alecto's eyes glared into Croft's, then she closed them. She slowly raised her other arm and placed her other hand at his temple, his head held between her hands like a vice.

Croft squirmed, but her grip was firm. His face contorted in pain.

Alecto's face too scrunched up in agony. "It will pain you less if you stop resisting. I will retrieve the information, one way or another."

Croft let out a throaty, primal growl. His hands closed around Alecto's tiny wrists. He pulled and kicked feebly with his legs. His arms shook from the effort of trying to free himself from Alecto's grasp.

Alecto's body trembled as well, but she did not let go. Her eyes were open now, wide and determined.

Croft's voice was hoarse and small as he tried to scream out, "She's killing me."

"Stop," Anna cried. "I have to get answers."

Alecto did not stop. Croft slid even further down the chair, his arms now loose at his sides. His legs had stopped kicking. Tears of pain rolled down his face. Still Alecto held his head tightly in her hands.

Jack grabbed Alecto's arms and tried to yank her away. "Stand down. That's an order. We need more intel before he can be terminated."

Alecto released her hold, her hands hovering in the air on either side of his head. She was still and quiet, as if frozen into place.

Croft's head lolled to the side. His eyes were open, but his body was still.

Jack felt his neck. "He's still alive. But I'm not sure what you'll be able to get out of him. He's non-responsive. I think she short-circuited his brain."

Anna's voice was full of rage. "Alecto, why didn't you stop when I told you? There were questions I needed him to answer. Not only about the antivirus and Dr. Montoya's stolen research, but about his plan and...and about my mother."

Alecto wobbled on her feet and looked near to passing out. Jack helped her back to the couch to sit. He yanked the pack from his back, found a water bottle and handed it to her.

Her hand trembled as she drank deeply. Once the bottle was drained, she said, "I know the location of the antivirus."

Anna's hands were on her hips. She loomed over Alecto, her eyes two large, dark pools. "That's something, but it's not enough. I needed time with him. You ruined any chance I'll ever have to know exactly what happened."

Jack gently placed his hands on Anna's shoulders and turned her to him. She turned her angry glare on him, but he didn't shrink away from her. "Back off, Anna. She did the best she could. I know you want answers, but remember the primary reason we came down here. Remember the people who need that antivirus."

The storm in her eyes blew away. A fresh fountain of tears welled in her eyes, and she let out a ragged breath. "You're right."

Jack wiped a tear from her cheek with his thumb and pulled her to him. "It will be okay. I've got you."

She shivered beneath his arms. Long sobs wracked her body.

Alecto's voice was hoarse. "I know answers to your questions," she croaked. "I could not trust him to speak the truth. I had to go deeply into his mind. To bypass lies so large he believed them. You see why I had to do it, don't you? He would have lied. But I found the truth buried inside him."

Anna unpeeled herself from Jack's embrace. "I'm sorry. I should not have snapped at you like that."

"Human emotions are volatile. I am accustomed to humans acting in irrational ways." Her voice held no bitterness or rancor.

"What did you learn about my mother?"

Alecto rose from the couch in a swift, effortless motion. "Your mother is indeed dead."

Anna's hand flew to her mouth as she gasped.

Jack put an arm around her shoulders and drew her into him.

Anna's voice cracked as she spoke. "So what he said earlier was true. But I can't believe she took her own life. Did he kill her?"

Alecto glanced at Croft, still slumped in the chair like a sack of flour. His eyes were open, but he stared blankly. "No, he did not."

Alecto dispassionately recounted Croft's memories. "They had been talking about your father. About how they both missed him. Croft apologized. He had not ordered Lizzy to do that. He referred to Robert Sturgis as his oldest friend."

"That seems hard to believe, seeing as how his goons at the penthouse were pretty intent on killing your dad," Jack said.

Anna nodded.

Alecto continued. "Croft promised your mother that he would take care of you, Anna. And Thomas. He turned from her for a moment, and when he turned back, she drank her tea. He noticed a small empty vial on the table next to her cup. He watched her die."

"He made her drink poison? So he did kill her." Anna pulled the gun from her holster and aimed at Croft. "Vegetable or no, I'm – "

"He was surprised. He had no knowledge of the poison she had hidden. He cried. He loved her."

Anna's quaking arms slowly lowered. "I didn't think this monster could love anyone." She put her gun back in the holster and rubbed at her temples. "None of this makes sense. Why would she kill herself?"

"She told Croft that she wanted to join Robert."

Anna fell onto the couch. "Tell me everything. From beginning to end of their last meeting."

Alecto recounted the encounter as if describing a live-action play. She described body language, recalled dialogue and Croft's emotions. It would have been more entertaining if Alecto had not told it as if reading the stock market report. But Jack was glad Anna had the truth now. Any missing pieces of the story of her mother's death would have haunted her for the rest of her life.

Anna knelt at Croft's chair. She took his hand in hers. When they arrived he had looked virile and strong, especially for a man his age. But now he looked fragile and old.

"Can you hear me?" she asked.

Croft's eyes roamed lazily as if he was coming off of anesthesia. They finally landed on Anna. "I know you?"

Anna nodded. "Yes. I'm Anna."

He frowned. "I don't know any Anna. I..." Tears welled in his eyes. "I don't know—I don't know you. I don't know anything." His eyes were wide with panic. His hands flew to his head, and his eyes scrunched up. "When I try to remember—" He groaned in pain. "It hurts. Oh God, it's agony." He wept. "Make it stop. Anna, make it go away."

Anna rose. She wiped her nose on her sleeve and took the pistol from its holster again. She aimed at Croft's head, holding the gun with both hands. Her arms quivered, and the gun shook.

"I...I can't do this." Her arms dropped to her sides.

Jack put his hand at the small of her back and took the gun from her trembling hand. He wiped the tears and kissed her lightly. "You don't have to."

"But it's not right to leave him like this. He's suffering."

"You don't have to, because I will."

Her eyes met his, and fresh tears welled. "But Jack – "

"Go with Alecto. Find the antivirus and Dr. Montoya's research. Meet me back in the foyer."

"Alecto could do this. Maybe she could even heal him."

"The damage is not something I can repair," Alecto said.

"And I need her with you in case you run into trouble." He kissed her forehead. "Now go. I've got this."

Anna kissed him again, more deeply this time, her hand at the back of his head, pulling him to her. She held him there, their foreheads touching. "I love you."

The three words he had said to Erika, and she'd gotten scared and pushed him away. But Anna wasn't scared of his love, and she certainly wasn't pushing him away.

"I love you too," he said. He hoped it wouldn't be the last time he got to tell her that.

She left with Alecto and closed the door behind them.

Alecto could have finished Croft off without expending much energy, and they could have left together to retrieve the antiviral. But he needed to do this. He'd once let Erika down when he hadn't been able to pull the trigger. He wasn't about to let Anna down too.

It would have been easier to pull the trigger though if Croft wasn't an unarmed, severely injured man. And Jack had already done far more killing than he'd ever wanted. Hell, even one death was more than he'd ever planned on.

He'd shivered from the cold only seconds before, but now he wiped nervous sweat from his brow. He tried to focus on his mom's death. On how Croft was at least partly to blame seeing as how he backed the Conexus plan.

But even his anger, hurt and grief didn't override the fact that the man slumped in the chair was not the same guy that had schemed with the Conexus. Alecto had already killed Croft. The shell of a man before him was only an old man in tremendous pain.

Croft looked up at him. His eyes were rimmed in red. His nose dripped and his face twisted in agony as he tried to understand who Jack was and why he had a gun pointed at him. "Robert. Is that you, Robert?"

Jack wiped his face with his shoulder. "I'm Jack. Robert's dead."

Croft cried in earnest then. "Dead? Oh, Robert." His hands were at the sides of his head again. He looked up at Jack with wild eyes. "Whoever you are, please use that gun. I beg of you. I don't know who I am. I don't know." He screamed out in pain, a long yowl like an injured animal. "Make it stop!"

Jack fired the gun. The blast echoed off of the high ceiling and plaster walls. He wiped the blood spatter from his face and walked out without looking back.

There was no feeling of relief within him. No weight had been lifted from his shoulders. He felt no satisfaction that the man who had caused so much suffering for so many was at last dead.

There was only the hope that he would never have to take another human life again for as long as he lived.

Jack closed the door behind him to the room where Croft lay in a pool of his own blood. He slid down the wall and sat on the floor, the wall behind him holding him up. He tried to calm himself to get his breathing to return to normal.

He waited for nearly fifteen minutes and was about to go in search of Anna and Alecto when he heard footsteps coming from the upstairs landing. In the span of one heartbeat, he was on his feet, his gun drawn.

Jack eased silently toward a column and hid behind it. Alecto had said for all they knew, Croft could have more men hiding in an even deeper, more secret space. It seemed logical that if he had more men, he would have called on them when he was first in trouble. But Jack was on alert anyway. He peeked slowly around the column.

Anna bounded down the stairs, taking them by twos. Alecto had no problem keeping up with her.

Jack let out a relieved sigh and stowed his gun. He stepped from behind the column. "Were you successful?"

Anna raised her bulging backpack into the air. "We got what we came for." She beamed.

Her smile faded when she got closer to Jack. She wiped at the dried blood on Jack's cheek. Her voice was a whisper. "I'm sorry."

He held her hand to his cheek then kissed it. "I'm okay." He smiled at her. "We'll all be okay. Eventually."

She nodded. "But no rest for the weary. We finish one task but get called to another."

They left the Croft house and entered the eerie town once again. The bright overhead lights were on again.

"Looks like you were able to get hold of your Aunt Lilly and tell her the good news."

"Yes. And she had an interesting call while we were here."

"Yeah? From who?"

"Dr. Randall, of all people. Apparently he needs her help. At the VLA."

Jack kept walking.

Anna looked at him out of the corner of her eye. "And Aunt Lilly wants us to go with her." She continued staring at him, waiting to see his reaction.

But Jack did his best not to give her one. The truth was he didn't know how he felt about it. He was with Anna now and wanted to keep it that way. But he didn't relish seeing how Erika would react to him moving on so quickly and with a Sturgis no less. And for that matter, he wasn't thrilled about seeing Erika with Tex. He may have moved on, but pride could still be wounded.

"So? What do you think?" Anna asked.

Jack wasn't about to tell her the messy, complicated truth. He was far from an expert on women. Hell, he seemed to get it wrong most of the time. But he knew enough to know that Anna wasn't likely to be thrilled about the whole truth of his thoughts on the issue. He settled for a truth that avoided the topic of Erika. "I think it will be good to get the hell out of his stinkin' underground and back to hot desert sun. They need our help? Let's not keep them waiting."

Anna took his hand, and the three walked as quickly as they could out of Apthartos. They left behind the dank rot of the place and plenty of bloodstained memories.

Avoiding Erika had been difficult, but Tex mostly managed it. Every time he sensed her presence near, he found an excuse to go somewhere else. He locked himself in with a group of scientists and later General Hays. When she finally caught up to him on a gravel path leading from one building to another, her eyes shot daggers at him.

"You've been avoiding me." She stood with her arms crossed over her chest, her lips pulled back.

He considered for a brief moment telling her the truth. But he thought better of it. Saying to her, 'Yes, I'm avoiding you so I don't have to tell you the truth' didn't seem like it would go over well.

He settled instead for hugging her to him. Her shoulders relaxed beneath his arms, and she let out a deep breath. Her tears made his chest wet.

He had not expected her to cry. He had no time for her emotions today. He pushed back from her.

"I'm sorry, Erika, I know you want to talk, but I must go see Dr. Randall right now. Time is of the essence and—"

Her eyes were rimmed in red and narrowed at him. "Fine. Go. I only sat in the cold, freezing my ass off for more than two days waiting for you. That M'Uktah creature attacked me. Did you know that?"

Tex shook his head. His mouth was open to apologize, but he couldn't get a word in edgewise.

"And even after the attack, I went back out there to wait for you. I was there when you landed. Did you know that? Do you even care?"

He hadn't known that she had waited for him. Joy filled him. He wanted to hold her. To run his fingers through her hair. To kiss the tears from her cheeks and the anger from her brow. But he had no time for a languid afternoon with Erika. He settled for an attempt to at least get a reprieve from her anger at him.

He softened his eyes, wrapped an arm around her waist and kissed her. She was rigid at first against him, but her muscles relaxed, and she finally kissed him back.

He let her go, and her eyes were still closed.

Her eyes opened languidly. "Don't get into the habit of thinking you can kiss my anger away."

The *pfft, pfft, pfft* of helicopter blades interrupted their conversation. His recent history with helicopters caused him to instinctively search for a place to hide. He mentally chastised himself. It was likely Commander Sturgis arriving.

"Come. You will want to see this." He walked briskly away, leaving Erika to jog behind to catch up.

Dr. Randall had not only been successful at convincing Commander Sturgis to bring Alecto to the VLA, but she arrived in a Blackhawk helicopter just under three hours after Tex had met with Dr. Randall.

And she brought Jack and a young woman named Anna with her. Tex felt a slight twinge of lingering jealousy when he saw Jack. But it was clear from the moment he saw Jack with Anna that the two of them were a couple. That eased away his old, harsh feelings toward Jack. The guy had never done anything against Tex other than be the object of Erika's affection. But their recent kisses showed that Erika was no longer thinking of Jack.

The arrival caused a stir for everyone at the tightly controlled compound. General Hays was in the middle of going ballistic when Commander Sturgis' feet hit the ground. Once he saw her, the general's mouth closed like it had been sewn shut.

Sturgis was decked out in Air Force blue, her blond hair upswept into the French twist she had worn nearly every day of Tex's life. Her Air Force cap was arranged on her head perfectly and must have been pinned tightly since the chopper blades did not even threaten to blow it from her head. She pulled her jacket down as she walked briskly toward the general with Alecto on her heels. Jack jumped out of the copter and held out his hands to help Anna Sturgis out of the black craft.

Erika stood beside Ian, and Tex watched them watch Jack. Ian said something into Erika's ear, and he waved Jack over to them.

Erika's mouth was set in a thin line, and even from thirty yards away, Tex knew that she seethed.

It was obvious, even to Tex, that Jack had a new love. The way he held Anna's hand even after he had helped her from the chopper. The way she smiled up at him as her long hair blew away from her face in the breeze caused by the chopping blades.

Ian and Jack clasped hands and hugged briefly. He then stood in front of Erika and simply stared down at her smiling. Erika's chin was tilted up, her lips in a thin line. It was clear she was trying to wear a mask of indifference, but from where Tex stood it didn't seem that she was pulling it off very well. Jack said something Tex could not hear, and he held his arms out to his sides. Erika rolled her eyes and gave him a brief hug. Jack then introduced the young blond woman at his side to Erika. The two women shook hands briefly. Erika's eyes were narrowed, her lips pursed. But Anna wore a wide smile, her eyes sparkling.

The brief happiness Tex felt that Jack Wilson was finally no longer in the picture evaporated as soon as he realized Erika's anger was caused by jealousy. No matter how far they had come together, it seemed that Jack Wilson was a part of her that she was not willing to let go.

Erika must have felt his eyes on her. She looked over the crowd and directly at him. Her eyes caught his, but her face still held anger. Tex looked away and hurried to the general's side. He had no time for drama with Erika and Jack. He had a galactic portal to close and a meeting with his estranged family to attend.

Tex met the general back at the same conference table they had used before. Erika and Jack had angrily argued for their right to be at the table.

"I'm the one that brought him to you," Erika had said.

But both General Hays and Commander Sturgis were firmly in unison that Tex was the only teenager they would allow at the meeting that they were deeming classified. As the doors closed, the last thing Tex saw was Erika's face.

As the meeting began, it was clear from General Hays' uncharacteristic deference to Commander Sturgis that they had history together. Tex would never know the story, though he figured it was probably an interesting tale. At times it seemed that all of them—Dr. Randall, Commander Sturgis, Generals Hays and Bardsley—had long histories each with the other and many unspoken stories between them.

General Hays seemed genuinely flustered as they took their places at the table. Tex wasn't sure if it had to do with his history with Commander Sturgis or due to Alecto's shiny black eyes on him. Tex was in his more human form, and though his eyes were still quite large, overall he looked more human now than Conexus.

But Tex had always looked more human than Alecto. With her shiny, bulbous, bald head, black, baseball-sized eyes and grayish skin, it was clearly hard for the general not to stare.

While the general's eyes were fixed on Alecto, her eyes were glued to Tex. He tried to probe her mind, but she blocked him. *Her powers have grown.* Though he had become more adept at reading human emotion from their body language and facial expressions, Alecto was as much of an enigma to him as he had been to humans. Her eyes showed no emotion. Her face was a smooth mask. Tex had no way of knowing if she would be eager to help him or try to terminate him at the first opportunity.

As they took seats, General Hays finally managed to choke out some words. "Lilly—" He coughed. "I mean Commander Sturgis." His face colored. "To what do we owe this pleasure—I mean, honor?"

For her part, Commander Sturgis had never looked more confident, cool and in control. She sat board straight, her face a cool mask of indifference to the general. Not a hair was out of place, and her skin was smooth, pink and hydrated without a trace of her usual pale, lined pallor.

"It is good to see you again too, Ralph." She brought forth then a fake smile, her lips parted in a nearly seductive way as she slowly batted her eyelids at the general.

If Erika had been there, she would have sighed loudly and probably would have commented out loud on how fake it was. Even Tex nearly rolled his eyes. But the general seemed to eat up the attention like a toddler sucking down ice cream. His face turned two shades darker red until he looked as though his head would pop like a blood blister.

While Hays shifted nervously in his seat and pulled at the collar of his shirt, Commander Sturgis moved away from idle small talk and launched directly to the heart of things.

"I understand that my son has asked for use of your radio telescopes and has been denied access." She spoke slowly and nearly purred the words. She indicated Tex with a slight wave of her hand.

"Now look, I've got no time for more games with the boy. He helped us come up with a good idea to plug up that hole that these bastards are flying out of. I grant him that. But we've got to move on that idea, and I've got no time for experiments to slake his curiosity or anyone else's." General Hays looked at Dr. Lewis as he said the last of it.

Drs. Lewis and Randall tried to speak at once in protest, but Commander Sturgis, while moving nothing else, simply raised her hand at them, and they both stopped talking.

"General Hays, you know my credentials and that I am a loyal servant to this country and a patriot."

The general nodded. "Of course. I have never questioned that."

Sturgis nodded curtly. "You, more than most, also know that when I say I will do something, I mean it."

The general swallowed hard as her eyes bored into him. Tex knew that stare of hers. It had made his bowels turn to water on more than one occasion.

She rose in one swift motion from her chair, her hands pressed firmly to the table and her body thrust toward the general. "I did not toil below ground for nearly thirty years in preparation for this war only to lose the last battle because a two-bit general made a grab for power."

The general's face turned another shade of red, and he was on his feet as well. "Who do you think you are, accusing me. I'll have you know that—"

The general's words were caught in his throat. He grabbed at the side of his head, his mouth contorted in pain. He fell back toward his chair, missed and was on the floor, where he writhed in agony from Alecto's virtual icepick to the brain.

Tex knew that feeling as well. He had endured it in his battle with Alecto in Apthartos just before he boarded the Conexus ship. He was made of different stuff than the general and was able to endure the pain better than most. He didn't figure the general would tolerate it long before the pain was too great and his heart could take it no longer. He should have intervened but found himself lacking the will.

Dr. Lewis was on her feet.

Dr. Randall shifted in his seat. "Lilly."

Commander Sturgis pulled the hem of her jacket down. "Stand down, Alecto."

Alecto had sat quietly and not moved a muscle. There was no outward sign that she had even heard Sturgis, but the man's screams of pain ceased.

He gasped and spit. He reached for the back of his chair and pulled himself up.

The general's hair was mussed, and his face was still purply red. He nearly fell into his chair, pulled a handkerchief from his back pants pocket and wiped his wet forehead. He coughed and finally managed to get words out between rasping breaths. "If it's so powerful, have it kill the murderous bastards." He pointed at Alecto. "But don't you come to my compound and use it to threaten me."

Commander Sturgis' fingers were steepled under her chin, her elbows resting on the table. "I do not make idle threats. You will cooperate and provide the tools and manpower that my son needs to complete his task."

The general put his hanky back in his pocket. His face had returned to a nearly normal shade of pink. "How about I tell you to go to hell."

Commander Sturgis rose. "By the way. Her name is Alecto. I will leave her with you as you ponder your choice, general."

Dr. Randall took Dr. Lewis by the elbow and steered her out of the room. Commander Sturgis followed on their heels.

General Hays attempted to get up to leave, but he was unable to move. Tex knew that feeling too. He had spent many days bound by the invisible restraints put on him by the Conexus. The man's eyes flitted from side to side in panic. He even resorted to pleading with Tex. "Please. Call her off." He squirmed and tried to twist himself up from the chair, but it was no use.

Tex turned his gaze to Alecto and caught her eye. "Do you require assistance with this task?"

"I do not," she replied. Her voice was calm and measured.

Tex rose then too and walked out of the building, leaving Alecto to her work. If Erika had been there, she would have raised loud protest. Jack and Ian too would have been appalled and likely tried to stop it.

At times Tex wished he had the sense of morality that they had. But he had been trained to look at the big picture. To do difficult things sometimes—even horrible things—if it meant saving the lives of many. *The needs of the many outweigh the needs of the few,*" Commander Sturgis had told him repeatedly.

He ignored the general's screams of pain as he closed the door behind him.

In less than twenty minutes, General Hays relented under Alecto's influence and relinquished control of the telescope array to Drs. Fisher and Lewis. They had already put their team to work calculating where to aim the radio telescopes and in what configuration to maximize amplification of signal to the Mocht Bogha galactic gateway.

While Alecto dealt with General Hays, Tex paid the captured alien a visit. He had come out of surgery and was recovering in a heavily guarded room in what used to be the visitor center of the VLA. General Hays had left orders that Tex be allowed access to the prisoner.

"You want one of us to go in with you? For protection," one of the military guards asked.

Tex stifled an incredulous laugh. The man could be excused for his ignorance. He had no idea who—or what—Tex was.

"I think I'll be okay," Tex said and entered the room.

The M'Uktah prisoner lay on two single-sized beds pushed together to accommodate his large frame. Even at that, his legs hung over the end. He was naked but draped with a sheet over the lower half of his well-muscled body. Chains were wrapped around his chest, hips and ankles, each kept shut tightly with padlocks.

The man's skin was smooth as molded plastic. There wasn't a hair on his head or face. No eyebrows or even the hint of hair growth shadow on his chin or upper lip. It wasn't that he had been shaved or waxed. There were no hair follicles at all.

He tilted his head up as Tex walked in. His orangey-yellow eyes were set wide on his large head, and his ears were like small dog ears sitting high, pointed and facing forward. His lips were wide and full. The alien uttered a low, guttural growl.

It was a sound that likely would frighten a human. But Tex was not afraid of the creature. He probably should have been, but instead of fear, Tex felt sad. He had been in the same position, both at A.H.D.N.A. and when he was with the Conexus. Strapped to a bed, unable to move while he was poked, prodded and pieces of himself literally removed. He did not wish the ordeal on anyone, even a merciless killer who had attacked Erika.

Tex approached the bed. He knew the alien would not understand his language. Dr. Lewis said that linguists had tried to communicate with it in all languages of Earth. But Tex wanted the man to hear his voice. "I am known as Bodaway. I will not hurt you."

The man's eyes coolly regarded Tex. The furrow of his brow lessened, but his lips were still pulled back in a tight grimace. He remained silent.

Tex reached his hand toward the alien's chained arm. The man tried to jerk his arm away, but he was pinned tightly to the bed.

Tex placed his relatively small hand on the man's thick forearm. It would have taken at least three of Tex's arms to make up one of this man's.

His skin was firm, smooth and warm under Tex's fingers. Tex wasn't sure what to do. He had communicated telepathically with both the Conexus and the Elosians. But both of those species had initiated the contact and had far more advanced telepathic abilities than even Tex. He wasn't sure he could be the one to begin the conversation.

Tex laid his other hand on the man's arm, closed his eyes and concentrated deeply. He reached out with all his senses and tried to find the thread of this alien man's mind in the quantum realm.

When he 'eavesdropped' on someone's private thoughts, it was generally like picking up a channel on an old AM radio. It was like he'd hear a faint signal, then as he homed in, he'd hear words, phrases, even whole conversations going on inside the person's mind. At times he'd have visions or images flashed in his mind's eyes.

He did not pick up this man's 'station.' It was like the quantum airwaves were empty.

Tex didn't know if that was because the man's physiology was incompatible with telepathic communication, or if the man was blocking Tex. He decided to try a different tactic.

Instead of being a receiver, he decided to send information. He called to mind all that the Elosians had told him about this prisoner's home planet, Uktah. Tex remembered the vision of the place that the Elosians had shared with him – of the man on the ornately carved wooden throne and the women in black robes with angry yellow eyes.

The man's pulse quickened beneath Tex's fingers. Tex opened his eyes, and the man was staring at him intently. He spoke to Tex in his language of clicks, chirps and many consonant sounds.

Tex again sent a message telepathically. He envisioned himself saying his name and explaining to the man what he was. He then imagined himself asking the man what he was called on his own planet.

Whatever barrier the man had put up, he released it. At least partially. He used the same technique to tell Tex that he was U'Vol Vree'Kah, Captain of the *Dra'Knar*.

Tex had not expected the prisoner to be a captain. General Hays would be ecstatic if he knew they had captured the captain of the alien vessel.

U'Vol's admission was followed quickly by a question. "How do you know of Uktah? Where did you get this information?" Even in telepathic communication, there was an alarm in U'Vol's voice.

"I will answer your questions, but you must also answer mine. If you cooperate with me, I may be able to help you."

Tex did his best to recall to his mind all that had transpired on Elosia, from landing there to his entire conversation with Cynothian. U'Vol showed no signs of discomfort from their telepathic communication as humans did. His facial muscles relaxed a bit as he took in the memories that Tex fed to him.

"I do not understand what the Elosians told me about your planet. Do you?"

U'Vol closed his eyes and breathed in deeply. When he opened his eyes again, they glistened. "I do not comprehend the full meaning. But one thing is clear. If I do not leave this planet, everyone that I love will perish."

"If I let you go, everyone I love will perish."

Their eyes were locked.

"I answered your questions. Now it is time for you to answer mine. What are the plans of your people for this planet?"

To Tex's surprise, U'Vol answered. He showed Tex his memories of preparations for the voyage and mission; of readying the *Dra'Knar* and krindor armors; and of his meetings with the Council of U. "The hunt is merely the first phase, you see. Cull the herd and subdue the population. The second phase will begin breeding for farm stock. In the final phase, the planet will be a M'Uktah outpost and the Sarhi that live here a domesticated food stock."

U'Vol's visions, imparted to Tex, chilled him to the marrow. He could practically see Erika in chains, confined like a breeding sow to deliver child after child only to be raised for consumption by the M'Uktah.

"This sickens you, yet you Sarhi eat your own animal food stocks. How is it any different?"

Tex was close to emptying the contents of his stomach. He swallowed to force the bile down. "There is no time for a morality debate. You have shown me the plans of your people. Now let me show you what will in fact happen."

Tex allowed the horrid memories of his time with the Conexus to flood his mind. He shared with U'Vol every minute of his torture, and along with it, the vast store of unbroken knowledge from thousands upon thousands of years of human history and the evolution that led to the Conexus timeline.

Tex felt U'Vol's pulse quicken again beneath his fingertips. His eyes widened. "This cannot be."

"It can be. It will be if things proceed as your people have planned. You weren't supposed to live, were you?"

U'Vol's eyes narrowed.

"Perhaps this woman in the black robes from my vision knew you would raise your voice against continuing the harvest here. Sounds like she wanted you out of the way."

U'Vol remained silent, but he did not disagree with Tex's assessment.

"There are two critical differences between this timeline and the one that leads to the Conexus."

U'Vol tilted his head quizzically.

"I did not exist in the Conexus history. And you – "

"Likely died on this forsaken planet."

"Yes. But what if you don't die? What if…"

Tex imagined a new history yet to be written. If he succeeded in closing the vortex of warped space that the M'Uktah used, it would close off their ability to send more ships. At least for three years, apparently, until the Mocht Bogha appeared again. That would buy the people of Earth valuable time to prepare.

But what if he failed? It was a fear that nagged at Tex. U'Vol would be a prisoner, and many of his men would die. But more ships would enter Earth space. More M'Uktah Vree would engage in a mass slaughter of humans. And as General Hays had already made clear, the nuclear option would be deployed.

"There may be a way that we can help each other. It goes against orders that both of us have been given. And we may both fail. But if it works, we will both get what we most desire."

"What is that?"

"Protection for our loved ones."

He had U'Vol's full attention.

Tex left his interrogation of U'Vol exhausted. General Hays found him when he was on his way to his bed chamber.

"What happened in there? Did you learn anything?"

Tex turned his weary face to the general. "No." He rubbed his temples. "I did my best, but the beast is clearly unable to communicate on a telepathic level. I'm sorry."

The general kicked the gravel. "Dammit." He narrowed his eyes at Tex. "That girlfriend of yours said you could communicate with anyone—even aliens—using your mind powers. Was she lying just to save your ass?"

Tex had never heard anyone refer to Erika as his girlfriend. He liked the idea of it but his cheeks colored.

"She did not lie." *But I lie to you now.* "I can communicate with people telepathically. But this creature's physiology is quite different from ours. And remember, the Conexus that I was able to talk to – they are simply our future selves."

Hays put his fingers to his temples and took a deep breath. "This whole damned thing gives me a migraine."

"As it does me," Tex said. "General, you must excuse me. I am quite tired after trying to speak with the alien creature, and I have to regain my strength by the morning." He didn't wait to hear the general start in on how his mission to close the Mocht Bogha was a waste of time and resources.

Tex spent the rest of his daylight hours in quiet meditation in his room. He skipped the evening meal. As the hour of his mission drew near, he sought solitude. Though he wanted more than anything to be with Erika, he knew that even the sight of her could crumble his resolve to do this thing that must be done.

He forced himself to release thoughts of her as he sank more deeply into meditation and removed himself from the world. *I only hope she'll forgive me some day.*

43
ERIKA

Tex's considerable and consistent effort to avoid Erika made it plain he did not want to be near her. She had risked her own life multiple times to save his. She'd slept on the ground, in the cold for Christ's sake, for two damned nights waiting for him when everyone else had given up on his sorry, skinny ass. And this was how he repaid her. Avoidance.

To add insult to injury, Jack had breezed in with Erika's sworn enemy, Commander Sturgis, and fawning all over her niece, this Anna chick. Erika disliked her from the minute she laid eyes on her. Of course, the minute she laid eyes on her was when Jack's hand touched hers and he pulled her from the copter and oh, she practically fell into his arms all smiles.

Ian reminded her that she had put Jack in the friend zone. That she had fallen for Tex. And he was right, of course. Damn him, he was always right. But that didn't mean that it didn't hurt to see him so happy. So effortlessly happy while she was trying to be in a relationship with someone who had never had a normal human relationship before. Trying to be with Tex was like carving a marble sculpture with a butter knife.

As Tex worked to avoid her, Erika did her best to dodge Jack. She skipped dinner and did her laundry instead. She sat atop a washing machine and watched her clothes spin around in the dryer. At least it was warm, which was more than she could say for the rest of the barracks building. She was only slightly warmer sleeping inside the barracks than she'd been on the cold ground.

Erika took the warm laundry back to her room in a ball in her arms and threw it onto the bed. She was tempted to leave it there for extra warmth, but she folded the shirts and placed them neatly into her duffle bag. She had no idea how much longer she'd stay, but she figured that if Tex's plan to shut down the Mocht Bogha didn't work, they'd all be escorted off the premises sooner rather than later. Maybe that was for the best. She wasn't sure what she could do to help, but she had been sidelined long enough. If Tex failed, she'd leave the VLA and find some way to help her species survive.

She was balling up a pair of socks and was ready to toss them into the open duffel when she heard someone at the door. Jack stood there, his back resting against the doorframe, his hands across his chest. She hated the brown color of his hair but had to admit he looked better than he had when they first met. He was slimmer and more fit. It suited him.

"Hi, Erika."

'Hi, Erika'? The last time they'd seen each other, Erika had disappeared in the Conexus ship. She had been to hell and back. Both of them had lost their moms, and the world was ending around them. *Yet all he can say is 'Hi, Erika'?*

She turned her back to him, grabbed another pair of socks, balled them up and threw them toward the duffel. She missed.

Jack sauntered in and grabbed the errant sock ball. He dropped it into the duffel and smiled at her. "Talk to me, Erika. Yell at me. Call me names. Beat me up even, but don't shun me. We've all been through too much to ignore each other."

She wanted to do all those things – to yell at him and pound his chest with her fists. She was mad and not even sure why because as he stood there she knew that she didn't love him anymore. She probably never did. Not really. Not the way she felt about Tex.

Erika sighed and threw a sock ball at him. "Why'd she have to be so freakin' pretty? I mean seriously, Jack. I'm not even into girls, and I think she's hot. And she's a Sturgis. I mean—why? How?"

He began to speak, but she cut him off.

"On second thought, don't answer those questions. I don't want to know."

His face lit up with the easy smile that she knew and loved. He was still Jack, and he still had a way of bringing the happy out in her despite herself.

"I hate you," she said. She threw another sock ball at him.

He caught it. "I know. Sometimes I hate me too." His smile melted, and she knew what he said was true. And she knew exactly what he meant. They had all had to do things that they never wanted to do. Things they weren't proud of. Things they would never talk about.

"If you got to know Anna, I think you might actually like her. Believe it or not, she probably hates the Sturgis clan as much or more than you do."

He said it with complete sincerity and probably even believed it. But Erika didn't plan on being besties with Anna. It was petty of her and she knew it. But making nice with her old boyfriend's new lady was not the Erika Holt way. She glared at him, and it took about a nanosecond for him to drop it.

"Are we good?" he asked.

She wanted to throw more socks at him because that had felt good, but she was out of socks. She searched her feelings for reasons to say no, but she didn't have any. They had started out friends, and as he stood there, she knew that she'd be lying if she told him she didn't want to be his friend anymore.

"Yeah," she said.

"Good. Then in classic Jack Wilson style, I'll now tell you something that will likely make you rethink it and throw me out."

Erika grabbed a pair of jeans to fold and didn't look up. "Oh no. What now?"

Jack yanked the jeans from her hands, forcing her to look at him. His eyes were soft, his lips curled into a warm smile. "Stop being a prideful and stubborn goat and go to him."

She frowned at him and yanked the jeans back. "No."

"Why not?"

Erika dropped the unfolded jeans to the bed and tried not to cry. "Because he doesn't want me, okay? You have Anna and she has you but I've got like only half of that equation, Jack. He doesn't want me."

Jack laughed so loud and hard they probably heard it two buildings over.

"Stop laughing at me. It's not funny."

Jack wiped at his eye with the back of his hand. "Darlin', I'm not laughing at you. I guess girls sometimes don't know anything more about guys than we do about you all."

He knelt on the bed facing her and took her hands in his. "Erika, I don't think I've ever seen a guy more in love with a girl than Tex is with you. Not want you? Girl, he wants you so bad it scares the shit out of him."

Erika shook her head. "You don't know him anymore, Jack. His time with the Conexus changed him. And since his sweat lodge experience, I think he's taking this messiah thing seriously. I mean, look at him. Sometimes even I start to believe he's a demigod or something."

Jack shook his head and smiled at her. "He's no god. He's just an eighteen-year-old guy that's in love with a girl."

Erika peered up at him, and he tucked a strand of her hair behind her ear. "You speak from experience?" She may have given him tacit approval to pursue Anna, but it still made her heart twinge to think about it.

Jack nodded. "Look, everyone has been vague about what exactly he'll do to shut down that portal. But my guess is that he's putting himself in danger. He's probably scared, Erika. Maybe he's trying not to be with you so he doesn't hurt so much. But I bet you anything that a part of him is right now wishing he was holding you." His eyes misted. "I know that if my life was in danger, I'd want to hold her one last time."

"Damn, you really love her, don't you?"

"Nearly as much as Tex loves you."

Jack's words echoed like a gong in a vast empty hall. *Tex loves you.* She recalled the kiss Tex had planted on her before he ran from her again. His actions were certainly confusing to her, but she had never been kissed that way before. Her cheeks flushed thinking about it.

Jack planted a light kiss on her warm cheek and let loose her hands. "After all we've been through, I feel like I know less than nothing these days. But I know this. If you don't go to him tonight, you'll regret it the rest of your life."

Regret was a word you used when bad things happened. "Why? Do you think he won't survive this?" As she said it she realized she wasn't sure what the "this" truly was. Tex had done a good job of keeping her out of the loop of exactly what he was going to do.

Jack looked away. "Hell, I don't know if any of us will survive this."

That was a truth they had all avoided speaking out loud as of late. But Erika's feet remained planted.

"What's stopping you?"

She didn't know. Fear of rejection? Maybe. But more than that, she feared he'd allow her entry. She had a history of avoiding intimacy. And being with Tex was more than just intimate. He could get inside of her mind and manipulate her in a way that horrified her.

"I've got reasons."

Jack went to the door and was about through it when he stopped. "It's time to allow yourself to feel, Erika." He gave her a weak smile before he walked away.

Tex had curled himself into an egg-shaped mass on his bed, resting his head on his thighs, his arms at his sides. It was a position that he found restful.

He tried not to think about what would happen to him tomorrow. Each time a worry came to his mind, he refocused instead on the technical aspects of how he would achieve the energetic resonance he needed to close the portal that the M'Uktah had referred to as the Mocht Bogha.

He was in deep meditation, his conscious mind left behind as his subconscious swirled in the heady quantum realm. But a light touch on his back pulled his attention back to the physical world around him.

At first he ignored the touch. It was likely a breeze.

There it was again. The touch warmed his skin. He became aware of scent, and his nostrils involuntarily flared from the heady aroma that filled the air. It was a scent he found intoxicating. His meditation was at an end, his concentration shattered.

Her hand traced a line down his naked back, touching on each vertebra. Shivers ran up his spine.

His attention was fully in the room with her now. In one swift motion he unwound himself and turned over to face her. Her hair was free of its usual band holding it back, and she wore a loose-fitting black T-shirt and jeans. Her face was finally free of bruises and cuts. Her eyes were clear and bright. Erika looked clean and rested and more refreshed than he had probably ever seen her. And she looked at him expectantly.

His voice came out low and hoarse, a side effect of the deep relaxation he had just experienced. "What do you want, Erika?" The words came out more biting than he had intended. He wanted to touch her. To wind himself up in her and never let go. But Tex didn't think he could take any more hurt or rejection. Not now. Not when his life—and the life of everyone he cared about—depended on his ability to believe in himself.

She jerked her hand back. "I'm sorry." She bit her lip. "I just – I wanted to say—wanted to know—"

"What do you want to know?"

She sighed. "I don't know why I came. Jack said I should."

"Jack?" *She still cares about him.* "Did he send you here to distract me? To finally have me out of the picture. He always hated me."

Erika rolled her eyes and set her jaw. "Dammit, I'm tired of you acting like a toddler, jealous over someone else getting a bigger piece of the cookie. You make it all so complicated, but it's not. Do you want to be with me or not?"

As usual, whenever they spoke, he managed to make her angry with him. It seemed that words were useless. If he could only speak directly to her mind. With telepathic communication, he didn't have to rely on only twenty-six letters to speak of all that welled inside him.

He closed his eyes and tried to regain the composure he had felt before she walked into the room. "I do not want to anger you. I never want to anger you."

"Jack doesn't hate you, Tex. He told me to come here because—well, he seems to think that you may feel about me the way he feels about Anna. He seems to think that maybe you'd want to spend what may be your last night on Earth with me." She stared at the floor. "Is he wrong?"

Tex hated to admit, even if only to himself, that Jack Wilson was right about anything. But Jack was right.

He took her hand in his. It was warm, soft and dry. *So small.* Erika's personality made her seem bigger than she actually was.

He held her hand up and inspected it. Tex had never had the opportunity to look closely at her before. He put his hand up to hers and marveled at how his—a hand he had always considered small—was so much larger than hers.

He took her other hand and did the same with it. Erika watched their hands, and he felt the tension in her muscles ease. As he held her hands up to his, he pulled her into his arms.

"I want to know you," he said.

Her breath was ragged and warm against his cheek. He bent his head and kissed her deeply. Tex felt her legs give way beneath her, so he pulled her closer into him and held her at the small of her back.

"Don't let go," she whispered. A tear rolled down her cheek.

Tex wiped the tear with his thumb. He reached out to her mind. It was something she had never wanted him to do, but he had to. He had to know if she truly wanted what she said she did.

But if he searched her mind without permission, she would be furious with him, and it would wreck everything he wanted. "I want to know all of you. Words seem to get me into trouble. May I interface directly with your mind? I promise I won't hurt you."

She nodded slowly.

As he probed her thoughts, the sensation of his touch at her back reflected back to him. He felt her warmth beneath his fingers, but he also felt the tingling sensation of her back being touched by him. He kissed her again and found that he experienced the kiss also as a double sensation. He felt his own feelings, but hers as well.

And oh, what she felt. Her mind was singly focused on want. Her desire was whole and pure and white-hot.

Tex did not think he had asked a question out loud, but she answered him as though he had. "I want only you."

And he knew it was true. There were no thoughts of Jack. No lingering longing for the guy that she'd once been with or anyone else for that matter.

Tex ended the interface both to save his energy but also to ensure that he did not harm Erika.

"You don't have to read my mind to know what's in my heart," she whispered. "Feel it."

Erika kissed him deeply as she had in the dream they'd shared during his sweat. Her hands found his waist, and she ran her fingers over his back.

He deftly pulled her T-shirt over her head and drank in the vision of the moonlight against her pale skin. His fingers shook as he touched her collarbone then traced the line of her shoulder. Erika gasped at his touch, and her head fell back, her mouth open.

He caressed her waist and arms, her shoulders and back. He felt the wounds U'Vol had given her and the stitches that had sewn her flesh back together. It took only a few seconds to heal her completely. She moaned at the warmth of his fingers as he erased the evidence of the razors-harp claws that had sliced her. Tex moved his fingers over her as if he read braille, memorizing every line and curve, every nuance of her form.

Erika's fingers shook, but she smiled as she reached out to his face. She traced lines over his cheeks and lips. It was as if she, too, wanted to remember each detail of his face; as if she soaked in memories to last her a lifetime. "Isn't this better than a dream?" Her voice was throaty and deep.

Tex had lived much of his life in a dream. Lulled into a slumber during his time at A.H.D.N.A. by the sedation of the humidity. Maintained in a dreamlike trance while with the Conexus, experiencing only what the Regina allowed him to know. He had thought that his time there was full. He had thought he had known love with Xenos because of the synthetic memories the Regina planted in his mind.

But in the moment that he and Erika became one, he knew that he had never truly lived before. Her lips were soft beneath his. Her breath was hot and ragged against his neck. Her skin was smooth and warm under his fingers. This—Erika—was real.

She loved him. And he gave himself to her wholly.

Erika's head rested on his chest, and she snored lightly. Tex stroked her hair. The silky feel of it stirred him, so he stopped. She was tired and needed rest.

Tex should have rested, but he could not find the path to an easy mind. Each time he tried to focus on what he must do in the morning, his thoughts wandered to the newly created memories he had made with Erika.

He wanted to scoop her into his arms and carry her away. They could run to the farthest corner of Earth, away from scientists and military brass and M'Uktah ships. There had to be some remote place where the M'Uktah would not bother to go.

Tex had lived for years wanting nothing more than to be free of A.H.D.N.A. and control. He had not considered having a relationship with a human.

But as soon as he'd met Erika and observed the relationships between Ian, Jack and Erika, a desire to be loved had welled in him.

As he looked down at her sleeping face, he knew that love was all that he had ever wanted. She was there in his arms, and it was all he desired.

Erika shifted, and her head rolled into the crook of his arm. Her small face was upturned to him. The beauty of her peaceful face drew tears from his eyes.

If only I could keep her life this way for her forever.

But he couldn't. She was going to know hurt. One way or another.

Tex rose about an hour before dawn. He gently let her head fall to the pillow. Erika began to rouse, but Tex put his hand on her head and bid her mind to rest easy.

He dressed in loose-fitting cotton pants. They were black, not puke green, but otherwise they were similar to what he'd always worn at A.H.D.N.A. He put on a black T-shirt as well and a pair of flip-flops. He laughed to himself. For years he had hated what he was required to wear at A.H.D.N.A., but when given a choice, he ended up in essentially the same outfit.

The barest hint of the first light lit up Erika's face. She wore a contented look, even in her sleep.

He bent to her, kissed her forehead and drank in her scent. It took every ounce of strength in his being to remove his lips from her cool forehead. He placed his hand at her temple and entered her mind with his.

As she dreamed, the memories they had just created were woven into the folds of her gray matter like new threads added to the weave of a sweater. Tex saw himself but through Erika's eyes, and it brought water to his eyes. In his original form, he had imagined himself as a hideous monster in the eyes of humans. But within Erika's mind, as she had kissed him, she had seen him not as he currently was but in his original form. She saw his true nature yet loved him anyway. To Erika, Tex was H.A.L.F. 9, and he was beautiful.

Tex wiped his eyes with the back of his hand and set about rewiring her memories as he had done to Smith. He took from her the beautiful memories they had just created with one simple word. "Forget."

After leaving Erika in his bedchamber, Tex sought out Alecto and Commander Sturgis. Drs. Lewis and Randall had filled them in on what he needed Alecto to do. The professional stuff had been attended to. This visit was personal.

He found them together in a room with two small beds thrown into it tucked into a corner on the first floor of the bunkhouse building. It looked like a room that had maybe been used for storage but hastily made ready for two more people.

Alecto was on one of the beds, balled into an upright egg-shaped blob. Tex was glad to see that she was resting and preserving her energy. He needed her to be at peak performance in the morning.

Commander Sturgis sat quietly upright on her bed. Her eyes were closed, but it was unclear if she was asleep or just resting. Her suit jacket was hung neatly over the back of a wooden chair at the end of the bed, but she still wore her shirt buttoned up, her hair still pulled tightly into a twist at the back of her head. The immaculately coiffed hair was in strange contrast to her legs in a lotus position, her pencil skirt hitched up on her thighs.

She knew immediately that he stood in the door. Her eyes opened slowly. "Hello, 9."

He did not answer but entered the room on swift feet and stood at the end of her bed facing her. "I must speak with you."

"Of course." She did not uncurl her legs or get up. She indicated he could sit in the chair with a motion of her hand.

Alecto remained in her tightly coiled position, giving no indication that she was aware he was in the room.

Tex sat on the chair, his legs straddling it. Sturgis looked at him evenly but without the cool mask of indifference he usually saw her wear. If anything, he thought she might have looked sad.

"I need you to do something for me," he said.

"I will do what I can."

He hesitated. He had never wanted to ask her for anything. She had been the last person he wished to show any weakness or request any favors from. He wasn't sure what moved him to come to her in the first place, but some part of him had forced his feet on the path to her door.

"The task before me tomorrow..."

She waited patiently for him to continue. "Go on," she said finally.

"I must not...Clothes, even hair can catch fire at high temperatures."

Her eyes softened, and he thought he heard a small gasp escape her lips. But the sound may have come from Alecto. He glanced over at Alecto, but her head still rested on her knees, her arms wound tightly around her body.

"Will you—cut my hair?"

A rogue tear filled the corner of her eye. "I would be honored."

And he believed she meant it.

She rose from the bed, slipped on her shoes and left him there. "I will be back soon. Stay here."

As soon as Sturgis departed, Alecto slowly raised her head. She blinked her eyes a few times as if trying to clear her vision. She cocked her head to the side and regarded him. "Your attempt to pass as a human is unsuccessful. You are still H.A.L.F." There was no judgment or sarcasm in her voice.

"I know."

"Does your new form please her?"

"Are you speaking of Erika?"

Alecto nodded her large head slowly.

"I am not entirely sure. Strangely, I don't think that she minded my original appearance."

She sniffed. "An odd girl, that one."

Tex smiled and nodded. "Probably why I enjoy being with her so much."

Alecto sat cross-legged, her back erect, her neck long and her bald head held high. "Commander Sturgis said that you no longer need fear water. Is that true?"

"Yes."

"Did you know that I was cured too? Commander Sturgis created a gene therapy that Dr. Randall administered."

"That's wonderful." Tex smiled widely, but she did not return the smile. Her emotions seemed as blunted as ever.

Tex truly was happy for her. Without the threat of being rendered as useless as a car without wheels simply from a dousing with water, Alecto could achieve a free life if she wanted it. Tex was surprised though that Sturgis would voluntarily take away the one method of total control of Alecto.

Her dark eyes drilled into him. It seemed she had something she wanted to say, but she remained quiet. Tex attempted again to probe at her mind, but she still blocked him. She was unwilling to communicate with him telepathically.

"Do you ever wish that things..." Alecto said.

"Wish what?"

"That it could be different? That we were—"

"Human?"

"Yes."

Alecto picked up a water bottle from the small table next to her bed and took a long draw. "This thirst. It is an unpleasant sensation."

"Agreed."

"Every step I take into the human world brings with it a host of unwanted feelings. It was easier below ground."

He could not share her sentiment. Tex had never found life below ground easy. But he decided not to argue with her over it. "Maybe."

They sat in silence a few minutes more. Alecto, apparently tired of looking at him, began to pull herself into a ball again.

"There's one thing—a thing I've wanted to say to you. For a while."

Her arms were wrapped around her legs and her head was almost to her knees, but she looked up at him, waiting.

"I wish things could have been different with us. That we could have been friends. After all, we are the only two of our kind in all the universe."

She silently regarded him. "Your attempt to seal the portal will put you in danger?"

He nodded.

"Should anything happen to you, I would then be the only one. I would be truly alone."

He nodded again.

"Then I shall do my best to ensure that you survive your endeavor." She then tucked her head down to her legs and withdrew all attention from the world outside herself.

A few minutes later, Sturgis returned with a plain white sheet in one hand and a pair of scissors in the other. She had him move his chair to the center of the small room and asked him to sit. She draped the sheet around his body and let its loose ends hang at the back.

Her cool fingers ran through his hair, combing it gently back away from his face. The touch reminded him of the feeling of the Regina's touch. The memory sent a shiver up his back. He forced the memory from his mind.

No words passed between them. There was only the sound of the scissor blades clanging against each other and the gentle swoosh as locks of his hair were snipped and fell to the floor. His neck prickled from the cool air.

Commander Sturgis whipped the sheet off of him and brushed the back of his neck off with her thin fingers. He stood and realized that he was now taller than she was. Somehow she looked smaller to him. He had a slight urge to hug her but thought better of it.

"You can have the hair. I think you'll find a use for it," he said.

She bit her lip and nodded. "Yes. I know exactly what to do with it."

It was clear that she fought back tears. If he hugged her, the tears would fall. But that was not how she would want him to remember her. He knew that much.

Instead he nodded back at her once and left her surrounded by the white-gold locks that she'd shorn from his head.

Pale-pink light filtered through Erika's eyelids and beckoned her to open her eyes. She was drowsy like she'd taken nighttime cold medicine, but she couldn't recall taking medicine. Her vision was bleary, and her head throbbed. With great effort, she hoisted her legs over the side of the bed, her head cradled in her hands.

She was still dressed in the clothes she'd worn the day before. She wasn't even under the covers. *What did I do last night?*

Erika pushed herself up off the bed and grabbed her toiletry bag. As she shuffled down the hall to go to the bathroom, she became aware of the eerie quiet of the place. She stood still and listened. The only sound was the whirr of warm air blowing out of the heating register.

The bathroom was empty and as cold as ever. She quickly took care of her business and brushed her teeth, eager to get back to her warm room and layer on more clothes before breakfast.

Her head still throbbed like she had a terrible hangover. But she couldn't recall drinking anything the night before. She pulled her hair back into a tail while trying to recall the previous night. The last thing she remembered, Jack was in her room. He had told her to go to Tex. *Did I?*

As she tried to recall whether she had seen him or not, her head throbbed. Then it hit her. It was the day Tex was supposed to close the portal. He was supposed to begin what he called Interface just after dawn. Her clock read 7:30. *He could already be gone.*

Erika pulled on a loose-fitting jacket as she ran down the deserted hall of the bunkhouse. She pulled her shoe on as she hit the top of the stairs. The building was the quiet of a deserted school on a Sunday. *Where is everyone?*

Each time she wracked her brain to remember what had happened to her the night before, her head throbbed. And each time she thought of Tex, the pain nearly made her pass out.

But she couldn't help thinking about him. There was something important about him. She knew it was there, but her recollection was hazy like a dream from years ago, vivid at the time but faded now to vague and hazy.

The gravel courtyard was empty as well. No one sipped morning coffee or scurried on their way to work. It was as though the entire place had been abandoned.

Erika ran past the long building that housed the computers and equipment that were the brains of the VLA and wheeled around the corner toward the first dish in the array. She felt a low thrum in her stomach like the rumble of far-off thunder. But the skies were clear. The sun was above the horizon now, and the distant mountains were purple silhouettes against a light-blue sky.

There was another blob on the horizon that had not been there before. As Erika ran to it, she realized it was a mass of people. A crowd had gathered, standing on the sandy soil while others were in the backs of jeeps or on top of vans. They formed a small mound of humanity all intently focused on the area around one dish aligned to the northeastern sky.

As she got closer, the deep rumble in her gut grew larger and more insistent. She tried to make out familiar faces. She searched the shapes, most facing away from her, for Ian, Jack, Dr. Randall or even Anna. No one in the crowd paid her any mind as she gently pried her way through them, searching for people she knew.

Erika worked her way forward through layer after layer of the throng. She hadn't realized there were that many people at the VLA, but between the military personnel that had descended on the place plus the regular cohort of scientists who were regulars plus her small band of friends, there had to be more than a hundred people crowded near the base of the dish.

Erika finally caught sight of Ian. His height made him stand out in the crowd. He was with Jack, Anna, Dr. Randall and Commander Sturgis. *Where's Alecto?*

She was glad to see them but also miffed that none of them had cared enough to make sure she was awake and there to support Tex. As she approached Ian, she had intended to give him a piece of her mind but was stopped short by the look on his face as he saw her.

Ian's eyes were rimmed in red and puffy, his cheeks wet. He didn't say a word but simply pulled her to him and enfolded her in his arms and stroked her hair.

The rumble in her belly was now also an audible hum. Erika pulled herself away from Ian and peered through the gap between the people in front of her toward where everyone looked.

Tex stood directly under the dish, his face upturned, his feet planted a few feet apart from each other, his arms outstretched to the sides. His head was smooth and shorn of hair. He was in his more human form complete with pale alabaster skin that practically glowed in the early morning light.

A low, guttural cry rose from his lips and filled the morning air. His eyes were open, and the skin on his face was mottled pink and red with blood that ran in a trickle from his eyes, ears and nose. Alecto was sprawled on the ground next to him, her hands wrapped around his leg. Her eyes were closed and her lips set in a grim expression, her brows knitted tightly together. She clung to him as though she was trying to keep him from flying away.

He opened his mouth, and this time the low guttural yell was an unearthly scream. It was a sound full of agony as if from an animal with its leg caught in a trap, tearing at its flesh as it tries to get away.

But no one rushed to his side. Erika turned to Ian and hissed, "Why isn't anyone helping him?" Without waiting for an answer, she took a step forward and was about to push the rest of the way through the crowd, but Ian caught her by the elbow and yanked her back.

"No, Erika. You can't." His voice trembled through tears.

"Let go." Her voice was a low growl.

But Ian didn't let go. He took her by the shoulders, looked down into her eyes and said, "He didn't want you to be here because he knew you'd try to stop him. He didn't want you to remember him like this. He's doing what he has to do, and you have to let him."

Her face softened, and Ian loosed his grip on her shoulders. Erika turned back toward Tex, and it was as though he was only a faint outline of himself but then solid again. There was a collective gasp that came from the entire crowd sucking in air all at once.

His body seemed to waver like heat shimmering on pavement, but it could have been the tears filling her eyes. She turned to Ian. "I can't just stand here and watch him suffer. He's hurt, Ian." She looked around them, and no one made a move to help him. Her voice rose in anger. "Sons-of-bitches, he has sacrificed for you his whole life, and none of you will raise a hand to help him."

A few turned to look at her, but she didn't pull their attention away from Tex for long. He let out another loud screech that made her heart drop to her stomach.

She flung herself forward through the crowd, but Ian surged after her. His legs were longer than hers, and he caught up to her within a few strides.

Ian grabbed her hand and pulled her back. "He ordered us not to interfere. And he specifically asked me to make sure you didn't try to stop him." Ian wiped at his eyes with his hand. "Do you want me to walk you back to your room?"

Erika looked across the faces of the gathered throng. There wasn't a dry eye to be seen. Even General Hays' eyes were red.

Ian still had hold of her hand, and Dr. Randall came from behind and took her other hand in his. "If you can bear it, I think you should stay," he said. His cheeks were wet. "On some level, he knows you're here, and that will give him strength." He smiled at her wanly.

A bolt of purplish-white light arched down from the sky and into Tex from above. It shot out of his hands and shook him like a dog shaking a toy, but he stood upright still, planted firmly on the ground despite the fact that his naked body smoked from the heat. Then he was a faint outline again, here but gone.

Despite the pain it caused, she forced herself to remember Tex as best she could while watching his body bleed and his voice call out. He was here, and she recalled the feel of his lips on hers. *Did that really happen? Or was it a dream?* His body began to disappear again, a faint outline of him remaining behind as though it was a placeholder waiting for his return. His chest was firm against hers, his skin ablaze with warmth. They had been in his room. *I was there. It did happen. We were together.*

His body was back, and his screams filled the air of the place. His nearly bald head was singed black, and smoke billowed off of him. Alecto's face was wet with sweat and tears, her knuckles white from gripping him.

"What is she doing?" Erika whispered.

"Healing him," Dr. Randall said. He wiped at his eyes, and his voice quavered. "Though it looks like she can't keep up with the damage this process is causing him."

"Can't keep up with the damage."

Tex screamed out to Alecto, "Let go!" His voice was scratchy and hoarse.

Alecto did not loose her grip on him. If anything, she clung more tightly.

Jack asked, "Should one of us go pry her off of him?" He seemed to be directing his question to Commander Sturgis.

Sturgis regarded him and appeared ready to step forward to retrieve Alecto. But before she could take a step, the space around them was filled with a thunderous rumble, and the ground shook. Alecto was flung away from Tex like she was no more than a tumbleweed bandied about by the wind. She toppled heel over head and landed about ten yards away from the edge of the crowd.

Drs. Randall, Sturgis and Lewis ran to her, but before they could determine if she had any injuries, the ground trembled again, and a more powerful shockwave emanated from Tex. He was jolted again by plasma that seemed to come from heaven itself. It filled him, and his mouth contorted in agony though no sound escaped his open lips.

Several people toppled to the ground, and camera equipment was shattered. Erika remained standing only because Ian held her upright. Her knees were jelly; her stomach a hollow pit.

Tex was surrounded by a glow of white-hot light. A man in one of the vans opened the door and shouted, "It's working!"

Tex's silhouette in the light was almost a shadow. His eyes had been pointed upward as though looking into the heavens. For the merest hint of an instant, he looked directly at Erika, picking her out of the crowd as if his eyes had a laser focus in them. And for that moment, her knees were steady and her tears stopped. The noise of the crowd was gone. There was only the rush of her blood in her ears and a lone voice speaking directly to her mind.

"I love you," he said.

But it was more than words. She knew his feelings for her as wholly as she knew her own feelings for him. And then, as soon as it had come, the moment was past. His eyes drifted away from her, and he was not quite gone but not quite here either.

In the next minutes, it was as though time slowed. Dr. Randall scooped Alecto up and carried her away from Tex, Drs. Sturgis and Lewis right behind him. An excited murmur erupted in the crowd at the announcement that Tex's efforts were doing what he said he could do – close down the galactic highway. With the gate closed, the M'Uktah harvesting plan would come to an end.

Erika was aware of her heart beating, but her breath had stopped. His voice, as plain as though he was whispering in her ear, said, "Goodbye, love."

The only word she could get to come out of her mouth was, "No." She pulled her hands away from Ian and Dr. Randall and flung herself through the crowd.

Her legs had never moved so fast. She remembered now and cursed him aloud for trying to rip those memories from her. "Don't you leave it like this. Don't leave me like this. Don't you go!" she screamed.

But the white light enveloped and obscured him. There was only a pulsating orb so bright that she had to shield her eyes. She could not go to him and put her arms around him. She could not stop him from destroying himself. The light exploded and threw her back.

She hit the ground hard. Pinpricks of light danced before her eyes as black played at the edges of her vision. Erika scrambled to her feet and made her way to the place where Tex had stood.

The ground was covered in a dusty white residue that resembled ash. A black burn mark covered the place where Tex had stood. Nothing remained of him but the memories that he had tried to take from her.

U'Vol lay in chains on the hard surface the Sarhi had strapped him to. His abdomen throbbed from where they had sliced into him. Their rudimentary attempts at healing may have saved his life, but he would be forever scarred from their crude surgery. *If I live long enough to scar.*

The strange being who called himself Bodaway had been able to communicate with him through U'Vol's neural implant. The neural implant also allowed U'Vol to block Bodaway from what he didn't want the Sarhi lad to know.

He was a strange Sarhi, that Bodaway. U'Vol didn't know why only one of the Sarhi had the ability to communicate with him in that way. And even stranger, Bodaway did not have a neural implant. In all the planets U'Vol had visited across the vast galaxy, he had never before encountered a being who did not need a neural implant to speak with others using only the mind.

Bodaway had confirmed U'Vol's worst fear. Doj'Owa was behind the mutiny against him. *But why?* And Bodaway had confirmed something else as well. If U'Vol didn't get home, his family was in grave danger.

Even after Bodaway shared with him memories of how he had gotten to the planet of the Grand Architects, beings that referred to themselves as Elosians, and all that had transpired there, U'Vol still had a difficult time believing him. If what Bodaway shared was true, it would rock the very foundations of the entire M'Uktah culture. If Doj was not the creator of their species, having endowed them with a special place in the cosmos to rule over all others, then the foundation of their hunter culture would crumble with the knowledge.

U'Vol was unsure if it was wise of him to even try to convince other M'Uktah of the truth of what Bodaway said. Perhaps it was better to leave such things alone.

But such philosophical questions mattered not if he was chained on K'Sarhi, far from his home. First he must escape.

Before Bodaway left him, the strange lad altered the structure of the chains that bound him. As advanced as the M'Uktah liked to think themselves, he had never known of anyone that could command the elements the way Bodaway could. In truth, U'Vol was in awe of the young man. He was curious about the strange youth. Under different circumstances, he would have liked to speak with the creature further and learn more about the so-called Elosians. He did his best to hide those feelings from Bodaway. He did not want to appear weaker than he already did to a Sarhi.

"In the morning, as the sun just begins to rise, the general and nearly all personnel will be out at the radio telescopes," Bodaway had said.

"Why?"

Bodaway shifted his memories and thoughts away from the radio telescopes, unwilling to share with U'Vol the nature of what would be happening there in the morning.

"It will be an opportunity for you to escape," he'd said. Bodaway moved his hands over the chains that bound U'Vol, closed his eyes and concentrated deeply. "Tin will be easy for you to break."

U'Vol had made a move to bust out of the chains but Bodaway shook his head and stilled U'Vol's arms.

"Not now. Remain bound until the morning. Your ship is on a flatbed truck. It will move out in the morning as well. Make sure you are out of here and to the truck before it leaves or you will lose your opportunity."

"Why are you helping me?" U'Vol asked.

Bodaway calmed his mind, carefully blocking U'Vol from knowing what Bodaway chose to keep secret. Finally he said, "If you leave and take your men, you are no longer a threat to the people of this planet."

U'Vol sensed there was more to the answer, but he would get no more out of Bodaway on the subject.

U'Vol had done as Bodaway suggested and waited to break the chains. Pink light filtered into the small room through a single window. U'Vol listened intently. The outer hall had been quiet all night, but feet scuffled. Sarhi voices rose. Laughter. A door slammed shut. The flurry of activity in the hall rose then fell off until it was quiet once more.

U'Vol filled his lungs and expanded his chest. The chains creaked. He pulled his arms outward, and the bonds broke, clanking to the hard floor. His hands now free, he ripped the chains from his hips and scissored his legs to unbind his ankles.

It took less than ten seconds for U'Vol to free himself of the bindings. The floor was littered now with bits of tin and the sheet that had covered him.

U'Vol stood to his full height, and his head nearly scraped the ceiling. The room was tiny compared to the spaces on Uktah, all built to accommodate people much larger than the Sarhi.

He quickly moved to the side of the door and waited. The clatter of his broken chains would likely get the attention of the guards that had been posted around the clock outside his door.

The door opened, and one of the Sarhi military men poked his head in. As he saw the empty beds, his eyes grew wide. His mouth flew open and he was about to cry out an alarm, but before he could, U'Vol grabbed the man around the throat with one mighty hand and snapped the man's neck. The pale Sarhi fellow dropped to the floor, his eyes open, his mouth still agape, his head twisted unnaturally to the side.

U'Vol stepped into the doorway and nearly ran into a second Sarhi guard. This one had his weapon in his hands. U'Vol smelled the sweat and fear pour from the man. The guard raised his weapon, but U'Vol batted it away as if it were a toy gun. The man said something in a loud voice, but of course U'Vol had no idea what the man said. Whatever it was, it was the last the man would ever say. U'Vol used both of his beefy hands to twist the man's neck until the bones snapped.

He dropped the Sarhi body to the ground and ran quickly down the hall toward the door. He hoped that Bodaway had been correct about most personnel being at radio telescope dishes. Though he had no fear of facing a puny Sarhi in close range hand-to-hand, without his krindor, he was vulnerable to their weapons.

U'Vol encountered no more Sarhi in the building. He ducked and had to go sideways to fit through the door, but he did so gingerly, trying not to make any noise. Though he weighed over three hundred pounds, he was light on his bare feet.

He stopped outside the door and sniffed the air. It was cleaner than the air where they had first landed the *Wa'Nar*. He filled his lungs with it. His ears twitched as he listened intently for any sounds of movement. It was quiet and still near him, but in the distance was a loud buzzing hum. As he analyzed it he realized it was more felt than heard. The Sarhi were powering up the telescopes again for some reason. *The same radio burst they did before.* But he had no idea why.

A part of him wanted to find the answer. But that was not to be. He had failed that mission even with his krindor and helmet. Without his armor, he was unlikely to survive a battle with tens of Sarhi.

His keen eyes roved across the landscape as he searched for the vehicle that young Bodaway showed him through the shared vision. He recognized the configuration of buildings and the courtyard. The vehicle carrying his Valo'Kar must be behind the building from which he had come.

U'Vol strode quickly in that direction. He covered two to three meters per stride, and in less than a minute he was around the building.

At the back of the three-story brick building, it looked like a warehouse for the squat, gasoline-powered Sarhi wheeled transports. Most of them were tiny. U'Vol would have barely fit into most of them, and at that, he would take up the entire vehicle himself with no room for passengers.

About fifty meters beyond he spied the Valo'Kar. The pod was just visible over the rows of Sarhi transports. U'Vol took the most direct path and leapt on top of a Sarhi vehicle in the first row. He bounded onto the next, leaping from cold metal roof to metal roof.

Each hop caused a thunderous crunch of metal as his massive form crushed the tops of the cars on which he landed. *If there are any Sarhi out here, this will draw their attention.* It was not what he wanted. He had not realized how flimsy their vehicles were, or he would have chosen to go around rather than over the sea of transports.

Excited Sarhi voices shouted. They were on the move. Without his krindor, he felt blind and deaf. His helmet would have been able to analyze exact distances, heat signatures and composition of weapons.

He kept moving, bounding as quickly as he could. His side burned as though it had ripped open, but he paid it no mind. Once aboard the *Dra'Knar*, the medical team would have his wound sealed in no time.

Even without his krindor, he moved far more quickly than the Sarhi, and his reflexes were sharper. There were a half-dozen of them ahead, all aiming at him. He leapt to the right then dodged to the left avoiding their bullets.

He got to the end of the roofs and leapt onto two of the Sarhi, knocking them down. There was movement to his left, and he swatted the weapon from a man's hand. It sailed through the air and had not even landed yet when he raised the man who had wielded it into the air and snapped his spinal cord with one jerk of his hand.

The danger he was in made his bloodlust run high. Blood rushed in his ears, and he panted with desire to eat rather than from exertion. He longed for the claws of his krindor. Without them he had no way to rip open the chests of these dead Sarhi and feed.

A bullet grazed his left shoulder, and tendrils of fiery pain threaded through his arm and upper back. He quickly closed the gap and took a man by the neck in each hand and ended them.

A lone Sarhi warrior was left. The man visibly shook, his rifle bouncing up and down in his hands. U'Vol smelled the acrid scent of urine. The lone warrior was soaked in sweat.

U'Vol let out a low growl, and before the man's primitive nervous system had a chance to register the movement, U'Vol swatted the weapon away with his giant paw of a hand. He snapped the man with two hands.

U'Vol leapt onto the flat bed of the transport in one easy stride. Chains and tightly woven straps held the Valo'Kar but he did not need to worry about them. The pod would be sucked into the portal of warped space created by the *Wa'Nar*. The Valo'Kar did not so much move through space as shift through time.

His meaty hand slapped against the smooth vrana material the pod was made of. The pod recognized him, and the door slid open. He slipped inside and used his handprint again to close the door behind him.

U'Vol breathed a long sigh of relief. He had made it. Though he was still a long way from making it home to Uktah, he was safe inside the Valo'Kar. The feeble bullets of the Sarhi weapons could not penetrate the extremely hard exterior of the pod.

U'Vol touched the wall and entered a series of numbers to power on the pod. He quickly opened a channel to the *Wa'Nar* and did not breathe as he waited for Tu'Rhen to answer his call. One second became two, and two bled into three. He was nearly to five and close to panic when Tu'Rhen answered his hail.

"U'Vol. By the blessed Doj'Madi, you are alive."

U'Vol resisted the temptation to openly scoff at crediting what he now knew was a fictional being with saving his hide. "Coordinates uploading. Open a bogha immediately."

"Yes, my Captain."

The comm links of individuals were powered by the same bioelectric energy as the krindors. The signal links were thus weaker than links with ships or other transports. U'Vol had been unable to reach Tu'Nai or the *Wa'Nar* without the electronics of his helmet to boost his signal. He did not know if he would be able to reach Tu'Nai. He hoped the Valo'Kar would strengthen the comm signal enough to reach Tu'Nai. He attempted to reach Tu'Nai while he waited for Tu'Rhen to power up the bogha generator.

The comm was silent.

A blue panel of lights blinked on then off. He waited patiently though it was difficult. Panic welled in him. The bogha generator aboard the *Wa'Nar* and Valo'Kar were relatively new technology for the M'Uktah. *And what if the Sarhi damaged my Valo'Kar?*

The light flickered again then stayed on. He was bathed in the low but insistent hum of the noise cancellation system. The *Wa'Nar* was locked onto the pod.

U'Vol breathed a sigh of relief.

The Valo'Kar rattled and shook. He could not fall over as there was no room to fall, but he held the sides of the pod to steady himself anyway.

His optical interface flashed yellow, and he blinked his right eye quickly to let Tu'Nai's message through.

"Captain, I feared the worst when we were unable to reach you. The *Dra'Knar* forbade us to send a rescue team. Tu'Vagh, that banch phisting—"

"Calm yourself, Tu'Nai. Gather your men now. Make haste. Get aboard the *Wa'Nar*. We must leave K'Sarhi."

"Captain? But we've not even filled the cargo bay fully and – "

"Do not argue or disobey me, Tu'Nai. I am still your captain."

"Yes, of course, Captain. Please forgive my tone. Kracht. I obey your command always, my captain."

U'Vol blinked and ended the connection, and just in time. The rumbling grew, and the pod quaked. The pressure was far more intense than he had experienced before. His hands flew to his head, and he yelled out a great cry of agony though no one, not even any Sarhi that might have been nearby, could have heard it. The Valo'Kar was soundproof.

His eyes were closed tightly, and he bent forward as far as the tiny compartment would allow. U'Vol writhed and squirmed, wishing the ordeal would soon be over. The alternating pressure and ripping pain was far worse than any slice, puncture, hit or projectile wound he had ever suffered.

At last the pressure in his head subsided. His ears rang, obscuring sound, and spots danced before his eyes as he blinked them open.

The door of the Valo'Kar opened, and he nearly fell out. Tu'Rhen grabbed him on one side while another crew member whose name he could not recall held him up on the other.

"Your krindor, Captain—"

"Is gone, Tu'Rhen. Have someone fetch me a robe for now."

After taking a few steps with assistance, U'Vol got his legs back beneath him. He shrugged off their help and barreled toward the command deck of the *Wa'Nar* with Tu'Rhen at his side.

"Are Tu'Nai and the ground forces aboard yet?"

"Tu'Nai is not aboard, sir. Most of the crew have made it safely aboard. Except, of course, the ones that are…"

U'Vol didn't let him finish the thought. "Hail the *Dra'Knar*. We'll depart K'Sarhi as soon as Tu'Nai and all Vree are aboard."

Tu'Rhen remained by his side.

"Do you wait for permission? Go, man. Each second on this planet increases the risk we will never leave it."

Tu'Rhen shot U'Vol a quizzical look. Seeing U'Vol's stern impatience, Tu'Rhen then burst forward, running now at full speed.

U'Vol did not stop even as a crew member dressed him in his red robes. A member of the medical crew used a small handheld device to measure his vitals. The med tech used a handheld laser tool to close the new wound on his shoulder from the last encounter with the Sarhi. He bade U'Vol open his mouth and popped a thin film of medicine onto his tongue.

"Let it dissolve, Captain."

The film dissolved into a gelatinous, bitter glob in his mouth, and he swallowed it. "Please tell me you did not just give me a painkiller. They make me groggy, and I have no time for mental fog."

The medical technician cowered next to him. The medical crew was not Vree. This technician had brown eyes the color of a raichta, small nuisance rodents on M'Uktah. His black hair was long down his back, but his knuckles barely had any hair at all. *He is young yet.*

"No, Captain, I gave you a tonic to devastate the bacteria in your system from the Sarhi attempts to provide you medical treatment."

The medical technician ran to keep up with U'Vol's quick walk.

"Do not give me a medicine again without first asking my permission. Now go. Healing must wait."

The medical technician stopped and likely bowed as was custom when leaving the presence of the captain. But U'Vol didn't see it. He was already three strides ahead of where he left the medical tech.

The doors to the command module opened, and U'Vol thundered into the room. It was built in a circular fashion with a captain's command console in the center. Technically, Tu'Rhen was commander of the *Wa'Nar* and usually occupied the captain's console on this ship. But he ceded his place to U'Vol and took up position at a station just to the left of where U'Vol now sat.

U'Vol put both hands flat on the console, and it powered on, recognizing his unique electromagnetic signature. His neural implant immediately began its interface with the *Wa'Nar* as he reclined back into takeoff position.

Tu'Rhen spoke to him through the comm. "I hailed the *Dra'Knar*. You're not going to like this, Captain."

"Speak."

"The *Dra'Knar* did not answer. Captain, the ship is gone."

A mixture of white-hot rage and fluttery panic welled in U'Vol. "What about the *Rik'Nar*?"

"Also radio silent. They appear to have left the planet as well, Captain. Long-range scans show no sign of either ship. They have likely already entered the Mocht Bogha to return home."

Tu'Rhen had given U'Vol this information on a closed channel shared only by the two of them as well as Tu'Nai, the third and final high officer of the ground crew.

Tu'Nai's guttural howl filled the comm bandwidth and buzzed in U'Vol's head.

"Where are you, Tu'Nai?" U'Vol asked.

He grunted and growled low again. "On the ramp. I've brought in the last of all who still stand, Captain. We'll be harnessed and ready for takeoff in less than two minutes. Though little good it will do, Captain."

Tu'Nai was right. The *Wa'Nar* was not built to withstand the rigors of traveling in the Mocht Bogha. Their hull was nearly full of food, enough to supply them sustenance on the months-long journey. But no one had ever tried to take a small ground based-ship through a warp gate before. The *Wa'Nar* could break apart or implode from the intense pressure.

And even if we make it back home, what will we find waiting for us there?

U'Vol chose to act as though he had not heard Tu'Nai's concerns. "Strap in, Tu'Nai. And do not tell the crew about the *Dra'Knar*. Not yet."

U'Vol's comm blinked yellow, and he allowed the message to interrupt. It was the warp fields officer. "Captain, the Mocht Bogha is showing unusual fluctuations, sir. This is most curious."

Curious wasn't the word U'Vol would have chosen. He had known that Bodaway was keeping something from him. He now knew what the massive spikes in radio waves meant.

The Sarhi are attempting to close the Mocht Bogha.

U'Vol gave the command for takeoff, and the ship lifted off. The comm was alive with chatter from Tu'Rhen to the men in the command module and to the rest of the crew.

They powered through the atmosphere of K'Sarhi, and the comm was silent for a time as the ship shook and rattled. As soon as they exited K'Sarhi's atmosphere, the comm crackled alive again with the noisy chatter of all departments reporting to Tu'Rhen.

U'Vol's interface flashed yellow. "The Mocht Bogha is unstable, Captain. Whatever is happening to it, if it continues, it will close before we can reach it, sir."

It was what U'Vol had suspected and feared. His mind raced with a solution. He ordered full thrust, but even at the *Wa'Nar's* maximum speed, the Mocht Bogha was at the outer edge of this solar system. It would take hours to reach it. They didn't have hours.

"Tu'Rhen, can we reconfigure the bogha generator to create a warp bubble around the *Wa'Nar*, rather than just a Valo'Kar?"

"It was not made to generate a field that large, Captain. That has never been attempted. It could—"

U'Vol took a breath to keep himself from flying into a rage at Tu'Rhen. "I do not want to hear the mights and maybes, Commander. If that gate closes, we are lost in space. Do we have any other options?"

The comm was silent for a moment.

"No, Captain. I have no alternatives to offer."

"Then do it, Tu'Rhen. Now!"

U'Vol continued to monitor all communications though it gave him a pounding headache to follow so many conversations. Tu'Rhen gave the command to power on the bogha generator and increase the field strength to take in the entire ship. He met resistance from the engineers. Tu'Rhen was even less patient with the engineers than U'Vol had been with Tu'Rhen.

"Do as I command, or your skins will adorn my walls," he barked.

The officer monitoring the Mocht Bogha continued to report its lessening strength. U'Vol closed off that channel. He did not need minute-by-minute reminders of their impending peril.

The floor beneath him shook, and his ears were accosted with an odious buzz. He had been reclined in the command chair as was custom during takeoffs and landings, but he made the chair rise, and he gripped the quaking armrests.

The engineers working on the bogha generator reported it was at fifty percent strength. The metal of the ship groaned in protest.

"Seventy percent."

The pressure made him feel as though all air had been pressed from his lungs by the hand of a giant. His ears had only just stopped ringing from his travel in the Valo'Kar. Now they rang again, only worse this time.

"Eighty percent."

The wound in his side burned as though he was again being torn open. His joints ached, and his head felt near to splitting. A few of his fellow Vree bellowed and held their heads from the pain.

"Ninety percent."

Black played at the edges of his vision. He panted hard, his knuckles bone white from grasping the console so hard.

The engineer did not announce one hundred percent. Likely he passed out from the pain as several of the command crew had. U'Vol remained conscious from sheer will alone.

The walls of the ship wavered, solid one minute, a shimmery shadow the next. The comm was silent, and the men around him appeared to move in slow motion. His eardrums had either shattered or they had entered a space in which they were ahead of the sound. Even the ringing of his ears was gone.

Time ceased to exist, and yet time was all that there was. Tu'Vagh's lips moved, but U'Vol had no idea what he said.

His head swam. Lights danced before his eyes like the pale yellow of the night bugs on Ghapta.

He was dancing with Eponia on the night of their tethering. Her pale hair had been braided, but one swift flick of his fingers and the leather wrap holding it was gone. He loved the feel of her silken hair in his fingers. He grabbed a handful of it gently in one hand as he pressed her close to him with the other. Flickering light of open flame candles twinkled in her golden eyes as she smiled up at him. He had gone through tethering four times before, but never had he enjoyed it half so much.

The lights flickered before his eyes. *Eponia.*

The lights were gone. Shadows played at the corners of his eyes and stole his vision. Eponia was gone, and he knew only cold and dark.

Jack stood in the rubble of what used to be the plaster façade of an eighteenth-century French apartment building. Truck backup beeping rang in the distance, likely clearing rubble. A dog barked. There were no sounds of car horns blaring or buses moving. The streets were not passable in this area.

He touched the screen of his phone and snapped a picture of Anna. She sat on a pile of bricks holding a tiny kitten and feeding it milk from a dropper.

A gaggle of children surrounded her, eager for their turn to play mama to the abandoned cat babies. Alecto stood with the children, barely taller than they were. Her thin lips were pulled back in a full smile, her expression as excited as the tots were to hold the baby kitten. The children and Alecto, like the kitten, were orphans.

He zoomed in and snapped a tight close-up. The photo didn't capture the pile of concrete and asphalt rubble behind Anna or the burned-out buildings. The pic was for Erika and Ian.

Jack had sent them a picture a day ever since he, Anna and Alecto arrived in France. At first, Jack's pictures had been shot wide, taking in the dead bodies and other signs of carnage. Ian and Erika had both asked him to scale it back. They'd seen enough death and destruction to last a lifetime.

There once was a time when a beautiful woman whose face was marred by an ugly red scar and a milky eye would cause children to stare and maybe even be afraid. But Anna was just one of many who bore the scars of the Alien War, as it had come to be known. Everyone assumed that she had been attacked by one of the biomechanical wolf men. She let people think that. It was easier than trying to explain how she'd gotten the wound from her cousin in a secret war that none of them would ever know about.

Anna and Thomas were both still wealthier than nearly anyone else alive. They had inherited both their father's Sturgis fortune as well as their mother's Croft holdings. But money hardly mattered to them even before the Alien War. It mattered even less now. Anna and Thomas created the Sturgis Foundation and poured nearly their entire fortune into it. The foundation would augment government efforts worldwide to rebuild infrastructure and provide humanitarian aid.

A few months after the Mocht Bogha closed, Anna and Jack set off to Europe to join humanitarian efforts to rebuild war-ravaged Europe. They spent their days digging in rubble searching for bodies, helping in makeshift hospitals and getting food and water to people in need.

Jack had been shocked when Alecto had asked to come with them.

"You said there are many sick people. Injured people. I can heal them," she'd said.

Anna had hugged Alecto. "Of course you can come. A brilliant idea. I wish I'd thought of it."

It was a good idea in some respects. Alecto was right. Her healing abilities alleviated suffering for hundreds, possibly thousands of people. But having her along meant having a third-wheel companion with them nearly constantly. Alecto knew little of the world. She was, in many ways, like a child, so he and Anna were like parents to her.

But Alecto learned quickly, and with each day she grew more independent. Jack enjoyed watching her learn and grow perhaps as much as Anna did. And when Alecto wasn't around, he was surprised at how much he missed her company.

Anna gently handed the kitten off to a little boy of probably four. His eyes were wide with wonder. His tiny hands shook with eagerness to hold the soft kitten. Anna showed the boy how to feed the kitten with the dropper. Alecto helped him feed the baby cat while Anna scooped up a little girl not more than two and held her close.

She looked up and caught Jack staring at her. He couldn't help it. He loved her so much it hurt. Anna put the little girl's hand in hers and made the girl wave in Jack's direction as she tickled the child with her other hand. The girl squealed with laughter, and a few kids at

Anna's side joined in the fun, tickling Anna's sides. Her head flung back, her laugh a harmonious melody that floated through the dust-filled air and burrowed into Jack's heart.

Someday they'd have children together. He could see it like a hazy movie reel in his mind, almost as if it had already happened. Sometimes he felt like he was living now just to get to that point.

But he was in no rush. They took each day—each moment—like it could be their last. Because they knew more than most that it truly could be.

49

COMMANDER STURGIS

Lillian Sturgis exited the house in Apthartos that had been built for William Croft and pulled the door shut. It had taken several liters of bleach to scrub away the stains of his blood, but she finally made it clean. It was her home now.

Her footsteps echoed on the brick sidewalks of the empty city as she walked toward the lab in the A.H.D.N.A. wing of the vast underground complex. Sewell had suggested she get an electric cart to drive, but she rejected the idea. "My work here is not done, Sewell. The walking will give me the energy I need to finish what I started."

Sewell had offered to stay on as her assistant. She didn't know if his offer was made out of the vestiges of his old loyalty or simply because in the rapidly changing world above, a denizen of the old ways had no place. She and Sewell had lived their lives preparing for war. The world above had nearly come to the brink of Armageddon and suffered horribly at the hands of the aliens. The people of Earth longed for universal peace, not more weapons of war.

But whatever the reason that Sewell asked to stay, Sturgis had gladly accepted his offer. As it was, at least until her clones were old enough to help, she and Sewell would need to do the jobs of a dozen or more people to keep Apthartos and their lab operational.

The world above would tire of peace. Sturgis was certain of that. Some country, faction or individual would agitate, and the world would be back to bombs and guns. But until then, she and Sewell devoted themselves to what they'd started.

Sturgis passed many doors behind which others used to work, but the offices were empty now. The high-speed train tracks were barren. The humidification system was in the off position. For the most part, A.H.D.N.A. now slept.

As far as the outside world was concerned, the H.A.L.F. program was no more and the A.H.D.N.A. facility was an expensive but empty hole in the ground. The train tunnel from the air force base in Tucson was sealed off. Anyone who had worked at A.H.D.N.A. was reassigned. Sturgis had once opposed the closure but in the end oversaw it herself.

The double doors leading to the main lab were open. There was no longer a need for key cards and secrecy. She and Sewell were the only ones there.

The aroma of freshly brewed tea wafted out. Sewell had a cup of Earl Gray steeping for her, sitting on her desk in the corner of the lab. Steam rose from the white porcelain cup. A silver spoon holding a single cube of sugar rested on the saucer. She gently stirred the sugar into the tea and took a sip. The warmth of her morning brew was one of the few small luxuries she afforded herself. After a few months up top, the damp underground world chilled her more than it had in the past. She drained the tea while reviewing data collected the day before about the status of the clones. She spritzed her orchids then delved into the inner lab room in search of Sewell.

Her heels clicked on the concrete floor as she walked. Sewell was standing at one of the artificial womb machines, his eyes riveted to the computer screen. He barely looked up when she entered.

"How are they doing today?" she asked.

Sewell swiped across the screen to turn off the computer and stowed it. "I've checked four of the six. C1 through C3 are all at optimum levels. But I think you should have a look at C4 here. The oxygen levels are in the low-normal range."

Sturgis moved closer to the oval-shaped glass receptacle that held the human-Conexus fetus. She peered into it. The being's thin arms and legs were tucked into its body, and it sucked on its tiny thumb. "Did you check the hoses?"

"Not yet, Commander."

Sturgis rolled her eyes. "How many times must I tell you not to call me that? Call me Lillian, or even Sturgis. But I no longer have anything to command."

Sewell handed her the electronic tablet he'd been holding so she could see the data he'd recorded that morning. "An old habit." He inspected the stainless steel tubing that ran from the glass womb to the apparatus below. He pulled a bright penlight out of his pocket and ran his hand along the tube. "No kinks or obvious holes in this one." He repeated his inspection with the other three tubes snaking from the bottom section of the machine to the top. "It won't be long and you'll again have people under your command." Sewell put his penlight away. "No obvious defects."

Sturgis' brows knitted together. "Up the flow rate by two percent. Check C4 again in two hours, and if the oxygen levels have not improved, do a scan of the lungs."

"Yes, ma'am."

While Sewell did as Sturgis had requested, she checked the vitals of C5 and C6. Though the six hybrids were clones with identical DNA, she had an affinity toward C6. Though it looked exactly like the others, it appeared to possess a more greatly developed telekinetic ability. Even though it was still only seven months old, it sensed her presence. As she pulled up the computer screen, C6 opened its eyes. The clone, a genetic duplicate of Alecto, stared directly at her with huge black alien eyes.

"Hello, C6," she said. She peered in, and a wide, genuine smile came to her lips. Sturgis marveled at the miracle of the life she had created. She gently placed her hand on the glass, her fingers splayed open.

C6, floating peacefully in the manufactured amniotic fluid, slowly reached its thin arm toward her. Its tiny hand, only a few inches long, touched the glass as if trying to touch her hand.

"It won't be long, little one," she whispered. "You and your sisters will soon be strong enough to leave your watery world."

Sewell coughed lightly.

Sturgis quickly removed her hand from the glass. "What is it, Sewell?"

"I've increased the flow rate for C4. How is C6 doing?" He peered into the womb from the other side, his face distorted by the glass into a strange wide shape with oversized eyes.

"She is perfect." Sturgis swiped the screen to view another page of graphs and data. "I've decided to name her Alexa."

"I thought you weren't going to name them."

Sturgis typed a note into her tablet. "Dr. Randall coddled 9." She looked up at the tiny clone. "I chastised him for it. I thought that if we treated them too much like children, that it would weaken them." Alexa reached her tiny hand out to Sturgis again. "I was wrong. 9 was..." Her throat was tight. She swallowed. "They're my children, Sewell. And I'll raise them as such."

Sewell smiled and peered up at little Alexa floating in her light-blue home. "Uncle Sewell."

Sturgis nodded. "I like that."

Sewell coughed, and his smile faded. "But to what purpose? The M'Uktah have been beaten. Humanity is safe again."

"For now," she said. "Sewell, we survived an attack by an advanced alien predator and learned the truth: we are not alone. Humanity is not unique. We are but one of many intelligent species in this universe. It will take a while for that to sink in up top."

"Yes, that's true. But what role will Alexa and the others play?"

"My life's mission was to save our species from extinction at the hands of aliens. But my clones have a new purpose." She once again splayed her hand on the glass. "One day Alexa and her sisters will save humanity from itself."

50
ERIKA

The ceiling and walls were rosy-pink with the glow of morning. Erika stood on the balcony with a hot cup of Kona coffee in her hand and peered down the hill toward the ocean churning toward the shore. She cupped her hand over her forehead to cut down on glare. Finally she spotted him. Ian was pretty far out, a tiny dot straddling his surfboard. He floated like flotsam waiting to be carried ashore.

His new friend Ryan was with him, no doubt. She was glad he had met someone new. It took the sting out of what Ben, aka Brad, had done to him if not eliminated it completely. She warned Ian to take it slow, which, in hindsight, was like asking matches not to set kerosene on fire.

But he'd be all right. He had made it through his time at A.H.D.N.A., the Conexus virus and being best friends with Erika. It would take more than heartache to break Ian.

She went back inside but left the sliding doors open. She liked the tropical breeze and moist air.

Erika poured herself another cup of coffee and began a fresh pot. Dr. Randall would be up soon, and like her, he needed a good half pot in the morning before he was firing on all cylinders.

By the time the coffee was brewed and her toast was up, Dr. Randall sauntered into the kitchen in his bare feet. He was groomed and dressed, but like the rest of them, he honored the Hawaiian tradition of not wearing shoes inside.

Erika grabbed a mug from the cupboard and poured him a cup. "Aloha, doc. Ready for another day in paradise?"

He muttered thanks and put coffee to lips. "Ask me that after I've drained this."

Erika had not stressed much about what she'd do after graduation, but it was a topic that had made her antsy. It seemed that everyone else had their futures figured out by the end of tenth grade.

But even at the beginning of her senior year, Erika hadn't a clue what she'd do with her life. She hadn't been thrilled with the idea of college. The only thing she'd been sure of was that she'd wanted to get as far away from Ajo as she could.

But she could never have dreamed that her first stop after high school would be to work as a research assistant to a man she was pretty sure was bat-shit crazy on a top-secret government project that did not officially exist. She and Ian were Dr. Randall's hands and eyes as they took apart M'Uktah biotech and worked to reverse-engineer it. As it turned out, she enjoyed the hands-on work and on-the-job training more than she would have enjoyed the stuffy lecture halls of college.

They were very close to cracking the technology puzzle that allowed the M'Uktah to control the flow of information to and from their retinal nerve via their neural and optical implants. It had taken nearly nine months, but they were closer than any of the other teams working on the issue. That meant they were likely going to be able to continue their work indefinitely and with little to no oversight. As long as they continued to produce, the powers that be didn't care if they worked out of a beach house in Hawaii or a lab in Minnesota. After decades underground, Dr. Randall had insisted on a view of the ocean. Erika and Ian didn't try to argue him out of it.

Since Anna, Jack and Thomas had personally seen to the destruction of not only William and Lizzy Croft but the dismantling of the Makers organization, Erika was fairly confident that the work she did with Dr. Randall was going to the right people. But even that was an idea fraught with potential contradiction. She once had thought that the government was the right people. Now she wasn't sure who the good guys were.

Thomas helped Erika set up their computer system. Everything they did was saved not only to encrypted servers they were directed to by the government, but Thomas also built in a coded uplink that tracked where the information went once uploaded. He even offered to track it for them. That way if he saw anything of concern, they'd know right away so they could work to keep the information out of the wrong hands. So far they had encountered no problems. But Thomas kept an eye on it anyway.

Dr. Randall was on his second cup of coffee and Erika on her third when Erika's cell phone rang. A quick glance at the caller ID, and she swiped the screen to answer. "It's Dr. Montoya," she said.

Dr. Montoya's voice was cheery. "Good afternoon. Oh, I guess morning there. So how's paradise treating you?"

Erika chuckled. "Paradise? Who has time to enjoy it? Dr. Randall keeps me working twenty-four, seven."

"Hey, you're the taskmaster," Dr. Randall said. He feigned a pout.

"I heard that," Dr. Montoya said. "Don't work him too hard."

Erika laughed. "Oh, I let him out of the cage to play occasionally. How's your work coming?"

"You know we've had setbacks getting the antivirus to some locations because of the destruction of infrastructure. But we're making progress. Our current projections are that we'll have ninety percent of the population inoculated within five years, and that will give us global herd immunity."

"That's amazing, doc."

"Well, we owe a huge debt of thanks to the Sturgis Foundation. Their funds and dedication to the work have allowed us to move more quickly than we thought possible right after the alien conflict."

Erika considered commenting on the absurdity of that statement. After all, Robert Sturgis had been a part of the Makers, a clandestine organization that had schemed for years to profit from the Conexus virus at the expense and peril of the population at large. And Commander Sturgis may not have known the full extent of Croft's plans, but she had been a part of a conspiracy to siphon billions in taxpayer dollars to create hybrid beings to protect the Makers, not the people. Having the Sturgis name affixed to a philanthropic endeavor was the height of irony.

But Erika held her tongue. Anna and Thomas were not Robert and Lillian. At least they were trying to right the wrongs of the prior generation.

After they finished their call with Dr. Montoya, Erika and Dr. Randall got back to work. She spent much of the day looking through a telescope at miniscule alien technology. The material the M'Uktah used had stymied them. Though its structure was mineral and was similar to a transistor, it behaved like an organic. It was fascinating work but tedious and eye-straining. By late afternoon her eyes needed a break.

"I'm heading down to the beach for a bit, doc. Wanna join me?"

Dr. Randall's face was only a few inches from his computer screen. Even with the thickest glasses, it was difficult for him to see print or numbers. "I'll take a rain check on that. It's going to storm."

The sun was bright, and there wasn't a cloud in the sky as far as she could see.

Erika planted a light kiss on his scruffy cheek. "Don't work too hard, doc. I'll be back in a bit."

He smiled, but his eyes remained riveted to the screen as she left.

The wind whipped her loose-fitting pants against her legs as she walked down the grassy hill toward the ocean. By the time she got to the bottom of the hill, clouds had gathered to the south. Lightning danced from the clouds down to the sea. When she felt the low rumble of thunder, her hand instinctively grabbed for the locket she wore around her neck.

Before Commander Sturgis left the VLA never to be seen or heard from again, she had stopped Erika in the gravel courtyard of the VLA.

"Miss Holt. Wait a moment."

Sturgis' voice made Erika bristle. Sturgis may have been there for Tex in the end, but Erika would never forget how the woman had once ordered Erika to be put to death. Erika stopped though and waited to hear her out. "What?"

Sturgis caught up to her. "I have something for you. Please. Hold out your hand."

Erika had no idea what Sturgis could possibly want to give her that Erika would want. She hesitated but finally put her hand out, palm up.

Sturgis pulled a lock of Tex's white-gold hair from her pocket, placed it on Erika's palm and closed her fingers over it. She gave Erika a wan smile and left without another word.

Erika wore that small remnant of Tex in the locket around her neck. Besides her memories of him, it was all she had left of their time together.

He never got to see the ocean.

"I think you would have liked the beach." Erika spoke it out loud even though Tex wasn't there to hear her.

She knew Tex was probably dead. Everyone seemed to think that he was. But she preferred to think of him alive somewhere. That the ball of light that had engulfed him at the end sucked him into another realm. That the ash pile left behind was not his remains but the residue of the plasma arc that he had created.

Erika smiled and rubbed the locket between her fingers as the waves washed over her feet. She dropped the locket against her chest and looked at the palm of her right hand. The compass tattooed there pointed north and she did too. Out across a vast, seemingly endless ocean, imagining that on the other side, Tex did the same.

THE END

NOTE FROM THE AUTHOR

Thank you for reading H.A.L.F.!

Dear Reader,

I hope you enjoyed **H.A.L.F.: ORIGINS** and the entire H.A.L.F. series. I truly appreciate that you spent some of your valuable time with my characters and you hung in there with them through to the end! To all of the readers who have loved the series, thank you. Reader support keeps writers writing, building worlds and creating characters that you love to love (and to hate).

When I wrote book one (*The Deep Beneath*), I had no way of knowing the support the series would get. But soon after *The Deep Beneath* released, readers began to contact me through email, Twitter, Facebook and my blog to talk about the story. I took to heart what readers said, and your comments and opinions changed some of what I'd planned for books two and three. In fact, it was fandom for Tex that led to H.A.L.F. 9 (aka Bodaway) becoming the backbone of the story. Believe it or not, when I first conceived the story, Tex was a sidekick to Erika rather than a co-lead character.

Now that you've finished reading the series, tell me what you liked, what you loved, and even what you hated. I'd also like to know if you are interested in a spin-off novella, novel or even series about the M'Uktah or Commander Sturgis and the clones. You can write to me at: NatalieWrightAuthor@gmail.com. You can also visit me on the web at www.NatalieWrightAuthor.com.

If you haven't already done so, please subscribe to my email newsletter. Subscribers receive access to exclusive content, subscriber-only giveaways, short stories, discounts and are always the first to hear about new releases. http://eepurl.com/gGHNL

Finally, I need to ask a favor. I'd love your review of *H.A.L.F.: Origins*. Honest reviews are always welcome as I appreciate any and all feedback. And reviews help other readers find books that they'll love. Please take a few minutes to go to my author page on Amazon where you can find all my books to review:

http://bit.ly/NatalieWright_Author.

And don't forget to follow me on Amazon so that you'll be notified of new releases in the future.

Many readers have asked, "What's next?" I have several intriguing story ideas in development. We'll see which set of characters "calls" to me the most. But you can bet that whether my next story is high fantasy, space opera or a young adult dystopian, I'll do my best to bring you an adventure set in a vividly detailed world peopled with intriguing characters.

Thank you for reading the H.A.L.F. series and spending your valuable time with my world.

In gratitude,

Natalie Wright

ABOUT THE AUTHOR

Natalie is the author of H.A.L.F., an award-winning science fiction series, and The Akasha Chronicles, a popular young adult fantasy trilogy. She lives in the high desert of Arizona with her husband, teen daughter, and two cat overlords.

Natalie spends her time writing, reading, gaming, traveling and meeting readers and fans at festivals and comic cons throughout the western United States. She is a frequent guest on blogs, internet radio and podcasts for writers, readers, geeks and book nerds. Natalie has appeared on shows such as Front Row Geeks, Speculative Fiction Cantina, The Creative Penn, iHeart Radio and others.

You can follow Natalie on Facebook (NatalieWright.Author), Twitter (@NatalieWright_), Instagram (NatalieWrightAuthor) or Pinterest (NatWrites).

Made in the USA
Middletown, DE
05 August 2020

14477654R00209